MERRY

Also Available by Susan Breen

Maggie Dove

Maggie Dove's Detective Agency

Maggie Dove and the Lost Brides

The Fiction Class

MERRY

A Novel

SUSAN BREEN

alcove
press

Published in the United States by Alcove Press, an imprint of The Quick Brown Fox & Company LLC.

Alcove Press and its logo are trademarks of The Quick Brown Fox & Company LLC.

Library of Congress Catalog-in-Publication data available upon request.

ISBN (hardcover): 979-8-89242-288-8
ISBN (paperback): 979-8-89242-193-5
ISBN (ebook): 979-8-89242-194-2

Cover design by Lucy Rose

Printed in the United States.

www.alcovepress.com

Alcove Press
34 West 27th St., 10th Floor
New York, NY 10001

First Edition: September 2025

The authorized representative in the EU for product safety and compliance is eucomply OÜPärnu mnt 139b-14, 11317 Tallinn, Estonia, hello@eucompliancepartner.com, +33757690241

10 9 8 7 6 5 4 3 2 1

For my treasures:
Savannah, Jack, and Avi

"In the cold wind, if you can lean against others, none of you will blow away."

—Anne Lamott

"But why do spirits walk the earth, and why do they come to me?"

—Ebenezer Scrooge

NEW YORK

CHAPTER ONE

Does Merry Bingham *need* to put up six Christmas trees this year?

No, of course not. Five would be more than enough.

Neither does she have to have put candles in each of the windows of her pink Victorian house. Or order vintage tinsel from a private supplier in New York City. Or buy presents for everyone at her office, especially given how notoriously particular antiquarian booksellers are. Or try to get her three grown children to smile in a non-snarky way for the annual Bingham Christmas card. Or make homemade sugar doughnuts to hand out to all the people who drive by her house every year to admire the lights and ask her how much her electric bill is.

This could be the year that Merry Bingham is sensible about Christmas.

She knows she's supposed to be sensible because everyone keeps telling her so. She's fifty-five years old, and she's supposed to be thinking about downsizing and cutting carbohydrates and being careful. She is not supposed to be crawling around on the roof, trying to attach Rudolph the Red-Nosed Reindeer to the eaves. Especially not in the middle of a windstorm, though she does so love the feeling of being up high, the Hudson River stretched out beneath her, waves cresting like little sharks.

She's never fallen off the roof before! Not even close.

So, all right. She was stupid. And she was lucky the yew bushes broke her fall. Now her ribs are banged up and she had to have an X-ray. She's back home and totally fine, except her entire body hurts when she breathes in, and she feels like she hears a train rushing through her ears.

You're not twenty-five anymore, her doctor said, which she thought was hostile. As though she doesn't know that. As though she does not know she is the same age her father was when he died. As though she has not spent the bulk of her life worrying about all the things middle-aged people are supposed to be worrying about. Whether she'll ever pay off her credit card bills and whether she and her husband will have enough money to retire on and whether her children will ever find happiness. Her beloved children who can't seem to look at each other without snarling. She knows perfectly well she overdoes it when it comes to Christmas, but how can she not?

Christmas is about a miracle. Christmas is about how the world changed completely over one silent night. Christmas is about joy, redemption, transformation, and yes, bells and whistles and lights and reindeer. Christmas is the exact opposite of being sensible, and Merry doesn't care if she goes soaring right off the roof again and again; she is not surrendering Christmas.

In fact, she comes from a long line of people who do not surrender.

Starting with her ancestor, one little Nora Villard, who at the age of ten, waylaid Charles Dickens on a train on his way from New York City and persuaded the Great Author to give her his copy of *A Christmas Carol*—which he autographed. This same volume has passed through five generations of Merry's family, each one of Nora's descendants more ferocious and persistent than the previous. They were the sort of people who dashed into collapsing buildings to save people, explored the Antarctic, flew airplanes. *Crashed* airplanes and then got back into other airplanes.

Bravest of all was Merry's father, Charles Dickens Villard the Third. Known as Trip. He was the bravest because the battle he fought was so secretive, so unrelenting, so poisonous.

Multiple sclerosis.

A terrible disease that grabbed hold of Merry's father when he was only thirty-two years old, wrestled him into a wheelchair and trapped him there for the final two decades of his life. Two decades in which he did not complain, did not surrender. Only tried to pass along his love of the holiday to Merry, who sat at his side each Christmas Eve, holding the family heirloom in her hands, praying that along with Scrooge's miracle would come a miracle for her father. Every single Christmas Eve she went to bed praying that the next morning she would wake up and find her father cured. A grown-up version of Tiny Tim, with his wheelchair cast aside.

Even though her father died before his miracle could take place, Merry has never stopped believing that Christmas is a time of magic.

She looks forward to it all year. She tries to welcome it into her heart. She starts listening to that Christmas carol station long before Thanksgiving. And if occasionally she feels as though it's more of a burden than it should be, if occasionally it feels like a bit of a landmine, then she pushes the thought aside.

Last year the arguing among her three children got so bad that Nick, her oldest son, clenched his jaw so hard he broke a tooth and needed thousands of dollars of dental work. Bessie, her middle child, and Song Lee, her youngest, got into a vicious argument because Song Lee had gotten a job at a lobbying firm in Washington, D.C., and Bessie said she was selling out, and Song Lee said that was better than sharing a five-bedroom apartment in Manhattan with four people who didn't like her, and Bessie said how did she know? Who'd told her no one liked her? Was it on Instagram?

That was when Merry's beloved husband locked himself in his office and put on music from the nineties. Merry's little dog started to twitch, and someone from American Express called to say that someone had stolen her card and was spending a lot of money, though that turned out to be a false alarm. It was just Merry spending all that money.

But that was last year and she's sure this year will be better The kids are all arriving in seven days, on the 23rd. Dr. Fiedler assured her her ribs would feel better soon.

She feels confident that this will be her best Christmas ever. She's bought everyone's favorite foods. She's spent hours thinking of the right gifts. She's made arrangements for them all to go Christmas caroling at a senior citizen center nearby; her husband has a beautiful tenor voice. She's even assembled costumes so they can put on a production of *A Christmas Carol.* She used to love to do that with her father. She'd dress up as Tiny Tim and he as Scrooge.

She's so caught up in the memory that it takes her a moment to realize her phone's ringing. The number on the screen is her doctor's. She assumes, foolishly it turns out, that he's calling about a book. In addition to being her doctor, he's also a book collector and she's been helping him build up a Dickens collection. So that's where her mind is when she hears Dr. Fiedler speak and realizes how wrong she is.

CHAPTER TWO

"So, I wouldn't say this is anything to worry about," Dr. Fiedler says, "but in reviewing your X-ray, we came across a nodule on your lungs."

"My lungs." Merry's never liked the word *lungs*. It's a word with an ugly aftertaste, but she knows they're important. Vital. "My lungs."

Merry looks around her, at the parlor, a room she's always thought was the prettiest room in the house, with its stained-glass windows and mahogany wainscoting and huge bay window. That's where she always puts her favorite Christmas tree. The one with the animal motif. But now it looks so unfinished. There's still so much she planned to do in this room. So much she planned to do with her life.

Dr. Fiedler clears his throat. She considers him a friend, but now he sounds more formal, as though he's distancing himself from her.

"We've found that many people have nodules in their lungs during this time of Covid. The likelihood is it's nothing. But of course, we want to be careful."

Who is this "we" he's talking about? She knows he has a wife, but she doubts she's implicated.

"Could it be cancer?"

"Merry, don't let your mind go there. Let's take this one step at a time."

"Don't let my mind go there? Max," she says, calling him by his first name because she feels like she needs to reconnect with the person who is her friend. She needs to take control of this situation. "I am the daughter of a man who caught a fever one day and was confined to a wheelchair for the next twenty years of his life. Don't tell me not to go there."

Merry sinks down into her antique Victorian tub chair, a flamingo-colored thing covered in damask that she bought when she was in Ohio looking for some Dickens ephemera. Dickens spent a lot of time in Ohio. Ohio has been good to Merry.

"I know," he says, and he does sound slightly warmer. His father was her father's doctor. Their relationship is generational. "Let's arrange for a PET scan and we'll get a better sense of what's going on. Look at it this way. You're lucky. If you hadn't fallen off the roof, we wouldn't have the X-ray and this nodule wouldn't have been discovered. Now at least we can do something about it. I'll send a script over to the hospital. Just call them and set up an appointment."

"Okay, but this isn't an emergency situation, is it? I mean, it can wait until after Christmas, can't it?"

Silence, and in that quiet, Merry feels so strange, as though she's on a plane and it's shifted levels unexpectedly. She was in one atmosphere and now she's in another.

"I wouldn't recommend it, Merry. It's always better to get in front these things."

A car drives by, lighting up the stained-glass windows. She pauses for a moment to watch the light arc, to admire the beauty of the windows. Hibiscus. Her father never got to see this house, but she bought it because she knew he would have loved it. He was a man who was always very clear about what he loved.

She's always assumed that death would be all right. That it would be like childbirth, except backward. That you would go back to where you came from, and she hoped that when she did, she would be with her father. That she would have the chance to apologize to him in a way she could not do in life.

It's just that she doesn't want to die *right now.* Not at fifty-five, not when her children still need her, not when so much of her life is still so unresolved. Not when it's almost Christmas.

Merry grips the soft pink damask on the chair. *Damask,* a word that she loves, that's husky and sensuous. Not like the word *nodule,* which is smooth and oily as a snake.

Her hands are shaking. She hates that. Hates being weak. She tries to hold them rigid, to seize control of her fear, but all that happens is that they look like claws. She doesn't recognize her hands. She doesn't recognize herself.

Which is the moment that her dog tiptoes into the parlor and says, "How can I help?"

CHAPTER THREE

Merry believes her dog talks to her. She's spent so much of her life in the world of books that she's never entirely sure what's real and what's not, but she's about ninety percent sure the dog talks. Seventy-five percent. He also speaks with a British accent, because why not?

A few years back she was at the Firsts Book Fair in London, talking to a lord who needed her advice about how to break up his library, and she was tempted to say, "You sound just like my dog." But she didn't. That was back when she had energy and self-control. Back when she didn't think she was dying. Back before the doctor called.

"I have a nodule in my lung and I have to have a PET scan and they are going to inject me full of radioactive tracers and if I have cancer it's going to light up. All sparkly and bright and deadly and vicious."

"You don't like the word lung," the dog murmurs.

"No, I don't."

He leaps alongside her, one swoosh of fur, and squeezes himself between her leg and the edge of the chair. He's so soft. She can never get over how soft his fur is, which is a constant source of aggravation to him. Because although his body froths with curls and his default position is to curl into a snail-like ball, he dreams of being a Rottweiler. Actually, he dreams of being Samuel L. Jackson. Never watch *Snakes on a Plane* with a cockapoo. He growls at larger dogs. He barks at the mailman. He throws out his chest, but, alas, he is defeated by his cuteness. No one fears him. All anyone ever wants to do is stroke him and kiss his nose. Another creature betrayed by his body, she thinks.

His name is Leroy.

"You will triumph," he murmurs. "You are the bravest warrior in the world."

"You're my dog, Leroy. You're supposed to think that."

Leroy is the one creature in this world who has never told her to be sensible.

His eyes pulse with adoration. Sweet little face. Sweet little nose.

"Remember the time you found that black thing in my fur and you got it out? With your bare hands?"

"It was an ant, Leroy. Neither of us was in any danger."

"And the time you thought a car was going to hit me and you pulled me out of the road?"

"Well, yes, but I should have been more careful. That was actually my fault."

She'd stopped to look at a vibrant chestnut tree and lost all sense of time and place. It was such a beautiful color.

"Or the time that big dog attacked and you threw yourself on top of me so he'd bite you and not me."

She still has the scar on her arm. A jagged lightning strike of a thing.

"All right, that was pretty epic," she acknowledges. Though, boy, had it hurt. She remembers lying on top of Leroy and kicking away the other dog. Screaming for help. Trying to grab on to a stick. She remembers how hard it was to keep struggling. To fight back. When she knew she was weakening, and all she could think about was how that dog would hurt Leroy.

She stares into her little dog's face and she knows he's trying to will her courage. He wants to help her. But she fears this may be a fight she can't win.

His nose makes little fluttering vibrations against her skin. There's something cooling about his breath. He smells floral from her deodorant.

He's spent so much time nestled against her that he has acquired the scent of her armpit.

He noses tears off her cheek, not licking them away, but rather sending them into the air. As though her grief and fear might fly away from her.

She can't seem to get her bearings. She's always known so strongly who she was: a wife and a mother, a book scout, a Christmas person. A descendant of the Villards. A strong-minded person with minor anger management issues.

But the call from Dr. Fiedler has shaken her. She feels different. More tentative. More frightened.

Or no, being honest, didn't it start before that?

Wasn't that why she climbed on the roof in the first place? Because she felt like something was slipping away from her? Because her body felt so strange, that odd roaring in her ear, the sudden tingling in her arm. She wanted to prove to herself that she wasn't falling apart, that she could still climb on the roof. She knew she was taking a risk, but it felt necessary. Because she was not about to take to her bed.

She thinks of a Samuel L. Jackson quote Leroy likes. *I don't mind dying. I just don't wanna go out like some punk.*

CHAPTER FOUR

Merry keeps her treasured *Christmas Carol* in the attic, in an ancient, heavy safe. In a perfect world, the safe would be on the first floor, but it was in the attic when she and Sully first moved in, and one does not easily move an ancient, heavy safe. The combination is 000. She's not worried about anyone stealing the book. Although there's plenty of thievery in the book world, it's more usually specialists who sneak into libraries and cut out pages. She can't imagine anyone tiptoeing up to her attic to steal her copy of *A Christmas Carol*. Plus, she can't figure out how to change the combination.

Now she tugs open the door and retrieves the special clamshell box. *Clamshell* is a word she loves. It makes her think of buried treasure and magic and mysterious sea creatures.

All it actually means is that the box has a hinge that opens and closes like a clamshell, but Merry has never been one to let reality stand in the way of magic.

The clamshell box is covered in silk. The sort of silk women used to wear to balls. Slightly frayed, slightly tattered, but still with that inner glow that only real silk has. Sensuous, seductive. You can't see that box and not want to stroke it.

Holding the box in both hands, she and Leroy then trudge back down the three flights of steps. She hears her husband humming from his office. Probably Gustav Mahler. He's a great romantic—both her husband *and* Mahler, come to that. One year, for her birthday, Sully arranged for the high school marching band to come play outside her window. The man lives in a dream state in which women are loved, children thrive, and dogs fetch. He does not live in a world of nodules.

They continue past him and she sits back down in the tub chair, Leroy tucking himself alongside her.

The top of the box is soft, weathered. Smells musty, but Merry doesn't mind the smell of dust. Couldn't be in the rare book trade if that were an issue. The dustier the book, the more likely no one's touched it for a while, the greater the possibility it might be an undiscovered treasure. She's just learned never to wear black clothes. Always wear gray.

Now she pries open the box, slowly, listening to the hinge wheeze.

And there it is, tucked inside.

The family treasure.

A seventh edition of *A Christmas Carol*. A surprisingly small volume, no larger than an address book. Covered in fine-ribbed pink cloth. Gold gilt on the edge of the pages. Gold-stamped on front. Merry loved all that gold, loved to run her fingers over it. When she studied Dickens, she learned that he'd designed the novel himself with the specific intention of making the physical book as beautiful as possible, so that people might buy it as Christmas gifts for their families. Because of that he'd earned little money on the book, although he desperately needed it. But growing up, all Merry knew was that it was the most beautiful thing she'd ever seen.

Merry opens the book to the half title page and touches her hand lightly to Dickens's signature.

There are people in this world who would consider that sacrilege. Who would only touch the book with cotton white gloves. But the tradition in her family has always been to handle the book—and Mr. Hong used to say that you could do more damage to a book with gloves than without. Easier to tear pages and easier to transmit dirt. Still, Merry is always careful to wash and dry her hands thoroughly before touching it. The book is worth about forty thousand dollars, according to the last person who offered, though Merry's never been tempted. This is her history. This is her legacy.

To Nora Villard. She who embodies persistence. Saturday Twenty first December 1867. Charles Dickens

How she loves that signature, which she's spent so much of her career tracking down in other volumes. Almost unreadable if you didn't know how to look at it. The C of his first name almost lowercase, all the letters crumpled together except for the D of his last name, which jumps up in the middle. The whole thing scrawled with tremendous forward energy and underneath, his famous flourish. That swirling tornado of lines that underscores all his signatures, though this particular signature is subdued. He was sick, tired, when he signed this book over to Merry's ancestor. Worn out from the tumult of deserting his wife. Stressed about being on a train after having survived the Staplehurst train accident. Charmed by a little girl.

Charmed by Nora Villard.

Whenever she holds this book, Merry can never get over the thrill of knowing that Charles Dickens held it—*owned* it—too. She breathes it in and thinks she smells him. A hint of orange, perhaps. Some rum. She pictures him sitting alongside her and it makes her feel stronger. Thanks to this book, she is part of something that is, if not eternal, at least legendary. Her name will be associated with Dickens's name for as long as this book exists.

She can almost imagine her ancestors circling around her, all five generations of Villards who have owned this box and the treasure inside. Five generations of lunging, leaping, foolhardy, brave, loving, passionate Villards.

Starting with Nora Villard, ten years old, face like a vampire if the old photos don't lie, who finagled her way into the train compartment where Charles Dickens was sitting, resting up after his contentious American tour. She told him that there were parts of *David Copperfield* that were slow and the great man said, "Tell me where." Then he took out a pen and paper and wrote down her thoughts, and at the end of the conversation he presented her with this book.

Nora passed it on to her brother, Nelson, a polar explorer who got left behind in Antarctica. He'd gone off to pursue a polar bear and disappeared. Everyone thought he was dead, and they left him there, but he managed to survive and spent the rest of his long life lecturing about this experience, at which point he left the book to his son, Charles Dickens Villard, a man who fought in World War I and was gassed at Ypres, and eventually died of his injuries, at which point the book went to his son, Charles Dickens Villard Jr., a stunt flyer who crashed three planes and survived two times, and from then on to his son, Merry's father, Charles Dickens Villard III, who eventually left it to her.

She imagines that someday her oldest child, Nick, will sit with his own children and tell them about her. He'll tell them how she loved this book, how it comforted her, how brave she was and perhaps how foolish. How she fell off the roof. How she once sold a book for a million dollars. How she had friends and a happy life, sort of, and a devoted husband and a restless cockapoo. She pictures a crowd of children by his feet. A wife by his side. Someone kind and loving and probably incredibly good-looking, given the women Nick seems drawn to. She imagines her other children and their families by his side. Bessie, with children or dogs or plants or whatever it is she will accumulate. Song Lee, her youngest child, adopted from Korea. Merry's always hoped she'd be the president of the United States. It would require a constitutional amendment, but Merry doesn't think anything is beyond her daughter.

For the first time since Dr. Fiedler's phone call, Merry feels like she has the courage to do what she needs to do. She calls up the hospital and makes an appointment for the PET scan, which she has to wait four days before she can have, which is both horrifying and a relief. She assures them she has not been near anyone who has Covid symptoms and has not traveled abroad and is not pregnant and does not have claustrophobia or any allergies, as best she knows.

"Though there's always a first time."

"Ha," the nurse says.

Having done that, she prepares to call Nick. She's ready to hand off the book. She hadn't planned to do it so soon, but the idea of him with the book comforts her. Now is the time to pass it down. This is the moment.

She knows she should probably think it over more, but it is not her way to think things over. When she believes something is the right thing to do, she does it.

So, she calls Nick and offers him her gift.

But his answer surprises her.

CHAPTER FIVE

Nick answers on the first ring.

Merry likes that about her son. He always answers her calls, no matter where in the world he is, and with Nick he could be anywhere. He leads adventure tours, so sometimes he's in the Himalayas and other times he's in the Grand Canyon and other times he's at his home, a small house in the middle of Oregon, surrounded by vistas of juniper grasslands and basalt canyons and herds of elk and mule deer. About as far away from her as he could possibly live and still be in the continental U.S., though she tries not to take it personally.

"Hey, Ma," he says. "All's well?"

She pictures him, her handsome son, with his long legs stretched out in front of him, head tilted back, long brown hair, heavy boots. He carries himself like a movie star, as though he just expects people to look at him. People are always asking for his autograph.

"Yes," she says, because the last thing she wants to discuss is her health. Not before Christmas. Instead, she chitchats a bit about the book-scouting business and he tells her about a man who broke his back on a bicycle trip and then they gossip about Song Lee, who is working in Washington, D.C., in a lobbying firm, and Bessie, who is working as an actor, which means she's unemployed but she finds random jobs. Nick heard she was working at a hospice, which surprises Merry and frightens her. Is it an omen? She's ridiculously superstitious. But then, so is everyone in the book business.

After a while he says, "So what's up?"

That's when she tells him she's come to the conclusion it's time to hand off *A Christmas Carol.* "I know it's more traditional to wait until I've passed on, but the fact is, I'd like to see you with that book."

Her voice throbs a bit on that last bit, remembering how moved she was when she inherited the book. Her father so suddenly dead. She in Gstaad, of all possible places. Skiing. She who'd never skied a day in her life. Her mother, who'd run off to Florida years earlier, flew back to her father's house in the Bronx to take care of everything because, as she said to everyone, she knew poor Meredith would be devastated that she wasn't there. By the time Merry succeeded in getting back from Gstaad (following the worst blizzard in decades) the house was emptied out of her father's things. Only the book remained, bubble-wrapped and set in the center of the kitchen table. There are still tearstains on it from how she'd wept. But it had been a comfort too. The one tangible thing she had from her father. A piece of his heart.

"No thanks," Nick says. "I don't want it."

That's not the answer she's expecting. First the nodule. Now the "no."

"I don't think you understand, Nick. I'm offering you the treasure of my heart. You can't say no." It never occurred to her he wouldn't want the book.

"You're always so overdramatic."

"That's true, but that's not the issue here. It's the family heirloom. It's been passed down for five generations. We're not talking about Grandma's bundt cake recipe here. You have to want it." When he was young, he used to torment his sisters over the fact that he was the oldest, and therefore the one to inherit the book. How Bessie cried over that.

"I can't take care of a book like that, Ma. I'm gone half the time. I'd be worrying about it. What if there's a fire? Or someone steals it?"

"You live in the middle of the wilderness in Oregon. Who's going to steal it, unless an elk wanders through?

He laughs, softly.

"You could put it in a safe deposit box. You don't even need to think about it, and some day, when you're older and more settled and have a family, then you can take it out and read it to them. It will mean something."

"I'll never have a family," he says.

"You're only thirty-two. You're young. Things can change, you can't be sure."

"I'm sure."

Merry can see the Hudson River from her parlor window, running so close she's often imagined she could jump into it. Today a tugboat bounces on top. Her husband once told her she reminded him of a tugboat, small and purposeful.

"Are you going to punish yourself for the rest of your life?" The question comes out angrier than she intended, but she's just so shocked. And hurt. And angry.

"I'm not punishing myself," he says, voice light, slightly ironic. As though *punish* is a word to laugh at.

"Yes, you are," she says. "For some reason you've decided you don't deserve to enjoy your life. You don't deserve joy, even if it's in the form of a book."

"For some reason? I think you know the reason."

"I do know the reason and I also know it wasn't your fault. You were a boy, there was nothing you could do."

"I was seventeen years old. Not a boy."

Four camp friends. A boating accident. Three drowned, one lived. She's grateful every day that Nick didn't jump in with the others.

"I lived because I'm a coward," he says, and for just a moment Merry hears something angry in his voice. Something red, something real. She wishes he would yell. Lose his temper. Let go. She's not always been proud of her own temper, but it's always seemed to her the most real thing about her. She wants him to scream at the terrible tragedy that engulfed him. *Rage* at it, instead of holding it inside, letting it build up a wall around him. He's stepped from the stream of life and has decided that from now on he'll just observe it, not swim in it.

A life in check. A life unlived.

Merry wants so much more for him. She wants everything for him.

"You survived," she said. "I don't care why. You've been given the gift of life—you can't just throw it away. You have to embrace it."

"By taking that book?" The anger has seeped out of his voice. Now he's back to sounding cool, detached.

"That book," Merry says. "That book. You make it sound like a relative with his hand out for money. It's our treasure, Nick. And it's a comfort."

"It's a book," he says. In the background she hears a bird screech by, making her think of the hawks that circle around his house. She's only been to visit him once in his compound in the wilds of Oregon, a place full of wild and isolated creatures.

"You could live your life in that book. You could change your life with that book."

"Scrooge and Tiny Tim will save my life." She didn't miss the undercurrent of contempt in his tone.

"They might. If you'd let them. They'd certainly open your heart."

He's silent then. She thinks of the ring of brambles that surround his house, imagines them drawing tighter and tighter. What if the day comes when he's completely imprisoned by his bitterness and guilt?

"You know what you should do?" he says. "Give the book to Song Lee. She likes things, and she's good with them. She's responsible."

"You're responsible too. You are precious. You are loved."

He starts to laugh. "You're starting to sound like a country song, Ma."

And she knows she's lost, because once he starts laughing, he's walled himself off again.

Her stubborn son. Her haunted son.

CHAPTER SIX

This is the day of Unbelievable Things, Merry thinks after the phone call is over.

First the nodule, then the PET scan. Now the rejection, and it's not even time for dinner. She considers calling Nick back and screaming, but she knows it won't get her anywhere. If anything, he'll just withdraw further.

She considers telling him about the nodule. She knows he loves her; she doesn't doubt that at all. But at this point she's not sure that telling him about the nodule would make a difference. He'd be sad, he'd feel guilty, but she's not sure he'd do anything because the fact is that he didn't jump into the water to save his friends. It was the right decision, but it was also a cruel one and maybe having made that decision, he's incapable of making any other ones.

But now that she's decided it's time to pass down the book, she has to do something. So, she thinks about what he said about Song Lee, that Song Lee would appreciate the book. And Merry has to acknowledge the truth of it. It's not a bad idea.

Song Lee is her only child not born to her biologically. The one she worries about the most, for just that reason. Because she is Asian in a country not always friendly to Asians. Because although Merry loves her desperately, she's always monitoring herself to make sure that the quality of her love is the same as what she gives to Nick and Bessie. Because although Nick and Bessie drive each other crazy, Merry knows they are bound for life, whereas with Song Lee she feels a bit more tentative. Because Song Lee does have a whole other biological family out there and Merry's read a lot of articles about Asian adoptees wanting to return back to their birth countries, because they feel more comfortable there.

And although Song Lee has said repeatedly that she does not want to do that, that she's happy with her lobbying job in Washington, and her jewel-like apartment in the Mount Vernon section of D.C., and the life she lives there and the Girl Scouts she mentors and the friends she has, Merry's not entirely sure Song Lee would tell her. She's always worried that Song Lee is waiting for her to die, and then, when she's dead, she'll leave the family. Merry's known other adoptive children who've done that.

So perhaps, in his roundabout way, Nick is right. Song Lee could be the perfect person to inherit the book.

In fact, now that she thinks about it, Song Lee was obsessed with the book when she first arrived. When she was two years old and didn't know English and Merry didn't know Korean, she'd take out the book and they'd look at the pictures. Song Lee loved the yellow of Mrs. Fezziwig's dress in John Leech's charming illustration. That was her first English word. *Yewwo*. Later Merry made Song Lee a yellow dress to wear to some Halloween party, though only she and Song Lee caught the Mrs. Fezziwig allusion.

Giving Song Lee the family heirloom would be the perfect way of saying to her, once and for all, you belong to us and we to you. You are a part of the family story. Wherever you go, whatever you do, a part of us will be with you.

The sky is darkening although it's only four in the afternoon. From her window Merry can see her neighbor walking her dog, a sleek Rottweiler. Leroy's obsessed with that dog, though Sophie won't give him the time of day. Whenever Leroy stays at the neighbor's house, which he does frequently because she's his dog-walker, all Sophie ever does is sniff his butt.

Merry looks down the street, at the few tendrils of Christmas lights that sway on most of the older houses. Nothing dramatic, the way it used to be. Now she's an outlier, her own personal Christmas village. She's heard about actual Christmas villages where people keep up lights year-round. It's a temptation, but she suspects she'd never see her kids again. They are way too cool for such effusions.

She could wait for tonight to call Song Lee and give her the news, but she knows Song Lee works from home a lot, and Merry's always excited to pass along good news. She needs to get her mind in a happy place. She can't be mired in death and nodules, and so she puts the book on her lap, resting her hand on it as though taking an oath. Leroy is standing at the window, watching. Waiting. Hoping. He looks a little like Thomas Jefferson, from this angle.

Excited, Merry sits up straight in her damask chair and presses in Song Lee's number.

CHAPTER SEVEN

"I don't think now would be the right time," Song Lee whispers.

Whispers? Song Lee never whispers. She is a person who speaks authoritatively. She is descended from invaders who swept into Korea millennia ago, destroying and crushing everything in their way. Triumphant, bold, powerful people.

"Is someone with you?" Merry whispers back, imagining Song Lee huddled in a corner of her beautiful little apartment. "Are you all right?"

"I'm fine," Song Lee says, though her voice is not fine. It's softer. More tentative. Merry wonders if it's possible that her daughter's being held hostage, though that's unlikely. Song Lee studied karate. She has a black belt. She would defend herself. And she lives in a well-guarded building in Mount Vernon, with a doorman and a concierge and an apartment on the ninth floor, so it's not likely someone would climb in.

Such a beautiful apartment. Only about 600 square feet, but so perfectly and carefully arranged. Diplomas and awards on the walls, certificates from Song Lee's years with the Girl Scouts, a letter from the president of the United States acknowledging her service to the Girl Scouts. A tidy bookshelf that features her small collection of French writers from the Belle Époque, a time period she finds fascinating.

"You don't sound like everything's fine."

How long has it been since Merry last talked to her daughter? Three weeks? Merry's just assumed Song Lee was busy with her new lobbyist job, working to influence education policy. She beat out 2,000 other applicants.

Merry figured they'd all catch up at Christmas, though she has sort of been worrying that Song Lee might bail. That some work deadline might come up.

"I'm fine," Song Lee says again.

Then silence. Merry can't see her daughter, but she has a pretty good idea what she looks like right now. Head thrust back a bit like a lizard about to strike, left eyebrow raised. She can be very intimidating.

"Are you at work? Is this a bad time?"

"No," Song Lee says.

A romance? Song Lee has always been so close-mouthed. She went to the prom with the captain of the football team, which was a revelation to Merry. That she wanted to go to the prom, and that she even knew the captain of the football team. Since then, she's tended to go out with older, high prestige sorts of guys.

Has she interrupted sex? But then why would Song Lee answer the phone?

"Song Lee, are we playing twenty questions? What's going on?"

"I was fired." Her voice is stripped of emotion. She might be reciting directions, and yet, there's a definite undercurrent of anger. But at whom?

If Song Lee were crying, Merry could comfort her. But she's not sure how to respond to this icy fury, and so she says what is probably the worst thing she could say: "You've only been there six months."

"Turns out you can be fired at any time." Snarky Song Lee is better than whispering Song Lee. Merry's grateful for that.

"But why?"

"Does it matter?"

"Well, yes. Were you a whistleblower or something?"

Song Lee snorts, but Merry can't imagine her being fired for cause. This is a child who has truly never caused her aggravation. She has worked and studied. She spent a few months after she first arrived having difficulty pooping, but you can't hold that against a two-year-old.

"Please tell me what happened."

A pause. "I plagiarized something."

"That's terrible," Merry says.

"Way to be supportive, Mom."

"Well, I am supportive. I guess. I adore you, obviously. But why would you do something like that?"

"Because I didn't think I'd get caught."

Merry starts to say something about virtue and ethics and the undying nature of a mother's love, but it's too late. Song Lee has ended the call.

"Wait, Song Lee, don't do that."

Though she has done it.

Merry calls her back. It goes to voicemail. She calls again and again.

When Song Lee was little and didn't want to go into her car seat, Merry remembers how she could turn herself into a plank, impossible to bend. The only solution was to tickle her. How long has it been since she's heard Song Lee laugh? Lately she's developed more of a snicker.

The rational side of Merry tells her that Song Lee is an intelligent and resourceful young woman and that she will figure this all out, whatever it is. She truly cannot see her as a plagiarizing person. But if she did, if she made some sort of mistake, there has to be a way to fix it. Song Lee wanted this job so badly.

Maybe she's joking with her? That would be easier to believe. Maybe she's decided for reasons of her own that she'd like to torture Merry. As a teenager she did once tell her she was pregnant and then started to laugh. Merry didn't think that was funny, especially, but she was relieved at the twist.

She looks at the ancient volume that she's still holding in her hands, clinging to it like it's the ledge of a cliff. None of the Cratchits did anything like this. They loved each other and supported each other and they all shared one meager little plum pudding without complaining.

Merry knows for a fact that once things start to go wrong, they can go wrong in a big way. She saw it with her father, pounded down by year after year of disease. She saw it with her husband, once so confident but undermined by a friend's betrayal. She sees it with herself, the way your entire life can change in one phone call.

But at least she has the book, she has her stories. What will Song Lee have to grab on to? What if this completely undermines her? What if she becomes a whispering sort of person? What if she loses her bold confidence?

Leroy starts to sneeze.

When her phone rings she answers it immediately, assuming it's Song Lee, ready to confide in her.

"I'm so glad you called," she cries out.

But it isn't Song Lee.

It's her middle daughter, Bessie.

"You were going to give Song Lee *A Christmas Carol* before me?"

CHAPTER EIGHT

Bessie's freckled face fills the phone screen. She always FaceTimes, which drives Merry crazy because instead of being able to focus on the conversation, she has to worry about making sure that the angle of her face is right, which it never is.

How did Bessie find out so fast? Merry wonders. How is it possible that Bessie knows so quickly that Merry offered Song Lee the book? She didn't even think Bessie and Song Lee were talking at the moment. Some dispute over a cactus that Merry still doesn't understand.

But she supposes that dirt on your mother trumps petty grievances. Or Nick might have called her. He's tricky that way. Likes to cause trouble.

"I didn't think you'd want it," Merry says, which is true. Bessie does not have kind feelings about Charles Dickens. She's been outspoken in her views about his treatment of his wife, which was awful. Deserting the mother of your ten children was bad enough, but he pushed her out of the family house and told his children to stay away from her. They didn't all listen, but still.

"That's not the point, Mom. You should have gone in sequence. Nick to me to Song Lee."

"I'm sorry," Merry says, and she genuinely is. She can understand why Bessie feels hurt. She also suspects that no matter what she does from this point on in her life, nothing will supersede the fact that when she thought about her legacy, she left out Bessie. Wars will rage, climate will change, disasters will occur, and yet she imagines Bessie holding the book in front of her children. *Your late grandmother didn't even think to give this to me.*

"You always go to Song Lee first."

"That's not true."

"Remember when you went to her swim meet instead of mine?"

"Well, that's true. But she was only five and I thought it more important that she have a cheerleader."

"You went because she always won. You've always thought I was a loser."

"Good grief," Merry says. "How can you say that?"

The sound in her ears is reverberating so loudly she's surprised Bessie can't hear it. She feels like the nodule is rocketing inside her. For the first time, she acknowledges herself as weakened. Sick. But now is not the time to succumb. Because it breaks her heart that Bessie feels this way and she knows she's right. Or she knows Bessie feels it anyway, and that amounts to the same thing.

How can you hurt someone so terribly without meaning to?

Merry wishes Bessie were right there, because Bessie is the one member of her family she could hug out of anger, but Bessie is in the city, out on a walk. Merry can hear people yelling at each other. Cars honking. The clatter of the clothing carts in the Fashion District.

"Leroy says our family has a toxic energy," Bessie says.

That gets Merry's attention.

"Leroy the dog?" Merry knows the dog talks to her, but she hadn't realized he spoke to anyone else. She looks over to him, but he stares back at her, liquid eyes merciless as death.

"I knew you'd say that," Bessie says.

"I don't know what you're talking about."

"My boyfriend. Leroy."

"You're going out with someone named Leroy?"

"Why did you have to give our dog a person name? Why couldn't you name him Spot?"

"Spot?" Merry says. She looks over at her little yellow dog. There's not a spot on him. Tufts of hair are standing straight up from his head. Static cling.

"I never thought it would be an issue. I just like the name Leroy."

Bessie leans forward, her entire face filling the screen, and lowers her voice to a whisper. Possibly Leroy the boyfriend is standing next to her. "Maybe for the time being we could call him something else."

Merry looks over to Leroy the dog, whose face has changed to one of irritation. The shape of it seems boxier, and his eyes glitter. Jewel-like.

"It's not like he knows his name," Bessie says. "He doesn't come when you call him."

"He's poorly trained," Merry remarks, "but that doesn't mean he doesn't have an identity."

She starts to laugh. She can't help herself. It's as though her body is betraying her. First the shadow that turned into a nodule and now this dog that has turned into a boyfriend. It is all just so ridiculous, this life of hers, that is going to end, and now she wants to cry.

"You're not taking this seriously," Bessie snaps.

This is the child who is most like her, she thinks. The one who is so full of heart and anger.

"Bessie, I'm genuinely sorry, but I cannot call that dog by another name. He's confused enough as it is." She feels like sand is seeping into her legs, she's so tired. "I want you to take the book, and I should have asked you first. Because really, you're the perfect person. You're the heart of our family and it belongs with you. I can picture the family congregating at your place in years to come, all of you together, acting out the story the way we used to do when you were kids. Do you remember? You loved that."

"I hated that!" Bessie says. "Nick always got to be Tiny Tim and I was always the Ghost of the Present. The most boring ghost. I couldn't even be the Ghost of Christmas Yet to Come because Song Lee wanted that. I don't want the book. All I want you to do is respect me and change that dog's name so I have a chance with my boyfriend and don't wind up alone. Is that really asking so much?"

CHAPTER NINE

Merry met the man who would become her husband at Ye Olde Christmas Shoppe in Yonkers, a huge store tucked between a Bagel Emporium and a PetSmart.

She'd begun working there after her father died. She could not possibly stay in his house by herself, so she sold the house in the Bronx, rented a small apartment in Yonkers, and worked during the day and went to college at night.

The Shoppe Ladies were the kindest people she ever knew. Like book collectors, though perhaps not quite so dusty and hunched over. But they had a similar obsession over accumulation. Merry can still remember the flurry when Hallmark introduced a limited-edition Babe Ruth ornament, and then it turned out that one of the Shoppe Ladies had been stockpiling them. The drama, the tears. The betrayal.

The Shoppe Ladies baked her cookies. They celebrated her birthday. They taught her to play canasta. They healed her from the grief that swallowed her after she lost her father. *Lost* being the proper word because for the longest time she felt like she'd misplaced him. He'd always been so sedentary—he quite literally couldn't move. She simply could not believe he was not there, and that she hadn't been with him when he died because she'd gone skiing in Gstaad.

Back then, Merry's favorite Shoppe Lady kept trying to set her up with her son. Sullivan Baker Bingham. A superstar lawyer who'd gone to Yale Law School and was now an associate at a big New York law firm. On top of being brilliant, he'd also been a catcher for his university baseball team. He played the piano and the piccolo, and he volunteered as a reading tutor.

It all sounded a bit much to Merry, but one day, when she was working at the cash register, a slender brown-haired man approached, holding in front of him a little ornament of a mouse on a computer. He held the ornament a distance in front of him, as though it was contagious. She noticed he had nice arms and that, slender though he was, his cotton shirt stretched against the muscles in his chest. He put the mouse down carefully on the counter, looked across at her, and said, "Wow."

Sully proposed a month later. They married in December, of course. And his mother arranged the wedding. Merry's mother couldn't come. She was planning her own December wedding. You'd think she would postpone her wedding under the circumstances, but Merry's mother was not then or now a postponing sort of person. She assured Merry they'd catch up. She sent her a huge bouquet of lilies, the sort of thing you'd stand up at a funeral. Merry donated them to the Shoppe Ladies, who were always visiting someone who needed flowers.

Now this very same slender brown-haired man smiles up at Merry when she bursts into his home office. He has a little gray in his hair now, but it makes him look thoughtful. Beyond that, his face is unlined. He looks a bit like Atticus Finch, if he were a geology teacher. Sully has ink on his hands; he grades his students' papers with fountain pens, which they love. They love *him*. His students are always emailing him heartfelt appreciations. He's always invited to their parties. Weddings. Baptisms. Bar mitzvahs. There's a slew of invitations on their refrigerator. The wall behind his desk is filled with letters from his students and their parents. *Thank you, Mr. Bingham.* And his Yale Law diploma, which he didn't want to put up but Merry insisted. He might have been cheated out of his law career, but he should still be recognized.

On his desk he keeps the little mouse ornament that first brought them together. He still finds the combination of the mouse and the computer charming. Since then, he's also bought her a mouse and cell phone ornament and another with a flashlight. Also on his desk is a nice three-volume set of *The Complete Works of Benjamin Franklin*, published in 1806. It's bound in straight-grained Moroccan leather with gilt edges, the last from a later owner, but Merry approves. She always goes for gilt. But the part of it Sully loves are the thirteen engraved plates that show Franklin's engravings and drawings. He's that rarest of things, a person who actually reads rare books. She bought it for him right after she went to work with Mr. Hong. One of her first big purchases.

"Is our family strange?" she asks. "Or is it me?"

"I thought it was me," he says, but his eyes shine when he looks at her. She's never seen anything but love there. "Song Lee talked to you?"

"You know about her?" she says, though of course he knows. If a tree falls in a forest, it calls Sully. People tell him everything, ask him everything. Trust him.

"She's strong, Merry."

"She can't be that strong or why did she plagiarize?"

He nods, stands up, and holds out his hand to her, taking her over to a little blue velvet bench tucked in the corner. She'd intended to buy an authentic Victorian one, but it wound up being more economical to buy from Wayfair. Still, it has the right look and lots of gilt ornamentation.

She loves sitting alongside him, leaning into him, breathing in the coffee smell of him. His breath is always warm, as are his lips.

"What's wrong?" he asks.

"What's wrong? My one daughter has just been kicked out of her job for plagiarizing, my other one is mortally wounded by my actions, and my son is mired in a morass of unending grief."

He nods. "That's true, but that wouldn't normally bother you."

Now would undoubtedly be the moment to tell him about Dr. Fiedler's call. The nodule. The PET scan. All the things she's been holding back.

The words are dancing on the edge of her tongue, but she can't speak.

Because the moment she says the words, her entire life will change.

She will no longer be Merry Bingham, successful book scout with clients all around the world, the mother of three lost children. Instead, she will be poor Merry Bingham, cancer patient and mother of three lost children. She will be pitiful, and there is absolutely no word Merry likes less than *pitiful*. Even *nodule* is better than pitiful.

"Is it true you're planning to give away the book?" He leans closer to her. Some of their fall hydrangeas stretch along the window, their faded maroon blossoms always reminding her of the leather of an old book.

How she hated the way people used to look at her father. That mincing tone of voice, the way they'd pitch their voices a little higher, a little louder. Sometimes they'd pat his head like a dog. Her father, who when not sitting was six foot two, was a strong capable man until the disease took all that away from him. She remembers how people used to flinch against the smell of him. How she used to flinch against that and didn't want to bring friends home. How she felt ashamed.

She cannot face that. Not from Sully, of all people.

Damn her eyes for filling with tears.

He puts his hand on hers, his gold wedding band glowing against his long fingers. She's so tempted to surrender. But she can't. Because once you surrender, you can't take it back.

So Merry does what she always does when she's upset. She goes on the offensive.

She points at the recycling bin alongside Sully's desk, which is filled with reams of paper and one bright glittery red envelope. "What's that?"

CHAPTER TEN

Sully's fast, but Merry's faster and she has better knees. She gets to the bin before he's out of his seat, retrieving the sparkly envelope from the rest of the recycling.

What she sees is truly the last thing she's expecting.

She'd thought one of Sully's tenth graders sent him a card. They're all in love with him, and with her too. They're so confused.

But the moment she sees those teeth, she knows who the card is from. The Campion teeth. The orthodontia that probably cost the equivalent of several mortgages. The smile of betrayal. Oh, how they smile as they stab you in the back. Not the children, actually. But the parents.

There they all are, arranged by height. All four of the Campion children, with Phoebe and Al at either end of them, like bookends. All of them wearing ugly sweaters, because they are a fun family and do stuff like that. They wear bright green and red sweaters, and they're proud of it. There's even a grandchild. A perfect grandchild with blonde hair and a full set of Campion teeth.

She hates them. Not the children, she has no quarrel with them. But Al, who had been her husband's best friend, and Phoebe, who had been hers.

"You still get cards from them?" she demands of her husband. How long has it been? Twenty years?

She looks at the back of the card. A handwritten note, of course. No printed-out letters from them.

Hey, prof. How's it going? Bet you're changing some lives. I'm still doing the corporate thing. Money, money, money. Nothing useful at all. We're all headed to London for the holidays. Bought a house in Mayfair. Lots of respect for you, man. Love to Merry and the kiddies.

"Why does he sound like he just graduated from Dartmouth? Do you send them a card? You do, don't you?"

Sully shrugs. "It's Christmas."

"You send the *Campions* a Christmas card? The people who ruined our lives? What do you say? *Ho, ho, ho, bitch*?"

"Merry!" He looks so genuinely wounded. In Sully-world everyone is genteel and forgiving and people do not swear.

"Sorry, but seriously, what do you say? Do you tell them about me? The kids?" She tries to remember the card the Binghams sent out last year. It didn't have of photo of their kids. They'd revolted. Said they were too old to get together for a family photo. She imagines what they would have said had she asked them to wear ugly sweaters. She'd sent out a card with glitter in the envelopes to make up for her hurt, but the glitter sprinkled all over people's floors. One woman thought it was anthrax.

"I just say best wishes and I tell them about my classes."

"I bet they love that. 'Good old Sully Bingham. Devoting his life to doing good. No need for us to feel guilty about getting him fired.'" Suddenly winded, she slumps back down onto the velvet Wayfair bench, which clatters against her movement because it is not the solid antique Victorian divan she wanted to buy. "'Maybe we'll even donate some of our millions to an impoverished geology teacher fund.'"

"It's Christmas, Merry. The time when we're supposed to forgive." He's clasped his hands together, pleading.

"Do not do your Bob Cratchit imitation for me, Mr. Bingham. My anger is righteous."

She can't take her eyes off the Campion faces. They look so joyful. So open. So receptive. They look the way she wants her family to look. She tries to imagine asking Song Lee to wear an ugly sweater. Or Nick to have a grandchild. Or Bessie to smile in a photo like a normal person instead of someone striking a pose. The last time she sent an official photo, which must have been four years ago now that she thinks of it, she had to take twenty shots just to get one in which no one looked irritated.

The Campions even have a confident-looking dog, one of those smooth-talking creatures with pricked-up ears and a lifesaving disposition. He probably patrols the house, saving babies in danger. He probably has a proper name. Like Lassie.

Merry imagines them traveling together, each one taking turns holding the baby, who sleeps throughout the whole flight. No projectile vomiting from her. She sees the house in Mayfair, which they probably bought without a mortgage. Such a jingly, sparkly sort of life, without shadows and nodules and PET scan appointments scheduled for the 18th, and she feels frustrated and envious, which is so irritating because she doesn't want to be that person. She is generally not that person.

But turns out she is that person, and she feels ashamed at herself and angry at them, and envious. Oh, so envious.

If only, she thinks.

If only Merry could take her family to London for Christmas. The things they could do! Walk under the angels that fly above Oxford Street. She loves those angels. Wander around Hyde Park. Listen to the bells from St. Paul's. Have tea at Kensington Palace.

Go to the Dickens Museum. Is there any place better to visit for Christmas? To walk the very floors he walked. To see the desk he wrote on. The Fezziwig etching is there, which always gives Merry a thrill. The dining room table set for Christmas dinner. So many seats crammed with family and friends. You can actually hear their voices. Or she can.

A welcoming front door painted bright red. A hallway filled with knickknacks: a wallet made out of safety pins, a nutmeg container to get rid of bad smells, a theater pass made out of ivory. She could meet with her outspoken friend who works as a guide there, who's still mad the Dickens family didn't bury him where he expressly wanted to be buried, which was outside in a quiet part of Kent. Instead, he was buried at Westminster Abbey. "Was he not clear?" she expostulates to everyone who comes by. "Didn't he say he did not want pomp?" They'd stop by Mary Hogarth's room, where there waits an ethereal docent with passion in her eyes. She tells the tragic story of Dickens's beloved sister-in-law, who died in that very room, she whispers as she points toward a piece of holly on Mary's small bed, worried perhaps at disturbing her ghost.

Then, to the library, where there is an Arthur Rackham illustrated edition of *A Christmas Carol*, not quite as valuable as her own but appealing for all that. Dark and Nordic and somewhat frightening.

Then, perhaps, inspired, they could put on their own production of *A Christmas Carol*, like they did when the kids were young and agreeable. She'd make up costumes and Sully would play the piccolo and they'd dance around and celebrate. How wonderful it would be to do that again, to get away from this nodule for Christmas. Have one last Christmas with her family filled with joy instead of sorrow and terror. Feel the holiday as she has not felt it for so long. Oh, what a dream that would be. To have a perfect Christmas. To have the children all around, and happy. Then she would have the energy to fight for her future. Then she would be ready to battle, and she could go to her death safe in the knowledge that she had given her children the most wonderful Christmas of their lives.

But she can't.

Because they have no money. And she has a nodule. And she must have a PET scan.

And her daughter has been fired because she's a plagiarist and her son is alone and depressed and her other daughter isn't speaking to her.

There is a train running through her head and she is just so angry and frightened.

Christmas feels so far away.

CHAPTER ELEVEN

Everything feels better the next day when Merry arrives at her office Christmas party. How can it not? The office itself is in one of the most elegant brownstones on the Upper East Side. And Augusta Hong is at the door to greet her, decked out in a bright red velvet maternity dress, high-heeled sparkly shoes, and a tiara. Gussie is the only person Merry knows who likes sparkly things as much as she does. Her young friend glitters, which is funny given that her father, the late great Julius Hong, had all the sparkle of a boulder.

Merry adored Julius Hong. He gave her her start. But he was not bubbly.

Had she been asked as a child to project the direction of her life, Merry would have said that she planned to be a librarian. She knew she wanted to do something with books, and that was the only career involving books that she knew about. That or working in a bookstore, which would have been okay too. But there was something secretive about librarians she found appealing. Librarians were privy to people's borrowing records, knew their secret histories. Ideally, she'd be a spy librarian, if such a career existed.

But then Mr. Hong introduced her to book scouting.

Turned out there was a career where you could be paid to be a scavenger hunter. Not paid a *lot*, but paid. Like the old joke said: *How do you make a million dollars in bookselling? You start with two million.* Still, it was about the joy of the hunt, of rustling through old attics, of meeting with passionate and eccentric collectors, of prowling through abandoned storage units and tracking down forgotten books. A job where people told you their deepest desires and asked you to help find them. A job where you actually had to seek out incunabula, those lush, beautifully illustrated books printed before 1500. Now that was a word. *Incunabula.*

"Merry," Gussie Hong burbles, her voice like a song. She drapes her slender arm around Merry's shoulder, then spins her around so she can admire the office decorations. They are extensive.

In the corner of the room, facing onto the grand windows that overlook East 79th Street, is a Christmas tree that is only slightly smaller than the one in Rockefeller Center. Wide strands of satin ribbon wrap around it. Masses of lights encircle it. On it are ornaments of books. Gussie makes them and gives them as gifts to the staff every year. Books they've loved, books they've sold. There are stars and bells and explosions of red bows. It is stunning and cheerful and over-the-top, just the way Christmas should be.

The bookshelves, normally so imposing, built to echo the ones in the Morgan Library, are now bedecked with chubby little angels. Music is coming out of a speaker somewhere. Something Merry doesn't recognize, but it's cheerful. There's a trumpet, which she loves, and a bass. It makes her feel like dancing, and in fact, some of the younger employees are doing a tango.

For the first time since Dr. Fiedler's call, the nodule has faded from the forefront of her mind. It hasn't disappeared, but it's taken a step back. Surrounded by so much love and splendor, how can a whisper of the Christmas spirit not make its way into Merry's mind?

The other book scouts, all draped around the floor like cats, grin at her and salute.

They call Merry "Captain." Affectionately. She has been the residue of wisdom since Mr. Hong died. She is the one who remembers the stories, and bookselling is all about stories and people. They come to her often and ask her, "Is this true? Did this really happen? Do you think he would sell this? Do you think he would want this?"

Normally she bakes stained glass window cookies for this party, a laborious effort that involves melting candies and pouring them into dough. But this year, nodule and all, she was not up to that, and so she got them all gift certificates at a local coffee shop, and thank God she thought of that. She didn't think of it until she walked by the coffee shop, but the staff is appreciative. Grateful.

They are all enthusiasm. There is no ennui in bookselling; it's all about hope and possibility, and for all it seems dusty and dry, it's actually the most exciting of professions. Whole new worlds are opening up. Books and stories from other cultures, other people. They are rewriting history. Creating a new history.

Crystal, draped across the settee, is working with a woman collecting the works of all the women writers Hemingway knew. Pedro specializes in memoirs from queer Latin Americans. Derek specializes in unusual playing cards, a section of ephemera that is booming.

"Just ran across someone who wants to buy your *Carol*," Gussie says. She's now moved on to the floor, her belly rising up like a mountain.

Someone is always asking to buy Merry's edition of *A Christmas Carol*. Dickens is never out of favor, no matter how times change, and that book in particular is a favorite with collectors.

"No thanks. Not for sale." Automatically Merry puts her hand to her bag, which feels warm. She has the book with her. She felt the need to have it nearby. She knows she runs the risk of someone stealing it, but she doesn't think your run-of-the-mill mugger will care about a seventh edition of Charles Dickens's great work. She has a hundred-dollar bill in her bag, and she figures that if she's attacked, she'll just throw the hundred at the robber.

The PET scan is in three days. Dr. Fiedler said he should know the results quickly. Merry will be able to view them on her medical portal, or if there's "anything to talk about," he'll call her. *Anything to talk about.* So, if she doesn't hear from him for two days after the test, all is good. All she has to do is pray the phone doesn't ring.

"I told them you didn't want to sell," Gussie says, "but they said to let them know if you change your mind. Nice family."

Merry nods. Gussie thinks all families are nice, either because she comes from a nice one herself or because she's willing to give some slack to people willing to part with so much money. Like so much in bookselling, it's a mixture of idealism and a desperate grab for cash.

But the conversation has moved on to a possible Shakespeare Folio that may or may not be authentic, and a letter from Anne Boleyn that may or may not be authentic, and the surprise that a letter from Frederick Douglass that was definitely authentic sold for so much money.

Merry is coasting along, relaxing, sort of, thinking of Mr. Hong and how he used to rule over these Christmas parties from his giant leather chair, which now sits empty in the window. He so wanted Gussie and Song Lee to be great friends, but although they were perfectly polite with each other, they never connected. Still, if it hadn't been for Song Lee, Merry would never have had the courage to approach Mr. Hong. They were both volunteering at a library sale, sorting through the literature selection. She had no idea that he was one of the foremost booksellers in New York. She just thought he seemed like a kindly Asian man, and she was always trying to surround Song Lee with Asian people. She wanted Song Lee to feel connected to her cultural heritage, to know she came from a vast and proud population of people, even if there were not many of them living on her street.

Merry and Mr. Hong wound up talking about Dickens. They both adored *Great Expectations* and then they got to talking about *A Christmas Carol* and she told him about her vampire ancestor Nora Villard and her autographed copy. After the sale was over, she began visiting him for lunch at his mansion on the Hudson and one thing led to another and he hired her to be his assistant.

First thing he did was send her to the London Rare Books School, where she immersed herself in classes on First Editions, Provenance, Bookbinding, Illustration, and Paleography—the study of ancient handwriting, for which she discovered she had a strange aptitude. Put her in front of one of Dickens's letters and the script seemed to unfurl in front of her. While she was in London, she also interned for Amos

Gaudy, a friend of Mr. Hong's, who had a small bookshop not far from the British Museum. Mr. Gaudy gave her the task of sorting 4,000 pamphlets relating to social unrest in the 1860s into some sort of order, which she did, and which he then sold to the British Museum for $10,000. He gave half to her, and it was one of the most generous gifts she'd ever received. Not just because of the money, though that was very useful, but because it made her feel like she truly had a place in this book community. It changed the direction of her life.

She's so immersed in thinking about Mr. Gaudy that it takes Merry a moment to realize that someone is talking about him.

"It's terrible," Gussie is saying.

"What happened?"

Merry starts, worried at first that Mr. Gaudy's died. But no, in some ways it's worse.

"Stuggot dropped him."

"Stuggot dropped him?" Merry repeats. Lately she's been hearing so many sentences she cannot process. Nodules and rejections and now her dear friend is to be betrayed by a man he's worked so hard to help. "How is that possible? Stuggot would be no one without Mr. Gaudy."

Edward Stuggot was a struggling collector with an interest in Middle Eastern works, from back when such books were not much in demand. Mr. Gaudy worked with him, gave him a place to stay, helped him build up a collection, which is now worth a fortune. Stuggot took up so much of Mr. Gaudy's time and energy that more than half of Mr. Gaudy's income has come to rest on his collecting.

"How will he be able to survive without him?" she asks.

"Stuggot decided to go with one of the bigger houses. They can do more for him," Gussie says.

"That's so unfair."

"I know," Gussie says. "Terrible."

She looks sad for a moment and then they all begin talking about some other bookselling trauma, but Merry can't let go.

Her mind froths. It's so wrong. She pictures poor Mr. Gaudy, the gentle look on his face, his huge plastic glasses that magnify his eyes and make him look like a grasshopper. He's one of the kindest people she knows.

"How is he going to be able to pay for his new space?" she asks.

"Who?"

"Mr. Gaudy. Didn't he just move to some new space in Paddington?"

"Oh, I don't know," Gussie says. "That's too bad." She looks up at Merry, worried. They all look worried, because they care, but not really. Sort of care. They like Mr. Gaudy and don't wish him harm, but the fact is he's been overtaken by a series of unavoidable events. A natural victim. Sort of like Merry's father, come to that. An innocent.

"There must be something we could do to help him."

"Of course," Gussie says. She takes out her phone and types in a note. Her nails are painted with silver glitter. She'll probably send him flowers.

"Something substantial," Merry presses. She knows she's ruined the vibe. It's tactless to hijack a Christmas party by dwelling on some poor old guy's troubles. She's supposed to be cheerful. It's that time of year. She has to move on and think of something else. But it really bothers her to think of Mr. Gaudy betrayed. It's wrong. It makes her angry. "What if we were to throw some work his way? Remember how I was going to meet with that hedge fund guy who wanted to start a collection of *Harry Potter* books? He seemed so eager. Maybe I could refer him to Mr. Gaudy."

Gussie nods thoughtfully. She looks so like her father in that moment.

"Frederic Lion, you mean? The one from Silicon Valley."

"Yes," Merry says, though she knows this is not going to fly. Gussie is kind, but she's not likely to want to surrender an enthusiastic multimillionaire. Merry gets it. She knows they're in a tough business, they're all struggling. But Mr. Gaudy's something special. A force for good. "It's just that if people like Mr. Gaudy are wiped out, if good people are beaten down without anyone standing up for them, then where are we? First, they come for Mr. Gaudy, but then they come for us."

Her young friends stare at her bug-eyed. She's gone too far. She knows it. She always goes too far, and now, worst of all, she feels like crying. Because it's so sad and so wrong, and she wants to do something for Mr. Gaudy but doesn't know what, and then young Pedro starts to cry.

"I didn't want to say anything, but my mother just found out she has cancer."

"Oh, Pedro," they cry out and then Crystal's broken up with her girlfriend and Derek is suffering from anxiety and then Gussie starts to cry because she misses her father. By the time Merry leaves, they're all depressed and she staggers out onto the street feeling a bit like the Ghost of Christmas Yet to Come. She has turned into the person who sucks joy out of the holiday. She is death.

CHAPTER TWELVE

Now Merry's striding down Madison Avenue, heading for Grand Central. Might as well take the train home. She's not doing any good here. Though she's not sure she's ready to go home.

Everywhere she looks she sees drama and pain.

She could go over to Rockefeller Center, but then she'd be trampled alive by the crowds. She would go look at the windows at Lord & Taylor, but Lord & Taylor has been closed for years. She could head down to the Morgan Library. That always makes her feel better. They own the original handwritten manuscript of *A Christmas Carol*, and every year they put one of its pages on display. Merry always loves to look at it. Or actually what she loves is seeing all the people lined up to look at it. Usually that fills her with optimism about the future of books, about the future of Dickens.

But she's too depressed to want to cheer herself up. It would feel like a lie. What she wants to do is help Mr. Gaudy. She thinks of that multimillionaire in California. Frederic Lion. She calls and gives him Mr. Gaudy's information. "He's first-rate," she tells him, which he is.

Like most multimillionaires, Frederic Lion does not burble with enthusiasm. He says thanks and closes the conversation. Yet Merry suspects he will call Mr. Gaudy immediately. She wonders what

Gussie will say when she hears. Merry will have to figure out a way to apologize. Fortunately, Gussie is one of the very few people in the book business who is not struggling, so Merry suspects she'll forgive her. Anyway, if Merry's dying, what does it matter?

Her phone buzzes. Bessie sending a text. *Sorry, didn't mean to argue.*

Sweet girl, Merry thinks. So quick to find offense, and yet so quick to apologize. Heart so open. Merry presses a heart emoji. She considers calling her but knows Bessie's going to start in on the Leroy thing and she's not up for that. Merry's sure to start crying, or laughing. Either one would get them nowhere.

Nick doesn't text, but when Merry checks her email she finds he's forwarded her an article about trees, which is his way of reaching out.

Song Lee sends her her Wordle score, which she does every day.

The kids are each showing their love in different ways, and Merry appreciates it, but it doesn't stop her from feeling aggravated because it's not what she wants from them. She knows she loves them. She knows they love her. She's not worried about love; she's worried about life. She's scared about death. She's worried about people who think the way to show love is through texting. She wants something grand for them, something majestic. She wants them to live big, openhearted lives with joy at the center of them, and Christmas and Dickens and legacy and history. In that context, these texts feel like mosquito bites. Little stinging reminders of what will not be.

Wind roars down Madison Avenue, battering Merry, knocking her from her direction, though she doesn't actually have a direction. She can barely see where she's going due to the snow slapping into her face. Shards of snow. There's nothing soft about these flakes.

The street is empty. Who would be walking around in this? She clutches her bag against her, thinking of the treasured book that rests protected inside of it. How she wishes she were a child again, sitting alongside her father, mashed up against him in his wheelchair. She needs to sit, and yet she's afraid to sit. She feels off-balance, weak. She wants her father. She's afraid to die. Her ribs hurt from when she fell on them. She feels the nodule like a ghost inside her, infiltrating her body.

She doesn't pray a lot, not as often as she should. But she's desperate now and pleads for help, her voice absorbed into the roaring of the wind.

Immediately her phone rings.

Merry's so startled, she drops the phone in the slush. Grabbing it up, excited, she thinks the call might be something wonderful.

But then she looks at the name on the screen and realizes her prayers have not been answered at all. This is the complete opposite of what she wants.

CHAPTER THIRTEEN

"Merry Christmas, Meredith," her mother says.

For some reason her mother finds it amusing to wish her Merry Christmas every time she calls. Even in July. Merry has put that on the list of things not worth arguing about with her mother. It's a short list.

"And to you, Lana," Merry replies, as she always does.

She hears salsa music in the background. It could be the start of a party or the end of one. There's always a party going on with her mother. As she has made perfectly clear, life is to be lived once and enjoyed.

"You don't sound well. You're wheezing."

"It's cold," Merry says. "I'm walking in the middle of a snowstorm."

"Why? Call an Uber."

Her mother loves Uber. It's designed for her. Practical and easy. Merry knows it's a good idea, but she's stubborn. Something in her mother brings it out in her. Funny how when she talks to her mother, even now, at fifty-five, she reverts back to adolescence. Back to when she was in high school and her mother announced she was leaving Merry's father for her boss, Jack Gutiérrez, the CEO of the manufacturing firm where she worked as an administrative assistant. "Jack's my soulmate," she'd said by way of consolation. "I would have left your father whether he got sick or not."

"I want to walk," Merry says,

"That's your martyr complex at play. Lean into it." Her mother caws at that. She finds herself amazingly funny. Her own best audience.

"No one would accuse you of suffering from that," Merry says.

"Too right," her mother says.

She pictures her mother, tanned and toned, hair tinted just the right shade of blonde. Elegant. People have always said that Merry gets her looks from her mother, but that's because most people hadn't seen what her father looked like when he was young and handsome and strong.

"So, I told Bessie flat out that she's crazy if she thinks you're going to change that dog's name. You're besotted with that dog."

This is the thing that absolutely confounds Merry. Although she is a horrible grandmother and never remembers anyone's birthday or goes to graduations or does anything you can rely on, the kids adore her and call her whenever there's trouble.

"You know me," she goes on. "I always take your side. But I told her I'd talk to you and see if maybe you'd change his name. He's just a dumb animal, right?"

"I am not changing the dog's name. It's ridiculous. She's gone out with five different guys and two women this year. Next, she'll probably go out with someone named Spot."

Her mother laughs at that. She finds Merry very funny. "You might regret that, baby. She seems to really like this fella. They're talking about marriage."

"How long as she known him?"

"People fall in love. There's no timetable for that."

"And I guess there's no timetable for falling out of love either."

How she'd begged her mother not to leave her father. She was only seventeen, and she worried about him so much. It tortured her seeing how much he suffered, each day losing strength until he could no longer move at all. Not even his hands.

Merry slips across a manhole covered by snow. She twists to right herself, in the process twisting the exact spot where she hurt her ribs. It feels like fire. It hurts so bad.

"You okay, Meredith? Have you gone to a specialist?"

"Why are you calling?" she snaps.

A cab skids in front of Merry, splashing her with slush, pellets of ice shooting out like bullets.

"Oh, and I told Song Lee she could move down here," her mother continues. "Stay with us for a while."

"To Florida?" Merry asks.

"Why not? There are plenty of felons down here."

Everything's a joke with her. Everything's something to laugh about. "She's not a felon. She plagiarized something. Once."

"Once?" her mother says. "Oh, I thought she said she'd done it a lot."

Merry hears Jack humming something in the background. Jack Gutiérrez, a man about as different from her father as it would be possible to be. A man who is all about movement and grace. Even when he's barbecuing, he looks like he's dancing.

"It's not a joke," Merry snaps. She's heartbroken that Song Lee has plagiarized once, but terrified that she's done it repeatedly. That would mean there was something seriously wrong with her, and it hurts her that she'd tell Lana before her. She would fight to the death for this daughter of hers, but what if Song Lee doesn't trust her? Is it ridiculous to feel terrified and jealous at the same time?

Her mother sighs. "You take everything so seriously."

"Yes," Merry says. "I do. I think things matter. I think when you work for your whole life to get a job and then you mess it up in one day and you may be banned from ever again doing the very thing you've dreamed of doing, that it matters. What if she can't find herself after this? What if she drifts? What if she's lost?"

"Good Lord, Meredith. Do you always expect the worst?"

"It has been my experience," she says, "that terrible things happen. That people you love get sick and suffer. Or they struggle. Or they're betrayed. Or things come up out of the blue." She puts her hand over where she thinks the nodule is, though fortunately her mother can't see her. "And you can't make jokes about it and you can't ignore it. You have to deal with it."

Her mother laughs. She is impossible to offend. "Honestly, Meredith, to hear you talk you'd think I left your father on the street. We weren't compatible. We would have gotten divorced one way or the other. If anything, I stayed with him longer because he was sick."

"That's a tremendous consolation."

Merry doesn't know why on earth her mother bothers to call her since all they do is argue. She's not entirely sure why she answers the phone. Except that her mother is her mother and she supposes she has this idea that someday that will mean something.

Her mother sighs. "But why are you getting rid of that book?"

Ah. That's what this call is about. There's always a reason. She wonders if her mother would take it. Probably. Her mother has never said no to anything that Merry can think of, beyond her request to please not leave her father.

"I'm not getting rid of it. I'm handing it down. It's my legacy."

"It's so unlike you to part with anything," her mother says.

"If you mean I'm loyal, that's true."

"You've always said you wouldn't part with that book until you were on your deathbed. You were such a morbid little girl. Remember when you made up that calendar that showed all the days of your life and you figured you'd die when you were eighty-four?"

"Surely it's not surprising that when you grow up with the sort of childhood I did, you become preoccupied with health."

"Are you dying?"

Merry starts at that. Sometimes her mother scares her with how accurately she observes her. Sometimes she wishes that they were close and she could lean on her. Sometimes it all just seems so sad, and that's where her fury is really useful.

"Good Lord. What a thing to say!"

"You had a bad medical test? Something you're worried about? You know how overdramatic you are."

"I'm fine," Merry snaps.

"Suit yourself. But go easy on yourself, baby."

"No," Merry says, loudly now. "I am not going easy on myself. It is *not* the point of life to go easy on yourself. It is the point of life to *push* yourself. To make yourself better than you are."

"Okay," her mother says. "You do you. Just consider this," she adds. "Who's the one yelling in this conversation?"

CHAPTER FOURTEEN

Merry turns off the phone. She needs to have one moment of peace.

One moment when she's not scared that a doctor or hospital is going to call her. One moment when she doesn't need to deal with arguing. Or blame or grievance. Or the Campions. The evil and betraying Campions. If she lets her mind go there, she'll truly be lost.

She must try to get her mind back to Christmas, but she just can't do it.

It's just out of reach.

Her mind boils. Every time she reaches for it, it slips away, and yet, she remembers how wonderful it was. That's the worst of it; she remembers a time when Christmas was so easy. When all you had to do was open yourself up to it and it was there. When everything felt magical, like an unopened gift. Everything colorful. Everything dipped in joy. Everything uncomplicated.

She remembers the cold of her father's steel wheelchair, which seems like it should have been harsh, but wasn't because her own warmth burned into it. The glow of his merry cheeks was reflected off of it. Even the sound of his deep singing voice seemed to chime from it. She clutches her bag. Presses the book against her heart. Feels the tears.

They mix with the snow that's falling harder.

They blur her eyes. She cannot see.

She can't get London out of her head. London at Christmas. She's visited there so often at Christmastime. Always a lot of bookselling going on then. It's magical and she's so desperate for magic. She wishes she could talk to Charles Dickens; he had such a love for Christmas. She's always loved reading the stories of how he celebrated it, with plays and parties and dinners and revels. How on Christmas Eve, he would take all of his children to a toy shop and let them each pick gifts for themselves and their friends. He kept his love of Christmas all his life, even though he went through some hard times.

If Merry could talk to Dickens, maybe he could tell her how to find that feeling again. Maybe he could tell her how to share it with her children. Maybe he could tell her how to get rid of this hollow space in her heart that is actually even more terrifying to her than the nodule. The place where Christmas used to be.

Merry staggers forward, conscious that she's made her way south of Grand Central. Somehow fury has propelled her forward. She's starting to shiver and knows she should turn around and go home. She's about to turn back when she notices a homeless woman sitting on one of the bronze plaques on Library Way.

Automatically Merry puts her hand in her pocket. She always carries a bunch of dollar bills there for just this situation. The weather's raw and the woman's covered up with a blanket. She's wearing a Santa hat and holding a book.

Merry always notices the books people are reading, but this one resonates especially because she *knows* this book—this particular copy. She bought it at an auction for $3,000. That was about three months ago, at the Swann Gallery. She was with one of her clients, Sheila Hobbs.

Merry gets closer. It's unmistakable. Sheila is one of the best-known collectors in the world of fore-edge paintings, books that have drawings painted on the edges of the book, so it looks, when you hold the book in front of you, as though a whole world is contained within it. Which is the truth.

This book, a collection of poems by Samuel Rogers from 1838, is bound in beautiful burgundy Morocco, the painting on its edges of

Boston's state house and New York's City Hall. The drawings are beautifully done, and unmistakable.

"Sheila?" Merry asks as she gets closer. It's hard to make out her features because her hair has blown in front of her face. The Santa hat drips gray liquid, some of which has fallen on to this woman's chin. "Sheila Hobbs?"

That's when Sheila looks up at her with her baby-blue eyes. "Merry," she says. "You look awful."

CHAPTER FIFTEEN

"Why are you sitting on the street?" Merry asks Sheila, alarmed.

"I'm not on the street. I'm on Library Way. On Francis Bacon, I believe."

The sidewalk is filled with plaques featuring quotes from famous writers.

"Even so," Merry says, scrunching down to get closer to her friend.

"Financial difficulties," Sheila says.

Sheila speaks with a slight British accent. Merry's never been entirely sure about her backstory, though she's spent a lot of time listening to it. According to Sheila, she attended a boarding school in England and a finishing school in France. She's descended from Charles Dickens's illegitimate eleventh child, she was the principal of a private school in New Hampshire, she's fabulously wealthy, she invented the internet. Only this last is Merry fairly sure is untrue. And, she supposes now, the part about her being wealthy.

"What would you think to getting some food?" Merry asks. In addition to the Santa hat, Sheila's wearing two pairs of mittens, sweatpants, and a heavy coat. "I'm starving."

"Not one of those Thai places," Sheila says. One time they were on a shopping hunt in Niagara Falls and Merry took Sheila to a Thai restaurant. She'd never seen anyone with such a bout of indigestion.

"How about that diner on 40th Street?"

"With that handsome maître d'?"

"He's quite unpleasant, as I recall, but the food's good." Merry tries tugging Sheila to her feet. Sheila's not heavy, but she's off-balance and can't get her footing, so they have to do an awkward sort of dance for a few moments until they get themselves right. It's not helped at all by the wind tearing down Madison Avenue, which nips off Sheila's hat; Merry automatically goes after it, grabbing it as though it were a football, and plants it back on Sheila's head.

The diner has a Christmassy sort of vibe. The waiters have on Santa hats, the waitresses have low-cut green tops and are supposed to look like elves. The diner pulses with lights. Tourists clutch Macy's bags that crackle and tear.

But the maître d' is a spitting, judging sort of man. A porcupine with a large gold cross around his neck.

He assesses Sheila's appearance and tells them they have no room at the diner, which is plainly not true. There are empty tables all around them.

Merry nods at his cross. "No room at the inn?"

He reddens. Then looks at Sheila and he sniffs, loudly. But Merry prevails. Her profession has taught her a quelling look that comes in useful in such situations. He seats them by the kitchen, where the door whacks into Merry's back every time a waiter goes by.

Soon after, he stalks up and flings two menus onto their table, the menus skimming like hockey pucks and banging into the sugar shaker.

Merry's about to leap to her feet, but Sheila looks up at him sweetly and says, "Thank you. I'm very hungry." Then she tilts her head coquettishly. "Such big menus," she says.

Sheila has curly gray hair and although she must be past seventy, her face is unlined. She's a bit musty, like a doll that's been left in the attic. Now she holds the menu in front of her, reading out loud. She will get the grilled cheese and French fries, Merry knows, because that's what she always gets.

"So, what happened?" Merry asks. How long can Sheila have been living on the street? That auction they went to was only three months ago. Merry's seen her buy hundreds of books. Some expensive, some not, and even as she thinks about it, she realizes that is probably the source of the problem. Nicholas Basbanes wrote a book on that very topic. *A Gentle Madness.* All about the obsession that holds book collectors in its grasp. An addiction that can be as intense as the one that grabs hold of gamblers or alcoholics. Merry can imagine Sheila going through all her money in pursuit of these fore-edge books. Putting up a brave front. Selling off a book from time to time to raise some money until she ran dry.

Sheila sighs but keeps her eyes on the menu. "My landlord claimed I owed him money."

"Even so. They can't throw you out on the street, can they?"

Sheila nods. "That's exactly what I thought. Do you think the pot roast is good here?"

"Did you get a lawyer?"

Sheila shakes her head. "The landlord took all my books, except this one. Impounded them," she says, puckering up her lips to emphasize the "p." "They said I was a hoarder. A threat to the building's structural stability."

She's wearing the same clothes as when they went to the Swann Gallery auction, Merry realizes now that the blanket's been removed. A blue short-sleeved shirt and a pale blue pair of sweatpants. Come to that, she's been wearing the same clothes for as long as Merry's known her, though she hadn't really thought about it. People in the book trade are not renowned for their sense of fashion.

"Well, come home with me, at least. You can stay with me until you get this sorted out. I'm sure Sully knows a lawyer who can help you. Or he can help you."

Sheila shakes her head. "Your house is too messy and your dog is strange."

"Now just a minute," Merry says. "Don't start insulting my dog."

"I meant no insult. It just always feels like he's trying to talk to me."

Merry resolves to talk to Leroy. It's one thing to talk to her, but she doesn't think he should make a practice of it.

She puts her hand on Sheila's. It's so cold. Her knuckles feel like marbles.

"Seriously. Come home with me."

Sheila shakes her head. "I have a place to live. Up in Harlem. It's a shelter, but it's quite nice. Lots of people with interesting stories. One of my roommates doesn't talk, but I'm teaching her to write. And my brother claims to be coming up soon to kidnap me to Virginia, so I can live with his wife and children." Her eyes cloud a bit. "It seems as though I will have to leave this beautiful city one way or the other."

"We can fight this," Merry says.

The waiter looms over them, like the solemn Ghost of Christmas Yet to Come. Except this looming phantom talks. "Have you decided?" he demands.

Sheila smiles up at him tremulously, like the heroine of a Dickens novel. An older and sadder version of Esther Summerson. She places her order, as does Merry, and then he stalks off as though a request for grilled cheese is in some way offensive.

Merry wants to grab him by his slippery lapels and demand that he recognize who he's talking to. That this woman of whom he's being so dismissive is one of the preeminent fore-edge collectors in the world. That there was a time when her presence at an auction was enough to give it authority. That people sought her out.

"You're glaring," Sheila says.

"Am I?"

"You're not going to get in a dispute with him, are you?"

"I'll try not to."

"I'd rather not get thrown out of here. Remember the time you got us thrown out of that restaurant in Ohio."

"In fairness, I still think that waiter spit into your soup."

"But you couldn't prove it without a DNA test."

Come to think of it, Sheila's looked down on her luck for a while now. Maybe what Merry thought was quirky was really a sign of poverty.

Merry nods. "I just destroyed a Christmas party. I'll try to hold it in."

"Good," Sheila says. "I'm hungry."

The door to the kitchen slams into Merry's back. She imagines it knocking the nodule loose.

The waiter slaps down the food and Sheila sighs with pleasure and begins eating her grilled cheese. She closes her eyes briefly with each bite. Merry has no appetite herself, but she takes a bite of toast and feels like she's being stung by bees. But she does feel pleasure in watching Sheila. Never has anyone enjoyed a sandwich so much. The cheese is an unnatural shade of orange, but it's warm and gooey and you can almost feel it flowing into the cracks inside her. Healing her. The bread itself sizzles with crunchy butter. It's unhealthy and yet nourishing, and the orange seeps onto her lips, like lipstick. Merry's egg-white omelet, by contrast, looks like a set of whitened lungs.

How is it possible, she wonders, that this woman who has lost so much seems able to find the joy of Christmas, while Merry is so unhappy? The waiter walks by, still glaring, and it seems to her that that is what Christmas has become. A glare, a bark, an egg-white omelet. Where there was bounty, there are now egg whites.

Merry doesn't even realize she's crying until she catches Sheila looking at her and realizes she must have been sobbing for the last ten minutes.

"Sorry," she says. "I'm having a crisis."

"What's wrong?"

"It doesn't seem right to complain to a homeless person."

Sheila laughs at that, great rolling peals of laughter. Joyful sounds, like bells. "Tell me about your problems," she says. "I'm so tired of thinking about my own."

And so Merry tells her about the son who is so miserable in Oregon and Song Lee plagiarizing and Bessie so unhappy, and Sully and the Campions, and poor Mr. Gaudy, and then she tells her about her nodule, and how it's probably nothing, but it could be something and there are going to be radioactive tracers put into her and she's so scared and how can she possibly die with everything so unfinished and how she wanted to give the children her book, but nobody wanted it. So here she is wandering around New York with an autographed copy of *A Christmas Carol* and she has absolutely no idea what to do with it.

Sheila looks at her solemnly, and then she says, "You have it with you?"

"Matter of fact, I do."

"Can I see it?"

So, they take turns going to the restroom to wash their hands, then have the plates taken away and set some napkins on the table. Then Merry switches seats, so that she's sitting alongside Sheila.

And she takes out the book.

She'd put it in her laptop sleeve for protection, but now she carefully draws it out.

"Ahh." Sheila sets her worn hands on the book and turns it open, stopping first to look at the signature. She whistles in a breath. A team of touring students go stomping by, but Merry barely hears them. The waiter swoops by but leaves them alone. She feels like she's in a bubble. New York, the nodule. Everything fades away.

Sheila purses her lips. She's the right person to show it to. Merry sees the love in her eyes as she gently turn the pages. She thinks of what she said to Nick about how in this book you could find life, and she believes it. There's a largeness of spirit in this book that is what is lacking in her. Looking at this book, Merry feels more joyful than she has in a while.

As she touches the book, she feels the force of her ancestors around her. She thinks of little vampire child Nora Villard, who hurled herself at the great man on the train. Who saw what she wanted and went after it, and then passed the book on to her brother, Nelson Villard, who almost immediately took it to the South Pole. So ridiculous. So easy for the whole thing to be lost, but it didn't get lost. Somehow both Nelson and Dickens made it to the South Pole and back. There's a little ice burn on the page, which she's often loved to feel, imagining him in a tent with nothing but fire and coffee to sustain him. Imagining his intrepid foolish wild spirit.

The book then passed on to Charles Dickens Villard, one of the first Americans to sign up to fight in World War I, all of them so willing to live life large. That's what she wants, she realizes. She doesn't want to curl into a ball and die. *I don't mind dying. I just don't wanna go out like some punk.*

If she has to go out, she's going to go out swinging. She refuses to drizzle her way into death. She is going to fight for Christmas. She is going to fight for her children. She is going to make this the best Christmas ever. Even if she has to sacrifice the possession most dear to her. Because what could possibly be more valuable than her family?

LONDON

CHAPTER SIXTEEN

Sunday

Merry vibrates with excitement the moment the plane touches down in London on December 21. She's done it. They are here. Sully holding her hand, Bessie and Song Lee whispering behind her.

Leroy the boyfriend is here too—on screen. Bessie was texting with him the whole six hours to London, and now he's on FaceTime. Nick is on his way; he had to go from Yakima to Seattle to London, but he's supposed to arrive soon. They will all be together, celebrating Christmas, in London.

It was an unexpectedly easy feat because Song Lee said yes immediately. Merry suspects her youngest daughter was feeling vulnerable about the plagiarism issue, or possibly she was inebriated. She kept forgetting words during their conversation. After the first yes, everything fell into place. Nick will always do whatever Song Lee does and Bessie will do anything anyone does. Her worst fear is of being left out. Even selling the book was easy because Gussie had that offer on the table. She wanted to run it up, get more money, but Merry didn't have time to delay. This may be the last Christmas of her life.

She had the PET scan two days ago, on Friday. Dr. Fiedler said he would only call if there was news and she hasn't heard from him yet, so that has to be good news, doesn't it? Surely bad news finds you quickly. She has to believe that's true. She so wants this trip to be about joy and magic rather than anxiety and death.

She so wants to open herself up to this moment. To embrace it.

It does feel strange to no longer own the book. If she thinks about it too much, she feels panicked, but she knows, absolutely, that her ancestors support her. She feels the breath of their love on her back. She feels them lifting her. She sort of imagines she sees them, little Nora in particular. That little vampire girl, whispering her support. *You did right to sell that book*, they tell her. *Be bold. Never surrender.*

They are urging her on. Pushing her onto the moving walkways at Heathrow. The walkways go so fast, and she is jumping from one to one. She's always loved to jump. The one and only time she went skiing she went jumping right off a black diamond mountain. She was fearless. She feels a similar sensation now: air, wind. Excitement. Song Lee and Bessie running behind her, trying to catch up. Song Lee wearing knee-length white boots. Posters on the wall exclaiming, *Everything is Great. Britain!*

A bright pink Christmas tree materializes in front of her, like something out of Dr. Seuss. So artificial, so bright, so miraculous.

There's no time to admire it because she's caught up in the surging motion that is Heathrow Airport. Everything funneling in one direction. Merry is so much about motion and here there is so much of it. Jumping onto the moving walkways that go on forever, and then to the signs directing her to customs, and then on to a long winding line for the e-gate, which sputters along quickly. Then through the passport scanning machine. A triumph of getting it to read her passport on the first try. Look up. Don't smile. But she can't do it. She has to smile.

"Madam, if you smile the machine won't work."

But how can she not smile? All she can do is hang on to Song Lee and Bessie. At this moment, no one's mad. Song Lee might have had a little too much to drink on the plane, but that's okay.

"Why are you here?" a guard asks them.

Merry's tempted to say, "To find the joy in Christmas and save our lives," but Sully responds, "Tourism."

She would like to talk longer, but the guards are not actually that chatty, and so they move along to baggage claim, where there are islands of marooned bags. Theirs come vaulting out of the metal birth canal the moment they get there.

It's a good sign. The world is with her. The world is all about finding good signs. It's something you learn early on in the book trade, where simply happening to look in the right direction or at the right bookshelf can net you a valuable find. Or lose you one.

For just a moment she sees the technician's face from the PET scan. A tanned young man with a face sculpted into one expression. Competence. If that's a look. She wished for something about him to falter, so that she could get some sense of how it went, and she tried to throw him off course when she left. "Everything okay?" she lobbed. But he didn't play back. "The doctor will go over the results with you." She remembers the way he looked at her. No one had ever looked at her like that before. She's been looked at with love, with anger, with envy, with admiration, but never with cold indifference. It was a look that said she was nothing more than a body, a collection of cells. That she was being erased.

Now Sully's lifting all the bags off the conveyor belt.

Bessie only brought one backpack, but Song Lee has three white-lacquered bags. She seems to have rebounded in a major way. Gone is the timid wavering person Merry spoke to on her phone. Now she is Song Lee on steroids. Or maybe Song Lee on a lot of free champagne. Thank you, Virgin Atlantic.

Song Lee looks stunning. Tall and thin as a model, she's decided to armor herself with an outfit designed to stop any onlookers or potential critics in their tracks. A low cut stretchy, button-down dress that is open right down about as far as it can go. She has no cleavage so there's nothing to see, except for a lot of skin. Sully says she's wearing a body suit under the dress, but Merry doesn't think so. She doesn't think body suits glisten like that.

Bessie, meanwhile, is wearing a black sweater and khaki pants. She will wear the same clothes all five days. She is passionate about rewearing clothes and cutting down on water usage. She also drinks the same cup of coffee all day. She's never truly happy unless it has mold, or so Merry is convinced. She still has her phone in front of her. Leroy the dog has gone to stay with her neighbor, Darcy the dog walker—the one with the Rottweiler. The one he adores. But Leroy the boyfriend is with them, his voice a constant murmur to Bessie. Merry can't hear what he's saying, but Bessie listens to him rapt.

Merry's bag bulges. She has two pairs of pants and two sweaters and a dress and a complete set of costumes for a production of *A Christmas Carol*—cane included, and that wasn't easy. She plans for this trip to culminate in a family production of this play. Charles Dickens used to do it with his children, she used to do it with her father and also with her children, when they were little and malleable. She wants them all to breathe and speak Dickens's story. To feel his words in their heart. The words from the book—

They no longer have the book.

That takes her breath away. Makes her stumble. They will act out this play.

She's also written up an entire schedule for the five days. Which she has laminated. And put glitter on. One for each of them. She's a little worried that might be just a bit too much, but she figured she might as well pull out all the stops. Maybe they'll take the schedule home and frame it. It's not the same as a seventh edition family heirloom of *A Christmas Carol*, but it's something.

Not that they have to follow the schedule exactly, but she does think there are things, such as the Dickens Museum or the Victoria and Albert Museum, that would be fun to see. She likes to have a plan.

But first they have to stop at Amos Gaudy's bookstore because they can't check into the apartment until late in the afternoon.

And what an apartment she's rented. A glorious place on Hyde Park with five bedrooms. One more than they need, but she wants them to have space. She wants them to feel expansive. The place has red furniture and a red-walled kitchen. She loved that. So Christmassy and excessive and red, and that's what she wanted. Christmas should be over-the-top, shouldn't it? If she could climb to the top of their Airbnb and hang up a reindeer, she'd do it. But she's gone one better.

She's splurged for a stocked refrigerator. Champagne and cheddar cheese and fennel and garlic salami and sourdough crackers and cans of baked beans and Northumbrian Pantry Red Onion Relish Chutney.

She has truly tried to give her children the best Christmas she can. At least she knows she has not held back on anything.

There is no Plan B.

She cannot undo what she has done. She cannot get that book back. She no longer has the money to buy it back, and she's sure it's already gone up in value.

She has one chance, and this is it.

CHAPTER SEVENTEEN

Merry's husband is a man of unusual passions, and one of those passions is the Heathrow Express, which is nothing more (or less) than a train that takes you from the airport into Paddington Station, in the middle of London, in under twenty minutes. It is, essentially, a very nice train, but her husband loves it as though it were the Hogwarts Express. He subscribes to their newsletter. He emails the chairman encouraging notes. *Can I tell you what a great job you're doing? I hope the Elizabeth line isn't cutting into your business.* He actually donates money to a Fund for Retired Conductors and has his name on a list of Heathrow Express supporters.

Merry spends a fair amount of time with obsessive people, so she accepts her husband's quirks. He is not as bad, after all, as one of her clients, Lord Crenshaw, who devoted ten years of his life to buying up Dickens's visiting cards. Beautiful little calling cards that had his photograph on them. *Cartes de visite.* They're not that hard to find now—you can just go on eBay—but when she was starting out, the online market was not so dominant. She had to spend vast quantities of time visiting homes that Dickens might have visited, or churches and antique stores near homes that Dickens might have visited.

One day she found a card Dickens had autographed to Nelly Ternan, Dickens's mistress, or his possible mistress. It was a treasure. She knew Lord Crenshaw would love it and he did. The minute she gave it to him, he wrote her a check and then he shook her hand and said, "I am done collecting." And so he was. He never bought another thing, after spending thousands and thousands of dollars over the years. He said he was complete.

Afterward, she could have kicked herself for bringing him that treasure. She should have known that there would be nothing after that that he would want. She could have strung him on for years. Certainly, she could have used the income, but she couldn't help herself. When you're a book scout you get as caught up in the hunt as the person who hires you. Even knowing how it would turn out, she still would have handed over the card. She does miss him though, and looks forward to the Christmas cards he sends her every year. Always signed, "Sorry."

All of which is to say, she finds her husband's obsession with the Heathrow Express charming. Passion is always charming, even if it means that instead of simply taking a taxi from the airport to Mr. Gaudy's bookstore in London, they are roaming around the bowels of Heathrow Airport, dragging their luggage.

The champagne is catching up with Song Lee. She's starting to list. She looks like she's walking on a sinking boat, and when Bessie goes up to her and asks if she'd like to lean against her, Song Lee pauses.

In the normal course of events, Song Lee would say no. Would snarl no. Song Lee does not like to be helped, and she especially does not like to be helped by Bessie.

Poor Bessie. No one wants her assistance, which is too bad because she wants nothing more than to be useful. She's always the first to volunteer for anything. She tried to sign up to donate a kidney when she was a teenager. Tried to save someone's life when she was on spring break and wound up being arrested because she had some weed in her pocket. No matter how many times she offers her heart, people are invariably saying *No thank you*. Merry's not sure why, except that there's something about Bessie's eagerness that's a bit off-putting. There's a neediness to it that's frightening.

Automatically Merry cringes against the rejection to come. But instead, miraculously, Song Lee says yes to Bessie. The joy of yes!

"Knock yourself out," she says and drapes her long body over Bessie's compact one. They look a bit like a semicolon, Song Lee circling around the dot that is Bessie. The look on Bessie's face. A stillness so different from her usual animation, as though the only way to accept this moment is through quiet. Merry thinks it's one of the most beautiful things she's ever seen.

She admires Bessie's courage. It takes courage to keep asking when you know people are going to say no.

They continue along through a series of ramps, Bessie doing her best to hang on to Song Lee, who is dragging her forward, but Bessie's game. Song Lee in one hand, Leroy the boyfriend in the other. Bessie keeping up a running commentary for Leroy, describing what she sees. Posters. People. Smells.

He seems pleasant, this virtual boyfriend. A bespectacled young Black man. It's not a word she generally uses, but in Leroy's case, *bespectacled* fits. His glasses make his brown eyes seem huge, and she suspects they're already big. He's crouched over all the time, riding a bicycle as he talks, with sudden interruptions as he dodges a car. Merry hopes he sticks around. But she's afraid to bond with him because Bessie does have an awful track record. Plus, she maintains friendships with all her exes, so she's invariably bringing one or more of them to family occasions. One time Merry was talking to someone she thought was an ex, but he wasn't—yet. She never heard the end of that one.

When they get to the turnstile, Sully stops, as he always does, to chat with the guard. He could just download the tickets onto his phone, and scan it onto the machine, but he prefers the physical tickets, which give him the opportunity for human contact.

Contacts.

He puts every single person he meets into his contact list. His personal goal is to win the Guinness World Record for contacts. When they have parties, the house is filled with people he's met at random locations. The guy from the Apple store who sold him his phone, a physicist from Skidmore, the guy who plays the violin at the train station. That man does not see boundaries.

He tells the ticket agent how much he admires the Heathrow Express and thanks him for his service. Merry notices for the first time that Song Lee has a line of dirt on her hem. Would she really go to Florida and live with her grandmother? They've always had a special bond.

But now they proceed toward a large elevator with one button on it. No indication as to whether it goes up or down, which Merry finds unnerving. She is most definitely a person who likes to know directions.

The doors to the elevator open. It's a large space and fifty people pack in. Immediately Sully strikes up a conversation with a couple from Iowa.

"It's a crime that Kennedy Airport doesn't have this," Sully says, and they're off.

The elevator is full. Everyone now talking about Kennedy Airport. Everyone enraptured by Sully's description of Heathrow. The elevator comes to a stop and the doors on the opposite side of it open and everyone pours out, though it seems to Merry that they're changed. That the interaction with Sully has changed them. Made them better. He grins at her. A handsome boyish man with no sense of boundaries.

Song Lee and Bessie seem stable as they finally make their way to the train platform, now with a gaggle of tourists behind them. Everything is going right. No phone call from Dr. Fiedler. Christmas all around them. London pulling out the stops.

Lights begin to flash, there's a whoosh of air, and then it is there, gleaming, beautiful. The Heathrow Express.

"Look how clean it is," Bessie whispers to Leroy.

Sully grabs up their luggage and puts it on the racks. Then he sits down alongside Merry and wraps his arms around her. "Isn't this just the best?" he says. So happy. So much happier than he normally is. Which makes her think of the Campions, but no. Not now.

He kisses her hard, surprisingly hard.

Then he leans his head back against the window, sighing with contentment. In front of them is a video screen in which cheerful British people are suggesting things to do while in London. There's also a QR code that allows you to scan interesting articles, which Sully immediately does.

She catches sight of her reflection in the window. Her face is pale from exhaustion and red from anxiety, an interesting combination. Her eyes, which she thinks are normally warm and friendly, now look like old marbles and her chin has that soft feeling. She needs a shower and some lipstick and a tranquilizer gun. She's excited. She's happy. She feels like she's walking on the edge of a cliff, holding a baby chick in her hands. She could plummet.

The train bursts out of the tunnel and into the open air. It's early, only around eight in the morning, so the city glows with a milky light. It makes her think of a Turner painting with those yellows and blues.

Past sleek new buildings, car dealerships. Rows of old brick houses bedecked with thousands of little clay chimney pots. She loves those pots. They make her think of pipe organs, as though all of London is singing her its song.

And then there's the beauty of all that green grass, even in winter. No snow. The silent hush of the train. They're approaching Paddington Station. She always loves the station names, which make her think of Agatha Christie. Bakerloo and Little Wapping. She can't wait to see the stocked refrigerator. Maybe because she's hungry. Undoubtedly because she's hungry, which feels good because she's been so unhungry the last few days. It's practically the only time in her life when she hasn't craved food, but something about isotopes and shadows will do that to you.

Suddenly the train stops. They're on the outskirts of the station. Around them are wires, railings, and a stone wall. Not the most attractive part of the journey.

A few minutes tick by. Sully starts looking at his phone as though the chairman of the Heathrow Express is going to text him an explanation.

That's when Merry notices a man standing on the outer edge of the train tracks, near the old brick wall. It doesn't look dangerous exactly but doesn't look legal either. Merry presses her face against the window, grimacing as she tries to make out what he's doing. Should she contact the police? Is he in trouble? Is that why the train's stopped?

Then he turns and she's startled because he looks just like a young version of Charles Dickens. She's seen so many paintings and sketches of the great man that she knows exactly what he would look like. The long curly hair, the pointed chin, the leaning forward, the trim figure. Dickens as he was when he was in his early thirties, when he was writing *A Christmas Carol.*

How odd.

Dickens had ten children, so there are bound to be descendants floating around, and that's assuming he didn't have additional children with Nelly Ternan. Though that's a whole other story, of course.

Then there are the man's clothes, which seem old-fashioned. A black frock coat and a blue cravat and bold striped pants.

Merry knows she's suggestible. She's been thinking of Dickens and now she's seeing Dickens. It all makes sense.

But then he looks directly at her.

She's losing her mind.

The eyes are unmistakable. Eyes that seem to burn with a yellow flame. Gazing right at her.

Or not gazing. *Glaring.*

Merry turns her head, certain he must be looking at someone behind her, but there's no one behind her except for Sully, who's looking at his phone.

Like an idiot she points at herself and mouths, "Me?"

He draws his brows together and scowls.

The ghost of Charles Dickens is mad at her. Unbelievable. For what? What has she done? Yes, she sold his book, but he understood money problems better than anyone.

"Now that's just wrong," she mutters, consumed with fury.

"What?" Sully says.

It's so unfair. She has sacrificed absolutely everything to come on this trip. She has held back nothing, and now the ghost of Charles Dickens is glaring at her. You'd think the least Charles Dickens could do is offer her a little support. Back her up. Mentor her. Smile at her. Give her a thumbs-up.

"What the hell did I do to you?" she cries at him, causing her whole family to stare at her agape and for Sully to whisper, "Merry. We're on the Heathrow Express."

She glares at her husband. "I saw—" she starts to say but thinks better of it. She sold the book, they're in London, and she wants to have a good time. She doesn't want everyone to think she's crazy.

She worries she *is* crazy. Talking dog. Angry Dickens. Nodule.

She glances back out the window. The man is gone.

"Sorry," she mumbles.

CHAPTER EIGHTEEN

Amos Gaudy's new bookstore is above a shop that sells Tower of London Christmas ornaments, tea towels with the late queen's picture, corgi stuffed animals, red phone booth magnets, woolen hats with the British flag on them, maps of London, Covid tests, passport photos, and, randomly, green bags of potatoes. Everything is a bit dusty, potatoes included. Merry's not sure they're at the right place until Bessie notices a little plaque in the corner of the front window: *Amos Gaudy Books: By Appointment Only.*

She shivers. It's chillier out than she'd expected. Not the raw ice of New York, but a sneaky sort of cold that she can feel burrowing into her bones.

Mr. Gaudy has fallen such a long way from the days when his sign hung on an ancient oak door in a tony area across from the British Museum. A charming blue building that looked like it had been dropped into its location from a balloon. Mr. Gaudy occupied that space for decades, not long after moving to London from India. From Shimla, to be specific. One of the hill stations in the Himalayas. He'd grown up dreaming of opening a bookstore in London, but he faced unbelievable obstacles when he got here, starting with a lack of money and ending with the fact that he was a person of color and the antiquarian world was not receptive. He began buying up books that no one else wanted. Books about Africa. Books about the Middle East. Slowly, he built up a network of sellers and buyers who could find things at his store they could find nowhere else.

One day he was going through a library dispersal that had already been picked over pretty thoroughly. But, being tall, he was able to run his hands over the top shelf and he found a book there that looked intriguing. He bought it for five pounds, just because he liked the cover and had a buyer who might be interested, and then discovered that tucked inside the book was a letter from Arthur Conan Doyle. An amazing find. The money he made from that sale launched his business.

"How do we get to the bookseller's?" Sully asks a group of young men standing by an assortment of backpacks.

They gesture toward a corner, and so Merry, her family, and their suitcases make their way toward a set of stairs so steep they look like they belong on the side of a pyramid.

Sully huffs and starts making his way upward and Song Lee sprints beside him. But Merry falters in front of the first step.

She can't catch her breath.

The stairs seem to unfold in front of her. They elongate. The lines appear to be converging toward the center. Merry feels a sense of terror swipe into her. She can't do it. She can't climb those steps. She feels like a train is going to race right through her. She feels like her body is being turned inside out, as though she is aware of every single thing taking place inside her. She feels exposed, vulnerable. Ill. Weakened. One terrible word after another. For the first time, she realizes just how sick she is. Or might be.

And yet, she has to go up those stairs.

Having come all this way, she cannot simply halt the trip due to some personal weakness. She tries to call up her ancestors, her father, her anger, which is usually enough to propel her. She takes a step, but still she can't get her breath. She's going to have to tell her family, which she has not wanted to do. She does not want this trip ruined by her mortality.

But there's no way out of this. She'd hoped to put it off until after the trip, but she doesn't see how she can avoid it. She's standing there, time slowing, when all of a sudden Bessie's hand is underneath hers.

"Hey, don't worry about losing your temper in the Heathrow Express," she's saying, as she tugs Merry up the steps. "It's emulsifying. Is that the right word, Leroy? Leroy knows everything. He knows more words than anyone I've ever met."

"I've never heard it in that context," Leroy says, "but I like it."

"No, I'm thinking of purifying, like a cleanse?

Her strong arm is tugging Merry forward, upward.

"Nonflagellating," he says, and she laughs and tosses back "ethnocentric," and soon they are tossing one word after another at each other, both of them burbling with joy.

And somehow, buoyed by Bessie's love and good nature, Merry makes it up the steps.

CHAPTER NINETEEN

Mr. Gaudy's bookstore smells of oiled leather and honey and grass and vanilla. It took her years to figure that last out, but it turns out that as old books break down, they release all sorts of chemicals, and one of them is related to vanilla. Which is one of Merry's favorite smells in this world. Vanilla brings back memories of baking with her father. *For* her father. He loved chocolate chip cookies, and they would often spend entire weekends trying out new recipes.

It's a magical smell, and the moment she breathes it, Merry feels as though she's walked into a magical world. Which she has.

She's just so relieved to be up those steps. Relieved that Bessie didn't notice her struggling. Relieved that it's not a thing.

There are stacks of books all over. On one stack is perched a sign that reads, "Signed by the author." Another proclaims First Editions. The largest stacks contain books about India and Africa. Another shelf is wrapped with yellow crime scene tape. This is where the mystery novels are shelved. In the corner is a plush red sofa. Romance section.

And there is Mr. Gaudy, scuttling toward them.

Has he always been so delicate? He looks like dried paper, his skin the color of old vellum. He seems almost transparent. But then she notices he has a kitten perched on his shoulder. And such a kitten! A little ginger-colored puff of a thing that mews softly and bats at his cheek. A man with a kitten on his shoulder is a man you cannot help but like.

"Merry," he says, and swoops in on her. "You found me."

He speaks with a musical Indian accent, his voice raspy. She's surprised at how slight he feels when she hugs him. He seems to have shrunk, along with his bookstore. He feels dry, almost flammable. He crackles, as though his clothes have too much starch in them. She wonders if he's spent so much time among old books that they've leached the moisture out of him. But he still glows with an inner light. He radiates kindness.

"Oh," she says as she launches herself into his arms. "It's so good to see you."

"Merry," he says. "Merry."

He takes off his glasses and wipes his eyes with a handkerchief. The kitten peers down at her from his shoulder.

"May I hold her?" Bessie says.

"Of course," Mr. Gaudy says. "This is MoMo." But MoMo has her own agenda. She leaps off Mr. Gaudy's shoulder, sails through the air and into Song Lee's arms. She staggers backward with surprise, but she catches the kitten.

"Why does no one like me?" Bessie mutters.

But the kitten knows no guilt. She surveys the company from Song Lee's arms. She and Song Lee have the same expression, the same way of rearing back their heads. The same look of divine contempt. Song Lee looks unsettled, as though uncertain what to do, but Mr. Gaudy just beams at her benignly. "Such a pleasure to meet you, my dear Song Lee," he says. "And Bessie." He bows slightly before her. "I have a present for you."

"For me?" Bessie looks so happy that Merry feels a spasm of guilt. The poor thing is so desperate to be loved and noticed, it makes her wonder if she ignored her through her childhood. She thought she was paying attention. She intended to pay attention. It's just that Bessie needed so *much* attention and it seemed as though no matter how much Merry gave it wasn't enough. How is it possible to love your kids so much and still disappoint them?

"And this is my boyfriend, Leroy," she says, thrusting the phone, and thereby Leroy, right in front of Mr. Gaudy's face.

"It is my great pleasure," Mr. Gaudy says.

"Thank you, sir."

"The world's strangest family," Song Lee mutters, but without true malice as her attention is engaged by MoMo.

Mr. Gaudy goes on to shake Sully's hand. They've met once before, and Mr. Gaudy told her afterward that he found Sully manly. Now he grabs up Sully's hand in a double-handed clasp.

From the back of the bookstore, Merry can hear some old voices talking. She recognizes them. Mr. Gaudy's posse. A group of collectors who seem always to be in a corner of his bookstore, wherever his bookstore is. Arguing over politics or the World Cup or royalty or how many angels can dance on the head of a pin or if there really is an undiscovered Shakespeare First Folio out there and whether the book business is falling apart and on it goes. She peeks over and waves and they wave back. "The lovely Merry," they say and they get up and shake hands. She loves them, these people of the book.

But Mr. Gaudy pushes them away, fussy, insistent. No, no, no time for talking. Merry's family must have tea. They must be tired. They must put away their luggage. He fusses and flutters, little butterfly taps hovering around them, his fingers so long and delicate, whispering against her skin. He steers them over to an empty corner of the store, which she suspects he has spent hours cleaning out for them. Poor thing must have moved the entire mystery and thriller section. She notices a little Christmas tree in the corner and knows he put it there just for her.

Bags deposited, he guides them over to a small table. A very small table that calls to mind parent-teacher conferences at the elementary school, but they make do, scrunching around. Only Sully remains standing; he cannot bend his legs like that. After you've played catcher in college, there are only so many knee bends you will ever do again.

Mr. Gaudy starts to head off in search of a better chair, but Sully stops him, puts his hand on Mr. Gaudy's shoulder. Insists he's all right.

Mr. Gaudy shivers with indecision, but Merry stands up to help him with the tea, and they soon fall into a familiar rhythm. She fills his electric kettle with water as he sets out the ancient silver tea service he brought with him from Shimla. Silver mugs engraved with scenes of the four seasons. Set upon a burnished silver tray. Cubes of sugar in a bowl. Tongs. A pitcher filled with cream. Another silver tray covered with a doily and stacked with ginger cookies.

As he leans down to set the tray on the table, the little kitten purrs loudly.

"Ah," he says to Song Lee. "Would you get her some milk?"

"I'll do it," Bessie says, jumping up from the table, causing everything to shift and sending the plates spinning. Everyone holds their breath, but fortunately nothing breaks. "When do I get a turn to hold MoMo?"

The Girl Whose Heart Is Too Big for Her Head. That's what Sully used to call her. Or one might say, The Girl with No Boundaries, The Girl Who Does Not Know When Enough Is Enough. The Girl Who Needs and Needs and Needs.

But Mr. Gaudy is unperturbed. He gets up and disappears behind a closet, then returns bearing a stack of presents. He hands the first to Bessie. "For me?" she croons. "First!"

She sets the present on her lap and props the phone across from her, so that Leroy can observe. She begins unfurling the brown wrapping paper, taking pleasure out of every moment, until a colorful volume emerges.

"Open the book," Mr. Gaudy whispers.

Merry recognizes it. A Lothar Meggendorfer pop-up book that probably comes from the Maurice Sendak collection. A treasure.

When Bessie opens it, a 3D world emerges. Magical. A world full of theatrical creatures that move around as you pull on tabs. Bessie is transfixed.

This was, parenthetically, the response Merry was hoping for when she offered her the family heirloom *Christmas Carol*, but all right, she's happy to see it now. The wonder. The dreaminess of Bessie's expression, as though she would be content to spend the day in this imaginary world.

To Sully, Mr. Gaudy hands a box that contains a small leaflet. Sully's hands are shaking as he removes the leaflet from the box, and then he whistles. He's awed at what he sees. It's one of the original pamphlets from the opening of the Heathrow Express in 1998. A garish technicolor brochure that shows Big Ben and the Tower of London emblazoned in shades of fluorescent green and pink. On the top, it reads, *The Fastest Way from the Airport to London.*

"How did you find this?" he cries out, as he embraces frail Mr. Gaudy. Merry feels what can only be described as a fizzle of joy. Like the bubbles you get when you open up a can of club soda. Something bubbly and salty at the same time.

Then Mr. Gaudy comes to Song Lee, who has little MoMo curled in the crook of her arm. It's the only time Merry has ever seen Song Lee look awkward. Even when she first strode off the plane from South Korea as a two-year-old, she seemed in command of her environment, but now she holds herself at an awkward angle so as not to disturb the little kitten.

"I'll hold MoMo for you while you open the present," Bessie says. The Girl Who Is Relentless.

Song Lee doesn't even respond. She simply drifts out her elegant left arm and undoes the present one-handed. She wrenches off the paper, MoMo eyeing it suspiciously, and then she withdraws what looks to be an old journal. She reads out the foreign words on the cover. *Federation Francais des Eclaireuses Collection.* Then she translates it. "French Federation of Girl Scouts"?

"Your mother told me how much you love the Girl Scouts, and how you're mentoring a troop in Washington. This comes from a group of Girl Scouts during the 1940s, during the Occupation in France. I thought it might inspire you in the good work you're doing."

Song Lee swallows so hard that the noise echoes off the wall.

He has no way of knowing that she's had to leave Washington, that she's been uncovered as a plagiarist, that she will have to leave her

Girl Scout troop behind. But he's sensitive enough to know that something's wrong. Merry's not sure what to do.

"This is a very valuable gift," Song Lee says. "I'm no longer with the Girl Scouts, but I treasured my time with them. This will be a memory of that."

"Wait, what?" Bessie says. "Why aren't you with the Girl Scouts? Does everyone know?"

"Not now," Merry hisses.

"Of course, oh, of course," Bessie says. She looks flustered, embarrassed, as though she knows she's making a scene but can't help herself. "What have I said? What have I done?"

All Merry can do is move forward. This is all she can ever do.

Mr. Gaudy hands her a present for Nick. Tells her to be sure to give it to him.

"I have a gift for you," she says to him.

"Ah," he says. He does love a present. He's almost childlike, clapping his hands, and she's excited because she knows she's giving him something he'll like. Like many people who are great gift givers, he has no expectation of getting a gift himself, and now she hands over to him the gift she's been saving for almost a year.

"What is it?" he asks.

"You'll see."

The cluster of older people who have been chatting in a corner have now magically transported itself around them. So much tweed and gingham and one woman who looks a bit like Ruth Bader Ginsburg, all in black. Merry enjoys the moment. Tries to put aside the whispering sounds of Bessie talking on the phone to Leroy. "What do you think happened? What did Song Lee do?" Of course, Merry's track record with gifts has not been phenomenal of late, but this one she feels sure about, and true enough, when he opens it, he gasps.

"Where did you find this?" Mr. Gaudy asks.

"One of those small online auctions. The moment I saw it, I thought of you."

It's a guest book from a hotel in Cuba, dating from May 1958, shortly before the revolution. The leather cover's beat up a bit, the hotel's name has flaked, but when you open it, the register pages are pristine. Name after name signed in dark blue ink against rich white paper. The date the hotel guest arrived, the place they came from.

Mr. Gaudy collects hotel guest books from all over the world, but he especially values ones from eras of historical significance. He loves looking at the names inscribed there and imagining their lives, and what happened to them in the historical convulsions that followed.

"All these lives," he murmurs reverently.

She knows he'll spend hours, perhaps days, thinking about those signatures and the people that went with them. He'll put it with the other guestbooks from Egypt and Russia and India. He'll imagine their fates.

Suddenly, she feels frightened. She's sitting in a place so familiar to her, surrounded by the smells and voices she loves, but she doesn't feel right. She's not in pain, though she's afraid pain will come. But she's hyperaware of her body. Feels conscious of every breath. Senses the nodule inside her. Feels like she can even taste it in the tip of her tongue, or perhaps that's residue from the radioactive isotopes they injected into her just two days ago. She'd actually asked the nurse if she'd set off a security alarm at the airport.

"No," the nurse had said and squeezed her shoulder.

Soft filtered sunlight comes through the dusty windows. Out the window Merry can see a bright red pub. The Pride of Paddington, and a strange clock that looks like it has a man trapped inside it. A shadow of a man who paces back and forth behind the face of the clock. Unhurried, watchful, patient. Could it be Dickens? Stuck inside a clock? Would that be significantly stranger than Dickens standing outside the Heathrow Express?

They're all exhausted. The plan was to wander over to Buckingham Palace and kill some time until they could check in to their fabulous apartment, but Merry can see no one is eager to move. She certainly isn't, and when Mr. Gaudy asks if they'd like to help him unpack some things, they're all amenable. So he guides them over to a stack of cartons and begins explaining to them what he wants them to do.

She can't move. She settles back in the chair, feeling depleted.

Calm, she supposes, like that man stuck in the clock. She is a shadow too. That's what she feels like, that she is not herself but a reflection of herself, and yet. Even so, she hears her family's voices and they pull her back toward light.

Her family is working together. There is love there. Of course, Nick will come and blow the whole thing to smithereens. Such an aggravation that he's not here right now, but this gives her hope that it will all work out, and she feels for the first time that this trip will be a success. Something in Mr. Gaudy's kindness has made a difference, and perhaps that's what they needed. Perhaps this is bringing her closer to what Christmas means. Peace and kindness. She so wants it to be so.

She sinks more deeply into the chair, exhausted. Her family and Mr. Gaudy have wandered over to a remote part of the store. It's early Sunday afternoon, but she's been up for almost twenty-four hours and that's leaving aside the twenty-four hours she was up before the PET scan. Still no sign from the doctor. When he said he would call within two days, did he mean that time precisely or could it be forty-nine hours he had in mind? Or fifty-three? How elastic is he? What about factoring in all the changes in time zones?

She could, of course, check her computer. She has her own private medical portal. Her report may be uploaded there already. It will tell her the results, but it won't interpret them. It will simply tell her the numbers, and she cannot bear to be told her future by looking at some dispassionate screen. Dr. Fiedler is someone she knows. Someone she sort of likes. Someone who collects books. If she must get a death sentence, she would rather it be from him. She would rather wait. She is a coward.

Her moment of peace disappears.

This panic is so strange. Not like anything she's felt before. There's something malicious about the way it seems to hide behind corners. Waiting for her to feel calm for a moment and then creeping up beside her.

She's being stalked. By fear.

She should fight back, and she knows it. She should call Dr. Fiedler right now and just ask him about the results, but she just cannot do it. She's never known fear like this before and it both scares and angers her. It's as though her insides have been hollowed out. It burns. It hurts.

Is this what Nick felt when he sat in his canoe, afraid to jump into the water and save his friends? A fear that takes over your mind, that blocks out anything else. Love, loyalty.

She can't take it. There's only so much self-hatred she can deal with on a beautiful Sunday afternoon in London. She needs to talk to someone comforting.

Merry decides to call her dog.

CHAPTER TWENTY

Darcy the dog walker answers the FaceTime call, of course. Even in Merry's imagination, Leroy the dog is not yet up to pressing buttons on a phone.

"Do you want to talk to your baby?" Darcy croons. She's wearing her pajamas, Merry assumes, because they are pink and have dogs all over them. Her hair is twisted in a topknot and she's holding the largest cup of coffee Merry's ever seen. "Let me go find him," she says.

Darcy actually found Leroy for Merry. She volunteers at a shelter. She called Merry one day and said she'd found a dog she thought she'd like. Merry didn't believe her. She'd had a dog when the kids were young, a golden retriever, and she adored him, although he didn't speak to her. When he died, she didn't think she could deal with that grief again. She was so devastated. But then Darcy introduced her to this little fluffy thing with molten brown eyes and Merry'd cuddled him in her arms and that was when he first spoke to her. He jumped out of her arms, shook himself so hard that his ears rattled, and he said, "I am not a baby."

And off they went.

Which was when she decided to name him Leroy. He had to have a man's name. She couldn't name a talking dog Bubbles. Or something cute.

The only worrisome thing about Darcy is that she's been estranged from her family for years, over an inheritance. Merry can't understand how someone as kind as Darcy cannot find a way to forgive her own family for what they might have done, and it worries her, because if Darcy cannot figure it out, then how will her own contentious children navigate the future? This is her worst fear, that her children will become estranged from each other. Or from her. What frightens her is that it seems to happen so easily. One comparatively minor grievance and the next thing you know, a family splits apart. It would break her heart.

But now there's a bit of commotion on her screen and then Leroy the dog appears in front of her.

How good it is to see him, though he looks a bit different. Darcy must have fluffed up the tufts of hair on his head. Or is he doing that himself to look more attractive to Sophie the Rottweiler? He looks a little like David Bowie. His face looks squarer. He begins licking his paw.

"How do you like his new look?" Darcy says. She kisses Leroy's nose and says, "We want him looking extra handsome for Sophie the Rottweiler, don't we?"

He has a blue bow on a tuft of hair on his forehead.

"It's so much fun having a little dog to play with," Darcy says. "Sophie's way too big to put on my lap."

"Darcy, I wonder if I could just have a moment alone with Leroy."

"Of course. You miss your baby, don't you?"

One of the many things she likes about Darcy is that if you call to talk to your dog, she won't say anything snarky. There's not even a passive-aggressive undercurrent to her voice. She just plops Leroy in front of the iPad and leaves.

"I'm so sorry," Merry tells him. "I promise I'll give you chicken every day for a month when I get home."

"I want to chew her hands," Leroy says.

"I can imagine."

"There are morkipoos here. They think they're so cool. They yip."

"I'm sorry, my friend." She'd had to make the travel arrangements so quickly that she didn't have a chance to ask Darcy what other dogs she'd have boarding with her.

He twists his lips in a way that reminds her of one of her father's friends blowing cigarette smoke out of his mouth.

"Well, how's Sophie?" she asks.

But suddenly Darcy is back, grabbing up Leroy from his perch, cradling him like a baby, which Merry knows drives him absolutely crazy.

"How's our sweet boy?" Darcy croons. "Did you talk to your mommy? Did you tell her that you wuff her?"

Leroy's eyes have turned into hard, burnished stones. Merry once met a man just released from jail who had an expression like that.

"Sorry to interrupt," Darcy says, "but I forgot to tell you. I went over to your house to check that everything was okay and there was a message on your phone from a Dr. Fiddler."

Merry feels like she's in a plummeting elevator, as though part of her has left her body. "You mean Dr. Fiedler?"

"That's it. I knew it was something musical. Anyway, he said he'll call you after the holidays."

She told Dr. Fiedler to call her on her cell phone. She told him twenty times that she wouldn't be home, that she would be in England, that he would need to reach her there. Why would he leave a message on her landline? Why does she even have a landline?

"Tell me exactly what he said," Merry snaps.

"Just that." Darcy shrugs, unaffected. "Oh, and he wished you a Merry Christmas. He said to enjoy the holiday."

That's ominous. Is it because it'll be her last holiday?

"He didn't say anything else? How did he sound?"

Darcy pauses. "Is everything okay, Merry?"

"Of course," she says, though she doesn't want to talk to Darcy now. Doesn't want to explore the situation. Can't deal with it.

She says goodbye and then calls her home voicemail to check on her messages. It hadn't even occurred to her Dr. Fiedler would call there. It takes her a minute to remember the number to access the messages. Then she has to sit through a new message from Optimum about changes to her internet service, and then finally she gets to old messages and hears his voice.

It's exactly as Darcy said.

"Sorry to miss you, Merry. I'll talk to you after the holiday. Have a Merry Christmas."

She listens to the message five times, listening to the nuances of Dr. Fiedler's voice. He sounds so genial, so friendly, so unalarmed. But why should he be alarmed? He's not the one with the nodule. If everything were fine, he would say so, wouldn't he? *All's well. Have a Merry Christmas.* That would be his gift to her.

But he's going to call after Christmas. He has further news to impart, and it can only be bad news.

That's when she feels something tapping on her knee, and it's not the Ghost of Christmas Yet to Come, as she first thinks, but rather poor Mr. Gaudy, who has come creeping back to the table. But that doesn't stop her from screaming.

CHAPTER TWENTY-ONE

"Oh dear," she says. "I'm sorry. Thought you were someone else."

Her heart is tumbling through her body and she expects it to land at her feet.

"Who?" he asks, waving away the elderly book club who have come to investigate the source of the noise.

"Death," she says. "Ha. Ha."

Mr. Gaudy doesn't look agitated, but she knows he is. Knows how he worries about her. She has spent too much time working alongside him to not be aware of the signals, the slightly louder breathing, the mashing of his lips together, the blinking of his eyes. She smiles at him to reassure him. "Jet lag," she amends.

He looks like he would like to say something more, but he pivots. "You haven't asked about your present, Merry."

"I knew you wouldn't forget, old friend," she says, though she's thinking that the only present she would actually have liked to get was a message from Dr. Fiedler saying she was fine.

He hands her a book wrapped in purple tissue paper. When she opens it, she sees it is the only thing it could be. A copy of *A Christmas Carol.*

Not the volume she owned and sold, not the one that had Charles Dickens's autograph, but still. A lovely edition, the Heineman edition from 1915, illustrated by Arthur Rackham.

Automatically she looks at the drawings. That's always how she enters the book, even though she loves the words. She always starts with the illustrations.

These drawings are different from the ones she's used to. Less colorful, darker. Instead of the vibrant yellow picture that starts off the Chapman edition of the Fezziwigs at the ball, this one begins with Marley's first visit to Scrooge. Dour. Scary. Marley washed out in white, Scrooge in profile wearing a blotchy night dress, his old hands gripping the edges of his chair. His feet in old slippers.

She flips through. The major drawings have tissue paper separating them from the rest of the pages. She loves the feel of it, the way you have to peel it off. She's always had a thing about tissue paper. Her mother used to wrap her clothes in tissue paper before packing for a trip. Each individual piece of clothing separately. It's one of the very few things her mother ever did that installed in her a sense of awe.

"It takes a little getting used to?" Mr. Gaudy suggests.

"Not at all," she says, putting her hand on his. "To tell you the truth, this version speaks to me now. It may well be the perfect *Carol* for me." Which is the truth. This is a volume that speaks more to the terror of the story, Scrooge's fear of death, to the moment she's in now.

Mr. Gaudy settles back into his chair. He looks so emaciated that she half expects him to disintegrate. His eyes are big and watery, an occupational hazard of being in the book business. Though the business is about so much more than seeing. It's about smell and touch and intuition and Merry feels her friend directing all of those talents her way.

"What's wrong, Merry?"

She's incapable of not answering a direct question. And anyway, she suspects that this moment is why she came here in the first place. Because she knew he would be a safe harbor. Because she trusts him and she feels as though somehow he is going to make this all better. Because clearly, she is incapable of doing it herself.

After checking to make sure her family is not within earshot, she tells Mr. Gaudy everything. From the falling off the roof, to the X-ray, to the nodule, to the PET scan, to the message on her phone, and she even throws in angry Dickens on the train tracks for good measure.

She expects him to hug her, to pray for her, to console her. But she doesn't expect what he says next.

"What does your family think?"

She shrugs. Feels like a teenager.

"You've told them?" He levels her with his assessing gaze. She knows that gaze. It's his take control of the negotiation gaze. There's only one way to respond to it and that's to look right back at him.

"No."

He flinches, slightly.

"I mean, I will, of course. But I don't want to do it now. If I tell them now, all the joy will leach right out of this trip. It will be the Merry Bingham Death March and I'm truly not up to that. I need time to come to terms with this myself before I can help someone else come to terms with it."

"You don't trust them?" he asks quietly.

From the window she sees the man trapped inside the clock. She knows it's supposed to be charming, but it's sort of threatening too. What if you were stuck in a clock? Why has everything in her life become a bad omen?

"Trust doesn't really come into it. I love them with all my heart. They *are* my heart. I'd sacrifice anything for them. In fact, I *have* sacrificed everything for them."

Mr. Gaudy nods. "Ah, you're angry at them."

"I am *not* angry at my family," Merry retorts. "That's ridiculous. I mean, yes, I'm annoyed that I had to sell my book, so I suppose I'm hurt. But angry? No."

A phone rings several times, but he doesn't go to answer it. Instead, Bessie picks up the phone. She has a voice that carries. "Can I have him get back to you? Will you give me your contact information?"

Merry lowers her voice further. "I just can't tell them yet, that's all. It's for self-preservation. That's my right, isn't it?"

"Merry, you *must* tell them."

"I know!" she mutters. "I know. Believe me, it's on my mind."

She feels flustered. Is she truly yelling at Mr. Gaudy? That's not possible.

Is she angry at her children? Her husband? Is that possible?

"I've got to fight this, Mr. Gaudy, and I don't know how and all I know is that right now I need to handle it myself. I can't have people pitying me or giving me advice." This last comes out sharper than she intended.

She notices that everything has quieted. Stilled. It's time to go. They're running late. It's time to check into the apartment. Mr. Gaudy stands up, wanting to hug her, and she does, of course, because she would never not hug Mr. Gaudy, but it's a brittle hug. There's space between them, and she pulls away from him more quickly than she ever has.

"I've got to go," she says. "We have to get to our apartment. We have to check in. We have to get moving."

"Now you are angry at me."

"No!" she whispers. "No."

Mr. Gaudy squeezes her hand, more tightly than she would have thought him capable. "Merry, anger is not a bad thing, but you have to tell them."

"I can't," she says, as she heads toward the door, to grab up her wayward family and take them to the apartment. "I cannot."

CHAPTER TWENTY-TWO

The cab driver can't find the apartment.

Is everything converging to drive Merry crazy? Dr. Fiedler and Charles Dickens and Mr. Gaudy and who knows what else?

Merry knows exactly what the building looks like. She has always dreamed of staying in such a building and was delighted to find it online.

A grand white brick building, facing Hyde Park. A doorman with a top hat. A circular driveway out front. She loves circular driveways. There's something so hopeful about them. You never have to back up. All you can do is go forward.

But the building does not seem to exist.

She knew someone once who wired money to an Airbnb and it disappeared. What if the money is gone? What if she's sold her family heirloom for nothing? It cost so much money to rent this place, and the thought of that money disappearing makes her ill. It would be so cruel, so unfair.

Mr. Gaudy's words rankle. The look on his face when they left. Not so much anger as disappointment. So what if she's made the wrong choice? She's made the choice that's right for her and it's her choice to make. It's hard enough keeping her family knit together when no one's upset. She can't deal with it. Doesn't want to deal with it. And it's *her choice to make.* That's the bottom line. If you have a nodule in your lung, don't you have the right to figure out how to deal with it?

"Leroy says we're near," Bessie says. For a moment, Merry thinks her daughter is talking about her dog, but then she realizes that she's talking about her boyfriend, who has now been on the phone with them for more than twenty-four hours. Is that strange? Yes, and yet he doesn't seem strange. He seems a quiet young man. But he's a playwright. Maybe he's writing a play about them. Maybe he's taking notes.

There is Hyde Park, to the left. The Winter Wonderland glitters at the edge of it, just a little bit like heaven. Even with the windows closed, she can hear laughter. Smell chestnuts. They pass by a red phone booth, a concrete water trough, scores of young Muslim women with silk scarves, people with dogs. Palm trees. She's always loved all the palm trees in London. There's the Russian embassy. People protesting. There's a random Christmas tree on the corner that has an obscene looking slash in its middle.

"It's for taking selfies," Leroy says. "You're supposed to stand in the middle of the tree and smile and take your picture."

"Jesus," Song Lee says. "I keep forgetting he's there."

"He can hear you," Bessie hisses.

Sully puts his hand on Song Lee's knee. "We're very glad you're here," he says to the phone. "Nice to have a new perspective."

"Exactly," Bessie says.

They are surrounded by everything in the world you could want for your London Christmas experience except the building for which you have transferred an inordinate amount of money and had the refrigerator stocked. With sausage and cheese and champagne. Perfection is within reach, if they could just find it.

Song Lee has her head pressed against the window as though she is stranded on a rowboat and waiting for an ocean liner to show up. Her left arm is still curved into the position in which she held MoMo. Bessie is sitting across from her in a seat that folds out. She's clutching her phone. The driver is getting tense. Making U-turns that seem incredibly dangerous.

"There's a bus coming at us!" Merry yells.

Those buses look evil. It's very cute when you see the big red things lumbering by in movies, but when they're bearing down on you, yellow eyes gleaming, they look like death.

Of course, everything looks like death lately. This could be Merry's last Christmas and she just wants it to be perfect. Is that asking for so damn much?

"Something's wrong," Bessie says.

"Of course something's wrong," Merry snaps. "We're roaming around London lost."

"No. Not that. Something more serious. What I want to know is . . ."

The inside of the cab silences. Even the driver stills as though they are all listening carefully to Bessie's words. Merry wants to put her hand over her breast, cover up her nodule, but knows that to do so will draw Bessie's attention. This is the problem with having actors in the family. They are so intuitive. They pick up on every nuance. They are hyperalert.

That's when the cab slams to a stop. "We're here."

"Oh my goodness," Sully whispers.

CHAPTER TWENTY-THREE

The building is completely covered in scaffolding and plastic tarps. It looks like a gigantic Christmas present that costs $2,000 a night. The circular driveway is closed off with sawhorses. If there is a doorman with a top hat, he is in hiding.

Merry feels her family's eyes upon her. You do not need to be a mind reader to know what they are thinking. *All this talk about a perfect Christmas and we've wound up in a construction zone.*

But Merry is just so relieved to know that a structure exists. She will make it work. They will have a place to stay. There is room at the inn. Possibly a danger zone, but she can deal with it. She doesn't need a lot of hope. Just a little.

So she catapults herself out of the cab, remembering, as she does so, one of the stories from a book she bought for one of her clients for his William the Conqueror collection. The great warrior jumped from a boat and fell onto the mud, but instead of being embarrassed he lifted up his hands and said, "I need to feel the earth." Trust William the Conqueror to put a good spin on things. He would have known how to handle Dr. Fiedler. She remembers that he used to throw ox bones at people who annoyed him. He would have bullied the man into giving him good news.

The building lobby, once you get through the scaffolding, is stunning. Marble walls, checkered floors, gold leaf ceilings. At one time, possibly around the time they took the Airbnb photos, it must have been incredible. So too must have the doorman.

Now the poor man just looks overwhelmed by fate. He's a large man with a gentle face. No top hat, but he does have a desk, which he clings to for support. He smiles at them gently.

"We've reserved an apartment," Merry says. "You have our key."

He nods sadly. She suspects he's been on the receiving end of a lot of disappointed patrons. He bows his head. Meanwhile Sully is lugging in all the luggage, Song Lee helping him. Bessie's prowling around, showing Leroy the space, holding her phone up to the wall.

"Yes," he says. "I have your key. Let me find it."

He has the air of a man who has been yelled at a lot. He looks defeated. She's seen dogs who looked like that. Leroy the dog once looked like that, when she picked him up from his previous owners, who didn't like him. She's never understood that.

"Take your time," she says, though you wouldn't think finding a key would be a difficult job. You might argue that it's the one job the doorman has. That and opening the door, which he also didn't do.

He sighs, as though agreeing with her that he is incompetent.

She forces herself to keep her body calm, to not lunge at the desk, which is her first impulse.

Bessie swoops by. She smells sweet. Like a donut. "Don't worry, Mom," she says as she hugs her. "This isn't your fault."

"I didn't think it was."

"Oh. Good."

"It had seventy-five five-star reviews."

"Good," she says, and swoops off.

An elevator opens and two drunk women fall out, which Merry finds tremendously reassuring. People are living here. They have not entered the twilight zone.

Finally, the doorman pulls out an envelope that's been taped closed.

Merry grabs it from his hand. "Thank you."

"Merry Christmas," the doorman says. "No trees allowed in the building."

"What?" Merry says. She's packed her bag with an ornament for each child. She's brought with her tinsel and lights that will work with British sockets. She'd also brought a dust buster, for the tinsel. She'd planned a tree-trimming night. Thought it would be a good way to kick off the first night here. She figured it would be fun to do while they drank from the Prosecco in the refrigerator and munched on the cheese and sausage. Get them in the mood to perform *A Christmas Carol* on the night before Christmas.

"Fire hazard," he says.

"We won't put up lights." That would be a blow, but she could deal with it.

The doorman coughs, hard. The sort of cough that comes from deep inside and isn't a sign of anything good. Will she sound like that? she wonders. If the shadow that is now a nodule turns into something even more serious.

"We've got that tree," the doorman says, pointing toward a tree that Merry has somehow not noticed, though usually she's like a heat-seeking missile when it comes to Christmas decorations. How did she miss it?

The tree tilts against a side wall, like a drunk at a party. Poor thing looks undernourished, as though someone has come through and swiped its needles. It's been rubbed raw. Neglected. Feral. And yet, strangely enough, it's real. If ever there were a place for an artificial tree it would be this lobby, but no. This little tree is still alive, somehow.

At that moment Nick texts to say, *Good news. Plane finally leaving Seattle. On to Dublin. Hope to be in London tomorrow morning.*

Dublin, she thinks. That wasn't on the itinerary.

Safe travels, she texts back. *Love you.*

She rubs the needles. She can never walk by a tree without touching it. Only seven ornaments hang from its branches, bland gold bobs. A set bought on sale, she imagines, and dropped somewhere, so that the eighth ornament broke. Two wrapped presents have been tossed onto a phosphorescent red skirt. For whom? There are two blank gift tags taped on.

"This is not acceptable," she whispers to the tree. "You deserve more than this. I'll figure something out."

The tree doesn't say anything in response, though Merry does pause. Just in case. But the tree is silent, sad, deserted, dying, depressed, alone.

"Okay," Sully says. "Here's the elevator.

CHAPTER TWENTY-FOUR

The elevator is about the size of a coffin for a thin person. It's ornate, gilded, mirrored, confining. There's definitely not enough room for all four of them to fit in. Not with all the luggage. Merry says she'll take the next one, but Bessie tugs her in. "We're not going to leave you behind, Ma."

So they all cram into the elevator, which almost immediately gets stuck between the third and fourth floors.

"This is all my fault," Bessie says, tearfully. "I should have waited for the next one myself."

Song Lee clears her throat. But whatever remark she's about to make, she swallows, to Merry's great relief.

"I'll call the doorman," Sully says. "I have his contact number."

Merry nods. She thinks she smiles, but she's not sure because at that moment she's engulfed with terror. All she can think of is the PET scan. How she had to lie, arms stretched over her head, in a white cylinder. Waiting for the tech to say breathe. Don't breathe. His voice so mechanical, coming from a microphone. Her feeling radioactive, toxic. Scared.

She starts to take deep breaths.

Of course, the doorman doesn't answer his phone. Merry suspects that's because he's operating the pulley that runs this elevator and can't hear the ringing. They are in London, she reminds herself. They are in a city with a viable emergency system. They will not be trapped here forever.

She has to get out. Now.

That's when she hears Bessie say to Song Lee, "What's wrong? What don't I know? Were you fired? Is that why you're no longer with the Girl Scouts?"

Why does she always have to ask these things in public situations? Merry wonders. Why can't she just pull Song Lee aside in a corner?

Song Lee stares at her with a look so implacable and intimidating that only Bessie would not be intimidated by it. The face staring at her is the one that the Moghul warriors wore when they swooped through Korea. But Bessie is undeterred.

"Did you do something wrong?" Bessie continues.

"I got fired for plagiarizing," Song Lee says.

The air around Bessie seems to still. She goes quiet as a bird dog with something in her mouth. Then she hurls herself at Song Lee.

"That's terrible. You poor thing. Are you going to sue? You have to fight this, right? If you need a place to stay you can stay with me. I know my apartment's tight, but if I move the plants, we should just be able to do it."

Merry's touched that it never occurs to Bessie that Song Lee might actually be guilty. Or maybe she doesn't even care.

"Leroy knows a lawyer. A good one. Top of his class at NYU. He does intellectual property, but I'm sure he'd handle your case as a favor. Oh, but I'm going on and I know that annoys you. Thank you for being honest. Thank you for telling me. I will do whatever I can to support you. Leroy will too." She's somehow holding the phone over her head, so Leroy's smiling down benignly at them all. A Christmas angel.

Bessie wraps her arms around Song Lee's waist. She's so much smaller than Song Lee that you'd think she'd look ridiculous, but her passion is so grand that it bulks her up. She looks like she's lifting Song Lee off her feet.

Merry cringes. She waits for the explosion, knowing how vigorously independent Song Lee is. So proud. So in control of her fate and generally so contemptuous of Bessie for being so dramatic.

And yet, Song Lee seems to soften. She looks down at Bessie and smiles. Then she strokes Bessie's hair.

There's something so tender in the gesture, so pure, that you could live in that moment forever. *This* is the love Merry wanted to kindle. This is exactly why she wanted to come on this trip. This is why she doesn't want to bring up the nodule. There's no room for a nodule in the midst of this beauty.

Grace comes in unexpected moments, she thinks, and whispers a prayer of thanks.

The elevator begins to move.

CHAPTER TWENTY-FIVE

Merry's first impression of the apartment she's rented is that it looks red. Very red. That might be because her eyes are blurred with tears, or because it does in fact look like a Valentine's box.

She reserved the place knowing about the kitchen, and the furniture. She should have extrapolated. What had seemed elegant and cheerful in the pictures online now looks like a place that hosts bachelor parties. No way in the world would she put her hand under the couch cushions. It smells of cologne, and she feels confident that young men have sat here watching porn. Is that a stripper pole?

She goes to the refrigerator and opens it.

Empty.

Where there was supposed to be a carefully selected box full of sausages and cheese and other British tasty things, there is now just an open bag of broccoli and a bottle of champagne. Which Song Lee grabs.

"It still has fizz to it," Song Lee calls out, swigging from the bottle. She and Bessie, now best friends, run off giggling, to check out the rest of the rooms.

Merry feels staggered by the emotion of the day. The joy, the anger, the fear. A few weeks ago, she was a more or less normal person living a more or less normal life and now she swings from joy to terror and can't find middle ground.

She circles the room. It is big. And if the windows were not shrouded by scaffolding, it would have a terrific view. Through a bit of tarp, she can just make out the Winter Wonderland in the distance. Sees the lights and movement of it. On the street she sees hordes of tourists, all of them holding bags and laughing. She thinks for a moment that she sees Charles Dickens. He doesn't look angry from this vantage point, but it's worrisome that he's on her street. Which would be worse? she wonders. An angry Charles Dickens or a stalking one?

She's so preoccupied that she doesn't hear Sully come up behind her. When he wraps his arms around her, she jumps.

"Good-sized room," Sully says. She hears the smile in his voice. Not a man to be upset by his wife inadvertently renting a brothel.

"Clean windows," she points out, leaning against him. She feels him vibrating; someone is always texting that man.

"The electricity works."

"And it's not on fire," Merry observes.

He laughs, and she turns toward him, looking up into those eyes that have warmed her for three decades. "And we're all going to lose a lot of weight because I'm never going on that elevator again," she adds, but then realizes that she doesn't have a choice. She'll have to take the elevator again because she can't climb five flights. She barely made it up to Mr. Gaudy's second floor bookstore.

"You okay, Merry?"

"Yes," she says and presses her head against his chest so that he can't see her face. He knows her too well. "That was nice the way Song Lee and Bessie hugged," she says, knowing that it will divert him. Also because it's true. "I didn't see it coming. I thought Song Lee was going to smack her."

"There's a gentleness to Song Lee that doesn't always come out," Sully says.

"And a toughness to Bessie."

"Where's Nick going to sleep?" she hears Bessie yell out. "I thought there were five bedrooms, but it looks like there are only three."

"No, wait," Song Lee says. "This isn't a closet, it's a bedroom."

The girls begin laughing hysterically. The sound of it pulsates in the vastness of the living room.

"You know, Merry," Sully says, "I have to confess, I thought you were sort of crazy when you planned this trip, but now I think you might be a genius."

"Genius or fool," she says. "They're the same thing."

"You hold us all together. Your strength, Merry. I don't know what I'd do without you."

She presses more tightly against him, squeezing her eyes shut so her tears won't drip onto his shirt. He smells so clean for a man who has been traveling for so many hours. So healthy.

"Hey," he says. "Is that a stripper pole? Remember when you and Phoebe took that class? She was right about one thing. It did add a spark to our marriage," he murmurs. "I wonder if it's like riding a bicycle. If it would all come back to you."

He leans down to kiss her, but she pulls away, saying she hears the kids coming, which she does, but she also feels unwilling to be touched. She feels lethal, toxic, contagious, and also slightly angry. Because why doesn't he know? He who knows her better than anyone else in the world—how can he not guess her secret? Why is thc burden on her to tell him?

CHAPTER TWENTY-SIX

They wind up at the Swan for dinner. The prettiest pub in London. A place that does Christmas the way it should be done: a Christmas tree in every room, all of them overflowing with satin ribbons and colorful lights and reams of ornaments and bows. The walls, already papered green, are now festooned with garlands of berries. And the paintings on the wall, which are primarily of dogs and ducks, glitter with little fairy lights. Almost everything else is wearing a Santa hat, including the stag head mounted on the wall across from Merry.

Merry wishes there were a way to kidnap the poor tree in her apartment building and bring it to the Swan. Here the tree would flourish, though the logistics of getting it here would defeat her and she feels like she's already bitten off a lot. She could steal some decorations from the Swan and put them on the tree in the lobby, but that doesn't feel right either.

At least Song Lee and Bessie are still getting along. They're sitting alongside each other, almost touching. Song Lee and Merry have gin and tonics. Bessie ordered the Special Drink of the House. No matter where she is, she orders the Special Drink of the House. Bessie's always dreaming of something magnificent with umbrellas and cherries, but at the Swan, the specialty of the house is a gin and tonic.

Sully has gone off to the bar to chat with the fellas about cask ales. He'll be there for an hour, she suspects, and will return with ten new contacts on his phone and stories about the Blitz.

Meanwhile, a waiter has brought over a plate stacked with all sorts of cheeses and breads and sausages. Everything is creamy or tart. Nothing tastes of iodine and fear, and Merry finds herself settling back into the sleek tub chair into which she's sunk. A beautiful sunny-colored chair upholstered with patterns of trees and foxes.

Now would be the moment, she thinks, to discuss the schedule for the next four days.

Merry knows that no one wants to be scheduled on a vacation, but this trip to London is not truly a vacation. It's more like a quest. Because there is a destination in mind that is going to change their lives and she just doesn't think you can wander your way into transformation. There has to be some sort of intention, doesn't there? There has to be a plan.

She clears her throat.

"What?" Song Lee says. She's in one of her dressed-to-kill ensembles. A cornflower blue dress that extends the entire length of her body and shows every single flaw, of which there are none. Hair blown out, eyes made up. Beautiful eyes, so different from Merry's own round blue ones. Eyes that she kissed all the time when Song Lee was little, hoping that love would be enough to protect her.

"I've made up a schedule," Merry says.

"For vacation?" Bessie asks.

"Yes."

"Did you laminate it?"

"Yes, Song Lee." She became a lamination addict when Song Lee was in Girl Scouts. She was the mother in charge of laminating, and she excelled.

Merry pulls the schedules out of her bag. They make a thumping sound as she stacks them on the table. Each day is written out in red calligraphy, and a photo inserted of the highlight of the day. Starting with a Christmas tree, for Sunday night.

Song Lee and Bessie exchange glances.

"Tree trimming on Sunday night," Song Lee reads out.

"Well, I had to cancel that due to circumstances out of my control," Merry says.

"What's the special boxed dinner?"

Merry shakes her head. "Forget about Sunday. Move on to Monday."

They both squint, as though reading the schedule from a great distance. Bessie holds her phone over her head so that Leroy will have a better view. It reminds Merry a bit of a client who used to keep a parrot on his shoulder. He collected books written by authors who personally knew the Brontë sisters. An interesting quest.

"That looks beautiful," Leroy says. "A real keepsake."

"Thank you!" She smiles at him, making true eye contact with Leroy for the first time. She likes what she sees. There's a good humor in his expression she wasn't anticipating. Most of Bessie's relationships are with angry people. Of course, he could simmer with unexpressed anger. But she doesn't think so. In fact, he seems to be the most enthusiastic person on the trip, and enthusiasm is a quality she admires greatly.

"You know, Leroy's family lives in a Christmas village."

"You're kidding," Merry says. "I've heard of them. but I thought it was an urban legend. You mean they actually keep their Christmas decorations up year-round?"

"And Hannukah decorations too. For my Uncle Leroy," he adds.

She can hear Sully laughing at the bar. He's made some friends. The waiter swoops by. He has a definite Artful Dodger vibe. Not hard to imagine him running stolen goods up and down London.

"Anything else, ladies?"

"Just keep them coming," Song Lee says, handing him her glass.

"Ah," he says, and looks at her with fascination, much in the way Leroy the dog stares at Sophie the Rottweiler, and with probably as much a chance.

"On Monday morning," Song Lee reads, "we're going to the Victoria and Albert Museum in the morning, then on a Scrooge walking tour, and then to dinner at Rules." She looks up at Merry. "Rules?"

"One of the oldest restaurants in London," Merry says. "Dickens used to go there all the time. They still have the table where he used to sit."

"I love the V&A," Leroy says. "So eccentric."

"Exactly," Merry says. The V&A is one of her favorite places in the world. That insane ceramic staircase, an explosion of tile and color and lushness that makes her dizzy, and that was even before her nodule. All the strange Victorian artwork, the huge silver tureens, big as bathtubs. The rows and rows of cobalt plates, the mirrors, the furniture, and the gift shop. All the gewgaws and detritus that make the Victorian age so fascinating. That bring Dickens alive to her and will hopefully get her children excited about the trip. "I don't think you can understand Dickens, or the Victorians, without going there."

"Why do we have to understand Dickens?" Song Lee asks.

"Because he wrote so beautifully about the joy that is at the heart of Christmas. Because if you can feel that joy—"

"Wait," Bessie says. "Didn't you once get ejected from a Scrooge tour?"

Merry tries to pivot from the topic of joy. "That was a long time ago. I've since matured."

"Didn't you punch him?"

"No, I did not punch the Scrooge tour guide. He was the one who hit me. With his cane."

The man was a complete idiot. Looked a bit like a cross between Jack the Ripper and Scrooge. She suspected he led both walking tours. First thing he did was announce that he didn't particularly like Dickens, which annoyed Merry. Then he said that Dickens's birthday was on February 5.

"No, it's not," Merry'd said. "It's on February 7."

"An expert," he'd grumbled, as though it were a crime.

"It's one of the most famous birthdays in literary history."

Then he said that Dickens wrote *A Christmas Carol* right before he died. Merry pointed out that, in fact, he was a young man when he wrote *A Christmas Carol*, at which point he asked her to please stop interrupting him and that was when he whacked her with his cane. Playfully, though it hurt, and she went to grab the cane from him and someone from the tour company showed up and asked her to please leave.

"I've chosen a different tour group this time."

"What if they have you on a blacklist?" Bessie asks. "What if they have you on a list of troublemakers? Oh no," she says then, her face reddening. "I didn't mean anything about you," she says to Song Lee.

"What do I have to do with Scrooge?" Song Lee asks.

"No, right," Bessie says. "Exactly, and I'm sure there's no blacklist for you."

Song Lee downs the rest of her gin and tonic. Is she up to four? Merry wonders. She doesn't seem drunk, but Song Lee is one of those quiet drinkers.

"On Wednesday night we're putting on a performance of *A Christmas Carol*," Song Lee reads.

"I don't even think it would be legal to have a blacklist. No matter what you did," Bessie says, relentless. "I would fight that."

"Enough about the blacklist," Merry snaps. "You've made your point, Bessie. Now drop it."

"But I wasn't *making* a point. I didn't mean to say anything."

"You mean," Song Lee says, putting her head in her hands, "that because I plagiarized, I'm going to be on a blacklist."

"But you *shouldn't* be—*that's* what I'm saying."

"Is it possible you are as stupid as you seem to be?" Song Lee says.

"That's not fair," Bessie says, clearly hurt. "I'm trying to be supportive."

"Enough!" Merry shouts. "Enough. Song Lee is not on a blacklist and if she is, there's not a damn thing you can do about it, Bessie, and let's just hope she doesn't wind up in jail, and Song Lee, would you please slow down on the drinking so we don't have to call an ambulance and get your stomach pumped and could you both please stop this foolishness and focus on the matter at hand, which is this schedule and the joy of Christmas."

"I did not have to have my stomach pumped in Aruba," Bessie says. "It never came to that."

"Bessie!"

They all look somberly at the schedule. Merry can see Bessie has tears in her eyes. Song Lee looks like she's going to throw up. Merry looks over to the bar. She can hear Sully laughing but doesn't see him.

"Who's going to play the part of Tiny Tim?" Bessie asks. "On Wednesday night. When we put on *A Christmas Carol*."

"I figured Nick."

"Why does it have to be a male? Tiny Tim was traditionally played on stage by a woman," Bessie says.

"It's true," Leroy adds. "I have a friend who wrote a PhD thesis about that."

Song Lee snorts. For such an ethereal looking person, she is capable of making very guttural noises.

"You think *you* should be Tiny Tim?" Song Lee says to Bessie. She clicks her jaw. Her tell. The thing she does when she's aggravated. "I'm the one who's an orphan."

"You are not an orphan," Merry snaps. "And neither is Tiny Tim. He simply has health issues."

"You always do that," Bessie says. "You have to make the conversation about you."

"Hey," Song Lee snaps. "I'm not the one carting around my make-believe boyfriend on a phone."

"He's not make-believe. He's real and we can't be together for the holiday because I have to be here, so what would you suggest we do?"

Does Song Lee see herself as an orphan? Merry wonders. She's never considered that possibility. Does she feel unloved, unwanted?

"You always side with Nick," Bessie cries out. "Always the two of you against me. But I'm going to take my stand here. I'm a natural Tiny Tim."

"Of course you are," Song Lee snarls. "Because you love to be a victim. You need as much pity as possible."

"That's not true. I've suffered a lot."

"How have you suffered?" Merry asks. "If anyone's suffered, it's Nick. He's the one who's gone through more than any of us combined."

"How did he suffer?" Bessie shouts. "He had a terrible thing happen, but it's not like he was injured. He didn't do anything, and anyway, that was years ago and he's the only one who blames himself for that. He should let it go, but he's obsessed with death."

"Are you truly that self-absorbed?" Some rank odor is pouring off of Song Lee. Maybe from all the gin she's drunk.

"You have to stop this," Merry hisses before one of them says something impossible to heal. "What is wrong with you two? Why can't you see how much you love each other?"

"Wait, does Nick know about your job? The plagiarism? You told him, didn't you? I wasn't the first to know. Did you tell him in person? Did he let you come visit him? What did he say?"

Song Lee rolls her eyes. "Seriously? That's all you care about. That I might have told him first."

"Did you tell him before Mom?"

"Are you crazy?"

"Don't you see what you're doing?" Merry says. "Getting swallowed up in these grievances. It's Christmas and we're in London. Can't you put all this aside?"

And it is at that moment, when they are truly at their worst, that she feels her husband's hands on her shoulders. She jumps up, startled, practically out of her wits, and when she turns, she sees Sully beaming with joy.

Standing alongside him are Phoebe and Al Campion. And their four smiling children. And one smiling granddaughter.

"Look who I found, Merry!" Sully says. "Can you believe it?"

CHAPTER TWENTY-SEVEN

The Campions look like they just stepped off a ski slope, though this being London that's unlikely. Though there is a ski ride at the Winter Wonderland, so perhaps they did.

They have that tactful, encouraging look on their face that people get when they find you doing something stupid, like arguing with your grown children about who should play the part of Tiny Tim.

The Campions do not argue. They do not quarrel. They are the perfect family. Their only flaw is that they have this tendency to stab you in the back.

The memory of the betrayal is so strong that Merry feels rocketed back in time. To when she was a young mother and Sully a rising star at the law firm, on track to make partner in five years, which was unheard of. Al Campion was his best friend and Phoebe hers. They did everything together. They loved each other. And then one day Al Campion came to Sully and said he'd heard about a young lawyer being harassed by one of the partners.

This was before the #metoo movement. This was when women were just supposed to deal with it, but Sully and Al Campion had worked with this young woman. Carly Fisher. They knew how good she was at her job and it bothered them to see her treated like that.

Bothered Merry and Phoebe too. They felt they were in a position where they could take a stand. The partner involved was a creepy old guy. They could make a difference.

So Sully and Al Campion asked to speak confidentially with the firm's managing partner.

Things got tense, but Sully didn't hesitate. This was the right thing to do, and anyway, he and Al Campion were the future of the firm. They billed over two thousand hours a year. They were untouchable. Together.

Except that on the day of the meeting with the managing partner, Al didn't show up. He called in sick that morning. Sully was going to have to do it alone. Merry knew Sully would be slaughtered. Al was always the more politically savvy of the two of them. Once she learned that Sully would have to go solo into that meeting, Merry quickly drove to Phoebe's house, banged on the door, begged her to get Al over there. She couldn't leave Sully to do this alone.

"I'm sorry," was all Phoebe said, and Merry knew in that moment that Al wasn't sick after all.

Never, until her dying day, will Merry forget the look on Phoebe's face when she turned her down. A mixture of sorrow, pity, and hate. Or the smell of the apple pie she was baking at the time. Merry can still smell it. Phoebe believed strongly that a house should smell like home; she was always baking something. Merry hasn't eat apple pie since.

Sully strode into the meeting himself. Her gallant knight. The managing partner heard out Sully. He thanked Sully for bringing the matter to the firm's attention. He complimented Sully for being a man of such high ethics and told him that Sully truly exemplified the core principles of the firm. Soon after, the firm gave all the lawyers a crystal paperweight engraved with those core principles.

The firm transferred Carly Fisher to the Cleveland office and sent the creepy partner on a three-week rest and relaxation retreat in Arizona.

But then Sully's work began drying up.

Partners stopped asking Sully to staff new M&A deals. He wasn't invited to client meetings on the matters he was already working on.

His billable hours plummeted. He was radioactive. He endured three years of that until one day, coincidentally the day Al Campion made partner, the managing partner called Sully in and said that the firm thought highly of Sully, but he was no longer on partner track. But they had high regard for him as an excellent lawyer and would provide him support as he looked for a new legal job.

Sully left the firm. He moved to a smaller one, but then the recession hit. That firm folded, and he moved to another one, but by that point he was getting too old to make partner. He drifted for a bit and then decided it was time for a radical change. He went back to school and got a teaching degree.

He's happy teaching. He says he loves it and Merry believes him. But he was such a good lawyer and such a proud man and they took that from him. It's unforgiveable.

Worst of all is that the divine providence that should have struck down the Campions has not struck. Al Campion has rocketed to success. He is now managing partner of the entire firm. His investments have paid off. His life has gone straight forward without any hitch and even his family seems to be perfect. It's so wrong that it drives her crazy, and meanwhile Sully has stayed in touch with Carly Fisher and guided her toward all sorts of opportunities, so much so that she made partner at her current firm. Meanwhile, the Binghams are still struggling to pay off dental bills. And she had to sell off her precious heirloom just to get her family to London for five days.

She feels bitterness festering inside her. Maybe this is what caused the nodule in the first place. But what can she possibly do except say, "Why, hello. Merry Christmas."

CHAPTER TWENTY-EIGHT

"You look wonderful," Phoebe says, leaning toward Merry and clutching her in a CPR-level grip. "Do you take antiaging pills?"

"Ha," Merry says and she smiles and her children smile too because that is the first rule of family. Even if you are on the verge of killing each other, you smile when a stranger asks you how you are.

"We couldn't believe it when we saw Sully at the bar," Phoebe says.

She looks just the same as she did twenty years ago. Even better. More toned. More cheerful. Though she was always cheerful, even when she stabbed Merry in the back.

She even smells the same. She'd always ordered her perfume from a special place in Paris. *My one extravagance!!!* Phoebe was into self-love before it was a thing. "Oh, I've missed you," Phoebe sings.

Merry looks at her husband and wonders what is going on in that man's mind. Has she not been explicit over the last decades about her deep hatred for the Campions? Whatever Merry's flaws, she is not wishy-washy. What she believes, she believes. And she believes these people are evil.

But Sully just floats there in his happy place. The man is incapable of holding a grudge. Possibly for a year or two, but after five, he folds. He's impossible when friends divorce, cannot choose sides. Always wants to stay friends with both parties, which Merry firmly believes is impossible. For a man who's been through so much, she can't understand how her husband is so innocent. Or does he just choose not to see what's in front of him?

Meanwhile, Al Campion looks much older. He's a large man, but he's softened around the edges. He looks seedy. Threads of his suit coat are hanging loose, though a man who can buy a house in Mayfair can surely afford a tailor.

"You must be Bessie," Phoebe croons. "You don't know us, but we're your biggest fans."

Bessie looks around as though waiting for someone to smack her. She's always afraid of being the butt of jokes, possibly because she is so often the butt of jokes. She looks tentative, vulnerable.

What she doesn't know is that Phoebe never jokes.

"We went to see you off-Broadway. We loved you in *Drunken Shakespeare.* You were absolutely the best person in the show. I couldn't believe it when I saw your name in the Playbill. I said to the kids, that's Merry and Sully's daughter."

Bessie laughs loudly. "Then you're better than my parents. They wouldn't come to that show."

"Didn't want to see her drunk on stage," Sully says.

"Oh, but she handled it so beautifully. You should have gone; it was a once in a lifetime experience."

Is she trying to make her feel guilty? Merry wonders. Seriously?

How she'd pounded on their door when she heard Al Campion wasn't going to be at that meeting. That he had the flu. How she begged Phoebe not to let Sully walk into that meeting by himself. "I'm sorry," she'd said. Oh, it's so easy to be sorry. That was something her father used to say: "Don't be sorry. Just don't do it."

Roaring anger mixes with the roaring in her ears. She feels like the nodule is giving her a superpower. There's a hot little bullet of death inside of her, and she's ready to shoot it.

Merry tries to grab Sully's attention, but that's hopeless. He's transfixed by the oldest Campion son, who's studying to be an astrophysicist. Show Sully a kid with a dream and he's all in.

Meanwhile Al Campion begins clapping his hands to get the waiter's attention. It's something she'd forgotten about him—he doesn't speak a lot, but when he does speak, he demands. He wants the waiter to bring over "a gaggle of chairs."

A gaggle?

"Honestly, I never would have known you were drunk if it hadn't been in the title. How were you able to drink so much liquor and still act so beautifully?" Phoebe asks.

And Bessie is off, telling her all the tools of the trade, telling her everything, loving her. Introducing her to Leroy, who proceeds to tell them about his own successes.

"A scholarship from NYU!" Phoebe screams. "You're going to be the power couple of the American theater."

When Bessie thinks a person likes her, she bonds with them immediately and to Bessie that means information sharing. After a few minutes, Merry half expects her to give out all their Social Security numbers.

But then, Phoebe turns her attention to Song Lee. It's a little like watching a tank in one of those old WWII movies. Slowly the gun shifts direction.

"And you must be Song Lee?"

"How did you guess?"

Blink, and move on.

"My gosh, we haven't seen you since you were little. I watched Bessie and Nick when your parents went to Kennedy Airport to get you. What a brave little tiger you were."

"I think I remember that day," Bessie says. "Did we play hide and seek?"

"You could be a model," Phoebe goes on. "What a beautiful outfit. Rag and Bones? Casey lives in Georgetown and she loves to shop there, though I can't say I've ever seen anyone wear it as beautifully as you."

But Bessie, having tapped into the fountain of love, is not going to let her moment be ruined and so she breaks in, now talking about Nick. How he's living in Oregon. "We think in an area near drug dealers, though who's to say, though it seems odd to me that that land could cost millions of dollars when it's in the middle of nowhere, though I am in no way suggesting Nick is a drug dealer because we all know how ethical Nick is."

"Of course, of course."

"He'll be here tomorrow, we hope. He's never anywhere on time. You just have to accept that about him."

That's when Phoebe notices the schedules, which Merry has forgotten all about, which are lying on the table, a little damp from gin and tonic overflow.

She springs to attention, like an umbrella when you push its button. "Oh, Merry, I see you still like to laminate."

She holds up the schedule and Merry feels weirdly violated. These are her hopes and dreams put on paper. She's starting to get angry but she doesn't want to be angry because she wants to focus on Christmas and her children and not this horrible person and why won't Sully stop smiling?

"Your mother was a great one for lamination," she tells Song Lee and Bessie. "I was always afraid to give her a piece of paper, for fear that she'd laminate it."

That's when Al Campion decides to speak and he says to Song Lee, "You're at Grace and Naybor now, aren't you? Top rate lobbying firm. Impressive you got a job there. It's great, the way they're diversifying."

"How do you mean?" Song Lee asks, in a sweet submissive tone.

"New times," Al goes on, because the man is tone deaf. Probably the secret to his success. "No, I think it's great. Really. Jameson got rejected from there, but I told him, it's a new world. You just have to adjust. Good to have new faces."

"I imagine you found a job for him," Merry says. "You must have some friend at a hedge fund who would look out for Jameson."

She catches Song Lee looking at her, appraisingly. Merry remembers the first time she took her to a Brownie meeting. She was the only

Asian person there. Everyone turned to look at her, but Song Lee didn't flinch. She walked right to the part of the circle that was occupied by who were clearly the popular girls. The pretty ones with lots of barrettes. She began talking to them, laughing, and by the end of the night she'd been invited to two sleepovers. She stayed friendly with them through college. Nice girls, but still somewhat intimidating.

She will not lose her temper, but it drives her crazy when people imply Song Lee got her job because of some quota. Those little underhanded remarks that people make and get away with.

Al Campion grimaces. "Oh, Merry, don't get all bent out of shape again."

"Again?"

But then Song Lee speaks. Shoulders straight back, chin raised, her voice clear as ice. "I don't work there anymore. I got fired for plagiarism."

Finally, the Campions are quiet. Shocked. Uncertain. And in that moment of silence, Merry feels something bursting inside her that might well be the joy of Christmas. She feels ridiculously happy at the looks on their faces. To see the ground shift beneath their feet. She feels like she's won something, though she's not sure what. But she's so proud of Song Lee for being bold and unafraid that she sort of forgets how upset she was that she was fired.

And when Song Lee starts walking toward the door, Merry jumps up and runs after her.

CHAPTER TWENTY-NINE

They run out of the Swan, though no one is chasing them—unless it's the past. Or more likely the future. Merry feels giddy, Song Lee too. Laughing. They are making a scene and people are looking at them, a middle-aged white woman and an elegant young Asian one.

Merry got used to the stares when Song Lee was young. The people who asked her how they were related, like it was any of their business. The people who told her she was a saint for taking in Song Lee, like that's what every child wants to hear—that her mother is a saint for taking her. Or the ones who asked her why she couldn't adopt an American, or wanted to know why she adopted at all. First rule of motherhood: You will be judged.

Sully texts. *I'm coming. Where are you?*

Don't bother. I'm fine, she texts back. And then, because she can't stop herself. *You just stay there with your friends.*

A pause. Then Bessie texts. *What just happened? Should I come too?*

Merry texts back. *No, stay with Dad. I suspect he'll need your help getting home.*

Then Sully texts. *Merry, are you mad at me?*

Unbelievable. How oblivious is it possible for one man to be?

Is Song Lee okay? he asks.

Song Lee is fine.

Which is true. Song Lee is all energy, charging up Bayswater Road, moving so fast Merry expects her to take flight. Away from their apartment, striding past the fake Christmas tree on the corner, which has a line of people waiting to take selfies. Double-decker buses ram by, red lights gleaming like dragons' eyes, looking so different from the way they do during the day. Dangerous, large, insistent, whispering by so close that you can feel their hot breath as they go by. They stride past a slew of new buildings, of old Victorian buildings, crossing the street so that they are now racing past Hyde Park, which looms solemn and mysterious. Merry hears herself breathing loudly, but she doesn't feel it. There's no time to feel it. She has to keep up.

Normally you're not allowed to walk through the park at night, but for the Winter Wonderland, the gates are open. The closer they get to the Wonderland, the more clearly Merry smells chestnuts and cinnamon. She remembers reading that right around here, people used to buy milk from cows. They'd wait while the milk was squeezed from the cow. The Wonderland sparkles in front of them. Merry always feels better when she sees something sparkly. There is absolutely nothing sparkly about a PET scan. Or a hospital. Sparkle is life.

Walking into Hyde Park at night is like walking back into the nineteenth century. It looks the same as it must have done. It's always been Merry's favorite part of London. During the day it's filled with runners and dogs, but at night it's mysterious. The old streetlights cast a pale-yellow glow. The silhouettes of the trees seem to tell their own stories. It's easy to imagine the sound of horses going by. In fact, she does hear horses. There's a stable nearby. There's also Kensington Palace, which she didn't put on this laminated visit, but which she loves to visit. It's the most eccentric of the palaces. The place where all the misbehavers went. Where there's a painting of Peter the Great, who the tour guide referred to as the Smashing Prince, because when he stayed there, he smashed all the windows. Merry relates to him.

Song Lee finally slows down long enough to say, "She drives me crazy."

"Me too," Merry says.

"Why does she go on like that? Why does she make such a fuss over things?"

"She's hateful," Merry says, though her voice catches. She's been running for about ten minutes now.

"The whole stupid Drunken Shakespeare thing."

Suddenly Merry realizes Song Lee is talking about Bessie, not Phoebe.

"Oh," she says, or gasps. It's getting harder to talk. She's been running for a while and is starting to feel lightheaded. She needs to sit down but doesn't want to stop the conversation. But neither does she want to collapse in the middle of Hyde Park.

Song Lee's striding along, Merry running a bit to keep up with her. She wishes Song Lee would notice and slow down, but Song Lee is not a person who slows down, and Merry forces herself to keep up, though she is conscious of the nodule. A time bomb inside her. Her death inside her.

"Do you really feel like an orphan?"

They're alone, under a streetlamp. Song Lee bolts to a stop. "I knew you wouldn't let that drop."

"How could you think I'd let it drop? It's a powerful thing to say."

"I was just joking." She pounds out the words, angry, but Merry will not back off.

"Even jokes can have truth in them. *Especially* jokes."

"No, I do not feel like an orphan. If anything, I have too many mothers, not too few." Nick would have made that statement with an undercurrent of irony, but not Song Lee. She's stating a fact, Merry thinks.

Merry's trying really hard not to wheeze. This conversation is so important. A once in a lifetime conversation. She can't screw it up by collapsing.

"Have you found her?" she asks quietly. "Your birth mother?"

Song Lee shakes her head.

Something really bad is happening with Merry's eyes. She feels like something's whirling to her right.

Song Lee picks up her pace once more. "If what you're asking is, did I plagiarize because I felt like an orphan, then the answer is no."

Merry has so many questions, but she's having difficulty getting her breath. She's so damn annoyed. She wants to have this conversation with Song Lee, but she has a feeling it's going to kill her, literally, and she rages at the cruelty of it. She's only fifty-five, way too young to be going through this, especially after all her father went through, and all she wants to do is try and help this young woman who she loves so much and she can't because her goddamned body is giving out. And she absolutely hates to feel vulnerable like this. She has spent her life fighting vulnerability. She will not ask for help, she would rather keel over, but she worries that would scar Song Lee for life. She doesn't know what to do.

Merry wheezes then and her body makes the strangest sound. A sound like a duck quacking. It's as though the nodule itself is talking to her. Is that possible? A talking dog and now a talking nodule.

Song Lee stops again. "What's wrong with you?" she asks.

"Nothing," Merry says. "But would you mind if we sit down for a minute?"

She sinks onto one of the benches. She happened to be at a book fair in London when the queen's funeral took place. She remembers sitting on this very bench, watching the crowds of people go by.

Now it's so still and empty. She grabs on to Song Lee's hand.

"What is wrong with you?" Song Lee asks. This time more quietly. "Selling that book, going on this trip, getting all crazy about everything. Are you having an affair?"

"No."

"Are you dying?"

"No," Merry says, but even she can hear that her voice is not conclusive. This is the exact reason she does not go to auctions. Because she cannot keep a secret.

"Probably not," she amends.

"You might be dying?" Song Lee's jaw drops like she's in a horror movie.

"I don't know. I mean, I don't think so. Probably not." How can you talk about your own death? Merry thinks of Scrooge looking at his gravestone. She covers her eyes, but then Song Lee starts to cry.

Great gusting sobs. The sort of tears Merry's never seen from her, not even when she was two years old and so solemn and afraid. Or no—Song Lee was never afraid.

Merry starts to cry too, and meanwhile she wraps her arms around her daughter. She doesn't know what to do, but she feels like they're going down the rapids on a raft together, which makes her think of Nick, of course, and she has the strongest possible feeling that she's just screwed things up in a major way.

"What's happening?" Song Lee asks.

"I really don't want to talk about it," Merry says, though she recognizes things have gone too far for that.

So she tells her the whole story about the nodule and the PET scan and how Dr. Fiedler said he would call if there was any news to report.

"And he didn't call?"

"He did call, but he left a message on the landline, although I told him to call on the cell phone."

"What did he say when you called him back?"

"I didn't call him back."

Song Lee goes still. Merry's dog does something similar when danger walks by. But she doesn't think Song Lee is trying to make herself invisible.

"This may be my last Christmas," Merry tries to explain. "I want it to be a celebration. A gift. A transformation. Perfect. This may be the Christmas you remember the rest of your lives. I want it to be a happy memory. Not me running around trying to get hold of a doctor, which I'm not going to be able to do anyway."

Song Lee scoffs, almost angry now. "*This* is how you want me to remember you? Wheezing on a bench, afraid to call your doctor? What does Dad say?"

Merry pictures her husband, standing puzzled at a bar, trying to figure out why Merry's mad. He's so damned oblivious he's probably asking Phoebe what she thinks.

"You *have* told him?"

Merry shakes her head. "No," she whispers. "Not yet."

"Mom! How could you do that him? You know how upset he'll be."

"I do know how upset he'll be, and so I'm giving him the gift of a few more days of not being upset. I want to keep it that way. I know this is a big ask, but would you not tell him?"

"No!" Song Lee snaps.

"Yes," Merry says. "Listen to me. This is my death we're talking about and I can do it how I want and I don't want it to be all about drama. It's Christmas. My father died at Christmas and I wasn't there and the memory of that has haunted me all my life and I don't want to do that. I want you guys to have Christmas and joy in your life. Promise me you won't tell."

Song Lee stares at her. "Has it occurred to you how controlling you are?"

"That's not fair," Merry says, a little hurt actually. "No one teaches you how to handle these things. I'm trying to figure it out."

"By doing it all yourself. By not trusting us. By asking me to keep this huge secret from Dad."

"Just for a few more days. I promise I'll tell him the day after Christmas."

"This is so fucked up," Song Lee says.

"Please," Merry begs.

Song Lee agrees, but when they get back to the apartment, she drops Merry off and tells her she's going out. To a bar. "I need to be with normal people."

And so she leaves, and Merry's alone.

CHAPTER THIRTY

Merry knows she's wrong.

She knows she's put Song Lee in an impossible position. Though a part of her, and not the best part of her, thinks that Song Lee could give her a little break. Can't she try to understand that a mother cannot be perfect all the time?

But no. This is her daughter and she's vulnerable and Merry has dumped this whole thing on her. She can't even think how to fix it. Call Sully home from the pub, home from the Campions, and say, oh, guess what?

How has she become this angry person? Why did she sell that book? How did she give away the family treasure, and for what? That book was her anchor to the world, and now she's not sure who she is.

She doesn't recognize herself. Not only her body is unfamiliar to her but her soul. Perhaps the same thing happened to Scrooge. There he was, going about his story, happy enough with his life and then he turned into a mean old miser. One day, you're a sad little boy, wishing someone would take you home for Christmas. The next day you're pushing away your nephew, universally despised.

More than anything, what Merry wishes is that her father were there. He would know what to do.

She remembers how her father always wore a top hat when he read *A Christmas Carol* to her, because he said you could only read Dickens wearing a top hat. Odd words from a man who grew up in the Bronx, not far from Yankee Stadium. That was back in the time when stadiums didn't need to be accessible to people in wheelchairs, so they could never go to the games. But they liked to go to the stadium parking lot and listen to the games. He in his wheelchair and she in a lawn chair she'd dragged along. The parking lot guys were fun. A lot like book collectors, actually. Chatty, though in their case they collected cars. Or accumulated them anyway. She never knew a parking lot attendant who didn't own at least two cars.

Her dad was a man who truly kept the joy of Christmas in his heart. Who seemed to keep the flicker of Christmas alive in him no matter what happened. Whatever sorrows, whatever hardships came his way, there was always an inner light. He never even had any wrinkles. She's never met anyone like him, except perhaps Mr. Gaudy and Sheila. They come closest. She realizes she's always been drawn to that. To people who've struggled and yet maintained their heart.

But now she's floundering.

She knows this is important, but she doesn't know what to do.

Her father died alone on Christmas Day. Nothing has ever been right since that day. Another misstep she can't correct. Is this what it is to reach the end of your life, to be tortured by guilt and recriminations?

Somehow, her life went off course. Her *family* went off course. She is not who she should be, but she doesn't know how to get herself back on course. She's not acting the way she wants to, but she doesn't know how to get there. All she knows is that the answer resides in Christmas. If she could just get back that feeling she used to have. When it was all so magical.

She goes over to the window and looks out at the park, which you can sort of see if you twist your head to see through the tarp. Her mind is on her father and the Christmases that were so magical, so distant. But is it the time that's distant or is it her? They are almost done with their first day here, and she feels further away from

Christmas than ever. How can she give her children the joy of Christmas if she can't find it herself?

She looks out the window in time to see a woman jumping out of the way of a bus. Death is everywhere. Horror.

And that's when she sees him. Charles Dickens.

The man himself. Or the ghost. Glaring up at her. The same man from the train tracks. This time, she's certain it's him.

That is *it.* She's had enough.

She's going to find out what he wants if it's the last thing she does.

CHAPTER THIRTY-ONE

Merry dashes out of her apartment, races into the hallway, slams her palm against the elevator button, and the doors open immediately. Almost as though she were in a functioning apartment building. She plummets down to the lobby and goes out onto Bayswater, which is crowded with people. She doesn't care. She knows he's here. She will find him if she has to run down every street in London.

But first she takes a minute to catch her breath.

Tourists from a nearby hotel are sitting outside, drinking and eating. They have on their winter coats, but the weather is mild. A line of young men is mingling around an ATM machine. She thinks she hears bowling balls. Disco music. Hyde Park looms across from her. A man walks out of a doorway she hadn't even noticed.

On the corner is that strange looking Christmas tree, artificial, garish, with a huge slit in the middle of it. The selfie tree. A couple walks into the slit, holds up a phone, and begins filming themselves.

She stares at the couple for a moment, watches them leave, and then Dickens takes their place.

He seems more vivid than he looked at the train station. His suit coat is now bright green. She's always dreamed of seeing one of his outfits.

None of his clothes remain, except for a rather formal suit at the Dickens Museum that he once wore to a royal reception—way less garish than the clothes she knows he loved. But here he is, in all his glory, as he was when he was a young man. Movie star handsome. Those big eyes. The curly hair. The imperious nose. The slight figure. He could be in one of those boy bands.

But his eyes have a rim of gold around them. Lion-like. In fact, there's something distinctly animal about the man. She steps back. She'd not thought to be frightened by him, but she is.

But she *knows* him, she reminds herself.

She knows his every word.

She's read his words over and over again. They are a part of her. If you know a man's words, you know the man, don't you?

She walks toward him, slowly, until she is only a few paces away.

He smells like oranges and liquor. He radiates heat. She would have thought a ghost would be cold, but actually, he's hot. She feels as though he could tan her. Her own face feels bronzed in his presence. He's like a Tasmanian devil. A bit like Beethoven—wild but young. So different than he looked when he was older. She's spent a lot of time in midwestern barns, scavenging for books, and there's something familiarly earthy and animal about him. She wonders if in heaven you get to pick the age you want to be. Or is the choice hers? Does she get to pick the ghost she wants to see?

He stares at her intently. It frightens her being examined like that. Song Lee used to do that when she was little. She would stare at her, unblinking.

Merry wants to touch him, but she's afraid to. She finds herself thinking of the radioactive dye being injected into her during the PET scan. The nurse wearing gloves to protect herself.

"What do you want with me?" she asks, asking him the very same question Scrooge asked the ghost of Marley. But she's not running from her ghost—she wants him. She's ready for him. She wants him to tell her what to do. In fact, if Dickens were to take out a laminated schedule, she'd follow it to the letter.

But he does not seem inclined to speak. In *A Christmas Carol* the ghosts crackled with energy. Marley's pigtail was up, as was the night-cap on Scrooge's head. But this ghost does not seem electric. He seems catatonic. It's like talking to a teenager.

Nothing. For a man who is known to be chatty, he is saying nothing. Merry hates silence more than anything—or that's what she thought until she had the PET scan and had to listen to automated voices telling her what to do and then she decided that was the worst sound ever. But this lack of sound is pretty bad too.

He brushes away his hair. She sees the Mary Hogarth ring. The one that belonged to his beloved sister-in-law, who died so suddenly. Mary, whom he claimed to love for his entire life, which was a little hard on Catherine, his wife. The ring disappeared after he died. It's in someone's collection for sure, but Merry's never been able to track it.

"I need your help," she says. Because she does. She's starting to think he's the only person who can help her. Everything is going so wrong. She's broken Song Lee's heart, and who even knows what's happening with Bessie. Sully is off with another woman, and Nick hasn't arrived yet and he's the one she thinks of as a troublemaker. "I'm trying to show my family the joy of Christmas and I can't seem to do it. In fact, I think I'm making them miserable."

Nothing. Shouldn't he take the initiative? Isn't the very nature of a ghost to be proactive? You are doing the haunting. You are, in essence, a verb. How can he just not respond?

She starts getting aggravated.

She's conscious of lights and movement around her, and yet she feels as though she's in a blur. Is that death? she wonders. To be blurred?

Or is that why he's here? To take her to heaven when she dies?

Has she *already* died?

She's starting to become frightened.

"You do not need my help," he says. His voice is high pitched, so educated sounding. He must have worked hard on that. She recognizes the accent from the royalty she's met, but he wouldn't have been born talking like that. Or maybe he would; his mother was a woman with aspirations.

It's so hard to take it all in. That he's here. That she feels like she knows him so well, but he doesn't know her at all. But he's *here*.

"On the contrary," she insists. "I do need your help. In fact, you are the only person who can help me."

He shakes his head. His hair whirls wildly. "I wrote a book on the topic. You should read it."

"I have read it," she says. "*A Christmas Carol*. I love that book. It's been the most important book in my life. In fact, you gave a copy of it to one of my ancestors. It's been the family treasure."

She didn't realize this would all be so much work. She thought this whole visitation was going to be a sort of gift. She feels anger rising inside her but fights to keep it down.

He leans in a little bit. "Where is this book?"

Merry feels something burst inside her that could be her nodule, could be her temper, could be her growing fury at the ridiculousness of the situation. "I don't have it. I had to sell it to bring my children to London so that I could show them the joy of Christmas."

"You sold my book?"

There's something so theatrical about his expression that she thinks he must be joking, but there's no reassuring twitch of the lips. His brow is furrowed, his eyes blaze. A smoky smell seems to ooze out of him.

Is this going to be one of those Gift of the Magi situations? she wonders. She sells the book and because of that he won't give her advice.

"Now don't get all high and mighty with me, Mr. Dickens. You know perfectly well what it's like to be short of money. You've sold plenty of things yourself. In fact—" she starts to say, but cannot go any further because someone is tapping on her shoulder.

"What?" she cries out.

"Excuse me, ma'am, but we'd like to take a selfie. Will you be done soon?"

"No!" she yells. "No."

She turns back, but Charles Dickens is gone.

She's just yelled at her salvation, and he's left.

CHAPTER THIRTY-TWO

Monday

Merry wakes up Monday morning in a bed that smells of cologne. Her husband does not wear cologne. Never has. But she suspects that dozens, if not hundreds, of cologned young men have lain in this bed. Lain perhaps not being the operative verb. She's never been in a brothel, but she wonders if they smell like this.

The sheets are clean, so the aroma must have bled into the mattress.

Ugh.

Her husband snores rhythmically alongside her. He's wearing sweatpants and a T-shirt. His sleepwear is essentially a casual version of his day wear; he never completely shuts down.

He came home shortly after her Dickens encounter. She so wanted to tell him about it. In the normal course of events, she would have. Somehow, it felt easier to tell him about seeing the ghost of a major literary figure than to tell him about a nodule.

But his face looked unfamiliar to her. Not angry, precisely, but dissatisfied. Flat. He wouldn't meet her eye and he was excessively polite. He actually said "excuse me" when he brushed against her.

That night, in bed, he lay at the furthest edge of the bed, crossed his arms across his chest like a mummy, and closed his eyes.

Now the sky groans a dank metal color, as though all the industry that has taken place in London has leached into the sky. She suspects she looks gray too. A corpse. Nick is supposed to arrive today. She'll have to put on makeup. A lot of it.

She has to figure out what to do about Dickens. She's so sure that he holds the answer to her problems. It would be too cruel for him to show up to just torment her. But why is he so angry at her? And why did he disappear? Though it's true he was famous for cutting off people who annoyed him, casting off one son after another when they went into debt.

But that's a completely different situation.

Would he have responded differently if she still had her copy of the book?

Could she get it back? Gussie will know who bought it, but the price will have risen and anyway, she no longer has the money to buy it back, even at its original price.

She prods Sully. He groans and rolls over, toward her. The blanket shifts off his shoulders, exposing the muscles on his arms.

"Why are you mad at me?" she asks.

He opens his eyes, heaves himself up, back straight against the headboard. There's something almost military in his posture. Unyielding. Unsmiling. She realizes how much she's defined his face by his smile.

From outside the window, she hears some boys laughing, the sort of laughter that means trouble. That means someone's about to do something they shouldn't.

"Why do you have such animus against Phoebe?" he asks.

"Animus. Let's not mince words. I downright hate her."

"It's been more than two decades, Merry. You truly can't find it in your heart to forgive her?"

"No," she says, "and frankly I'm surprised that you, of all people, are even asking me to. She betrayed you most of all. The pair of them destroyed the career you worked so hard for."

He looks at her now. She's seen him give similar looks at parent-teacher meetings. Usually to parents of whom he disapproved. He also presses his shoulders forward slightly, as though pushing a boulder. She looks away, upward, and only then does she notice there's a mirror on the ceiling. How did she miss that?

"Merry, do you think I didn't know he was going to bail before that meeting?" She's surprised at the intensity in his voice. There's something sort of arousing about it. It throws her off.

"What do you mean?"

"I always knew what sort of man he was. I knew he was weak." He shakes his head, gives a dismissive laugh. In this moment she sees the arrogance that must have powered him through Yale Law School.

"You weren't surprised?"

She still remembers how shocked she was. Al Campion. Their best friend. The one who had always been just a little bit better than Sully. Just a little more polished, a little more political. More confident. The guy who always took the check.

"But then why did you go to that meeting by yourself?"

"Because it was the right thing to do. Because I hated what they were doing to Carly Fisher. Because I couldn't have lived with myself if I didn't speak up. Because it wasn't worth it to me to be a lawyer if I had to live my life like that. No one took my choice away from me."

She shakes her head. "No. I mean, I believe you and I admire you. But you cannot tell me that you would not have been happier as a lawyer."

She thinks of the man who went into that meeting and the man who came out. She thinks of how even his posture changed after that day. The way he still wears his suits to school, as though he can't quite give up that part of him. The way he still uses the language of a lawyer. The pride he takes in helping people with legal questions.

Maybe the loss of the money bothered her more than she realized. Maybe she's way shallower than she knew. She's willing to acknowledge that. She would have liked to have a roof that doesn't leak, and for her kids to have braces, and to redecorate the house. Money makes life easier. She knows they have a good life. She knows they're blessed in so many ways, but still. There's been so much unnecessary struggle. Maybe the nodule is a product of that.

"Wasn't it my choice to make too?" she asks now.

"Would you have asked me to make a different choice?"

"No. You did the right thing. I don't dispute that, but . . . Phoebe was my best friend. She was like a sister to me. And she wasn't weak. She could have pushed him."

"She feels terrible about it."

"You talked to her about me?"

Suddenly she feels slimy. She really wants to brush her teeth. She'd been so tired after the whole Dickens fiasco last night that she didn't do her normal skincare routine. Plus, she didn't sleep well and would rather not have this conversation looking haggard.

She glares at him, and he glares right back.

"She was upset, after you and Song Lee went running out. I had to say something,"

"No, you didn't. You could have just said goodbye and left. In fact, you didn't even need to say goodbye."

"She was crying, Merry. She loves you, and she feels terrible. She said it's terrible to live knowing that she betrayed her best friend."

"Then she should kill herself," she snaps. "That would resolve the problem."

"*Merry.*"

"What do you want me to say? She's had twenty years to apologize. But somehow, she does it when she's alone with you."

"This isn't like you, Merry. You've always had such a great heart."

She's so angry at him for not understanding, for being so oblivious. For living in his own perfect little world where everyone is good and forgivable. She imagines Phoebe going after him when she dies. The two of them on their honeymoon mourning wonderful Merry.

"They're having a party in a couple days and I want to go," Sully says.

"Have you lost your mind?"

He has that sullen look on his face that he gets when he's determined to do something stupid, like when he bought the thousand-dollar snow blower because it was such a good buy he couldn't pass it up.

"Think about it, Merry. It will give you and Phoebe a chance to really talk. To say what you need to say. Isn't that the sort of thing Dickens would want you to do?"

She thinks of the angry man in the green suit who walked out on her in a selfie tree.

"No, I doubt very much that Dickens would want me to see Phoebe."

Though even as she says it, she wonders if she's right. She's been so worried about atoning for what she did to her father. Maybe he's more concerned about her forgiving Phoebe.

No, that would be ridiculous. Phoebe never even cared about Dickens.

"Plus, think about what you'd be modeling for the kids. You wanted them to learn about the joy of Christmas. What could be more about Christmas than forgiveness?"

"I don't want to," she says. It seems so lame after his impassioned speech, but it's the truth. She's dealing with worrying about her father and her health and her future and her life and now she's got to add Phoebe into this mix. Toned and fabulous Mayfair-living Phoebe who does not seem to be lacking for anything.

And yet, there's a part of her that worries that Sully is right. That maybe some dramatic act of forgiveness will save this vacation. After all, he did walk into a lion's den to do the right thing, all those years ago. She absolutely knows that he would forgive Phoebe, if he were in her position.

If only she could ask Dickens if that's what he wants.

But no, she can't, because she's being haunted by a ghost who comes and goes as he pleases and doesn't say much. Scrooge's ghosts came once every hour.

"When is this party?" she asks.

"Wednesday night. Christmas Eve."

"Well, there you go. It's impossible because that's the night we're all going to be acting out *A Christmas Carol*."

He lies back down in bed and stretches. She suspects he looks very sexy in the overhead mirror. "I didn't think you were still going to do that. Not after all the arguing about Tiny Tim."

"It's the highlight of this trip," she says. "It's why I brought us all here. You seriously think I'm going to surrender that so we can go to Mayfair and watch Phoebe do her Lady Phoebe imitation?"

He sighs. Rolls over toward the window, which would have a fabulous view if it weren't covered with scaffolding. "Okay," he mutters.

"That's it. You have nothing more to say?"

He shrugs, presses the side of his face into the pillow. "I'm going to need to pick up Nick in a bit, Merry. Maybe I should just sleep in."

"Oh sure," she snaps. "Take a good long rest."

She stares at his back, covered in a harsh white blanket. She hopes to God someone has washed that thing in the last year.

Merry wants to shake him out of his smugness. She's tempted to hurl herself at him and tell him about the nodule, but it doesn't seem right to weaponize her body and anyway, she's starting to have trouble breathing. But as she walks out of the room, she thinks that first Phoebe ruined her life and now Phoebe's ruining this vacation—and possibly her marriage—and if the point of this whole haunting by Dickens is to forgive Phoebe, she's going to be furious.

CHAPTER THIRTY-THREE

The thing is, Dickens was not a forgiving man. Quite the opposite; he could be quite vengeful. When he separated from his wife, he vilified the poor woman in the press and cut himself off from anyone who didn't take his side. His worst anger he reserved for Catherine's mother, who had the temerity to suggest he'd been having an affair. Which he likely was. He forbade his children to ever talk to her again.

Is it likely that a man like that would come back now for the sole purpose of getting Merry to forgive Phoebe? It just doesn't seem reasonable.

But what is reasonable about a ghost?

The anger she feels toward Phoebe has been festering inside her for a long time and she can well imagine it accumulating into a nodule. In fact, she can imagine the nodule with Phoebe's face on it, with her teeth like a shark.

Merry's sitting in a room that looks like a bordello. Her ghost has disappeared and her husband is acting like a child and Song Lee is snoring loudly. Who even knows what time she got in? A strange groaning sound is emitting from Bessie's bedroom. And Nick is airborne somewhere over England. No one seems to care that even at this moment, according to the laminated schedule, they should be heading off to the Victoria and Albert Museum.

She hates being mad at Sully. She's never mad at Sully. She can't even remember the last time they argued. Possibly over a car, that time she backed into the garage door. Or when she said she wanted to have a third child and he said no, but then he changed his mind, as she knew he would. He is her safe haven.

Of course . . . maybe the point Dickens's ghost is making is that she should forgive *herself*. The only person Merry ever talked about Gstaad with was Phoebe, one rain-soaked afternoon when the kids were napping and they each had two glasses of wine and it felt like the most debaucherous afternoon ever. Phoebe's spinning wheel in the corner. Her handmade hooked rugs. A nice white wine, present from one of the clients. And that was when Merry told her about Gstaad.

One of the most luxurious places in the world, and somehow, Merry wound up there thanks to meeting a wealthy young Frenchman at her community college in the Bronx.

Talk about random.

There she was, living at home with her father, struggling to take care of him and get her degree. She enrolled in a French class and there was Phillipe. That should have been a tip off to the sort of person he was. That he was fluent in French and enrolled in Intro to French for an easy A, which, parenthetically, he didn't get because he didn't do the homework.

But he was so much fun and so handsome. He would do anything, and he adored Merry. He loved how serious she was and took her to restaurants in the city and skiing in Connecticut, and she discovered, to her surprise, that she was athletic.

She'd never known that. Somehow it seemed wrong to celebrate the body when you lived with someone who couldn't use his. But with Phillipe she discovered she loved skiing and skating and hiking and running and even rolling down hills. They loved that. Clinging to each other and just going as fast as they could.

She didn't tell Phillipe about her father. Didn't introduce them, and her father didn't press it. Of course, he had to know each morning when he saw her, rosy cheeked and happier than ever, that she was seeing someone. He arranged for his aide to come more frequently. Merry didn't adore the aide, but she thought her capable, even if she did take a lot of smoking breaks.

When Phillipe asked her to spend Christmas with his family in Gstaad, she said yes.

She was forced to tell her father then, but it turned out he was thrilled for her. "I want you to be happy. Merry, you have one life. You love this man."

"Yes," she'd said, because she did. Though afterward she realized that she didn't love him at all. She was awed by him, she desired him, she wanted to live his life.

"I'll call you on Christmas Eve," she'd told her father, "and we'll read *A Christmas Carol* together. Just like we always do."

He'd laughed. "It will cost a fortune to make that call."

"You're worth it."

She asked her mother if she'd come up and spend that Christmas with her father. She didn't like to think of him by himself. With only the aide. But Lana couldn't do it. She and Jack Gutiérrez were having a party for two hundred people. The invitations had already been sent, and the moment Merry got to Gstaad, all her worries went away.

It was so beautiful. So pristine. Since then, Merry's been to a lot of lovely places as a book scout, but nothing compared to Gstaad at Christmastime. The lights, the sheer cleanliness of it, the smell of it. Like a giant Christmas tree.

Phillipe's family was charming. They spent days skiing together and nights talking around the fire at the chateau they'd rented. They ate raclette.

On Christmas Eve, she tried to call her father, but this was back before cell phones, when circuits jammed. Too many people calling home. She tried for a while, but there was a Christmas banquet to get to. Nighttime skiing. A party.

The next day, Christmas, her mother called her.

"I have some very sad news for you, Meredith."

He'd died on Christmas Eve. "He just went to sleep," her mother said. "You know how sick he was. This was a blessing. His suffering was over. Oh, and you know what, he had that book in his hands. That must have been a comfort to him."

But all Merry could do was picture her father, sitting by himself, on Christmas Eve, waiting for her to call.

She gets a notice on her phone that her PET scan results are in. *Click here for your results.*

CHAPTER THIRTY-FOUR

Something like a shard of glass feels like it's puncturing Merry's spine.

She's a person who lives by words, so seeing these words in front of her makes the danger of the nodule clearer. *Meredith Bingham. Your test results are in. Please press the following link.*

She will die as Meredith. Not Merry.

She goes to the site and logs in. It's called *My Health*, which is sort of funny because the only reason you'd have to go there is because you don't have health. There's a link called Test Results and she clicks on that. There it is. PET Scan Results. A live link. All she has to do is press it. *Easy peasy*, as Mr. Hong used to love to say. All her questions could be answered if she would simply click on that link.

Just one click, but she can't do it. Her hand hovers over the screen, but she just can't press it. It's so impersonal. So cold. So terrifying. She feels dizzy.

Any moment she can put it off is one less moment that she's dying.

There was a time when she considered being a doctor herself. Considered applying to medical school. She didn't like science, but she liked the idea of helping. Unfortunately, molecular biology did her in. She fell asleep during the midterm and never looked back.

She remembers talking to Dr. Fiedler about it. Not her Dr. Fiedler, but her father's doctor, her doctor's father, a man who dressed like Columbo and smelled of smoke. Her mother was always convinced he was a moron, which maybe he was, but he was kind, and he was willing to try anything. She remembers how he went with her father to Mexico one year, because there was some sort of therapy that could possibly help patients with M.S. It involved drinking snake venom. Only years later did it occur to Merry what a bizarre thing that was to do. But she understands now how desperate her father must have been to live. To be cured.

The odd thing was that years later, she read something in the *New York Times* that suggested snake venom actually had chemical properties that may help people with M.S.

Her finger hovers, she's trying to press the button, when her phone erupts into sound.

Incoming call from her mother.

And for the first time in decades, she greets her mother with genuine joy and emotion. Anything to get away from that screen.

"Hello!" she cries out. "Good to hear from you." What time is it in Florida? Must be three A.M., but then her mother has never needed a lot of sleep. That was actually reassuring when Merry was a girl, that when she woke from nightmares, she could invariably hear her mother talking.

"You sound happy. Good sex?" her mother says.

"Mom."

"Oh, I'm sorry, I forgot you don't have sex."

"Mom." That brief moment of good will is dissolving.

Her mother begins to crunch. She's eating almonds, surely. She loves almonds. Always has a packet of them with her. Instant energy, and her mother needs instant energy because she's always on the go. Lana is about movement, fun, change, transition, excitement.

She and Jack live off a golf course. One time, when Bessie was visiting them, someone shot a golf ball right through their window. Occupational hazard. They had the ball mounted in a plastic cube. Thought it was all good fun. Lucky Bessie didn't get hit in the head.

How could you live in a place where there was a realistic possibility that a bullet of a ball could come and shatter your skull?

Merry doesn't understand her mother's life choices.

"That husband of yours is pretty good looking. I hope you take good care of him."

"Is there a reason you've called?"

"So, I've been thinking, do you want me to buy the book back?" her mother asks.

Her mother is the only person Merry knows who has the sort of money that would enable her to buy the book back. She suspects her mother would do it. She's never been a person who minded about money. Even though she left her father for a much wealthier man, Merry doesn't think that was a factor. She fell in love with his vitality and health. The money was a bonus.

But it doesn't seem right to ask her mother for money when she's spent years being horrible to her and anyway, is the meaning of Christmas to go borrow an exorbitant amount of money? It can't be that. She must be missing something.

"No, thank you," Merry says. "I made my choice. I'll stand by it."

"What a martyr complex you have. You must be feeling guilty about something, but I don't know what it is."

Of course she doesn't know what it is, Merry thinks. Because her mother doesn't understand guilt. It is not an emotion she suffers from, so how could she possibly understand how much it's haunted Merry. And if she were to try and explain it to her, Lana would laugh and say she's being ridiculous and it's time to move on and everyone makes mistakes. That she just wanted to have fun in Gstaad. That she had no intention of hurting her father.

But would that be true? That's what tortures Merry. That maybe on some level she *wanted* to hurt her father. That maybe she felt anger at him in ways she still can't acknowledge.

"You wouldn't understand," she says to her mother.

"I'm sure," her mother agrees. *Crunch.* She moves on to a friend of hers who has a valuable old Bible. "Could it be worth a lot of money?"

"No," Merry rasps. "It's not worth anything. They're never worth anything. Everyone thinks they're valuable because they're old. But they are also extremely common. It's rarity that you're looking for."

"Meredith, you're sounding upset."

"I'm *Merry*," she shouts and slaps off the phone.

She has to get out of this apartment. Has to get out of here. Has to find Dickens. Has to find out what he wants from her.

She has to talk to him. And not in a selfie tree.

CHAPTER THIRTY-FIVE

He could be anywhere. He lived all over London, except for that most upper crust part, Mayfair. So that's probably one place she could cross off the list. But it still leaves a vast number of places he could be.

Merry paces around the living room. She would make herself some coffee, but the machine looks like it requires a nuclear code. She would brew some tea, but she can't figure out how to turn on the stove. It's electric, but there's no on/off switch. It's disturbing to think of a bunch of carousing bachelors able to brew tea and coffee without any trouble. She hates to be incompetent, which is yet one more irritation. Illness. Incompetence. Incontinence.

She knows at least a hundred Dickens experts who would have an opinion, but she would probably get a hundred different opinions. She has Claire Tomalin's biography of Dickens with her; there's a map in the front of it that shows all the places in central London that Dickens lived, but that would just prove what she already knows. Which is that he lived in a lot of places.

She decides to call up Mr. Gaudy. He's not a Dickens expert, but he's sensible. And anyway, she wants to apologize to him for getting mad.

"It is I who need to apologize," he says. "You're right. You have to handle this your own way."

"You sound cheerful."

"I am."

Turns out he had some good news, which is that the Milagro family is going to let him have first look at their collection. Sergio Milagro was one of the most mysterious collectors in the world. He never sold anything, just bought and bought and, since he died, everyone has been curious to know what he has stored away in his house.

"What a coup!" Merry says. "Do you have any idea what he could have in there?"

"No, no one knows. Not even his widow. He was so secretive, but he spent all those years in the Middle East and those books are so hot right now."

Hot. They're selling for millions. Wealthy Middle Eastern investors are looking to bulk up their libraries, and Sergio Milagro was making connections there before anyone else was even thinking about it. His books could be worth a fortune.

"You deserve this, Mr. Gaudy."

He gives his papery laugh. "You know, I think I do, Merry. She's giving me four hours on Wednesday. All to myself."

"That is truly wonderful."

"You're the one who turned my luck, Merry. When you put me in touch with that *Harry Potter* collector, Frederic Lion."

"Well, the less said about that the better. Probably." She still has to discuss the whole thing with Gussie.

"Of course, of course."

She feels so energized after talking to Mr. Gaudy. Perhaps things are coming into alignment. Things can go from bad to good.

She goes to the window and peers out as best she can; there's the edge of Hyde Park laid out in front of her. Rolls of fog float over it, making it look like it holds within it the gates to heaven and hell.

Dickens is out there, she knows it.

That's when she remembers a quote she used to love from the famed book collector Basie Bales Gitlin. *Your vision is guiding where you're looking, and not everyone has your vision.*

Isn't that the very heart of her career? That she's always had the gift of being able to sense where a book might be. Or as Mr. Gaudy used to put it, her hands start to tingle when she feels like a good book is nearby. She can actually put her hands in a box of books and, without looking, pull out the most valuable book in the box. It's an instinct that she's learned to trust.

One of her fondest memories is of a road trip that she and Mr. Gaudy and Mr. Hong took some years back, around the midwestern towns where Dickens spoke on his first reading tour of the United States. They drove around Cincinnati and St. Louis and spent four days in Lebanon, Illinois. They'd wanted to stay at the Mermaid House Hotel, which was where Dickens had stayed and was, miraculously, still in existence, but not as a hotel anymore, so instead they stayed at a Hampton Inn and every morning they drove around looking for church sales and attic sales.

Then they began knocking on farmers' doors. Merry was always the person who knocked, Hong and Gaudy hulking behind her. They joked that they were like the Men in Black, though as a practical matter none of them had any physical strength.

They would have run away at the smallest sign of confrontation. However, the people they ran into were kind and did not view them as threatening and were happy to talk to them about Dickens, who had left his mark on the town, even though he'd only spent a brief time there more than a century earlier.

People shared all sorts of anecdotes, but no one had any memorabilia or books.

They were getting ready to call it a day when they happened to drive by an old pink house. Merry couldn't say why she felt something at the sight of that house. Maybe it was just that she liked pink houses, but she told Mr. Hong to pull into the driveway and they knocked one last time.

A very old man and woman welcomed them. They didn't have any books to sell, but they were happy to tell them stories of Dickens, most of which Merry and Mr. Gaudy and Mr. Hong had already heard, but they were happy to hear again. As they were about to leave, the old woman, a Mrs. Bonaparte, said, "We do have something with his signature on it. But it's not a book. It's in the powder room."

They had followed her into the powder room—crammed in, come to think of it, like the elevator and the PET scan, though Merry had no fear of enclosures then.

And there, on the wall, was a framed poster announcing that Dickens would be coming through. Probably worth about five hundred dollars on its own, but with the signature, possibly $2,000. Mr. Hong offered them a thousand dollars. They had a collector who was desperate for ephemera. The Bonapartes were overwhelmed by their windfall.

"You have a gift," Mr. Hong said to her afterward and she felt proud. Because she'd *known* they'd find something there. She'd felt it.

Just as now she feels certain she can find Dickens's ghost. She's come to trust that tingling and she feels it now. And suddenly, she knows where to look.

CHAPTER THIRTY-SIX

Of course. It's so obvious.

Just a short tube ride. Merry can get there and back before anyone wakes up. She can resolve her entire life in less than an hour. That's not bad.

Her fingers are tingling. She feels like this is right.

She tiptoes into her bedroom to get some clothes.

Sully is still asleep. Or at least he's lying in bed, back turned to her, eyes closed. She doesn't know how to deal with him mad at her. They are not one of those screaming couples. Al and Phoebe used to be like that and she both admired and feared it—she thought it seemed passionate. But it was just never how she and Sully were. They never annoyed each other. Sometimes she felt like they were two sides of the same person, as though the line between where one of them ended and the other began was blurred. She wants to go to him, hug him, tell him that she's sorry she doesn't want to go to Phoebe's party—but she's *not* sorry and she can't see apologizing for something she's not sorry about. This is about Phoebe, who betrayed her, even as she told her her secret.

She still hasn't had time to unpack, and she grabs up her box filled with her good clothes. Something Song Lee has taught her about packing: compartmentalize. You put a particular outfit each in a plastic bag and then when you unpack, you don't need to unpack everything. It's great, although it doesn't allow for overlap. What if you want to wear the same pair of pants two days in a row but with different shirts? But Song Lee is not an overlapping sort of person. Never has been. Doesn't even like different types of food to touch each other. Does not like her steak to touch her mashed potatoes. She never liked Korean food, although they tried. Too much blending.

She grabs a pair of jeans and a gray sweater. Washes her face, puts on some lipstick. Her face looks like a stranger's. So pale. Ethereal. Almost as though she's become a ghost herself. She puts on a darker lipstick and some blush. Now she looks like she's going to a nightclub. She's overthinking this.

She tiptoes back into the living room and toward the front door, which she's just creaking open, when Bessie's door swings open and she stands in the doorway. Merry can't tell if she's just woken up. Her freckled, young face. A tangle of curls. A black V neck sweater. She wonders if she wears regular clothes to sleep. Is that a Generation Z thing? In her hand she holds her phone, on which Merry can see Leroy. Leroy, who seems to be riding a bike though it's only five A.M. in New York. Dark out.

"You're going to the V&A without me?"

The V&A. The laminated schedule. God bless her, Bessie's the only one who read the schedule.

"No," Merry says. "I'm just going out for a little bit."

"With Song Lee?"

"No," Merry says, looking into her daughter's earnest face. Always so afraid of being left behind. "Something else entirely."

"Can we go with you?"

The world seems to hush. How can she possibly say no to this child, whom she's already wounded by not offering her the family heirloom in the proper order?

But to take Bessie on a Dickens ghost hunting expedition is a different order of magnitude entirely. It will become a circus, it will be an event. It will be unsuccessful because as hard as it would be to find a ghost on her own, Merry feels certain it will be impossible to find it with her dramatic daughter and her boyfriend on her phone.

So Merry says the only thing she possibly can say. "Okay."

CHAPTER THIRTY-SEVEN

"Charles Dickens's ghost?!" Bessie roars. They're making their way to the tube stop by Lancaster Gate. Merry's plan is to take the tube to Charing Cross railway station.

Turns out Bessie and Leroy are into ghosts in a big way. They see them all the time at the hospice where they work part-time. They smell them. They talk to them. They watch souls leave bodies.

"Why do you think he'll be at Warren's Blacking Factory?" she asks.

"I had an epiphany," Merry says. They walk by the Italian gardens, wreathed with poinsettias. Past a strange little church that seems to lurk out of view, waiting to pounce. "I tried to think of places that would be so powerful they would draw him. A place that had a tremendous emotional impact on him. A place that haunted him all his life and colored everything he wrote. Once I figured that out, it was obvious it would have to be Warren's Blacking Factory."

A proud boy, she thinks, forced to put stickers onto bottles because his father was in jail for not paying debts. His mother was desperate for money and so she sent Charles out to work, and lodge in a stranger's house while she lived with her husband at Marshalsea Prison, along with their younger children. How he seethed at that humiliation. How he hated his mother for that and never really forgave her. His father caused him no end of embarrassment and yet he was able to move on. But not with his mother.

"And the factory is at Charing Cross station?"

"Well, no. The factory was actually torn down when Charing Cross station was built. But I have to assume there will be some sort of marker, or one of those blue plaques, maybe down in the bowels of the station. Something has to be there. Some brick. Some rock. Something that would draw him."

"And why do we want to find Dickens?" Leroy asks.

But Bessie interjects. "I think that makes absolute sense," Bessie says. "I would definitely go back to Aruba if I were a ghost. I'll never get over what happened to me there."

Merry thinks of the PET scan. But no, it would be coming home from Gstaad and finding her father dead. That changed her life, and who she became, and what she thought of herself. The PET scan just terrified her.

"Don't you remember Aruba, Ma?"

Merry blinks, trying to remember. "What happened to you in Aruba?"

"Don't you remember? That wet T-shirt contest and then it went viral. You don't remember that?"

"I do, I do," Merry says.

She does remember a lot of drama about Aruba. But there was also drama with the Bahamas. Those spring breaks were killers.

"It looks like the tube is closed," Leroy observes.

"Dang, they're on strike," Merry says. It's actually a planned strike. Who ever heard of such a thing? Isn't the point of strikes to surprise you? "Let's get an Uber."

"No," Bessie says. "Let's walk. It's so brisk outside. I need to walk off sitting on the plane."

Charing Cross station is about three miles away, Merry thinks, as she looks at the map on her own phone. She remembers how winded she got with Song Lee only the night before. Song Lee, who she's wounded so terribly, but if she collapses with Bessie, it will be so much worse. Bessie would no doubt flag down a royal helicopter. Merry feels frightened and then Leroy says, "Why don't we take a bus? The 94 will take you to Picadilly Circus, and we can walk to Charing Cross station from there."

"You're a genius," Merry says.

"Great idea," Bessie says, and as quickly as that, a bus is upon them. They climb on—to the top level, of course; even Merry can't resist that—and then they are seated. She's safe.

"You don't remember that woman wrote a blog post about me?" Bessie continues, once they are on their way. "How to protect your social identity when you're on vacation. It was the most horrifying moment of my life. Really transformed what I thought of my body. I can't believe you don't remember it."'

Bessie goes on in that vein for a bit. Merry's trying to pay attention, but she's distracted by a succession of ancient gnarled trees that look like they could offer advice. Perhaps they've seen the ghost of Dickens go by. Perhaps they knew him when he was young. After a bit, Merry realizes she hasn't heard Leroy's voice in a while, and when she looks at Bessie's phone, she thinks his face looks pinched.

"What about you, Leroy?" she calls out. "What moment would you haunt?

"Oh, yes," Bessie says. "Great question. What do you think, Leroy?"

He takes a moment. He's one of those public thinkers. Thoughts flash across his face like a slide show. Meanwhile, the bus has turned onto Oxford Street and Merry's entranced by the angels that float overhead. Even unlit, there's something so graceful and solemn about them.

Merry sneaks another look at Leroy's face and notices how frail he is. She just assumed he's strong because he's always riding a bicycle, but now he looks fragile. Perhaps migrained. Or perhaps her family has done it to him. She remembers taking Nick to the emergency dentist a few Christmases ago when he clenched his jaw and cracked a tooth.

Nick, who should be here in just a few hours. She hasn't seen him in a long time and she's so excited.

They've stopped at a traffic light. Merry can never get over how fast the traffic lights are in London. In New York, you have twenty-five seconds to cross a street. In London, ten seconds. Seems out of keeping with the historical vibe of the city, a city that is much more designed for strolling than New York. A group of young women all in white go dashing in front of the bus.

"I guess I'd go back to the hospice," Leroy says. "With Mr. Hurd."

"Really?" Bessie says.

"Who is that?" Merry asks.

They're at Picadilly and Merry has to wind her way down the stairs to the first floor of the bus. She clutches the railing tightly, but even so, she and Bessie practically fly on to the street. And right there is a pair of angel wings painted on a wall.

"Quick, Mom, let me take your picture," Bessie says, and thrusts Merry between the wings, and then there is more commotion, but Merry is able to guide them onto Regent Street.

Almost there.

"What about Mr. Hurd?" Bessie asks, drawing them back to the original conversation. *What moment in your life would you haunt?*

Suddenly Leroy looks eager. More eager than Merry's ever seen him. His soft brown face fills the screen, his eyes wide. "He was one of my clients at the hospice. Very difficult. Very angry. I tried to get him to talk. We were to work on a scrapbook together, but he wouldn't do it. Wouldn't look at me."

"Bigot," Bessie mutters.

"Every day for months I brought something for him to do. A record player so he could listen to his music. Books. I read to him. The doctors kept saying he was going to die."

"He should have died," Bessie says. "But he wouldn't let go."

Merry fights to not put her hand over where she believes the nodule to be. She's sure Bessie will observe the motion and draw conclusions. "He wanted to keep living?" she asks.

"No," Leroy says. "But he just couldn't let go."

"He wouldn't even let go of the bed railing," Bessie says.

They've made it past Trafalgar Square. To her right Merry can see the grand neoclassical building of the Athenaeum Club, of which Dickens was a member. Could he be there?

"I've never known failure before," Leroy says. "Never."

"Can you imagine?" Bessie says.

"And then Bessie came to my rescue."

"It was unresolved guilt," she says. "I knew it right away. Well, I've seen enough of it."

"Terrible story," Leroy says.

"What was it?"

Bessie gestures at Leroy to indicate he should speak.

"One day," Leroy says, "when he was a boy, he was running late to school. He had a violin lesson that day but he'd forgotten his violin and he could have run back to get it but he was already late, so he asked his older brother if he could take his. The brother's room was closer to the front of the house."

Bessie's nodding vigorously. Merry hears the coffee in her left hand sloshing. "It was a better violin anyway," she says. "I think they'd bought it for him."

"That's right. The parents had rented Mr. Hurd's violin, but they bought the one for the older brother."

"So he went to school, but he lost it. He left it on the subway and he felt terrible and he knew his mother would be really mad. So he told her that the older brother took it and lost it."

"Oh," Merry says.

"But here's the thing," Bessie whispers. "Her brother didn't tell on him. He took the punishment."

"Beating," Leroy says.

"It wasn't only that," Bessie says. "He became the kid who lost the expensive violin. He became the untrustworthy one. Even years later, the parents made the young brother the executor of the will."

"But couldn't the younger brother confess at some point?" Merry asks.

"I guess it had gone on too long," Leroy says. "By the time the parents died, the older brother was a failure. He lived into their expectations. And then the brother died. Hit by a car, but it sounded like he had a drinking problem. And it was all too late. Until Bessie got it out of Mr. Hurd. She got him to talk. It was the most amazing thing I've ever seen. I think I've never loved anyone so much."

"Lover," Bessie whispers.

"As soon as he finished talking, he died," Leroy says. "He was at peace. You gave him the gift of a good death."

"How did you do it?" Merry asks, looking at a daughter who seems to radiate happiness and competence. "What did you say?"

"Oh," Bessie says. "I told him about Nick."

CHAPTER THIRTY-EIGHT

Miraculously, they have made it to Charing Cross station. They've walked, bused, and walked and Merry doesn't feel tired. It's as though she's been bewitched. She's in Bessie-world, where anything is possible. Maybe in Bessie-world she doesn't even have a nodule.

The station is a gleaming monumental structure, but Merry is automatically drawn toward the incredibly strange Queen Eleanor Memorial Cross. It's a reconstruction of an earlier cross, built during the thirteenth century, then destroyed. This one was built by a Victorian artist and looks like it was placed there by a UFO.

Merry leans against it.

She stops moving. The crowd seems to stop moving. The only thing Merry can feel moving is her heart, and the train that sounds like it's about to roar out of her ears.

"Nick's a classic case of unresolved guilt," Bessie says, continuing the Mr. Hurd conversation. "I wish I could get him to talk about what went on on that camping trip."

"What do you mean what went on? Four boys went out in a canoe in choppy weather. Three fell into the water and drowned. Nick didn't."

It occurs to Merry that where they are standing now is exactly where the Thames River used to flow. The Victorians decided to move the river, and they did. Say what you will about the Victorians, they had get up and go.

Bessie nods, gazing over to Charing Cross station. "You can't think there isn't more to the story. Why didn't he jump?"

"Because he knew he would die too."

"But what if it's something else? Something like the equivalent of stealing a violin."

Merry notices that lines have appeared on Leroy's forehead.

"Bessie, let this go," she says. "Do not start in on Nick when he gets here. I want to have a nice time."

Bessie rolls her eyes. "Right, like anyone has ever had a nice time with Nick."

"If you start in on him when he's here, then he's going to shut down and it's going to be a disaster."

"He's holding the whole family hostage, Mom! We can never talk about what happened."

Merry shakes her head. "He's the one the tragedy happened to. It's his right to talk about it or not."

"It happened to *all* of us. All our lives were changed because of what happened to him. Except that he knows what happened and we don't. But if I could get him to talk—"

"Enough!" Suddenly Leroy's voice cracks into the air. He gazes at Bessie, a pained expression on his face. "Enough," he repeats. "Let's find the ghost."

Bessie seems to collapse into herself as though he'd punched her in the stomach.

"Just a minute," she says to Merry and walks over to the corner. Merry's relieved by the quiet. Yes, she's in the middle of London and there's a lot of commotion, but that's nothing like a conversation with Bessie. She thinks suddenly of a bookseller who was leafing through a biography of Jesse James and inside the book found an invitation to a hanging.

She can see Bessie has the phone pressed close to her mouth. Merry misses her dog so badly she could weep. Her eyes fog. She can smell him.

And then, Bessie is back. Smiling. And Leroy is smiling too, and Bessie sings out, "Who's ready to find Charles Dickens's ghost?"

CHAPTER THIRTY-NINE

When Merry finally has a chance to focus on Charing Cross station, the very vastness of it defeats her.

How has she seriously thought to find Dickens's ghost here?

It is as glossy as is possible for a railway station to be. So weird to think that there was a time, two hundred years ago, when this was one of the worst slums in London. When the Thames River, polluted with sewage too terrible to think about, flowed in this very spot. When young Charles Dickens sat in a window, humiliated and angry and putting labels on blacking jars. Desperately afraid that someone who knew him would pass by.

But now that's completely gone. Even the river is gone, redirected, and Merry's feeling overwhelmed. All this walking and talking and drama and she'd like to get a cup of tea, but Bessie is on a mission. They are here to find a ghost and she *will* find one. Dead or alive.

Bessie waves her hand to attract a crowd. She asks if anyone's seen Dickens's ghost. "He would be a short man, would you say, Mom?" And she holds up her phone, which shows everyone Leroy, who is himself holding up Claire Tomalin's biography of Dickens. Of course, she thinks. He comes from a Christmas village and he owns her favorite book on Dickens. She hopes this relationship lasts.

Bessie looks so excited and eager and moist. Like rising bread. Merry finds herself remembering how difficult a labor she had with her. Nick had been so easy. Popped out in just an hour and then he was sleeping through the night at two months. Breastfed immediately. She genuinely thought she knew what she was doing, and then came Bessie and it was a nightmare. Her head was too big so she needed a caesarian and then she screamed for months; you could not put her down. Merry'd always wanted to have a big family, but after Bessie she just couldn't deal with it, until she saw the ad for Song Lee.

Merry did prefer going to Song Lee's swim meets, she realizes. Because Song Lee always won. Bessie's right about that.

That's awful.

Next thing that happens, Bessie approaches a tiny woman wearing a bright yellow vest that indicates she works for the London Transport System. Bessie asks her if she knows where there's a blue sign for Dickens. To Merry's amazement the woman responds, in a heavy Russian accent, "Yes. Follow me."

Then she heads toward the door in the station that leads out onto the street. Not at all in the direction Merry expected, which would have been deeper into the station and probably down.

"No," Merry says. "This is not the right way."

But the guide continues, relentless. Heading toward the crosswalk, cutting across the Strand. As they follow her, Merry wonders if it's possible to walk to your own kidnapping.

"Do you think we should keep doing this?" she whispers.

"Yes," Bessie says. "I trust her."

"Why?" Merry asks, but Bessie is in the throes of a quest and when Bessie commits, she commits, and so they keep following this woman, who marches with purpose. They follow her past the police station, which is quite an attractive building. Merry finds this oddly reassuring. They keep going.

All of a sudden everything hushes, as London does sometimes, and Merry knows they're going in the wrong direction because the blacking factory was on the river and this cannot be right, and then they get to a quiet little corner and there is a charming tea place for children. It has nothing to do with Dickens, but Merry would love to go in there. A little girl walks by with her mother, wearing a splash of poppies and Merry wonders if that's the sort of thing Nora Villard would've worn. Maybe they've entered a time loop.

Now the transport woman stops so suddenly that they all pile into her. There's a locked door. A bag of trash. Ahead of them is the Lady Hotel, which looks beautiful, but they are in a square of gloom, and then she says "Look" and gestures upward. There is the blue sign.

In this place, Dickens worked as a boy.

Merry realizes where she went wrong. The first factory closed, was torn down to make way for the river, but young Dickens moved to a second place. Here.

She found what she's looking for. Sort of.

There's no ghost, so it's not a complete accomplishment. She still has no idea what Dickens is supposed to do for her and whether it involves Phoebe, and yet, she feels triumphant. She feels like she's in a better place than she was this morning.

"What should we do?" Bessie says. "Should we wait here?"

Merry offers the transport woman a five-pound note, but she waves it away. "Just buy train tickets," she says. "That's all the thanks I need."

She walks away and Merry feels exhausted. The way you feel after a six-year-old's birthday party. Like even your toes hurt. She wants to sit down. She feels like her voice is slurring. Her phone buzzes and Sully has texted her to say that he and Song Lee are picking up Nick at Paddington. No heart emoji. No smiley face.

She texts back. *We're not far from Rules. Want to just meet there?*

OK.

She waits, but there's nothing more. He's still angry.

That deflates her even more.

It's getting dark even though it's only a little past three, and they haven't stopped to eat. Haven't stopped to sit. She's not surprised Dickens isn't here. She suspects that her relationship with him, such as it is, is not a group activity. Having Bessie here, and the disembodied face of Leroy on a phone, cannot possibly be useful.

But now she doesn't know what to do. It's Monday the 22nd and they have only four more days in London. Two days until they're to put on the show. Nick will be here within the hour and he's certain to make the situation worse. She's certain that Dickens is there to help her, if he's real, but how can you tell if a ghost is real?

There is just no rule book for life.

She had thought that *A Christmas Carol* was as close to a rule book as she could find. It certainly seemed to be for her father. But now that seems to be turned upside down, and if she's reading this correctly, Dickens wants for her to apologize to Phoebe, which is just so wrong, but maybe she's supposed to go to that party. Maybe the Campions' appearance was not random. Maybe she's misread life.

Merry persuades Bessie and Leroy to walk around the streets near the blue sign on their own. Some clue may jump out at them. Meanwhile she creaks over to Saint Paul's, where she knows there will be peace and benches. There's maybe a half hour of light left. She feels like everything is ticking down.

This is not the famous Saint Paul's cathedral that soars over the London skyline. This is Saint Paul's church, or the actors' church, right in the middle of Covent Garden. Even though it's winter, the garden in the back is still green, and fairly empty. You can get into the church through a front door, but Merry's always preferred the secret black and white tiled alley that leads into it from a side street. She loves secrets, yearnings, locations with hidden meaning.

As expected, the church garden is quiet. Merry settles into a comfortable bench. Surveys the view.

This was all here during Dickens's time. Another potential haunting site. Plus, now she's on her own, but no. No Dickens. Is it possible that he only intended to have one visit with her and that was it? That would be so unfair. Or what if he plans to meet her at the Campion party? That would be worse. You would think if there were anyone she needed to apologize to it would be her father. He was the one she left alone to die. That is something she knows for a fact was wrong. She would give anything to be able to undo it. Surely that was worse than yelling at Phoebe in a British pub.

She calls her husband. "I'd like to go to that Campion party after all."

"No, you wouldn't, and I shouldn't have asked you. I'm just a cheap drunk. We will forget about the party and put on the best *Christmas Carol* ever."

"Yes, to the last part, but the fact is I would like to go."

"Why?" She pictures the smile on his face, remembers the way he looked when she told him she didn't plan to do it but it wouldn't be a bad idea to dig up Mr. Sedler's coffin because he'd been buried holding a valuable manuscript.

"This is going to sound strange, but I believe there's an outside chance that the ghost of Charles Dickens will be there."

"Wow. Didn't see that coming. I imagine there's a story."

He sounds so calm, and even amused. But then he's a man who works with high school students. He's certainly heard stories much more profoundly weird than anything she could come up with.

She puts her hand over where she believes the nodule to be. It feels warm. Why is it so much easier to tell him about a ghost than death?

"There is something serious I need to tell you," she says, finally.

She starts to cry. Convulsive sobs, as she tells him about the nodule and the PET scan and how she's been too afraid to call for the results, and he doesn't criticize her because he loves and understands her.

"I want to be with you when you get the results," he says, his voice husky. She imagines him crying too. "Don't worry, I won't pity you."

She rubs her eyes. He understands. He has been paying attention.

"I should have told you before."

"Merry. When have you ever done what you were supposed to do? Oh, here's Nick's train. I have to go, but you know how much I love you."

"I do."

"Does Song Lee know?" he asks suddenly.

She pauses. "Yes. It was awful of me to ask her to keep it quiet."

"I just wondered why she looked like she was crying. That means Nick will know. I'll tell Bessie."

"No," she says. "I'll do it. Now would actually be a good time."

Though, at the exact moment Merry is about to text Bessie and ask her to come sit with her, she hears her daughter scream, and when she reaches the place where her daughter stands, she sees the most remarkable scene she's seen in her life.

CHAPTER FORTY

Bessie stands in the middle of the Strand, traffic stopped, a child in her arms. The pose is so theatrical, Merry is reasonably sure she's seen a Rembrandt just like it. So like Bessie, except who's the child? And where's the phone with Leroy on it?

That's when she notices a double-decker red bus stopped not two feet away from Bessie. A crowd of people surround her, and an older woman, the child's grandmother perhaps, is weeping hysterically into a handkerchief. *She just flew out of my grip.*

"My God," another woman whispers, over and over, staring at Bessie in disbelief. This must be the mother, poor soul. She looks stunned.

Merry nears her, trying to figure out what's going on, relieved to see Bessie looks okay. Better than okay, actually. She looks empowered, revitalized. Heroic. Merry once saw Bessie play Cordelia in *King Lear* and she suspects she's channeling that. Angry, loving, tragic.

"How could you drive like that?" her daughter is yelling at a large, burly man. "You were an inch away from hitting her."

The bus driver is sweating, looking down at the ground. Opposite from them is a Burger King and a Pizza Hut, which makes everything feel that much more bizarre.

"What happened?" Merry asks one of the onlookers.

"It's the bravest thing I've ever seen," she says. "That little boy ran into the street and the bus was coming toward him and that lady ran right in front of the bus and saved his life."

"I've never seen anything like it," another woman says.

The child's mother now steps forward and takes her son from Bessie's hands. It's all so theatrical, Merry thinks, and yet true. This is, in every sense of the word, classic Bessie. Merry feels both proud and exhausted as she makes her way forward. When Bessie sees her, she grins and she is pure joy. She is like Charles Dickens Villard Jr., Merry thinks, who ran into a falling subway to save lives. She is like little vampire girl Nora Villard who approached the great Charles Dickens to talk to him about his book.

She is so proud of her.

She feels like even if she no longer has the book, the Villard spirit lives on. It's such a good feeling. She can almost feel the swirl of her ancestors around her.

Someone starts to clap, and then everyone around starts clapping and Bessie just glows and begins to bow. Merry feels so glad to be part of this moment, which Bessie is certain to be talking about for the rest of her days. The mother tries to give Bessie money, but she turns it away. "It was my honor, I was humbled." This is the Oscar speech she may or may not ever give.

One of the flower vendors comes up to her then and, bowing slightly, hands Bessie a bouquet. An effusion of colors. Everyone starts to clap again, and Bessie bows dramatically, with great flourish, and then they stay and mingle. Merry's in no hurry to go. She could drink this all in forever, but Sully texts. *Almost there.*

From triumph to death, Merry thinks. That sounds about right.

How is she supposed to tell Bessie about the nodule now? This has been such a triumphant moment for her and she doesn't want to ruin it. Merry's so happy for this daughter of hers who always needs love and attention and has now got it, in the right way. She suspects that Bessie will be more devastated than all of them by the news. That as angry as she constantly is at Merry, she also depends on her the most. Merry just wants to live in this moment of hearing Bessie bubbling away.

"I just couldn't believe it when I saw that little boy wandering into the street and nobody paying attention to him. The mother was on her phone and the bus driver didn't slow down."

"You could have died," Leroy says. His voice comes from her bra. She must have tucked her phone in there when she ran for the bus.

"Oh my gosh," Merry says, wrapping her arms around her daughter, so grateful that she's okay. The bouquet smells like a sachet. Perfect. "Listen, we should start to head for Rules. Nick will be there soon."

Bessie nods. "Of course. Nicky."

Bessie waves toward the last of the crowd. Street lamps turn on, guiding them to Rules. The street turns into cobblestones, and Bessie automatically grabs Merry's arm so she doesn't trip.

"Don't want you to break a leg."

She retrieves Leroy from her bra. There is that wide smile, the eager eyes, the sense of bewilderment. Merry figures she might as well say what she's going to say now, with Leroy there for comfort, because it's not like Bessie's going to keep this a secret.

So she says, "There's something I've been wanting to talk to you about. It's not terrible, but—"

Her words are lost. Bessie is in flight because she's just spotted Nick and wants to be first in his arms.

CHAPTER FORTY-ONE

It's always easy to spot Nick. Just follow who everyone else is looking at. It's not just that he's good-looking, though he is. But he has an aura to him. He looks like a model who's taken up lumberjacking, or the other way around. Plaid shirt, jeans, high boots, long hair pulled back, and those huge eyes.

People always make way for him. Smile at him. Give him a bit more latitude.

Merry remembers reading how people used to jump out of J. P. Morgan's way. When he walked down Fifth Avenue, the crowd would open before him. Something similar happens with Nick.

It's been the same thing all his life. When he got into trouble in high school, the principal let him off. He just had to write an essay, and Merry's pretty sure his girlfriend wrote it. Bessie had to go to summer school, and Song Lee never got into trouble. Ever. Until she decided to break the law and destroy her career.

The stakes always seemed lower for him. Up until that terrible day when he was at camp and tragedy hit, and suddenly the stakes were way too high.

Now he strides toward them with his distinctive lope, backpack shrugged over his shoulder. He's wearing the same clothes he wore the last time she saw him. She's not sure if that's because he wears the same outfits over and over again or always buys the same ones. She suspects the latter. He handwashes his clothes and hangs them on a clothesline. Always smells fresh, slightly of juniper. He and Song Lee smell similar, though in her case the juniper is from the gin.

Bessie rushes past her and hurls herself into his arms like a dove nesting. Then she waves her phone in his face. "This is Leroy."

"Why, hello, Leroy."

Song Lee walks behind him, wearing large sunglasses. She has on a camel-colored slip of a dress and thigh-high boots. She doesn't completely stop when Nick does, so she bumps into him. Merry watches his arm go around her, pull her close. And then he lets go of both his sisters and walks toward Merry.

He looks at her in a way that no one else does, with the possible exception of Leroy the dog. He looks thinner, but his eyes blaze. Two young women walk by and wave at him. He grins and waves back.

And she is with her boy. The boy she loves so much. The boy who lived. And as she always does when she sees him, she whispers a prayer of gratitude, because he is here. She is so grateful.

Only now does she notice some lines around his eyes and one or two strands of gray hair, and a bruise on his wrist.

"Dirt bike accident," he says, knowing without her saying anything what she's thinking. The Power of the Oldest Child. All the time they spent together. She doesn't think she's ever been so unfiltered with anyone. Bessie came along three years later, and then she had to figure out how to divide her time. How to be fair. How to manage. There was so much more to manage with two than with one. Nick became more independent. Started going off on play dates. Bessie had her own set of friends. The dynamic changed, but for those first three years, when it was just Nick and her, and Sully, of course, she felt closer to that boy than to anyone in the world.

"You look good," she says.

"So do you, Ma," he says, with the slightest throb in his voice that tells her that Song Lee shared her secret with him. How could she expect her not to? How could she have ever asked it?

"I am," she says. "I am."

Because this was what she wanted, wasn't it? To have them all together. For Christmas. In London. Just like the Campions. Instead of grinning insanely at a camera, instead of wearing ugly sweaters, instead of going for the shallow, they are going to do Christmas the way it should be done.

Dickens must be nearby. She can feel it. Her father too. They're circling her, loving her. London surrounding them, people walking by, but her family a perfect little microcosm of Christmas.

As they all weave themselves together, she pictures the way it will all play out. *She* will play the part of Tiny Tim. Song Lee can be Scrooge. That's the sort of mood she's in. Destructive and angry. Bessie can be the Ghost of Christmas Present. She is all joy and love and in the moment. Leroy could be the nephew, a small role and yet an important one. She doesn't have an outfit for that, but it doesn't matter because Leroy will just be on the screen. Sully was born to play Bob Cratchit. Nick can be the Ghost of Christmas Yet to Come, because he's spent too much of his life looking backward. What he needs to do is look forward and the Ghost of Christmas Yet to Come is not that scary because it points you in the direction of change. Of transformation. It's all so perfect.

It's all coming together.

That's when Nick looks at Bessie and says, "Hey, little sis. Why are you holding those flowers?"

Time seems to slow down. Bessie turns white, and she started off pretty white. She looks like she's seen a ghost. She starts to stutter.

Nick's not concerned. He looks at her with that wry look he always has, as though seeing the world through prismatic glasses. "Did someone propose?"

"Oh, I'm sorry, Nicky. I forgot."

"Forgot what?"

Now everyone is looking at Bessie, wondering what she's going on about. Except for Merry, who is beginning to have a clue. Who is desperately trying to think of a way to stop this train wreck, except it can't be stopped.

"Oh, I'm sorry," Bessie keeps saying. "I'm so so sorry, Nicky. I didn't want to upset you."

Now Nick is starting to look upset. As though some warning signal is going off in his head. Some memory of all the various times Bessie has brought disaster onto him.

"What is it, Bessie?" has asks, his voice hard now. His elbows tight. The bruise on his wrist now turning darker, pulsating with the blood that must be circulating through him.

"I saved someone's life," she mutters. "Oh Nicky, I'm so sorry. I saved someone's life."

CHAPTER FORTY-TWO

Dinner is quiet.

Nick is sullen. Bessie apologizes at least five more times, which doesn't help. Once words are out, you can't take them back, and anyway, the underlying problem is that her words are true. She did save a life and Nick didn't. You can justify it or deny it or be grateful for it or whatever you want. You just can't change it.

Three boys died on his watch. He didn't kill them, but neither did he run in front of a bus to save them. Cowardice? Common sense? Intelligence?

Four boys who'd been camp friends since they were little. Now counselors, on their very last day of camp. The last time they'd all be together. It had rained all that summer. One of those torturous summers where they had to spend days and days doing indoor games and everything smelled musty. Somehow, they pulled through, and the kids went home. The counselors had to stay behind to close up the cabins. Put all the equipment away for the winter. A bittersweet moment. The end of an era. The official end of their youth.

And then finally, after a whole summer of rain, the sun came out. They decided to go for one last canoe ride down the river.

They'd known that river since they were children. Knew every last tree and rock of it, but what they hadn't factored in was that the river was swollen with rain. The normally gentle currents were like whirlpools.

Matt jumped in first. He was always the risk-taker of the bunch and he wanted to swim in the waves, but almost immediately he was carried off toward a waterfall. It happened so fast. Jacob jumped in to save him, and just as quickly he was carried off. Tyler hesitated, but jumped in and just as quickly he was pulled under. Then, miraculously, the canoe got stuck on a rock. All of this information Merry knows from the police report.

Nick wouldn't talk about it then and he hasn't talked about it since. Except to a therapist.

All she knows for sure is that when they found Nick, hours later, he was lying down in the canoe, clinging to its edges, and wouldn't let go.

Now he clings to the table at Rules.

Merry watches pain seep across his face. She sees it in his jaws, clenched so tight that bones she's never seen before are jutting out of his cheeks. She can see the skeleton under his skin. It's like watching him die in front of her.

To make matters worse, the waitress at Rules took one look at Nick and immediately moved them to a better table. So they are right in the middle of the restaurant, for everyone to see. They are surrounded by all the sparkle that is Rules and it is sparkly indeed. Possibly the most sparkly restaurant Merry has ever seen. There are little lights everywhere and sprigs of holly. When you look up, you see a ceiling that Michelangelo would have painted, if he'd been Victorian. It is all so florid and festive and the room surges with Christmas joy, except at Merry's table, which is dense with silence.

No one has even ordered a drink, and they do have special cocktails here. They have something called a Rules Royale with Tempus Fugit liquor. Merry doesn't know what it is, but it sounds about right. Then there's a Black Velvet. Champagne and Guinness.

"Look at this," she says to Bessie, but all Bessie wants is water.

Merry orders one for herself. She feels the need to take some sort of action.

"Are you sure?" Sully asks, and she knows what he's thinking. *Should you be drinking if you have a nodule?* Could this get any worse?

Actually, it could. Because Bessie gets up then and gives the flowers to the maître d'. "Could you donate these to a deserving person?"

"I heard about what you did," he says. "You deserve them."

Song Lee pours a little salt on her hand and licks it, something she's not done since she was little. Merry has a feeling it was something the orphanage had them do. It makes Merry so sad, which is saying a lot, because she already feels sad, and angry.

The waiter hands them huge menus that are filled with extravagant dishes full of meat and cream, and Merry realizes that at least half the people at this table are vegetarian. What was she thinking? They should have all gone to the avocado bar across the street. Then at least they could have slipped out without any difficulty.

Out the window, Merry sees some girls on a bicycle singing songs from *Mamma Mia!*, and she thinks for a moment that she sees a man in a green suit go by. She wants more than anything to chase after him, to find the miracle that is Christmas. To heal this wound that is tearing them apart. To do anything.

"Look at that," Sully says. He points at a plaque across from them that says that a James Bond movie was filmed in that very location. Leroy the dog would love that, Merry thinks. Ian Fleming was also a great book collector and his nephews carried on the tradition. It was one of the more surprising things she learned when she became a book scout, but now doesn't seem like the moment.

"I think we should order the soup," Sully says. "Let's all get soup. Look, it has watercress and crème fraiche. That would be soothing."

They all agree immediately, for the first time ever in the history of her family. They'll probably order Caesar salads as their main courses. No dessert. Then race back to the flat and put *Home Alone* on the TV.

"So how did you save someone's life?" Nick asks. He looks Bessie in the eyes. His expression is mildly amused, but Merry notices him pressing his left fist against his right palm. He'll have stigmata before the dinner is done.

"I don't want to talk about it."

"You might just as well because we're all thinking about it, and until you talk about it, we're not going to be able to move on."

"I feel embarrassed," she says. Her normally curly hair looks matted. Her eyes look tired. Merry wonders if she's slept at all or if she was up all night talking to Leroy. "Under the circumstances."

"Under the circumstances," Nick mutters.

Sully clears his throat. Automatically, they all turn toward him. He's not at all an attention-grabbing person. He has on his dad face. His brows knit, his shoulders squared. He should be wearing a wool sweater, but the suspenders work well. He is completely unintimidating, Merry thinks, which is part of why she loves him so well. But it's also why she cringes as she waits for what's to come.

"Could we just think for a minute about all the effort your mother has gone through to bring us to this time and place? And what does she want? For us to have a meaningful Christmas. Is that truly asking so much, as we sit together in this magnificent place? After all, she sacrificed her most treasured possession to take us here."

Silence. For a moment. Then, the sound of a family a table away laughing. At another table, in the corner, a solitary gentleman eyes them appraisingly.

And then Nick says, "Her treasure and my inheritance."

"You didn't want it!" Merry cries out. She feels betrayed. Nick! The one who's always on her side. How could he be criticizing her?

"I didn't want the *book*. I didn't know I could sell it."

"You couldn't sell it. Only I could sell it, and that was for a higher purpose."

How is it possible for her to feel alone with the people she loves the most in the world, because that is the thing she thinks as she looks around at them. How much she loves them and how hopeless it seems to make them happy. They all just seem to dislike each other so much. They seem to dislike her. They have turned into the sort of people she used to gossip about.

The worst hour of your life is just sixty minutes, someone told her once. Which was completely wrong, she thinks. The worst hour of your life, the worst dinner of your life, can go on for hours, and it seems like this is going to. They are going to peck at each other.

"I never would have sold it," Bessie's saying. "I would have recognized it for an heirloom. I would have given it to a children's museum."

Nick snickers at that, and Bessie howls, "Why? I would have. That way everyone could benefit from our inheritance."

"Oh God, you are just so annoying," Song Lee snaps, which is actually reassuring because she'd rather a snapping Song Lee than a sobbing one.

"Oh, really?" Bessie says. "What would *you* have done with the book?"

"I would have burned it," Song Lee says. "Who cares about these stupid old things? They're a dead weight on all of us."

Merry looks out the window, at the beautiful lit-up street. Dickens loved this restaurant. He ate here often. There are private, plush rooms that you can reserve. She tried to do that, but they were already booked. But there's no Dickens here now, no hope, no joy. It all feels like dust. Maybe he's not coming back, which is so unfair. Scrooge got three chances and the ghost explained to him what he wanted. Why does she only get one chance and she still has no idea what he wants from her? Why does she get a passive ghost?

Heat from the soup rises up into her face.

Suddenly Merry blasts with anger. This is ridiculous. Only her family could get into an argument because someone has saved a life.

She has gone to a considerable amount of time and energy to get her family here and they are going to have a Merry Christmas if it's the last thing she does. She's done with tiptoeing around with their sensibilities, trying to bond with each of them, trying to care, trying to heal. This is about Christmas, and it may well be their last Christmas together and she's going to do it right.

"Now listen," she hisses, and they all look up at her, startled.

"We are done with this, all this carping and sniping and misery. I have given you all a gift and I have paid for all of us to come to

London and celebrate Christmas and we are going to enjoy it. We are going to stop whimpering and sniveling and we are going to go to the Dickens Museum first thing tomorrow because we are going to do one damn thing on my list, and then we're going to see a production of *A Christmas Carol* at the Old Vic that is supposed to be revelatory and then on Christmas Eve we are going to go to the Campions for a party and when that is all over, when the day is done, we are going to put on a version of *A Christmas Carol* just for ourselves. I used to do it with my father and it was the most meaningful moment of my life and I want you to have that too. And Nick, I'm telling you now, you are not going to be Tiny Tim. You are just going to have to deal with that, and I have no idea how many Christmases I have left because I have this nodule in my lung and Song Lee, I'm sorry I told you last night, and Bessie if you say one thing about not knowing first, I'm going to go screaming out of this restaurant."

When she's done, they all stare at her in awe. And possibly horror. And then Bessie automatically stands to clap.

And when she does, the phone goes flying out of her hand. They all watch as it sails through the air, like one of those Bounty commercials, and then lands right in Nick's soup. Which is steaming hot. All is silent except for the steamy, sizzling sound the phone makes as it dies, the last thing to fade being Leroy's face, which looks puzzled as he dissolves into the soup.

CHAPTER FORTY-THREE

Merry lunges for the phone. She burns her hands, but succeeds in tossing it to the table.

Sully yells, "Rice!"

Song Lee and Nick run over with their linen napkins and begin blotting at the phone, trying to dry it off, though the cream has oozed into all the crevices. It has become the Ghost of Phones Past. "Is that an iPhone 7?" Song Lee asks. "I didn't know they had FaceTime."

Meanwhile, Bessie lies with her head on the table like a fish. She makes no noise, which is what frightens Merry. She would have thought Bessie would be swimming in the drama.

They are the center of everyone's attention.

A waiter runs over with a bowl of rice, and Sully snaps, "No. no. Raw rice. And a plastic bag."

The waiter doesn't flinch. He acts as though they were the fifth table today to drop a phone in the soup. Within minutes, the waiter strides back with a bowl of raw rice and a plastic bag.

Sully takes the damp phone and puts it and the rice into the plastic bag.

"This will dry it out," he says to Bessie, who has not moved. "Though I don't know how long that will take."

At this point, they cannot resume eating. They really need to go, but Bessie doesn't look like she can walk.

Then Nick sits down alongside her. He puts his hand on her shoulder and hands her his phone, which touches Merry. He's never been the sort of person who likes sharing possessions. He won't even give you a piece of a New York pretzel and no one can eat a whole one of those.

But here he is handing his gleaming new phone over to Bessie, and Merry's surprised at how sparkly it is. There must be more money in leading adventure tours than she realized.

"He won't recognize the number," Bessie whimpers. But at least she's lifted her head off the table.

The waiter asks them if they'd like him to clear.

"And the check," Sully says.

"Text Leroy that you're using my phone," Nick says, patiently.

Which she does. They all perk up when the delivered sign comes up.

Then they wait for a response.

No response.

"Call him," Nick says.

Bessie takes several deep breaths and punches in his number, which rings and rings.

Damn, Merry thinks. She sincerely liked Leroy. He was the only person in the family who got her jokes and liked Dickens as much as she does. Though perhaps he was never part of the family. Maybe he's just a young playwright scouring for material.

"He's ghosting me," Bessie says.

Sully pays and they cart Bessie out of the restaurant. Merry has the sense that they all feel that what is about to happen should happen in private. Song Lee calls an Uber, which shows up immediately and they pack in.

"Try again," Song Lee says.

"I've already called five times and texted twice."

"Maybe he had to step out of the room."

"Without his phone?"

"Bathroom."

"He always has his phone."

Song Lee groans and presses her head against the car window.

Sully wraps his arms around Bessie. He's normally good at calming her. But not this time. She pushes his arms away.

"He's probably disgusted by our family." She looks at Song Lee. "You're lucky you're an orphan."

Song Lee looks startled.

"She's not—" Merry starts to say.

"Maybe he had a bike accident," Nick says. "It happens a lot when people are distracted. He could have been jolted when the phone fell in the soup. He could have hit a curb."

"Or a car," Song Lee suggests.

"No," Bessie says. "I would know if he was dead. I would feel it. He's dumped me. Like everyone else."

"Look," Sully says. "There's got to be an Apple store nearby."

"In Covent Gardens," Merry says. She's walked by it often. "It's huge. Right next to the Royal Opera House."

"This what we'll do," Sully says. "First thing tomorrow we'll go to the Apple store and see if they can fix your phone."

"You want to go to an Apple store two days before Christmas?" Song Lee asks.

"Would you mind, Merry? If we hold off going to the Dickens Museum?"

It's sort of sweet that Sully consulted the laminated schedule, she thinks. And anyway, there's no point in doing anything until this is resolved.

"Of course not," she says. Because as much as she loves that museum, this will still be an opportunity to be with everyone together.

Bessie shrugs. "Maybe, but I don't see what difference it's going to make. He's dumped me. That's all there is to say."

"Why would he dump you because you accidentally broke your phone?" Nick asks.

"You say that because no one ever dumps you," Bessie wails. "Remember when Ulysses dumped me because I couldn't find a parking spot at his sister's wedding?"

"Classic," Song Lee mutters. "Wait," she adds. "We don't *all* have to go to the Apple store, do we?"

"Of course," Merry says. "We're a family. If one of us is suffering, we should all suffer together."

"That's for sure," Song Lee says.

"You should be happy," Bessie says, suddenly grabbing Merry with her eyes.

"Why?"

"Because now you don't have to change your dog's name," Bessie says, and then breaks into a storm of tears.

CHAPTER FORTY-FOUR

Tuesday

That night, Merry dreams of Nora Villard, her vampire girl ancestor.

Unlike most of her dreams, which are surreal and involve her trying to escape from a hidden room, this one has the feel of a documentary. Even in her sleep, she can feel herself saying, "Wow, this is so realistic."

There, center stage, is Nora Villard. Ten years old. Small, elfin. Not so much vampire-like because in this version she's in color. She's mobile. She's active. Now she looks more like a fairy princess, and her hair, which looks so dark and dank in the one photo of her that Merry's ever seen, now looks luxuriant.

Nora wants to see Dickens.

Merry can relate to that. She wants to see Dickens herself. Except that in the case of Nora, Dickens is a living, breathing person, not a ghost that she's chasing around London.

The year is 1867. It's Christmastime and Dickens is going to be in New York, speaking at Steinway Hall, and her mother got tickets. But she's going with Nora's sister. Nora is too young, she explains, and anyway, there are other siblings and she couldn't possibly single out Nora.

But Nora is relentless. Nora is brave. Nora is a lot like Merry, she thinks as she watches her ancestor unfold in her dream. Except that this Nora isn't suffering from anxieties and doesn't have a nodule. This Nora is like Merry without the trauma—though Merry knows that Nora will have trauma. She knows what will happen. This little ancestor will have to call up all her bravery, but that's yet to come. For now, all she wants is to see Charles Dickens, whom she loves.

She's the sort of girl that Merry was, content to stay in her bedroom, reading a book. More engrossed in stories than in real life. Even as a child, Merry found life in books so much more true than real life. She's always thought that was why she had such trouble later on differentiating between what was real and what wasn't and why she feels like her dog is talking to her and why even this dream feels so real.

So Nora couldn't get tickets to see Dickens in person. But she was allowed to stand outside with her cousins and watch the building that housed the great man. She wrote down her memories of the experience. How cold it was outside. How people would run out and tell the passages he was reading and she knew them by heart, so she could follow along. Merry's seen posters of the event, has seen pictures of Dickens at his special podium, holding the book. Grizzly hair splayed out from the center of his head. So different from the ghost she's pursuing.

He didn't read from the book. He had it all memorized, so he didn't actually care which of his novels he held. On this particular night it was a seventh edition of *A Christmas Carol*.

After the reading was over, Nora and her mother had to head home to Massachusetts. They had to run for the next train, which they caught, and it wasn't until they were halfway home that they heard other passengers whispering that Dickens was on board. He too had to run for the train. He had to meet up with friends in Boston. He planned to celebrate Christmas with them.

Once Nora knew, she had to see him.

She didn't tell her mother her plans. She waited until her mother fell asleep and then she crept forward. He was one train car ahead.

But now everything turns red, and the realistic turns surreal. She's stuck in the train. The train's going to crash. She's lost. She needs help, but she doesn't know where to turn. She's calling for help. Her mind burns with fear.

Merry flinches awake, startled to find herself asleep on the red couch, mind clawing to orient herself. She is in the Christmas bordello, she has spent most of the night trying to comfort Bessie, who is distraught over the disintegration of her phone and her mother's nodule and the fact that she was the last to know. She meant to lie down in the bed, but she was so exhausted she only made it as far as the couch.

And her son is sitting across from her.

Her handsome son. Hair falling in front of his eyes. His frame is so slender. His arms are wiry. He has a tattoo she didn't know he had. A symbol. She doesn't know what it means. She doesn't know him. There was a time she would have said she knew him better than anyone in the world. That she could tell simply by looking at his face what he was thinking. When he was a boy, she used to hire a babysitter for Bessie, just so she and he could have time together. So he wouldn't feel lost.

"You were having a nightmare."

"A long one," she says.

He sits alongside her, stretching out his long legs. He wears a faded checked shirt that she knows is soft to the touch and a vest. She suspects he puts more care into his clothes than he would like people to think. She's spent enough time in the book business to know what people look like who genuinely don't care. Who will spend thousands of dollars on a book but have socks with holes.

She can't bear to look at him. She's worried she'll start to cry. She's worried she'll start to scream. She so wishes he was still two years old and all she had to do when she got mad at him was hug him tightly and never let him go.

She read parenting books religiously when the kids were growing up. She obsessed about whether they started speaking at the right time. Walked early or late. Got the right teachers. She remembers going to talk to the principal of the nursery school because she didn't think the teacher was challenging enough. She set up play dates. Wanted them socialized. Took them to Sunday school. Wanted them to have values. Took them every month to work at a food pantry because she wanted them to understand they were privileged. She organized elaborate birthday parties. When it came to Christmas, she was always over the top. Climbing all over the roof to put up reindeer, but also "adopting" a family each Christmas to give them gifts. She had her kids tutored for their SATs. When they got older, she worked more, but she doesn't think she missed anything major. She honestly does not know what she could have done differently. Most of all, she loved them. They were her favorite people to be with. Her idea of a good time was to spend it with the kids. One time she and Sully went away for the weekend, and she got so homesick for them she came home early.

But nowhere in any of the parenting books, in any of the discussions, does it tell you what to do when your kids are adults. She supposes it's because your job is done. They're adults and now you're supposed to focus on your career and take Viking cruises.

But what are you supposed to do if they're unhappy?

She doesn't recall any parenting book giving advice about what to do when your children grow up and they go in directions different than you intended. Different than you wanted. And all that love you thought you were spreading on them doesn't seem to be enough because each in his or her own way seems so lost and so unloved and so alone, and then you go and take them to London because you feel like that's the one thing that will pull them all together and it turns out that's the worst thing of all.

It turns out that's the final nail in the coffin.

Turns out there's nothing you can do to save them, and sometimes families just fall apart.

"You know what I realized at dinner," she says to Nick, when she finally gets the energy to push herself into a sitting position. She's reached the point where she genuinely can't tell if the drumming in her chest is from the nodule or anxiety.

"What?" Nick says, back to looking cooly ironic. Which is both a relief and a tragedy. Her handsome son, with those liquid eyes.

"I realized that our family is seriously messed up."

She expects him to laugh. He's always the one to laugh her out of her moods. But he doesn't laugh.

He just takes her hand and holds it. His hands so rough, so different from the little boy's hands that once reached for her through the kindergarten window.

"You have to be all right," he says. His voice so clear and direct, as though just by saying the words he could make it so.

"I want to be all right," she says.

"I couldn't live without you."

He looks so stricken that she starts to cry. Is that what she's been waiting to hear? That someone feels as bad about her dying as she does? He cries too, the two of them sitting there, and then he gives her his handkerchief and she blows her nose.

"I'm so scared," she says

"I know."

"Not about the nodule. I mean I'm not thrilled with that, but I'm scared about you. And your sisters. I love you so much and I'm just starting to feel like my love isn't enough."

"That's not so," he says. Sighs. Pulls back.

"Look at you," she says. "For fifteen years now, I've hurled myself at that wall of yours, trying to figure out what happened, and I'm no closer now than I was. I feel like we've all built these walls around ourselves and I don't know what to do."

He shakes his head. Smiles almost as though he's telling himself a joke. Then he takes a deep breath, and says, "What do you want to know?"

"Everything," she says. "Anything."

And for the first time in years, he talks. Really talks. And she stays up the rest of the night listening to his story. Which begins and ends with that long-ago summer. Of course.

CHAPTER FORTY-FIVE

The four friends had not been getting along well that summer. It had not been the idyllic last summer of their youth. Yes, the constant rain added pressure, but the fact was they were very different people who had forged a friendship together that was never going to last. And then there was the fact that Matt came out to them as gay.

"He was the one I'd always felt closest to. We were going to the same college. We'd planned it out that way, but once he told me I felt betrayed. It was like he wasn't who I thought he was. We'd spent so much time sleeping together over the years. Sharing bunks, taking showers, swimming, and suddenly it all seemed weird to me. I was an idiot. I know that now. But then I just felt so angry. I didn't want to talk to him. I didn't want to be with him, except there was no avoiding him because he was everywhere I went. We were counselors together and he wanted me to understand. He wanted to talk to me about it. One day I got so mad I punched him in the face."

Merry remembers that bruise. The police asked about it, but the boys' bodies were so banged up by the rocks in the river that they didn't pursue it.

"Tyler was so good with him. So was Jacob. They were supportive, said it didn't matter, but it did matter to me. So I began taking these stupid risks. I had to get out. I had to do something. I jumped off the top of Suicide Hill. I chugged vodka. There are parts of those summer I don't even remember. I started bringing girls from Camp Eastwood back to the cabin. I was such a jerk. But the worst of it was that everyone started doing what I did. Jack, Tyler, and Matt. Like they needed to prove something to me. They jumped off Suicide Hill. They started putting vodka in their water bottles. Not the girls though. That was the one way I could be alone.

"I couldn't wait to get out of there and go to college. That's all I dreamed about. Then came the last day and we were going to go on the river, but everyone could see it was dangerous. We'd never seen waves like that before. So big.

"I wanted to go out on it. When I saw those waves, I knew that's what had been waiting for me all summer. This was the challenge to end all challenges. So, I said I was going out and I expected them all to turn around and leave me, but they didn't. They stayed with me. Even Matt. I was so sure he would chicken out, but he didn't. He didn't even look afraid. They weren't going to let me go alone. They were going to support me. Through thick and thin, we were a team. We would always be a team. I couldn't stand it, so I jumped into the water.

"The current was terrible. Like being caught up in a crowd at a concert. I couldn't move, but right then, I rammed into a log and I grabbed hold of it.

"But they all came jumping out to save me. I screamed at them not to jump. I was safe. But they couldn't hear me.

"One by one they jumped in, and they were swept away. Over the falls. The roaring. I still remember the way Matt looked at me. Not scared. Not at all. It was like he forgave me.

"I held on to that log for a long time and when the river finally quieted, the canoe just floated over to me. I got on and I stayed there until they found me. They figured I was a coward and I figured I could live with that. It was a lot better than what I actually was.

"About a year later, I went and visited their parents and I told them what happened. I figured they deserved to know. That felt right.

But since then, I've just felt like I've been marking time. Someday I'll have to pay for what I did. I want to pay for it. But don't worry, Ma. I'm not going to kill myself. That would be a betrayal."

Merry doesn't know what to say. What is there to say? He was young. He has matured. He paid a terrible price for a terrible mistake, but those boys paid a far higher price. He does owe something to the world to pay for what he did. He will find the opportunity. She's glad he told their parents. She's glad he found the courage for that. She thinks about how one stupid decision can ruin your life. A trip to Gstaad. She thinks there are some things that cannot be forgiven. Not by her anyway. Maybe that's what Christmas is about, though she's not sure. She hopes so.

"I don't need to play the part of Tiny Tim," he says.

She laughs, jolted out of her thoughts. "How did you know I was thinking about that?"

"Because your face is like an open book," he says. "And because you're always thinking of that play."

Then his face seems to melt into itself and he starts to cry. She cries too. Barking sobs, and yet, underneath it all, she feels a kindle of joy because he is not lost. He is not lost. She flings her arms around him then, for the first time in a long time not worrying that he'll flinch. He hugs her back.

Two hours later, Merry and her whole family go staggering into the Apple store.

CHAPTER FORTY-SIX

Some years ago, Merry went to visit Canterbury Cathedral, which was the most awesome place she'd ever seen. It was hard to imagine human hands had made such a structure. A similar sense of awe goes through her mind when her family steps into the Apple store on Tuesday morning. She'd assumed it would be like the one she's used to back home in the Westchester mall in White Plains, but this is a whole other order of magnitude. You walk in and you have to look upward. This is the sort of awe that Merry's always loved about Christmas. The reason she's always over-decorated and over-celebrated.

Because it's big.

Because it's supposed to be big. Because it's transformative. Because so much of life is small and petty, but not Christmas.

She just stands there, taking it in. A vast brick building with ceilings that soar. On the first level is an assortment of boxes that are actually chairs, and a host of people sitting on them, and a woman at the front, giving a lecture about How to Use Your New Phone. Friendly looking people wander around with iPads, asking if you have any questions.

Everything smells so clean. Not clean like the hospital, which smelled like antiseptic, but rather clean like after a rain shower. Refreshed. But not natural. She can't figure it out.

She and Mr. Hong spent whole days trying to categorize the smell of books. *Bibliosmia.* They're all so different, because the moment a book is created, it begins to break down. So leather-bound books from the 1800s smell different than wood and metal ones from the 1500s, and they smell different yet again from seventy-year-old paperback ones. Mr. Hong was like a connoisseur, sitting at his desk with an array of books in front of him, holding them to his nose. *A hint of grass, Merry, do you think?*

Merry's so tired she feels like she's floating. She puts a foot down and isn't sure where it will land. It wouldn't surprise her to go plummeting through the floor.

But however bad she looks, Bessie looks worse. She's a zombie, with Nick's phone bolted to her hands, pushing redial over and over. Leroy has not picked up. Merry's thinking about how much of this vacation is revolving around phone calls. The one she desperately does not want to get from Dr. Fiedler and the one she desperately wants her daughter to get from Leroy. How could he disappear on her like that?

So now they are at the Apple store on the day before Christmas Eve, without a reservation at the Genius Bar.

"I don't know why you don't have a better phone," Song Lee says.

"Not all of us have a ton of money. Not all of us are working as lobbyists," Bessie says. "*Were* working."

"But I sent you money," Song Lee says. "For a new phone."

"I did too," Nick says.

Merry is confounded.

"I had some expenditures come up," Bessie says.

"Who did you give the money to?" Song Lee asks, now in district attorney mode. "Did you give it to Leroy?"

"He was desperate," Bessie wails.

"You gave him money." Song Lee is shaking her head. "Do you ever learn?"

"That's not fair. He loves me. This is serious. You can see how special he is, can't you?"

He did seem special, Merry thinks. When he was talking about writing a play for Bessie, he seemed so sincere. Plus, he laughed at all of Merry's jokes, which she considers a very nice quality in a person.

And his parents live in a Christmas village, which is awesome. They have Christmas decorations up year-round.

But why isn't he answering the phone?

"Are they going to be able to fix it?" Bessie asks.

Sully falters. Even his essential optimism, Merry suspects, is stretched by the idea of fixing this phone on the Tuesday before Christmas. They turn to look at the Genius Bar, which is encased with people.

Merry perches on one of the boxes. She hasn't eaten anything and she's starving. According to the laminated schedule, they're supposed to go to Ye Olde Cheshire Cheese, one of the oldest pubs in London, for lunch. It's another of Dickens's favorite places. She has this weird feeling that her future rests on the health of this iPhone. That if they can fix it, she will live. If they can't, she will die.

It's ridiculous, but she can't breathe. She feels as though even the nodule inside her is sentient, waiting for a clue. Dr. Fiedler is out there, with his information. She's so scared.

Suddenly Sully says, "I know what to do." He pulls out his own iPhone, which is the most modern phone available. No matter what is going on in his life, he's one of those people who will stand on line to wait for the newest phone, preferably in the newest color. This one is green. "He's in my contacts. I'm sure of it."

"Who?"

He begins scrolling, then punches in a number and he says, "Vikram. It's Sully Bingham. Yes. Yes. Oh, it was nothing. Happy to help. Say, did I remember that you were moving to the Apple store in London? No kidding? Is that right? I'm here now. Crazy, right? You're here! Now? Wait, let me see."

They all turn toward the Genius Bar, which is where Merry sees a tall Indian man with a megawatt smile waving at her husband.

"Vikram!" he exclaims, and the three children follow.

Merry's eyes fill with tears. She feels like she got a reprieve.

Nick stops. "Coming, Ma?"

"I'm just going to wait here for a moment." They all step toward her, eyes concerned, but she waves them away. "I don't want to deal with crowds right now."

"I'll stay," Song Lee says.

"No, seriously. Go. I'll watch you," she says, and then feels compelled to add, "I'm going to call Lana."

Now they halt. "You never call Lana," Nick says.

"Well, I thought I'd do it now."

"That's nice," Song Lee says.

"You sure?" Nick says, but she can see they're all dying to go to the front of the line to meet Vikram, and anyway, she loves to watch them together. There's something so beautiful about watching her creations. Bessie, the smallest of them, walking next to Sully, who has his arm around her. Song Lee and Nick walking side by side, both tilting toward each other as though drawn together magnetically.

Some lines from *A Christmas Carol* pop into her head, and she whispers them.

They were not a handsome family . . . But they were happy, grateful, pleased with one another, and contented with the time; and when they faded, and looked happier yet in the bright sprinklings of the Spirit's torch at parting . . .

"Amen," she whispers.

CHAPTER FORTY-SEVEN

Should she call her mother?

Now that she's said that's what she's going to do, she feels like she should, though she doesn't usually. She feels sort of proud of herself for answering her mother's calls at all, all things considered. Her mother actually threw her father's ashes into the ocean. When Merry finally managed to get back from Gstaad, the funeral service was over and her mother had thrown his ashes into the ocean. *You know how he loved the water.*

He hadn't loved the water at all. He grew up in the Bronx. Occasionally he went to a public pool. It was her mother's new husband who loved the water, who'd grown up on a boat.

But she hadn't told her kids about that; she didn't think that would add anything to the family dynamic. Because Lana is their grandmother and Merry doesn't want to be that person. But now, in this brief moment of tranquility, it seems like it would be the right thing to do to call her, especially since the kids have noticed that she doesn't call. She can't believe both Song Lee and Nick are sending Bessie money. She can't believe how much she doesn't know about her kids. She's always suspected they texted each other during the family Zoom calls.

Her mother sounds frantic when she answers the phone. So unlike her. "You okay?"

"Yes," Merry says, only then realizing that she's called her mother at five in the morning, Florida time, which is either very early or very late, depending on her mother's schedule. "I'm sorry. I didn't mean to wake you."

"No, we weren't sleeping."

"Okay."

"It's just that you never call. Can I get back to you in, say, ten minutes?"

"That's fine," Merry says and clicks off.

Please don't let me have just interrupted my mother having sex, she thinks.

Sully and the kids have connected with Vikram. She can see a lot of conversing going on, and some of the other Genius Bar guys joining in on the conversation. She suspects this is the sort of challenge they enjoy. They are all shaking Sully's hand. Five more contacts for his phone. She notices they are all eyeing Song Lee as well. Maybe this would be a good career pivot. She likes technology and they probably have good benefits and Merry's sense of the tech world is there's not a lot of concern about plagiarism. Though maybe she's wrong. She wouldn't have thought it would be an issue in the lobbying world either. Is that what she wants for her daughter? A job in a field where morals are elastic?

Merry's starting to feel antsy, or hungry, or anxious and that's when she notices a discreet glass stairway tucked in a brick corner. Merry loves discreet stairways. Many of her best finds have taken place in out of the way places. On bathroom walls or behind cabinets or in rooms that were blocked off by books so no one bothered to look in them. She loves a mystery, so she gets up and goes up the stairway. She has a thing about hidden places. She has the same tingling in her fingers that she gets when she's in a bookstore or a barn or a library, when she knows that something amazing is waiting for her around the corner. She runs her hand against the brick, some of it aged red and other an almost urine-colored yellow, which is still quite attractive. It feels old. They took it from somewhere ancient. She wonders what used to be on this spot. She has a map in her office of London during Dickens's time, but she can't remember what stood right here.

A woman walks by, looking maternal, carrying an iPad in front of her. She could be a robot. Or a ghost. Or just a woman with an iPad. Merry expects her to tell her to turn around and go back, but she doesn't even look at her.

From up here she has a panoramic view of the store. She can see her family, still chatting with Vikram, with now an even larger crowd around them. Above her she has a clear view of the vast row of windows that make up the roof. She loves it and is admiring it when her mother calls. She was right, Merry thinks. Whatever she and Jack Gutiérrez were doing did just take ten minutes.

"You're such a prude."

"I'm really not," Merry says. "I've had a number of clients who collected pornography. I just don't want to know about *your* sex life. Anyway, I was hoping I'd get some props for calling."

"You do," her mother says. "I give you props for everything. I adore you. So, you're in the Apple store, right?"

She knows everything, Merry thinks.

"Which of my kids told you about the nodule?"

Her mother is oddly silent. No crunching. No music behind her. "Actually, it was your husband."

"You talk to Sully about me?"

"I called yesterday and asked him if you were okay. You've seemed so strange. You're going to be okay?"

Her mother's voice shakes, which scares and annoys her. She wasn't having sex just before, Merry realizes. She was crying. Her call must have interrupted Jack Gutiérrez comforting her mother. She feels sad. And aggravated. Perfect. Now, on top of everything else, she's going to have to comfort her mother. It's going to become about her mother. She can just imagine her mother dressed in black at her funeral. The chief mourner.

"What does it matter to you?" she says. "What are you going to do if I'm sick? Move to Bora Bora?"

Merry expects her to laugh. She's never said anything that her mother hasn't laughed at, but she doesn't. Instead, she surprises Merry. "You know, he wasn't perfect."

"I never said he was," she replies, though she thinks her father was as perfect as it is possible to be. "But he was the best man I ever knew."

"You were a girl. The two of you were in a closed little bubble. You never saw him for what he was."

"That's not true at all. He was braver than anyone I ever knew. He fought that terrible disease all by himself. He never complained."

"He didn't complain to you, but he complained plenty to me. All he did was complain. To you he was all about the Villards, but to me he was someone different. And he was angry."

"He had a lot to be angry about."

"What he did to you was wrong, and you know it. He should have encouraged you to go away to college. He should have encouraged you to go out with friends."

"Whatever I did for him, I was happy to give."

She still gets upset just thinking about it. The grief and anger and desire to protect her father have been a hard nodule inside her for way longer than this current one.

"You were a child. You shouldn't have had to make that choice."

"I didn't have a choice after you left him. I could hardly leave him on his own."

"He would not have been on his own. He would have been cared for. You didn't need to sacrifice your life for him and he shouldn't have expected it."

"I loved him," she says, stubborn. "He was the best part of me."

Her mother sighs. "The world loves a martyr."

"What does that mean? You're always so hard on Dad, and he didn't deserve it."

"Answer me this, then," her mother snaps. "Why did you go to Gstaad?" Then she slams off the phone, leaving Merry standing there, gaping, unable to take it all in.

Her eyes sting. She feels like she can't breathe. She smells something rancid and wonders if it's her. Her mother is wrong. Merry knows better than anyone in this world what sort of man her father was. But she feels rattled, just the same. Because she truly didn't expect her mother to say anything like that. Because although her mother is not precisely reliable, Merry has come to trust her. In a way. She's become a part of her life through her children, and she can't understand why her mother would be so venomous.

She genuinely cannot think of one time she ever heard her father complain.

And yet her mother's last remark hits home.

Because she did leave him to go to Gstaad, and this has eaten at her all the years of her life. It's the one thing in her life she would do over, if she could. But she can't. It doesn't seem like you get second chances. Or it doesn't seem like she does.

And that's when Merry looks over and sees Charles Dickens. He's one floor up, standing on the top landing.

There's a sign at the bottom of the circular staircase that says, "Do Not Enter."

Merry goes around it.

"Mr. Dickens!" she calls out. "Wait!"

CHAPTER FORTY-EIGHT

She runs up the steps, which isn't easy. You'd think a ghost would have a little empathy for a woman with a nodule in her lung, but anyway, she gets up there, panting. And there he is, wearing the same green dress coat he wore before, though now, in the daylight, she can see his outfit better. Underneath the coat he wears a richly patterned velvet waistcoat that dances with roses and forget-me-nots. And his pants! How had she missed those? Gray with black stripes. No wonder people were always talking about his clothes.

But he also looks a little older than he did last time she saw him. His jaw looks swollen. His face ruddier. She hopes she's not aging him. She feels like in real life he would be a hugger, and she wishes she knew him well enough to hug him, but she suspects that they don't have that sort of relationship.

He stares out at the store and she wonders what he sees. She knows how he admired Niagara Falls, which he felt was the most miraculous thing he'd ever seen. But what does he think of this Apple store, which is in its own way just as miraculous? Maybe more so because this is an act of man. No god created this. Unless God inspired Steve Jobs, which is one way of looking at it.

"I'm so glad to see you," she says. "I was beginning to think you were a figment of my imagination." Though why on earth she would dream up a hostile Charles Dickens is beyond her.

"I'm not a fragment."

"No, I mean figment." She doesn't pursue it. He looks oddly vulnerable and reminds her for a minute of her friend Sheila, and the way she looked when Merry found her sitting on the plaque on Library Way. As though the ground had shifted beneath her. Bewildered. The way Merry felt when Dr. Fiedler called to tell her to schedule the PET scan, as though the rules of the game had changed. She's been so preoccupied with Dickens's anger toward her, or perhaps her anger toward him, that she hasn't really stopped to think about it. He still looks angry, yes, but he looks slightly unsure of himself. Vulnerable. It surprises her, though of course she knows he was a person who was vulnerable.

That's why she'd sought him out at the blacking factory. Because he was a person haunted by his past, like her. Neither could he forgive his past.

"I want to apologize for getting mad at you the other night," she tells him. "I have some anger management issues, but I shouldn't have shouted at you. I know you're here to help me."

"I cannot help you." He rubs one pale hand against the other, dismissively.

"Now you're just being downright disagreeable," she says. "Isn't the whole point of being a ghost that you are there to provide some sort of guidance to the living, and I am in desperate need of guidance and specifically from you?"

He just stares at her.

"It's to do with my father, isn't it? You're judging me about that and you're right. I was terrible to him. I left him alone on Christmas. He died holding your book, he must have been clinging to it for comfort. I hate to think that in the last moments of his life he was so hurt by me, and if you could just tell him how sorry I am . . ." Her words drift away as she gets a little choked up.

The store is hushed. The murmuring seems a form of a chant. She's conscious of a vast number of people below them, and yet it feels like she and Charles Dickens are the only two people in the world.

He's not crackling the way he had been. Now he seems solemn, mournful. The color of his clothes looks to be darkening, almost as if he's absorbing her news. A man who took in everything around him. "You think I'm a messenger boy?"

"No, obviously. You are the Inimitable, the greatest writer of your time."

"Of my time?" This is a look she recognizes from his many portraits. Proud and imperious and yet oddly benevolent.

"You are the greatest writer ever." Merry is used to people with egos. She once had to intervene in a fight between two billionaires about who bid first on a rare copy of the Declaration of Independence. She knows all you can do is shovel on the praise. But time is running out for her. Tomorrow is Christmas Eve.

So she pursues. "I don't have a lot of time. Only two more nights. If I can't figure this out, I'm not likely to get another chance. It's the only reason that makes sense for you being here, unless you'd like to enlighten me. No offense, but you could put an end to this whole thing if you'd simply tell me why you're here."

His face seems to change color. Yellow to green and then back to his normal pale shade, but the effect frightens her.

Meanwhile, Dickens turns away from her slightly. So that he is looking out over the railing, down at the people below. Perhaps at her family. At her dear son who is trying to struggle his way out of guilt and grief. At her daughter, who seeks love so desperately. At her youngest daughter, who is trying to find her place in this world. He must see them.

"I wish you could find a way to help me."

It's easier to talk to his profile than to his face. His eyes are so unsettling. They see into her, the parts of her she wants to protect, the nodule and the nodule of memory. Suddenly she realizes that he must know about her nodule, that he probably knows whether or not she's going to die. He must know the results of the medical tests. She smells something too. Something pungent. Cloves?

"I was with him when he died," Dickens says.

"You were with my father?"

He nods. "He loved me."

She's so incredibly touched to think her father wasn't alone when he died. To think that Charles Dickens was there, with him, to help him pass over. Because her father did love Dickens so, as does she.

As does she.

And in that moment, everything clicks into place. Dickens *knows* the results of her medical tests and they must be bad and that's why he's here. To help her die.

She steps back, away from him. "No!" she whispers. "Not right now. I cannot. I am not ready to die right now. You are going to have to wait."

It's so cruel, but she knows better than anyone that terrible things can happen even on Christmas Day. To the people you love most in the world.

She's all alone here, with only the ghost of Charles Dickens. His face seems to flash with emotion, from grief to anger to kindness to grief. He is changing, evolving in front of her. But what happens if he fixes on the final emotion, the emotion of judgment? What happens when his face changes to the one that will take her away? How horrifying that would be to see those stern eyes focused on her, that long slender hand reaching toward her.

No.

She has to get out of there. Has to get back to her family. He will not take her when she's with people, she thinks. He's only ever appeared to her by herself.

She just has to get out. She heads for the stairs.

"Wait," he says, his voice hoarse, almost as though he's crying.

"No," she says. "No. I will not die on Christmas. I know that I have to die but not now, and frankly it's infuriating that you of all people would do this. Knowing how much Christmas means to me."

She races down the stairs and gets to the Genius Bar desk, but they're not there.

She can see Vikram talking to someone. There are still crowds of people swarming around. But her family is gone.

CHAPTER FORTY-NINE

She is stranded in the Apple store, with the ghost of Charles Dickens seeking to harvest her soul or body. She's not religious enough to be sure, though she wishes she was. Her family's gone and it's Christmas. Almost Christmas. Her heart is pounding. Merry looks at her phone and sees that it's run out of power. Unbelievable. How did she let that happen? In the Apple store yet. She's normally so obsessed with charging her phone.

Perhaps Dickens sapped it out of her.

Perhaps he altered time. How long was she even on the third floor with Dickens? She checks out the time on one of the display computers. 11:15 A.M. More than an hour since she spoke to her mother. Why didn't her family come find her? Was she invisible? Everything looks different and yet the same. The lights, the chatter, the hum of everyday life, and yet she feels like a dark line has been drawn around everything. There is death here. Her death.

Where is her family? She needs them. Now.

That's when Merry looks out the window and sees an absolutely giant Christmas tree, right in the middle of Covent Garden. She's drawn to it as though mesmerized. It flashes different colors, not unlike Charles Dickens's face. This particular one seems to mock her. She grasps at the needles and they feel cold. So different from the spindly little tree in the lobby of her apartment building. She feels badly for all spindly little things. She feels defeated. She feels absolutely terrified.

But all is not lost, because suddenly Nick is there, triumphant. "I knew you'd be here. I knew wherever there's a tree, we'd find you."

"Just look for the tree and there's Mom," Song Lee says.

"Classic Mom," Nick adds.

All of them beam at her lovingly.

"We had such a great time," Bessie says. She looks so bright. Her face glows with good cheer. It's gotten colder out and she's all pink. "They can fix the phone, but it seems like it would be better to get a new one."

"Surprise," Song Lee says.

"But I can keep my old number. I realized that Leroy was hacked last month and he's blocked unknown numbers. I bet he's been calling me all the time. I bet there will be one hundred unanswered calls. And Vikram said he could give me a good deal. He's going to bring it to us at the restaurant. You have Ye Olde Cheshire Cheese on the laminated schedule. He's going to meet us there."

"No!" Merry blurts out, and they all gape at her. She shakes her head. "Not about Vikram. I mean I don't really feel like Ye Olde Cheshire Cheese right now."

That's the last thing she wants. To go to one of Dickens's favorite haunts. She might as well put a stake through her heart. She has to avoid him. In fact, she wants to spend the rest of this trip going to modern places, to places he wouldn't know. The Tate Modern. The London Eye. Or places he probably wouldn't have gone even when he was alive. Buckingham Palace. Mayfair. All the more reason to go to the Campion party.

"But I thought that was a place important to Dickens," Bessie says. "You said in the laminated schedule that he went there all the time."

"Yes, he did and it's a lovely place. But it's a bit of a walk from where we are and there's an Avoplace around the corner. Haven't you been wanting to try that?"

"Are you feeling okay?" Sully asks.

"Yes, I feel fine, but just a little tired and given that we have not done one thing on the laminated schedule so far, I don't see why we have to do it now."

That came off more hostile than she intended, but she's feeling hostile. Angry. Not at her family. Not exactly. Though you could make an argument that this whole disastrous trip could have been avoided had one of them just accepted the book. Her inheritance. It's entirely possible that they're killing her.

She thinks about the way Dickens's face looked just minutes ago. Her click of understanding about his purpose. The horror that this man, who has been the source of so much joy to her, should also be the source of so much fear. It's so cruel, but she knows how cruel life can be. She's seen it firsthand with her father. A man who loved nothing more than to work with his hands. Who was a genius with his hands. Who seemed on his way to becoming a successful display animator. Who worked with Disney, who had the world opening in front of him, and then, in the space of a month, his world collapsed.

He lost all feeling in his hands as the disease raced through his body. Before the year was out, he was confined to a wheelchair and then to his bed. Dr. Fiedler had never seen anything like it.

Why had she, of all people, thought there would be a set of rules? Why had she thought she had figured it out? Why had she ever thought she would figure out the meaning of Christmas when her father, the person who loved it most in the world, was defeated by it?

She's going to stop this ridiculous quest to find Charles Dickens.

She will not keep Christmas in her heart. Not if all it's going to do is set her up for disappointment. For tragedy.

And what did her mother mean by saying that her father complained all the time?

Merry is here, with her family, and they're doing okay, and thanks to Vikram's efforts, they're about to get a fairly inexpensive cell phone. Of such small details is life made up. She can live with this.

"Bah, humbug," she mutters.

Enough of Christmas, enough of Dickens, enough of the Villards. Merry Bingham is going to surrender, and it's all going to be fine.

CHAPTER FIFTY

Merry crams herself full of avocado. The Avoplace, at least, is all that it is intended to be. No irony, no subtext, no cruel twist of face. It is a place that sells avocados and only avocados.

Never has she realized the healing power of the fruit. She feels like she can't stop eating it. She ordered a dish that looks a bit like a funeral pyre, a mound of avocado that just goes up into the air. Something sacrificial about it.

The avocado oozes into her pores. It feels like plaster. She imagines it filling in all the cracks inside her. Smoothing over all the wounds. Healing.

Except that Bessie won't let Dickens drop. "What we should do, after this, is walk over to Ye Olde Cheshire Cheese."

"That's not necessary," Merry assures her. "It's all good. We don't need to do that. Anyway, you just told Vikram to meet us here. You don't want to confuse him."

"We could have Song Lee wait here for Vikram and then they could walk over to . . ."

"No!" Merry shouts. "No, this is really fine, Bessie."

"I just feel so badly," she says. "You've gone to all this effort and now we're not going to do anything on the laminated tour."

She will never laminate anything again for the rest of her life, Merry thinks, though even as she has the thought, she is reminded of those laminated cards they hand out at funerals. She fizzles with fear, automatically looks toward the window, expecting to see Dickens lurching toward her.

"It just seems so sad," Bessie says.

"For God's sake," Merry snaps. "Could you just let the whole thing drop? For once, just let it go."

The table quiets.

Bessie stares at her with Bambi-like eyes, swollen with tears.

"I'm sorry," Merry says. "I just don't want to go to Ye Olde Cheshire Cheese. Could we just leave it at that and move on? Move *on*."

"How about a glass of wine?" Song Lee suggests.

"Yes," Merry says. "In fact, a gin and tonic would hit the spot."

She notices Nick glance at the clock. It's 11:45 A.M.

"Would you like to make a comment about my drinking?" she asks him.

"Are you in pain?" he asks.

They all look at her with concern. Leaning toward her. So much love there, and she realizes they think she's suffering. That it's the nodule that's causing her anger. She *is* suffering, though not with pain. Rather, with disappointment and anger and she's not even sure what she's disappointed and angry about. She got what she wanted. Her family's in London. They are getting along reasonably well. Nick has made a breakthrough and she's happy about that but also disturbed. And Song Lee's plagiarism prickles her, and Bessie and this Leroy are disasters waiting to happen. She wanted a miracle and she got an expensive family vacation in London and worst of all is this brewing anger that seems volcanic. And she sold her legacy, the one miraculous thing she did own and the source of that miracle seems to want to take her soul.

"We don't serve liquor," the waitress says. A sprightly little thing who makes eye contact only with Nick. "But I can get her a matcha smoothie. Would she like that?"

Nick smiles back. Nice to know that if she's carted off in an ambulance, he'll find someone to flirt with.

"No, she would not," Merry says, and the waitress slips away.

An awkward silence descends. Bessie spills some avocado on her pants. Merry knows they are waiting for her to say something, do something. Fix this. But she doesn't want to. Not just because she feels exhausted, which she does. But because on some level, she wants them to suffer. Isn't that awful?

Merry scans the restaurant, unable to bear looking at anyone directly. She remembers then the avocado green of their house, growing up. Avocado dishwasher. Avocado refrigerator. Her mother loved it so.

She feels radioactive. She remembers the way she felt when the nurse injected her with the radiotracers. The nurse had to wear gloves, because touching the liquid was too dangerous, and yet they were injecting it inside of her. How can you express a thought like that? How can you make other people understand?

"Are you excited about *A Christmas Carol?*" Nick asks.

"What?" She looks at the man sitting next to her. He looks exactly like her son but so polite.

"The play you got those tickets for," Sully says.

"It's on the laminated schedule," Nick says.

"No one is to say the word laminated again. Ever."

"Vikram says it's a hot ticket," Song Lee says.

"When did he say that?" Bessie asks. "You've been texting him? Is my phone ready?"

"I looked at the seats," Sully says. "They look really good."

Good grief. She pulled so many strings to get those tickets. The performance is supposed to be transformative; she doesn't know why. But she loves the actor who plays Scrooge. She was so excited and now it feels like the last thing she wants to do. She has a vision of the Ghost of Christmas Yet to Come flying over the rafters and onto her lap, scooping her away. She can't go. There has to be a way out of this.

"What say we just stay home tonight and watch *Home Alone*?" Merry suggests.

They look at her, dumbfounded. Almost comically so.

"But you hate that movie," Nick says.

"I never said I hated it. I just said that I couldn't see how it's considered a Christmas movie. But now I've changed my mind." Safe, she thinks, in the bordello. With her family around her. "Anyway, I like Catherine O'Hara. She's worth the price of admission."

"But we're in London. All you've been doing is talking about this play and how transformative it's supposed to be," Sully says.

"I know. But now I'm thinking maybe I've gone about this whole thing the wrong way." She thinks of the look on Dickens's face. She thinks how terrifying it would be to have him come after her. She thinks of poor Scrooge coming to realize what the last ghost meant. That he was about to die. *Am I that poor man who lay upon the bed?*

"Maybe a night together as a family. Resting. That would be nice."

She feels Sully's eyes on her, watching her. She knows he's trying to work out what's going on and she can't blame him for feeling stumped. Killer Dickens would not be first thing on anyone's mind. But then her dear husband comes through.

"Of course," Sully says. "A night of popcorn and *Home Alone* sounds perfect."

"We can sneak down and decorate that tree," Song Lee says.

"Yes, yes, and we can practice for our own play." Then Bessie starts to cry. "I was so sure that Leroy would be Tiny Tim. He would have been so good."

"Now, now," Sully whispers.

The conversation moves on. They're talking about Vikram and how once he gets the new phone up and running and once Leroy sees her number, he'll be sure to pick up. Anyone can see how much he loves her. It's so obvious.

Merry feels herself spacing out. It's just nice to sit still for a bit and listen to the familiar waves of confrontation. Suddenly the strangest memory hits Merry of her father.

It was a warm summer night in the Bronx. Must've been the early 1970s. There was a lot of turmoil in the world then and in the south

Bronx, but in the east Bronx, where her family lived, all was relatively calm. They lived in a small three-story house on a narrow street. The neighborhood was packed with kids. She remembers baseball games in the middle of the street. Mothers standing as lookouts. Trucks that hauled carousels and rides. They would stop in the street and the kids would climb on. It was unbelievably dangerous. Other trucks that drove by spraying insect repellant and the kids would dance in the fumes.

Almost all the mothers stayed home, except for the divorced or widowed ones. Her mother was the best-looking of the bunch. Granted, Merry was biased because that was her mother, but she was an observant child. She saw the way the other women looked at her mother. The way they complimented her. The way they fussed over her and invited her to their parties and their dinners. Wherever Lana was invited, she would go. A stranger was a friend she hadn't met.

Their house had a concrete stoop out front with six steep steps. After her father got sick, that was a nightmare to navigate. But when she was young, Merry used to love to sit outside with her mother, and watch for her father to come home. The subway was a fifteen-minute walk away. There were no cell phones, so they would just sit there, chatting with the neighbors. Her mother was always jangling with her earrings and bracelets. Her father had even designed a special piece of jewelry for her that spread over her hand like a glove.

That night she wore high-heeled sandals. Toes painted Cherry. From one of the stoops came the music of Joan Baez singing "The Night They Drove Old Dixie Down." Merry loved that song although her mother said it was depressing. She would have been only four or five at the time, but it spoke to her. That one line about how in the winter of '65, they were hungry, just barely alive. She could sing it over and over again for hours.

The song was just coming to an end and the O'Jays switched on. "Love Train." Immediately her mother jumped off the stoop. She was genetically engineered for disco. She began swiveling and jangling and bumping, and at that moment, her father turned the corner.

Merry could hear her mother's cry of excitement. The way she ran toward him and jumped. The way he lifted her in his arms and the way they danced together. Locked together. The whole street sighing over how romantic it was.

That's when Vikram comes running into the Avoplace.

CHAPTER FIFTY-ONE

Vikram holds the phone in front of him in just the same way a doctor might hold a new baby.

"I've got it all set up for you," he says. "I transferred over all your contacts."

Bessie stands to receive it. She throws back her shoulders and breathes in deeply. She's truly incapable of doing something that's not a performance. Then she presses Leroy's number. It's on speaker. No point in even trying to maintain a semblance of privacy at this point.

The phone rings six times and goes to voicemail. It's not even Leroy's voice, but one of those digital answering machines.

"You have reached the home of Leroy Christmas. Please leave a message and I'll get back to you."

His last name is Christmas?

Could he have been one of Dickens's unwritten ghosts? The Ghost of Christmas Interrupted.

"Try again," Sully says. But Bessie just shakes her head.

"He's not answering. He's not going to answer." She sets the phone down on the table. It's such a sparkly, glimmering object, but it's brought her no joy. "I am the Unreturned Call. I am the Unloved. I am the Hopeless. I am the Despised. I am Lost."

Merry feels so desperate that she actually stops thinking about herself for a few minutes. Seconds. But the fact is they must do something to help her poor daughter. There comes a moment in everyone's life when they've been pushed too far, but she never wanted to see it with her daughter. Bessie yelling, Bessie crying. Anything is better than Lost Bessie.

Sully pulls Bessie to him, but she stays rigid, and he lets go. Settles for cupping Bessie's hands in his own warm ones.

This is just so sad. Merry's furious at Leroy. Not only has he apparently dumped Bessie, he's dumped all of them. They've admitted them into their inner circle. They opened their cantankerous souls to him and now he's shunned them. Of course, it is possible that he was hit by a car. That he's in a coma in a hospital. Leroy Christmas. Of all things. She should be able to track him down. This is the sort of thing she knows how to do.

How many hospitals are in New York?

But what will she do when she finds him?

Song Lee has gone wandering out the door and is chatting with Vikram. The waitress is circling Nick. They have to do something. Have to get out of there. Have to go somewhere, but try figuring out where to go in London that has nothing to do with Dickens.

"What would you think about the Tate Modern?" she tries.

"I just want to go home," Bessie says.

"No," Sully says. "We're in London and we have to get out and about. Leroy would've wanted you to do that."

Merry waits for her to erupt. To yell about who cares what Leroy would want. But Sully's decision to speak about him in the past tense seems to have been a wise one. Maybe it's easier for Bessie to imagine him as dead than as cruel. In every sense of the word, except for the actual one, he is dead. They won't see him again. He's gone.

"You know what Leroy really wanted to do," she says. "When he was here."

"What's that, dear?" Sully says.

Nick and Song Lee have wandered back to the table, curious about the direction the conversation has taken.

"He really wanted to go to this place Lock & Co."

"That hat store?" Merry asks.

She nods. "You know of it. He thought you would."

"Yes, it's not too far from here," Merry says. "But . . ."

"But?" Those round brown eyes are upon her, so like Leroy the dog's. How long has it been since she talked to her dog?

It is a glorious store. One of the treasures of London. She's been to the top floor where the women's couture hats are kept and it's like being inside an eggshell. There's a tiny little office and the end of the shop that has pictures of people who've bought their hats there. Royalty and actors and Sean Connery and famous authors.

Dickens loved it there. He loved hats. Colorful dandy things. Even for his time, he was mocked for his dress, and this was a time when men wore truly outlandish outfits.

If there were ever a place where Dickens would be waiting for her, it would be Lock & Co.

But what choice does she have?

"But I'm dying to go," she finishes.

"Oh, good. Leroy would have liked that."

CHAPTER FIFTY-TWO

A bright green door gleams in front of Lock & Co. The exact shade of green as Dickens's suit. Warning? Welcome? Merry doesn't stop to think about it. One thing she learned from her Villard ancestors is that if you're going to put yourself into a dangerous situation, you cannot stop and cogitate.

When Nelson Villard found himself abandoned on a polar exploration with only *A Christmas Carol* to sustain him, did he curl up and die? No, he pushed forward.

When Charles Dickens Villard found himself in the midst of a battle in World War I, did he run? Yes, but toward the fight.

When Charles Dickens Villard Jr. crashed two planes, did he refuse to go up again? Nope.

And poor little Nora Villard, who died in childbirth not so many years after meeting Dickens. Who lived long enough to clutch her little son and to proclaim herself satisfied.

No, none of those ancestors would have skittered away from going through that door, and the fact is that Merry doesn't feel so afraid anymore. She's sufficiently aggravated that it's giving her ballast.

So Merry pushes open the door and immediately a bell chimes and she screams.

Darn. She wasn't expecting a chime.

But then they all just stand there in wonder. In front of them is a long row of hats. Hundreds of black hats. Top hats. Bowlers. They gleam with an inner light. The glow that comes from the handmade. Merry has felt something similar when she's come across an old book, a treasure, and has felt some of the love that the owner had rub off on it. These hats have been carefully tended to, and she feels moved. Teary even. Wondrous. Sort of Christmassy, come to that. She never thought of Christmas as being like a new hat. She looks around at her family and sees that they too are swept up in this emotion. And then a large man appears.

A handsome man. One of those people who looks content with himself, as though he has stumbled into exactly the life he wanted. He glows with good health and purpose. Around his neck he wears a measuring tape. The buttons on his shirt are pressed so tight they look like they might burst. If ever there were a Ghost of Christmas Present, it is this man. Merry can picture him as the ghost in Leech's famous drawing: the green dressing gown, lined with fur, pulled open so that the hair on his chest shows.

"Looking for a hat?" he asks.

Suddenly Merry feels a sense of awkwardness descend upon them, that feeling that they are not the sort of people who belong in this sort of store. It's way too fancy for them. But this salesman must be used to people feeling that way because he offers to take them on a tour.

He radiates kindness as he begins showing them all the hats, telling them an involved story about Winston Churchill and a particular hat he wanted. Nick spies a newsboy hat and puts it on, and there doesn't seem to be any pressure to buy anything, which is good because the hats are quite expensive, but it is wonderful to try them and feel them. Sully puts on a hat from the James Bond collection. It's the type of bowler that one of the villains used to throw at people's heads. Sully is delighted by it.

"Let me get it for you, Dad," Nick says.

"No, I couldn't."

"The adventure business is good, and you've brought us all to London. It's the least I can do. Anyway, we can all wear them to the Campion party. I want to get you each a hat."

It's so generous, so exuberant, so unlike Nick. And the thought of them all showing up at the Campion party with hats! That's even better than ugly sweaters.

Nick winds up with the newsboy cap, and Sully decides on a less elaborate bowler. Merry can just picture him at the high school.

"Do you have a women's section?" Song Lee asks the salesman.

"No," he says. "We don't serve women."

"What?" Song Lee says, but he starts to laugh. "It's upstairs. Come, let me show you around."

He leads them to a little corner of the store, which is blocked off by a chain. He gestures for Merry to go in front of him, and there she sees a staircase. A steep winding thing that looks like it belongs in a horror movie. What treasures could lurk at the top of that? "Don't worry," the salesman says. "We've only had two people kill themselves on these steps."

An unusual sense of humor, she thinks.

She gets to the top. She's been here before, but it's still a revelation. She suspects it's the sort of place that will always feel new, no matter how many times you go.

It looks like heaven. Or a very close proximity thereof.

The room is in the clouds. No buildings block the windows. All she can see are the clear blue London skies. But it is the color of the room that strikes her. A creamy color, somewhere between white and yellow. A color so soft it feels like it should have a texture. The room glows, and around the room, propped onto perches, are an array of hats.

So many hats. Each one set off individually, like a work of art, which they are. Whispers of color. Merry feels like she's floating as she moves around the room. It's all so serene. There are a series of cloche hats, one of which reminds her of Sheila.

She goes over to it immediately and thinks of Sheila sitting on the bronze plaque on Library Walk. She holds the hat, thinking of how

Sheila set this whole trip in motion. How her enthusiasm inspired Merry. Had Merry not gone into the city that day, she would still be in her ramshackle Victorian house, dithering over whether she had enough money to reupholster her tub chair. She misses Sheila. She wonders if she'll see her again. She hopes her brother's come to retrieve her, but she can't imagine that she'll have a cell phone.

She notices Bessie trying on a hat that looks appropriate for a Victorian funeral. Lace hoods her eyes. There is perhaps a note of Miss Havisham about it. Bessie will wear that hat until her house burns around her. But perhaps it's a comfort. Perhaps there are times when all you can do is rip down all the boundaries.

Merry turns back to the genteel cloche she holds in her hands.

She's about to put it on, but suddenly the salesman is by her side.

"Not that one," he says, and guides her over to a hat set in a specially made indentation in the wall. The sort of place the crown jewels would be kept. She smells oranges, looks around.

"This is the one for you," he says.

He gestures for her to sit on a delicate little chair, and then he lifts the hat off its stand. It is a hat unlike anything she has ever seen.

Green velvet, but green doesn't do it justice. It's more than just a color. It's a sensation. It is plushness. And so whimsical. It looks like a question mark. The velvet circles around, but it's offset by a lighter material. A chiffon perhaps.

She will look ridiculous.

His arms block her view as she tries to look at herself in the mirror. She's afraid of what she will see when he pulls away. Afraid of what will be staring back at her when he's done adjusting the position of the hat. It takes him a while. There's a clasp that must be pressed into the back of her hair. There's a little string that must be adjusted.

But finally, he's done and she can see herself.

She sees the high cheekbones. She sees the way the color sets off her eyes. She sees the delicate beauty of the hat. She smiles at herself. Why, she's beautiful.

She looks around for her family, but they've all drifted into a corner. Song Lee is trying on headbands.

"It's perfect," the salesman says.

"It must cost a fortune."

"Not for you. Mr. Dickens chose it."

She jumps to her feet. "Is he here?" She looks around, blindsided not by fear but by anger. "Why is he playing these games?"

The salesman doesn't look troubled. Does this happen a lot?

She starts to take off the hat, noticing that her family is looking in her direction, heading toward her.

"But no," the salesman says to her, now looking troubled. Flustered. "This is his gift for you. He chose it especially."

"I don't want this gift, as he well knows. It's a different gift I want. Something bigger than this," she blurts out.

At which point, her phone rings. The caller is listed as a local hospital. She's so startled she almost drops the phone. She knows it's ridiculous. Dr. Fiedler would not be calling her from a British hospital. But who's to say what's possible at this point? So she answers the phone.

Turns out Amos Gaudy is in the hospital and he needs to see her.

"I have to go," she says to her family, and she dashes off.

CHAPTER FIFTY-THREE

He's at St. Thomas's Hospital, a sturdy white building that Merry's often noticed when she walks across the Westminster Bridge. It's associated with Florence Nightingale, though it has been a place of healing since the eleventh century. Mr. Gaudy would appreciate that, she thinks. It's the right place for him.

Except they won't let her into the hospital to see Mr. Gaudy because it's after hours and she's not a relative. She's standing there in the gleaming hospital lobby, ready to argue with the security guard, though she knows it's hopeless. This security guard will not bend.

Her hands are full of bags.

As soon as she got the word she ran to Waterstones bookstore and picked up a few books for Mr. Gaudy. She simply couldn't stand for him to be in a room without books, and she also picked up some Indian food because she knows, if nothing else, the smell of it will reassure him. So her arms are full when she gets to the hospital, and the security guard won't let her in.

He is one of those implacable sorts of people and it is clear to Merry she's not going to win this argument. And then she thinks of Lord Crenshaw.

The man who collected Dickens's *cartes de visite*. The man who has apologized over and over again for dumping her so precipitously after she brought him the Nelly Ternan *carte de visite*. He is always telling her that if there's ever anything he can do . . .

Merry doesn't know much about the British health care system, but she has a pretty good idea of how nobility works in the British culture, and so she calls Lord Crenshaw's private line and next thing you know she's in with Mr. Gaudy, and oh, they're moving him into a private room.

She thought she'd prepared herself, but she can't prepare herself for the sight of Mr. Gaudy looking so fragile. He looks like more of a ghost than Charles Dickens does. Though both their eyes shine.

He smiles at the sight of her and looks immediately at the books she's brought him. She didn't have time to think about the selection, but there's a new mystery about someone in the antique book trade. Also, a book by Winfred Rennick, filled with paintings of the American South. Joyful paintings. He breathes in the books, and then the food.

Then he smiles at her. "Stunning," he says. "Promise me you won't take it off."

She can't think what he's talking about until she realizes she still has the hat from Lock & Co. on her head. She's been running around London with a question mark on her head. Well, that's appropriate.

"How are you, friend?" she asks. "What happened?"

"I was carrying a stack of books and I fell over."

"I'm so sorry," she says.

Booksellers' hazard. Probably the number one way booksellers die. "They want to run tests. They won't let me go. I'm trapped here. Looks like I won't be able to go to the Milagro open house."

"That's awful!" His big opportunity to jump-start his business and now it's all screwed up. Of course. "Would Mrs. Milagro postpone it?"

"No, I tried. But she's arranged for all the other dealers to come, so she can't change everything for me. People are flying in from all over."

He rubs his hands against the books. Merry knows the feeling. How simply touching a book can make you feel better. How she misses her copy of *A Christmas Carol*. Nothing has gone right since she got rid of that book. She feels an ache inside her where the book once was. The opposite of a nodule.

"The food smells wonderful," he says.

"Shall I put some out?"

"Please."

The restaurant has packed plates and cutlery. Mr. Gaudy is a regular there, so when she told them it was for him, they didn't even let her pay. They've also packed in way more things than she ordered, and now she lays out the assortment, which is a feast. So many little containers.

"Let me see if I can microwave it."

"No, no," he says, "it's hot enough." He begins making neat little assortments of food on his plate. It smells like summer. She's only been to India once, but she remembers the colors, the heat.

Only then does she notice the windows in Mr. Gaudy's room, which are huge and look out on to the Thames and Parliament and Big Ben. It's the iconic London view. She remembers how Florence Nightingale believed it was important for patients to have light and beauty. It occurs to her that this is the view Merry was hoping for when she booked her bordello a week ago. A week ago! When everything seemed possible.

"Have some, Merry."

She puts some on a plate, but she's not really hungry. She leans back in the chair. Suddenly an idea hits her. "You know, I could go to that Milagro open house for you tomorrow."

Mr. Gaudy shakes his head. "I couldn't ask you to take precious time away from your family."

"No. Seriously. It would be fine. Maybe they'd come with me. I'd much rather do something positive than sit around stressing."

"Why are you stressing?"

"I'm not. Just a figure of speech." As it is, she had told all her troubles to a homeless person. She's not about to launch herself on an invalid.

"Would Gussie mind?" He looks over at a potted anthurium. Gussie Hong must have sent it. "If you went to the Milagros in my stead?"

"Probably. But I'll talk to her. She's essentially very good natured. What do you think I should look for?"

"You'll only have four hours."

"That's okay. I can do it. What was he like?"

"Secretive, Merry. Voracious. Rapacious. He would buy everything. He'd go into a barn sale and buy the entire contents, even papers lying on the straw, and he'd box it all up and then bring it home and spend the rest of the year going through the stuff. He could have everything. He could have nothing."

Merry nods. That's a challenge. But it's a challenge she understands. She can do this.

Milagro spent a lot of time in the Middle East, talking to people in the oil business, picking up maps and diaries and blueprints. These are the sorts of things that are incredibly valuable right now. The market in Middle Eastern books is probably the fastest growing part of the antiquarian book market, and if you can find something good, people will pay top dollar.

"He told me once about a book he got when he was in Dubai. He was with a petroleum engineer. The man had several books of maps and Milagro bought them from him for $10. Last year, one book just like that sold for more than $350,000 at auction. Who knows how much several of those books could be worth? If you could find them . . ."

She does the math. Mr. Gaudy would have to give the widow most of his earnings, of course. And if he brought it to one of the big auction houses, they'd take a big cut. Then he'd have to spend time researching its authenticity and provenance. But still.

This is the magic of book scouting. The hope. The potential for some money. For enough money to last until the next sale.

"I'll do it, Mr. Gaudy."

"Thank you." He clears his throat then, and looks at her. His skin has lightened in color, the way watercolors wash out a color. He is almost transparent.

"What's worrying you, Merry? Did you talk to the doctor? Did you get the diagnosis?"

This is the problem with working alongside a man for hours, days, years of your life. It's impossible to keep a secret.

"No," she says. "I have not yet mustered the courage to do that."

A nurse pokes her head in, but Mr. Gaudy waves her away.

"I'm just having the worst Christmas of my life." She laughs, though even to her ears it sounds more like a cry. "I thought that all I needed to be happy this Christmas was to have my family around me and bring them to London. I thought they'd be swept up in the joy of it all. That it would bring meaning into their lives that I thought they were lacking. I thought we would gather together and put on a play of *A Christmas Carol* and it would be transformative."

"And?"

"And they're doing okay. Surprisingly so. I mean, Bessie's a wreck because that boyfriend of hers ghosted her."

"That nice boy on the phone?"

"I know." She looks out at the London skyline, sparkling in front of her, and yet so far away. "That was so sad. I really liked him, but at least her siblings are being kind to her and that's a blessing. And Song Lee has the whole plagiarism thing going on, but at least she's resourceful."

"Yes," he says. "She told me about it."

"Really?"

"I like her," he says, as though settling a point.

"Well, yes," she says, "and Nick actually seems calm for once, and Sully is always Sully, but it's me. I'm just so angry. I'm the one who's always been the heart of Christmas. I've always loved Christmas. My happiest memories are of reading *A Christmas Carol* with my father. I used to put up Christmas lights before Halloween and now it just all feels like dust. I feel emptied out, bitter. Angry. I'm just so angry and I'm sure it has something to do with this nodule, though I don't even know."

He sighs. "I'm sorry, Merry."

"And worst of all is this ghost of Dickens."

"What?" He frowns slightly, as though dealing with a difficult client. She wants him to understand. She needs him to understand.

"This ghost. Charles Dickens. He's haunting me, but he won't tell me why. It's ridiculous."

Mr. Gaudy makes a soft sound like branches whispering in the wind. She wonders if he's laughing at her. She couldn't bear that. But he's not, bless him. There's never been any mockery in Mr. Gaudy. Now he leans forward and says, "What happened?"

So she tells him about how she's seen Dickens three times. The first time on the Heathrow Express. Then outside her apartment at the selfie tree. How she tried to get him to help her understand the meaning of Christmas and all he did was get mad at her for selling the book. The third time, that morning, at an Apple store. She was so sure she'd figured it out. That he'd come to help her apologize to her father, but then it turned out that she was wrong about that too, and now she just thinks he's here to take her soul.

"But that's so unfair. How can I die without Christmas? It's like everything I thought was important in my life is wrong, and then what am I leaving to my children?"

She expects Mr. Gaudy to reassure her. Instead, he rustles himself into a sitting position. He looks at her sternly. His glasses aren't on, which makes him look different. Instead of owlish, he now seems more of a falcon. "You have to find him."

"But if I find him, he's going to kill me."

"You have never been afraid, Merry. Not from the moment you came blasting through the door of my bookshop. Think of all those Villard ancestors of yours."

He starts to cough. She wants to call the nurse, but he waves her off.

"I'm getting tired of all those brave Villard ancestors. Maybe I'll break the mold and be the cowardly Villard."

"You must find him and say to him what you have said to me. You must get him to explain to you the meaning of Christmas. You cannot confront this serious challenge in front of you without the joy of Christmas. He is here for a reason."

"But I've tried!" she says. "This is what I'm saying to you. I keep trying and trying and things are just getting worse."

He looks at her sternly then. "Merry. Do not whine."

Mr. Gaudy is mad at her.

He shakes his head and leans against the pillow. He looks exhausted. She holds his hand, which seems to be turning into dust even as she holds it.

She knows Mr. Gaudy's right. He's always right.

The problem is, Merry has absolutely no idea what to do. She's already spent a considerable amount of time wandering around London looking for Dickens. She's drained. She sits there, watching as Mr. Gaudy drifts into sleep, and hopes, or prays, that some form of help will come her way.

Though, when it does, of course, it comes in the form of a disaster. Again.

CHAPTER FIFTY-FOUR

Wednesday

Merry has always loved Christmas Eve even more than Christmas, because this is the day that she always feels closest to the miracle. By Christmas, the miracle is over. All you can do is wait for the next year. But on Christmas Eve, anything is possible. Except for this year. This year she dreads what will come.

Now she watches the clock tick to midnight. It is officially the start of December 24. Hospital noises hum around her. Soft beeping sounds. Padded footsteps. A slight twinkle from a garland. There's a little tree near the nursing station. One of those modern trees that looks more like a sculpture. There are boxes of chocolates out, though weirdly, she's not tempted. You can spend your life trying to lose five pounds and only when you feel like you're dying do you get your weight where you want it.

She's spent so much time in hospitals over the course of her life. Her father was always being admitted to one for some reason or another. Sometimes for months at a time. They are places that are both oddly familiar and completely terrifying to her. Soon she will begin her own hospital journey; the thought of it makes her feel as though sand is pouring into her legs.

Meanwhile she's got to go to the Milagro collection and find Mr. Gaudy's miracle, which, under the circumstances, feels unlikely. Then she has to make it through the Campion party and then, somehow, she has to persuade her family to put on that play. Worst of all is the feeling that they'll do it just because they pity her. She will be the honorary Tiny Tim. Their last memory of her. Pitiful. Terrified.

She rages.

Something crashes, but the shattering doesn't come from inside her. She looks out the door to find out what happened, and sees that the nurse has bumped into the Christmas tree and knocked it to the ground. It lies there, arms flung up, ornaments shattered. Without thinking, Merry runs toward the tree and starts to scoop it up, but the nurse intervenes.

"Don't do that," she says. "Broken glass. You'll hurt yourself."

The janitor comes running by.

"It's a danger," the nurse says. "Be careful."

That's when the phone rings. It's Sully. "How are you?" he asks.

"Really depressed." Might as well be honest. "But I told Mr. Gaudy I'd go over to Milagro tomorrow. I think that will be a good idea. If I find the right book for him, I could change his life. And the kids could come too. They might enjoy it."

"That's a great idea, Merry. We need a change of focus here."

He's whispering. She hears the TV in the background. *Lethal Weapon*. She'd know Mel Gibson's voice anywhere.

"I don't know about a change of focus, but it would be a good thing. Certainly. Would get us all in the mood for putting on the play. Create the right vibe."

He's silent.

"What?" she asks.

One of the nurses swears. "I've got some glass on me!"

"You're going ahead with the play?" Sully asks. "After all this?"

"*Especially* after all this! What better time for it?"

"You're like a dog with a bone." His voice sounds tired, sad.

"What does that mean?"

He sighs. "Bessie wants to go home."

Home! No. That would mean the end of it all. Plus, there cannot be Christmas without Bessie. In a weird way, she's the glue that holds them all together.

"That's not possible. Bessie never gives up on anything."

"She wants to go to Leroy's apartment. She feels like if she can see him in person, she can change things." He pauses then. "She's struggling, Merry."

"I get it. This has been stressful. Beyond stressful. Possibly torturous. But we are going home in little more than a day."

"She insists she can't wait that long, and I'm worried about her. She's not in a good place right now, Merry. In fact, I'm thinking that I might go home with her. I don't—well, none of us like the idea of her traveling by herself right now."

"It would be impossible to travel now. Everything's booked."

"Nick and Song Lee were investigating it, and actually we could get a pretty good flight that goes through Germany. It wouldn't leave until six P.M. tomorrow. So we'd still have the day together."

"You're all planning to leave me alone on Christmas?" She knows she's being self-centered, but she's just so hurt. She has a nodule and she's scared. Don't they know that? She's spent so much of her life putting their needs first. Would it be asking so much for them to put her needs first, just for once?

Mr. Gaudy groans in his sleep. She squeezes his hand, he squeezes back. She hopes he's asleep. Hopes he's not having to listen to this.

"Of course we're not leaving you alone, Merry. Nick will stay with you."

"No," she says. "That is not acceptable."

"But Merry—"

"No. I am a potentially dying person and I have dragged myself and everyone in my family to London for five lousy days. To do so I have sold the thing most precious to me. I get first dibs. This could well be my last Christmas. It's not too much to ask that everyone make me happy."

"Merry. I know you too well. I know how upset you are, but there is nothing more important to you than family. Surely you wouldn't want Bessie to suffer."

"Do you remember that time we went on that family trip to Las Vegas and we had tickets to see Siegfried and Roy and then she broke her leg and we all had to come home?"

She hears a soft whooshing sound. Pictures him puffing up his cheeks and blowing out. The thing that could drive you crazy about Sully is the essential reasonableness of him. He's not a man to climb up a roof and try to hang a reindeer. But if you fall, he'll race you to the hospital. And if you get sick, he'll be with you every step of the way.

She knows he's right, but that doesn't stop the burn of anger from running through her. It's getting worse, this roaring in her ears. As though her heart is working extra hard to keep her going. She thinks of Dickens, lurking. Waiting for her misstep. Is this yet another test? Will she put her daughter before herself?

"Look, could you try to hold her off for a little bit?" Merry asks.

"Why? What are you going to do?"

"I'm going to try and get hold of Leroy."

Sully sighs. "He's not answering his phone, Merry."

"I know. But I have a plan," she says. "Please. Just let me try."

"Okay," he says. Then she feels his smile over the phone. "I have faith."

CHAPTER FIFTY-FIVE

The one relevant fact Merry knows about Leroy is that his parents live in a Christmas village. If she could get hold of his parents, she feels sure she could get through to Leroy. It's so often the family that's the key. But when she tries googling *places that celebrate Christmas year-round*, she comes up with an infinite variety. And not surprisingly, many of the people who live in those places have Christmas as their last name.

Normally, Merry likes a challenge.

It's the sort of hunt Merry actually enjoys. Like a scavenger hunt. Except that generally she has a lot of time to plan it out. Generally, she has more than a few hours to succeed, and there's not so much at stake, and she doesn't feel emotionally so ripped apart. She feels like this whole trip has been an exercise in flagellation, with bits of her being torn off at every turn.

Mr. Gaudy wheezes.

She looks at his kind face. The hooded eyes, the soft breathing.

And that's when the phone rings.

Her heart stops. But it's not Dr. Fiedler. It's her mother. She answers the phone. "How do you do that?"

"What?" her mother says. Her voice is husky, as though she's been singing at a bar all night. She's Mrs. Fezziwig on hormones. But Merry's kind of glad to hear her voice.

Merry might have responded, how do you know when I need you? But she confines herself to saying, "Know when I'm thinking about you?"

"Ah." Merry can picture her mother's face. Catlike, satiated. Her mother is all about satisfaction.

"You haven't just talked to Sully, have you?"

"No," Lana says, and Merry believes her. Her mother never lies, even at those times when it would be better if she did. "I have talked to Bessie though. She's in bad shape."

"I know. She wants to go home."

"Don't let her, Merry. You've worked so hard to pursue this dream of yours. Don't give up."

Oh my God. She agrees with her mother. The world is upside down. Nothing is right.

Maybe she *should* go home with Bessie.

"There's nothing wrong with putting your needs first, Meredith. What are you teaching your children by suffering all the time?"

"Hopefully I'm teaching them selflessness. That my own needs are not the most important thing. That there's something bigger."

Mr. Gaudy groans in his sleep. Merry reaches over to hold his hand. The bluish light of the hospital room drains the color out of everything, making them all look like ghosts.

"The best thing you ever did was go to Gstaad, Meredith."

All these years later, and she still sees so clearly the look on her father's face when she kissed him goodbye. Eyes that pooled with love. She still feels his eyes on her. It still breaks her heart.

"Deserting Dad?"

"That was the only way you could break away from him."

"I didn't want to break away from him. That's what you can't seem to understand. I loved him."

"Of course you loved him. No one disputes that. But he wanted you to give him your whole life and that wasn't fair."

"He never asked from me anything I didn't want to give." She thinks of him, alone, in that hospital bed. Dying. Clutching on to that book while the aide was outside smoking a cigarette.

"You were a child. You didn't know what you were capable of giving."

"I know this much: Ever since I left him, I've never had a day go by that I haven't felt guilty about it."

Her mother sighs, a strangled sort of sound. "There comes a point where guilt becomes a form of narcissism."

"I can understand why you would think that."

Her mother doesn't respond to the last statement. Merry feels so worn out. She feels like there are arguments that can take a lifetime.

"Do you want my help?" her mother says.

"How? With what?"

"I assume you're trying to find Leroy's parents. I can do that."

"How?"

"Because, baby, you get some of your smarts from me." She sucks deeply on a straw. Merry can almost smell the rum. "Where did Leroy go to college?"

"NYU. But I don't think they hand out addresses of their students."

"My famous Christmas party is going on now. And do you know who I'm standing right next to?" Lana erupts in laughter. "Get your hands out of there, Jackson."

"A pervert?"

"No. The uncle of the last provost of NYU. Hold on just a minute."

Merry sits there stupefied while her mother goes about her business. She wonders if Dickens really did sit alongside her father when he was dying. Does she hear Christmas carols?

"Ha." Her mother says, back on the phone. "He's going to call his nephew right now. What do you think about that, O Judgmental Daughter of Mine? Once I have Leroy's parents' number, I'll be able to get to him."

Merry feels the strangest flipping sensation in her stomach that might be hope or might be anxiety or might be both. Maybe they're inextricably linked. "That's a great idea, but I think I'm the one who should talk to him."

"No, Meredith, I'm the one who should do it."

"Why?"

"Because I'm the one who will understand what he must be feeling. I know what's it's like to be desperate to get out of this family."

"He's not desperate to get out of the family—there was a mishap with the soup and the phone, that's all."

She can practically see her mother's skeptical glance. "All right. So why isn't he answering Bessie's calls now?"

Merry has nothing to say to that.

"Just say thank you, Meredith."

"Thank you, Mom."

CHAPTER FIFTY-SIX

Merry wakes to the sound of Bessie laughing. Oh, joyous sound.

The aroma tips her off as to where she is. Cologne. Sully's soft breathing. The slinky touch of the sheets. But then, also, the smell of bacon and eggs.

She has never smelled anything so wonderful. Never felt so hungry.

How did she even get home? She must have sleepwalked into an Uber and crawled into bed. She's still wearing her clothes from yesterday. Her hat, however, is on the nightstand. That's a relief. Had she woken up with a question mark on her head that would have been way too on the nose.

"You did good," Sully says. "It's good to hear her laughing."

She jumps, turns toward him. "It was my mother, I guess."

Merry wants to take a shower, she *needs* to take a shower and yet that breakfast smells so good. Fortunately, she leans toward clothes that don't require ironing, so she thinks she's presentable. Enough.

What she finds in the kitchen is like a dream come true. Her three children, sitting on barstools, laughing. Nick with his shirtsleeves rolled up, waving around a spatula. For a period of time, he considered being a chef. So everything he makes comes with presentation, in this case a circle of red pepper around the eggs. Song Lee is wearing sweatpants. Sweatpants! Merry wonders where they came from. And there is Bessie laughing, holding up her phone with Leroy's face upon the screen. A more sullen Leroy than he has been, and yet, still Leroy. Hair pulled back. Eyes swollen. Tired.

"We're going to counseling," Bessie says. "We're both committed to making this work."

Leroy nods solemnly. "We have to."

Merry wonders what inducements her mother used on Leroy. Would she have threatened him? That's not really Lana's style. More likely that she would have offered him a million dollars not to break up with Bessie right now.

"I'm glad to see you," Merry says. "It wasn't the same without you."

"Lana talked to him and they had a really good conversation."

"I was feeling trapped," Leroy acknowledges.

"But that's in the past," Bessie says.

Song Lee doesn't actually snort, but Merry's so convinced she's snorting in her head that she actually hears it.

Her phone beeps with message from Mr. Gaudy. *How are things going?*

Oh, my God. She completely forgot about the Milagro collection. She was supposed to be there at nine. She was to have four hours.

"What time is it? she cries out.

"Eleven-forty-two," Sully says.

She's three hours late. She can't believe it. She's never late for anything.

She doesn't even go to the mirror. She goes running through the living room toward the door and her shoes. Everyone jumps up. "I have to get to the Milagro house."

"What is that?" Sully says, though everyone is following her out the door, into the elevator. She hopes someone turned off the stove.

She has three missed calls from Mr. Gaudy.

I'm on my way, she texts him. *So so sorry.*

"We'll come with you," Sully says.

"You know what?" she says. "That would be a help."

CHAPTER FIFTY-SEVEN

Fortunately, the Milagro house is not too far from where they're staying. It's easier to run than to find a cab and get stuck in holiday traffic. She'll have about fifty minutes to pick her way through a lifetime's worth of collecting.

Fifty minutes.

They get to the Milagro house, which must be the narrowest house in London. It can't be more than twenty feet across. Squeezed between two large buildings, it looks as though if the earth moved everything within it would be crushed.

Unlike almost every other house on the street, there are no Christmas decorations. Only books. She can see the books through the windows, stacked up.

She has fifty minutes to find a treasure for Mr. Gaudy. After that, all the other collectors will pour in. She sees some she recognizes standing in the street, waiting. She waves at one of her favorites, Sarah Marie. Then she goes tearing for the stairs, but the effort defeats her. For just a moment time stops, and she's conscious of being the center of attention and concern. She knows they're worried for her, but now is not the time. She puts out her hand to Sully and asks him to give her a tug, which he does.

"Hey, Merry," someone calls out, but she doesn't even wave. Though she does quickly send a text to Gussie Hong. "Must go to Milagro house for Mr. Gaudy. Will explain later."

There's a pause, and then Gussie texts back a heart.

She's a good one, Merry thinks.

Up the steps, and into the house.

It is the most disorganized thing she's ever seen, and she's seen a lot. You can barely move. There are little alleyways where Mr. Milagro and his wife must have made their way. Aisles carved out of books. And the smell! Usually, she revels in the smell of books, but this has undercurrents of body order and, oh God, urine. The books will have absorbed the smell. It's madness and nothing jumps to the eye. There is everything here. There is nothing here. You can spend years here and not begin to hack away at it. It is weighty. The odor feels like it's weaving its way into her nodule. She feels overwhelmed by the task of what she's taken on, but there's no way to tell Mr. Gaudy that. Back when she was young, she would have hurled herself into this, but she has no energy. She feels staggered.

But she must do this. She must help Mr. Gaudy. She owes him so much. And anyway, she loves him.

Merry remembers Larry McMurtry's famous words from his time as a book collector: "If you want to find something, look high and look low because everybody looks in between."

She scans the house. A staircase is in the corner. Who even knows how many floors there are, but one thing she feels sure of is that every piece of flooring, every step, every hallway is crammed with books. She's a little concerned that the building will implode upon itself. She's known plenty of collectors who've been ejected from their houses. Sheila, come to that, who was thrown out of her own building. It's a reasonable concern. Buildings can only hold so much weight.

She sees all the sorts of things she always sees. Books on botany. Bibles. Lots of Bibles. Biographies that might be worth something to someone somewhere but are certainly not worth a fortune.

She has forty-five minutes left.

"Where do we begin?" Song Lee asks. She's wearing a white lambswool sweater that is going to be destroyed.

"Just start looking for anything that seems to relate to the Middle East," Merry says, though even as she speaks, she knows the strategy is hopeless. And yet she feels sure that something's here. She feels it, almost as though the books are whispering to her. She stands there, in the entryway, trying to get a sense of it. She knows that there is something here and someone is going to stumble over it. Someone will turn over a book or a chair and it will be under there.

A little old lady walks toward her then. This must be Mrs. Milagro. She walks gingerly, careful not to go tripping over anything.

"You're late," she says.

"I apologize."

"You are supposed to find my husband's treasure."

Of course, Merry thinks, she's as desperate to find the treasure as Mr. Gaudy is. More so, probably. She must be in desperate need of money, and it will be an ordeal to get rid of all this stuff. There's no point to asking if there's any order to this collection, though Merry does ask, just in the interest of being comprehensive.

"He didn't tell you where he kept his special things?"

"No," Mrs. Milagro says. "He preferred to keep that private."

Not surprising. What better way to keep your secrets than to hide them in a pile of clutter?

Thirty minutes left. Not that it probably matters if a swarm of book buyers comes in. No one will be able to find anything. It's all down to luck.

But she owes Mr. Gaudy.

Bessie runs toward her then. "Mom, I found a history of Islam. Does that help?"

It's an attractive book. But not worth a fortune. "Start to make a pile," Merry says.

She forces herself to calm down. She has to get her mind working. She can do this. She's done this before. An idea occurs to her.

"Can you show me where he died?" she asks Mrs. Milagro.

The old woman looks at her suspiciously. Merry wonders how long it's been since she went outside. She's wearing a faded floral dress and her hair has obviously been self-cut. She turns and starts toward the flight of stairs, and Merry follows her.

Behind her Bessie calls, "I found a history of Saudi Arabia. But it looks like a textbook."

"Put it in the pile," she calls back, and follows Mrs. Milagro, who is muttering to herself as she huffs up the stairs. A hectoring sort of sound. Though whether she's criticizing herself or Merry, Merry's not sure.

The further up they go, the denser the air becomes and the narrower the passageways. How long has it taken to fill the house like this? There's no natural light at all. All the windows are covered by books. There are parts of the stairway where they have to turn sideways to make it through, and neither of them are big women. Merry hears something skittering in a corner and jumps, thinking perhaps it is Dickens, but she hasn't seen him in a day now. Not since the Apple store. He's waiting for tonight. Christmas Eve. She feels sure of it.

Another sound.

Who knows what is living here? She hopes there are no candles.

They finally make their way to the top floor. This is the most crowded area of all. They pass by a bucket filled with water that's ostensibly dripped from a leak in the ceiling, and towers of books. Merry has been glancing at the titles, but there is no order to them. College calculus books are alongside delicate treatises that seem hand-drawn. But just because something's old doesn't make it valuable. Someone has to want it.

Then finally they are at the bedroom. Mrs. Milagro stands back, shyly, and Merry walks in.

There is a bed in the middle of the room, surrounded by books. A boat surrounded by sharks. The bed is narrow, and there are books on the bed, but there is a small empty space—the only empty space Merry's seen in the whole house. Against the sheet is a body-shaped indentation. This must be where he slept and where he died. As so many book collectors do, he died surrounded by his books, comforted by the possessions he loved so much in life. How did they get his body downstairs? Where does Mrs. Milagro sleep?

Merry walks toward the bed.

The smell is oily, rancid. It reminds her of an old bottle of Crisco oil that she once accidentally poured into cookie batter. The shock of tasting it. The way it coated her tongue.

She approaches the bed.

Mrs. Milagro tugs at her arm. “Don’t touch it.”

“I want to move the mattress.”

“You can’t do that.”

But Merry has a feeling. That tingling in her fingers that she’s learned to trust. That’s been the making of her career. It’s here. She feels sure of it.

At Mrs. Milagro’s reluctant nod, she tugs at the mattress, which is light. In fact, she notices that there’s a slight bend in the pile of books that suggests that the mattress has been moved before. She feels a wash of excitement, feels lighter than she has for days, and as she tugs away the mattress, she sees beneath it a hollowed-out space. Inside are some books carefully wrapped in plastic. What looks like a drawing of an oil refinery on the cover. What looks a lot like the books of maps Mr. Gaudy mentioned that sold for a fortune.

Merry feels a sense of triumph she hasn’t felt in a long time. It steadies her, reassures her. “I found it!” she crows.

Something surges into her that feels like hope. Something just a little sparkly. Something that gives her the courage to move forward, which she’s going to need. Because she has the Campion party to go to tonight, and then the ghost of Dickens. And the nodule. But for the first time since arriving in London, Merry feels like herself. Like maybe everything is possible.

CHAPTER FIFTY-EIGHT

"How did you know they would be there?" Song Lee asks, as they walk back to their apartment on Bayswater.

Song Lee has one arm tucked in Merry's. Somehow, she does not have one speck of dust on her sweater. Nick walks beside her. Bessie walks alongside Sully, holding her phone in front of her like a talisman, so that Leroy can see everything that passes before them. Or does she not want to look into his face? It's a difficult relationship to figure out.

They could have taken a cab, but Merry loves walking through the park. She loves the trees and all the dogs that run off leash. Everything is movement and laughter. This is a good moment, she thinks, and she wants to enjoy it.

Even the roaring in her ears has settled into more of a murmur, like the tide coming in on a beach.

"A lot of book collectors die surrounded by their favorite books," she says. "Or maybe not a lot, but it's not unusual. I just figured I had one shot and that was the most likely place."

"Did you save Mr. Gaudy's life?" Bessie asks.

Merry smiles at her. This is how Bessie sees things. Against a life-or-death backdrop. But perhaps she's right. Perhaps it's important to pay attention to every small thing. Small things matter. The nodule matters. Would any of this matter if not for the nodule? Would they be here if not for that? Should she be grateful for that? Is that the point?

She places her hand against where she thinks her lung is. She thinks of that man dying alone in his revolting bed. She will not die alone. She is grateful for that.

"People have strange deathbed behavior," Leroy says.

Merry starts. He's been so quiet since his being in the soup, that she's sort of forgotten he's there. She's missed his voice, which is a nice tenor. High, like Dickens's, but without the threat.

"What are you talking about, lover?" Bessie asks.

"Remember Mrs. Davidson? She had her son with her all the time when she was in her last days. He never left her side. It went on and on and finally she told him that she wanted a Diet Coke. So he went to the cafeteria to get her one and when he came back, she was dead."

Bessie nods, her whole body bobbing with the motion. Around them Hyde Park flourishes, worn down by winter and yet still staggeringly beautiful. Merry notices two trees that seem to be tilting toward each other, the larger one leaning in toward the smaller one. Their branches reach toward each other in what can only be love.

"I remember that," Bessie says. "He was devastated. He'd been so devoted to her and he couldn't believe that she would die the moment he wasn't there. He felt so guilty."

"But the nurse told us that people often do that. They want to spare their loved ones the memory of them dying. Or they feel that it's something so intimate they want to do alone."

Like her father, Merry thinks. Alone. Was that intentional? Could he have chosen to die without her there? Do you have control over things like that? She's never considered that as a possibility and yet it feels right. It settles into her like syrup. Soothing.

Song Lee starts to laugh. "It wouldn't be a Bingham family vacation if we didn't all wind up talking about death."

Nick snorts at that, but it's a happy snort. Merry notices he's not making that grinding sound as much.

"Is every family as effed up as ours?" Song Lee asks.

Merry hears only two words in that sentence. As ours. *As ours.* They may be battered, they may be contentious, they may be self-destructive, but they are a family. *Ours.*

CHAPTER FIFTY-NINE

The Campion house is exactly the sort of place Merry has always dreamed of owning. That Flemish brick bonding that she loves. The arch over the windows, the bubbly glass. And the window panes shaped like diamonds, which are officially called quarrels, as she recalls. She's always liked that. A quarrel of windows.

Then a tidy little garden out front, gated off with a beautiful wrought iron gate. Nothing too showy, nothing ostentatious. Just perfect. Palm trees growing neatly at the edges, as though nature itself bows to Phoebe's wishes. And then, the Christmas decorations. Only now does Merry remember how Phoebe used to decorate for Christmas. She was the template upon which all Merry's efforts were based. The candles. The wreaths. The ribbons. All of it tasteful and somehow joyful. She cannot criticize a single thing.

It is perfection, and she and her family stand at the door and knock. Her beloved and imperfect family. She wants to hold up her hands to ward off anything critical Phoebe may say, but there is no need. Phoebe opens the door, and if she thinks it odd that Merry went screaming out of their last encounter, or Song Lee confessed to plagiarism, or Bessie's boyfriend looks like a ghost, she does not say so.

She just swoops in.

Merry is sort of glad that she has her hat on. Some sort of effort seems called for.

Meanwhile, Phoebe is dressed in a silver sheath. Up close Merry sees lines on her face that she hadn't noticed at the pub. Then, Merry's eyes had been so filmed over with fury that she hadn't really seen her. She's aged, but so has Merry. Al Campion comes over, squeezes Merry just a bit too hard. She struggles out of his grasp.

There's a string quartet. Of course. Never has Merry wished so desperately for her mother. This party could surely use a jolt of Lana and Jack Gutiérrez and their salsa. She pictures her mother swanning through this party and wishes she could summon her. Only now does it occur to her that her mother is quite fun. There's a reason her children like her so much. Come to that, her mother is a bit like Mrs. Fezziwig.

Waiters come over with food that could equally well pass as art. Celery bent into unnatural shapes. Chicken wings made out of tofu and tofu made out of chicken and who knows what else. The Bingham children fall on the food as though they were survivors of a Russian siege. But their appetite pleases Merry. An appetite is good, a sign of life. Such delicate little treats. Even Song Lee, who normally just nibbles, has a chicken drumstick by the edge and seems to be growling at it. There's something that looks like a house made of zucchini and Merry grabs two of those. The waiter looks at her and nods.

Good. She doesn't like judgmental waiters.

She's determined to be fun. This has been a miraculous day. She's hoping this will be a miraculous night. Maybe the ghost of Dickens will appear to all of them while they're putting on the play. Maybe he's not there to kill her but to direct her in a play. It's a long shot, but she's talking about the ghost of Charles Dickens. Is anything improbable?

Sully has gone off to talk to one of the cellists. A hunched-over man who whips his bow around with great passion. The kids are grazing for drinks. Leroy is offering commentary.

Merry automatically drifts toward the first place she goes whenever she goes into someone's house. The bookshelf. There's something so intimate about seeing a person's tastes in books exposed. These are grouped by color. Reds and greens and golds. Christmas books. She wonders if they went out and bought books that color or if they got rid of the other colors. But then she sees more books in the corner. Now she's intrigued.

There's a Russian edition of *War and Peace* that she's pretty sure she saw at the Firsts Fair a few months earlier. She'd had such fun at the fair. Had gone with Mr. Gaudy and listened to a lecture on bibliographies. Met with old friends. Looked at the bibliography winners. That was only in September. Three months ago, when she viewed herself as a normal fifty-five-year-old woman with a normal life.

She hears Song Lee's voice then, talking to someone she can't see. Telling him that Mr. Gaudy has offered her a job. Is that true? "He wants me to take over the shipping of books," Song Lee says with such pride in her voice. "I might also have the opportunity to write copy for the catalog."

Then Phoebe is there, smiling. "Merry, I'm so glad to see you."

And the strangest thing happens. Although Merry isn't precisely glad to see her, she does feel that sense of belonging that you feel when you're with someone from your youth.

Suddenly she's transported back to herself as a young woman, lugging Nick around. So unsure of what to do and so happy to have this friend who always seemed one step ahead of her, so assured. Who had three children, which just seemed monumental to Merry at the time. Who knew how to wrap his blanket and what to do if his nose got stuffy and how to deal with diaper rash.

She remembers them calling each other in the middle of the night, when both their husbands were working long hours. Phoebe was the sister she'd never had. Merry's mother had gone off to Florida by then and whenever Merry asked her for advice about child-rearing, she'd say, "Oh God, I don't know."

Meanwhile, there was Phoebe, willing and ready to do anything. Swim lessons and poetry lessons and trips into New York City. The Museum of Natural History and the Central Park Zoo. An essential part of her life.

Merry hugs her, more tightly than she intended.

"I've missed you so much," Phoebe says.

"Me too," Merry says. "Me too."

She tugs her over to a velour chair. Phoebe is the source of Merry's love of plush.

They sit down alongside of each other, knees against knees, Phoebe tilting in. That familiar aroma. The perfume she has made for her by a Parisian boutique.

"There's so much I want to tell you about. You'll be so proud of me, Merry. I went and got my law degree. Remember how you always encouraged me? You were the one who told me I could do it, even when I didn't believe in myself. Now I'm doing pro bono work. I know it's not as interesting as the work you do, but I enjoy it."

"I'm glad," Merry says.

"You know what I was thinking about the other day," Phoebe says. "That time we went to Yankee Stadium and you had to back into that parking spot."

Merry laughs.

What a nightmare. She'd been driving a Dodge minivan at the time. This was before Metro North stopped at Yankee Stadium. The only way to get there was to drive, which was all right, and to park, which was a nightmare. But she loved going to the games. Her father had been a huge Yankee fan and she always felt like she was paying her respects to him whenever she went there.

But the lots were terrible. Crowded. And this one particular time, the attendant insisted she back into the spot. A sadist. He said he'd park the car for her, but she was damned if she would give him the satisfaction.

This was before cars had back cameras.

So she did it, with Phoebe standing out front and shouting directions. The kids were glued to the window, watching and clapping. When she succeeded in backing into the spot, they'd all leapt around in exultation. She feels something similar now when she finds the right book for a client, or wins an auction, but she can remember the pure joy of that moment. That feeling of triumph.

A waiter comes by with a mound of pistachio bombs. Phoebe waves him away. "My thighs," she says.

The memories pour back. Merry hears the voices around her but isn't paying much attention. So caught up in the conversation and the memories.

"But you," Phoebe says, moving on to a different topic. "Your work as a book scout. It must be so fascinating."

That's another thing Merry has forgotten about her. The ability Phoebe has to get her to talk. She begins telling her stories, one after the other, about Mr. Gaudy and his travails, and going through the Milagro collections. Merry catches Sully's eye. He's smiling at her. He was right, she thinks. It is nice to catch up. Now is a time in her life for healing. Not for opening up feuds.

Merry's going on with some story about a Dickens teaspoon that someone just bought for $8,000, when Phoebe says, "We've gotten involved in the book business too. Though from a different end of it, of course."

"Have you?"

"Book collecting."

Merry's not surprised. She saw the books in the living room. She can imagine Phoebe getting caught up in the hunt, and of course, she has the money to pursue it.

"That's great. I think Sully said something about that. First editions?" That's how most people with money enter the market.

"We don't have a specific buying plan yet, but Merry," she says, tapping her knee, leaning forward excitedly. "You'll never believe this. We bought your book."

Merry tilts her head. "What book?"

"*A Christmas Carol.* The one Dickens signed to your ancestor."

Suddenly Merry smells onions. What a weird sensation. She feels her jaw drop. It's a cliché and yet it's real. Her jaw really does feel like it's become unhinged. Like Marley's ghost. *Its lower jaw dropped down upon its breast.*

"My *Christmas Carol*?" The words come out like a shriek.

Phoebe seems to falter for just a moment. A wrinkle surges across her forehead, but she dismisses it and presses forward.

"It was for sale. We got a phone call. You know how I always loved that book, and when we heard it was for sale, we took the opportunity."

"But you knew it was mine," Merry says. She must be speaking louder than she intended because people are looking at her. But she doesn't care. "You knew how much that book meant to me."

Phoebe looks confused. "But it was for sale."

"But you'd have to know that I'd only sell it if something desperate was going on in my life. Wouldn't you think to call me first and make sure I was all right?"

And there's the face Merry remembers. The one that haunted her dreams. Phoebe, implacable. Phoebe standing in the doorway when Merry went to her and begged her to do something to help Sully who was about to go into the meeting without Al Campion by his side. She didn't care what Sully said; Al Campion knew he was throwing Sully to the wolves and he should have been there with him.

What had Gussie Hong said? *A nice family wanted the book.* Oh, they were always so nice. All of them.

"I had no idea," Phoebe says.

Merry rises to her feet. "You had a perfectly good idea. You must have known I was in a bad way if I needed to sell the book. Did you even guess that I might have cancer? That I might be dying? That this might be my last Christmas ever? Did that even matter to you? Did I ever matter to you, ever? You just wanted that book and you didn't want to take the time to call me because then you might lose it. Because it was a hot property. More than friendship, more than anything else, you wanted that book."

All the anger that she's been trying to tamp down, to deal with, has come flooding up. She can't control it. She feels it washing over her. She wants to hit Phoebe.

Her children are around her. Her husband. They're angry too, their faces hard masks. Even Sully looks furious, the expression so unfamiliar that it looks like his face will split open.

They surround Merry and shuttle her out of the Campions' quaint house the way Secret Service agents get a president out of danger.

The party has gone funereal, everyone stopped in their tracks the way people do in that children's game. Halted in whatever position they were in before the fighting started, as though a giant curtain of gloom has settled over all of them. Christmas ruined.

Bessie slams open the door and they all stalk out into the chilly London air. A woman goes by, who really does look like royalty, and she squeezes Merry's hand and says, "I'm so very, very sorry."

Merry takes one final look back at the house after the door's closed. Its veiled eyes stare back at her blankly. It looks hunched over, dark, and silent.

She has become the Christmas Killer, Merry thinks. She goes where there is joy and she sucks it out of the room.

CHAPTER SIXTY

"What horrible people," Nick says.

"Hypocrites. All that Christmas stuff up and they're no better than anyone else."

"Worse," Bessie says. "Don't you think so, Leroy? Leroy? Are you okay?"

"I'm so sorry," Sully says. "You were right all along, Merry. I don't know why I didn't see it."

"It kind of makes you wonder about celebrating Christmas at all," Song Lee says. "You know it's really just a pagan holiday."

"Did you see all those fake angels?" Nick says.

"Leroy? Leroy? Don't get upset. You're not trapped." Bessie holds the phone over her head, Leroy's anxious face shining back at them like a deflating balloon.

"No!" Merry whimpers. This is not what she wanted. To ruin Christmas. She has no satisfaction in this turn of events. She wanted them all to have fun at the party. To ride that bounce of joy they'd been feeling since they discovered the manuscript Mr. Gaudy needed. She didn't want them embittered and cynical.

Automatically Merry looks around for Dickens, but she doesn't see him. She wouldn't; Mayfair wasn't a place where Dickens felt comfortable. It intimidated him with its rows of white houses facing each other like people at a dinner table.

He's not here, and she has nowhere to go. Even her laminated schedule is of no use to her in this moment. She'd planned to have them all performing *A Christmas Carol* tonight, after a dinner at one of Dickens's favorite pubs, the George and Vulture. But that's not happening. Everyone is far too brittle for that.

"Maybe we could sue?" Song Lee says. "Don't we have cause, Dad?"

"I'm so sorry, Merry," he says. He looks deflated. Older. "I never saw that side of her. You've been right all along."

Their faces are all contorted in anger. Merry aches at the sight of them. She has destroyed her family's Christmas. Now, whenever they think of it, they will think of the Campions and how her mother started to scream and shocked royalty.

She starts as she bumps into a wall, a furniture shop filled with the sort of Victorian furniture she loves. Just like the tub chair she has in her parlor at home. Her one great purchase.

No one noticed her collision. They're so turned in on themselves. Her head hurts. She puts her hand to her breast, below which lies the nodule. She feels like she can actually feel it pulsating. Taking over her life.

"Just because Phoebe is terrible, it doesn't follow that Christmas is terrible," she feels obliged to say. "Christmas is not about Phoebe."

"We should steal the book back," Song Lee says. "It would be difficult, but we could pull it off."

"So now you're a felon?" Nick says.

"Maybe I am. Maybe I'm more dangerous than you know."

"You've been drinking," Nick says.

"It's a party," Song Lee says. "You're supposed to drink."

"You're not supposed to have five Russian mules."

"You were counting?"

"They had Russian mules?" Bessie says. "I asked them if they had a special drink of the day and they said no."

"You had plenty to drink yourself," Song Lee says, looking hurt. She's not the one who's usually on the receiving end of Nick's snarkiness.

"No, I didn't," Nick said. "I just had Sprite."

Now Song Lee laughs. "You had plenty to drink last time I saw you. In Oregon. You weren't so high and mighty then."

"That's what made me realize I was drinking too much. I didn't like the way it made me feel. I started going to AA after that."

"Wait," Bessie says. "You've been to Nick's house in Oregon? I thought none of us were invited."

"Don't do this," Merry says, but they're off. Voices strident. Ripping away at each other. Tearing.

"When was this? Recently? You've been out there a while, but you told me no. You told me I couldn't come."

They're staggering through Mayfair, which is the most beautiful place in London, which is one of the most beautiful places in the world, and they're all so angry with each other. They pass by houses, lit with lights and laughter, that in any other context they would stop and admire. She thinks of Scrooge, wandering around with the Ghost of Christmas Present, stopping to look at the different ways people are celebrating the holiday but feeling cut off from it. That terrible barrier line that cuts you off from the rest of the world.

Her family is caught up in anger and ill will, but it is not their fault, she thinks. They were perfectly happy at the party. They were ready to celebrate. They were even ready to put on a production of *A Christmas Carol.* They have been ready to do everything she asked, but it is she who has been getting them roiled up. It's *her* anger and guilt that is tearing them apart. She is toxic in every sense of the word.

It's all so wrong.

They go through the streets arguing, and now even gentle Leroy has gotten into it, telling Song Lee that she should back off from teasing Bessie all the time. It's not her fault that she's high maintenance and that no one ever pays attention to her, and Nick says that's not fair, they all do the best they can for her, and Bessie says, "Leroy, what do you mean I'm high maintenance?"

Then Nick starts to laugh. "Here we go. Here we go. The end of yet another beautiful relationship. Though I don't blame him after you dumped him in the soup." His voice is raspy. His arm movements spastic. He looks like he's flailing, drowning. Some people walk by and go around him.

"He's depressed," Bessie says. "You have no idea what's going on in his life. I haven't wanted to say anything, but . . ."

"Don't say anything!" Leroy roars. His face is contorted.

"No, no, no, no, no," Bessie says. She's lost weight, Merry realizes. On a brief trip to London, her daughter is being winnowed away.

"Go ahead," Song Lee snarls. "Tell us. Or are you going to disappear again, Leroy?"

"That's so hurtful," Bessie whimpers.

"That's *enough*," Sully says. "This is Christmas and you know how important that is to your mother. You know she loves it. I want you to stop this now."

They do stop, for a moment. The way sometimes the TV freezes. Not so much a calming pause but a sharp break in the action.

Merry feels like she's gasping for air. A fish that's been flung onto a beach. She can't breathe.

"I'm going to move home," Bessie announces. "I'm going to put my career on hold and move in and take care of you, Mom."

"What career?" Song Lee says. "You've been in a total of two plays, and in one of them you were drunk."

"That is so not true," Bessie says. "My career is unfolding even now. I haven't wanted to bring it up, because there's still a finance piece to arrange, but Leroy is writing a play just for me. I'm going to be the star."

Nick starts to laugh at that, though it's not a joyful sort of laugh.

Leroy's shouting something, but Merry can't make it out. Everything has gone muffled, or muted, because of the roaring in her ears. She feels like everything is happening in slow motion.

"That's going to be a huge help," she hears Song Lee say. "You'll probably wind up killing her."

"Not in Mayfair," Merry says, though she knows that's a ridiculous thing to say and yet it's true. Not in this glorious and stately part of London. If her family is going to dissolve, it feels like it should be on the Embankment. Someplace crowded and dangerous. She was pickpocketed once on the Embankment. She swallows and can't seem to get her breath. Suddenly all she can think about is the pickpocket, a middle-aged woman at the end of her rope. Also, not an effective thief. Merry felt the tug on her pocketbook, saw the woman with her wallet in her hand and chased after her. She got her. The woman was no athlete. Merry caught up to her without difficulty, and when the woman looked at her, she seemed terrified and just threw the wallet at her. Pitiful, beaten down.

"How can you say something like that? I'm very good with sick people."

"You work with dying people, at a hospice," Song Lee snarls. "They have nowhere to go but down."

"That's terrible," Bessie yells. "You of all people should be glad that our family has a giving spirit."

Time slows. This must be what it's like to step off a cliff, Merry thinks. There must be a moment when you hover suspended, right before you plummet.

"What do you mean by that?" Song Lee asks. She's reared back, like a dinosaur out of Jurassic Park, ready to spew venom.

Merry watches it unfold and wants to do something. She has to do something. This is terrible. She opens her mouth to speak and nothing comes out. Maybe this is death, she thinks. When you've reached the absolute limit and you cross over.

Bessie falters. She is not a mean person. She looks to Nick as though seeking his support, but he just sneers at her and puts his arm around Song Lee, which is probably the worst thing he could do. Because now Bessie feels outnumbered. Now she's lashing out. Now she's out of control.

"I'm just saying you're lucky we took you in. Just think where you'd be if we didn't. Do you remember what your face looked like? With that scar on your lip?"

"That's enough," Merry rasps. She starts toward Bessie, thinking that maybe if she hugs her she can calm her down, but she can't move. She feels paralyzed.

The one taboo they have in the family is Song Lee's adoption. The unwritten law. Not that they don't talk about it. When you're a family consisting of four white people and one Asian one, it's fairly obvious that one of you is adopted. But never, *never* has Merry wanted Song Lee to feel they did her some sort of favor by adopting her. She came to their family in a different way than the other children, but she is just as much a part of it as they are.

This is what Merry has always believed. She thought her children believed it too. To hear otherwise, even in words spoken in anger, shatters the very structure of their family.

How can Song Lee come back from that? How can their family come back from that?

And that the blow came from Bessie, who is so good-hearted, and so wounded. And so cruel. How could she say such a thing?

How can she repair it?

Merry thinks of the day she got the flyer in the mail. Along with advertising for gutter repair and window cleaning. It was a glossy postcard with a picture of eight children on it. Seven of them smiling, desperately, into the camera. *Can you help one of these children?*

She was so intrigued by the unsmiling child, who wound up being Song Lee. She imagined that little girl must have tremendous strength of character to stand up to all that peer pressure to smile. She didn't pity her, she admired her.

Merry had never before considered adopting a child, certainly not one from a flyer. Sometimes she thought about having a third child, especially when Bessie started kindergarten. She had to do something with her life and she loved being a mother. Nick was already so independent and Bessie so popular. Invited to every birthday party.

Possibly a little needy, but everyone, or Phoebe anyway, said she'd grow out of it.

Merry had become pregnant with a third child but lost it early. Which hurt more than she expected. She mourned that little baby.

Something about that picture haunted Merry. She could imagine a future for that girl. In the way she squared her shoulders, in the way she scowled at the photographer, she saw Nora the vampire girl. She knew she could love her.

After Song Lee arrived, Merry tore up the postcard. She never wanted Song Lee to know that that's how she found her. She didn't want her to feel diminished. All she'd ever said was that she came from an adoption agency, which was more or less the truth.

Now, as Merry looks back on it, she can see all the ways in which she put a wall around Song Lee. Because she wanted to protect her. She never told the kids not to talk about her adoption. She certainly never hid it. But perhaps in avoiding the circumstances of Song Lee's adoption, she's implied there was something dodgy about it. That must be what Bessie picked up on, and her insult went right to the heart of Song Lee.

Meanwhile, Bessie seems to realize what she's just said. "Oh, Song Lee. Oh, I'm sorry. I didn't mean that. What am I saying? Oh, I'm sorry. I love you. I don't know what's wrong with me."

But Song Lee doesn't respond. She swallows. Merry does too, a swollen nodule of grief and anger making its way down her long throat. And finally Merry gets her voice back and she yells, "You are being hateful. Hateful! Stop it right now."

Bessie looks to be on the verge of saying something awful, and so Merry says the only thing she can think of to shut her down. "You were right," Merry hisses. "I did prefer going to Song Lee's swim meets—not because she always won, but because she didn't whine all the time."

A man walks past just then, looking suspiciously like the man who led the Scrooge tour, the one who hit her with a cane.

"Merry Christmas," he cackles, "and God bless us every one."

"Oh, shut up," Merry spits at him, but he's gone.

That's when the bells of Saint Paul's Cathedral start to ring. It is one in the morning. The exact time the first ghost appeared to Scrooge. The moment his salvation began. But there is to be no salvation for her. No Dickens. No hope.

CHAPTER SIXTY-ONE

Except.

Except, Merry will not give up.

She simply does not have it in her. Because she absolutely knows that there is a solution to this problem, and that it rests inside an invisible man with an attitude problem. A ghost who haunts but does not help. Who does not even point, mutely, toward her grave.

There has to be a reason Dickens is here.

At this point, even if that reason is to take her spirit, she's willing to risk it. She will not go down without a fight.

So when Song Lee heads off to a bar with Nick, and Sully climbs into an Uber with Bessie, who has stuck her phone, and with it Leroy, into her pocket, Merry remains behind. She says she needs some time to herself, and everyone is so distracted they don't fight her.

She watches her family disappear and then she closes her eyes.

She remembers once going to a corn maze with the kids when they were young. In Ohio. A pretty town she'd come across on one of her scouting expeditions. They got to the corn maze and could not find their way out. They spent hours there, going back and forth. Song Lee with a compass, Sully trying to figure out angles of the sun, Bessie crying, and Nick stressed. Hours went by, but Merry refused to surrender. She could not believe her family could not find their way out of a corn maze.

Finally, Sully had enough and began ripping the stalks out of the ground. The kids joined in. They decimated the maze, and none of them talked to her for the rest of the trip, and they never went to a maze again. All their activities from there on out had to have an exit strategy.

Merry tries to channel the feeling she had earlier that day, when she was at the Milagro house. She knows she can do this. She just has to follow her instincts, and right now they are telling her to head toward Oxford Street.

So she does.

CHAPTER SIXTY-TWO

Oxford Street sparkles. It is unquestionably the sparkliest place in London. Giant angels, wings outstretched, heads turned like swans, glitter for as far as Merry can see. This has always been her favorite part of London to walk around at Christmas time, though now she is struck by the solemnity of the angels. Underneath all the show, their faces are grave. Sorrowing, even. Their arms are in different positions, sometimes raised, sometimes outstretched, but always in the posture of surrender.

Around her pulses London at Christmas. Some of the stores are open, though it is late. People scream with laughter. A neon pink pedicab roars so close to her she has to jump out of the way. It all makes her think of Bessie, and all the brilliant courageous Villards, none of whom seemed to be plagued by depression or self-doubt. Maybe selling off the Villard *Carol* was the literary equivalent of Samson cutting off his hair.

Around her are some of the most expensive stores in the world, though nothing tempts her. Still, Merry looks in the windows. Seeking.

Nothing like this would have been here during Dickens's time. The street would have been filled with residential buildings. Near here is where Esther Summerson lived. From *Bleak House*. There would have been gas lamps. Toward the western end of the road would have been Tyburn, where public executions took place, though they had stopped, in that particular spot, by Dickens's time. Too much thievery took place during the executions so they had to be moved within jail walls.

She knows Dickens's world so well. She knows his words so well. She knows everything there is to know about Charles Dickens, except where he is and what he wants of her.

The noise is making her dizzy. She sees a quiet street and turns on to it. Duke Street. Beautiful, classical Mayfair. Hushed, wealthy, secretive.

A large baroque building looms in front of her with vitrine green doors. It's the sort of random structure that pops up around London, a gift from the Victorians who seemed compelled to make a decoration out of everything. It looks like a mausoleum, but she doesn't think it is. She doesn't see a plaque with anyone's name on it. She's near Grosvenor Square, so it would make sense that this would be Lord Grosvenor's tomb. Or the family mausoleum. But they don't seem like the sort of people who would hide their name.

She prowls around it and sees a sign warning to be careful of electric currents.

Is it an electrical station? A pump?

But it's just so glorious and monumental.

The doors are so beautifully wrought, with a punched-out pattern on them. Merry touches it. It's old. She's always loved the feel of old things.

On either side of the doors is a set of stairs. Steep stairs.

There's a sign that says it closes at dusk, but Merry can't believe that applies to Christmas, and anyway, Merry can never resist a secretive flight of stairs. Show her something hidden and she's on it.

But she's not halfway up when exhilaration fades and her body rebels. Damn, she thinks, as she stands wheezing on the steps, trying to catch her breath. This nodule is continually taking her unawares. Pulling her down when she's trying so hard to rise.

She finds herself remembering the night only a few weeks ago that she climbed up the ladder to the roof of her house, determined to put up Rudolph the Red-Nosed Reindeer in such a way that he would seem to be vaulting over the eaves and into the Hudson. She had the idea vividly in her mind and she was determined to do it.

The strange thing, what hits her right now, is that as she was falling, she felt rage. At her father.

What a weird thing. She'd forgotten all about it. She recovered from the fall and picked up the pieces of Rudolph, who had shattered on the lawn. Only now, in a similarly precarious position, does she remember the rage she felt. She's not even sure *why* she was angry at her father. The kindest man in the world, and yet. How is it possible to be angry at someone she loved so much?

But she was. As she was falling, when she'd thought she might well break her hip or worse, she'd seen his face and she'd screamed at him. Not at the gentle face which she knew and loved so well but at a needy, quarrelsome face. A whiny face. That was the last image that occurred to her before she could have died. Is that the direction in which she's headed now? To wind down her life in a ball of fury?

Merry's tempted to turn around and go home. That's where she should be, with her family. What good is she doing anyone by sitting here shivering? But what good will it be to go home, to surrender on Christmas? She makes a pact with herself that she'll go up the steps, and then will turn around and go back. She's proved her point, and she's lost.

But she can't turn around when she gets to the top because it's so stunning. It's a Christmas spectacular. There's a huge white-lit tree right in the middle of the space. Normally she prefers colorful trees, but this one seems to have the right vibe for the occasion. Modern, edgy. There are smaller trees distributed at the corners. They look like acolytes, as though they are moving toward the tree and plan to serve it. There's something secretive about them, as though they know Christmas is a mystery that not everyone understands.

Most amazing of all is the view that surrounds them. It's like having a private perch in the most secret part of Mayfair. She can't believe it. It's the best view in London she's ever seen. And she's seen a lot of views. She's climbed to the top of Saint Paul's Cathedral. But this is like something out of *Rear Window*, except that instead of watching a murderer, you have all the lushness of a novel set in front of you. So many stories. So many buildings. So many rich people. This must be what it's like to write a novel, she thinks. To have so many lives on display.

How did she never know about this? Or hear about it? Where is she?

She notices an arrangement of benches toward the edge of the rooftop. Thank heavens. She needs to sit. She starts to make her way over and notices a man sitting at the end of the walkway. She steers toward the left, so as to give him more room.

And that's when she notices it's Charles Dickens.

CHAPTER SIXTY-THREE

His back is to her and she doesn't want to startle him, having irritated him enough. Yet Merry's confident he knows she's there. She remembers that wonderful line from *A Christmas Carol* when Scrooge, looking through Marley's waistcoat, *could see the two buttons on his coat behind.* Surely the essence of being supernatural is to have superpowers. And yet, she does not want to quarrel with this man. She needs his help.

She needs to keep her rage under wraps. Although she feels like she glows with anger and depression, although the nodule feels like the glowing red button the president presses to launch a nuclear attack, she must stay calm.

As Mr. Hong loved to say, "Easy peasy."

So she walks across the stone blocks that cover the outdoor space. Someone paid a pretty penny for that. Her heels click against the stone. She's still wearing the clothes she wore to the Campion party, a silk gray dress and her question mark hat.

Dickens looks up at her as she approaches. His face is lined. Gone is the youthful man she saw a few days ago, face shiny as a boy's. This face is the one that Nora the ancestor must have seen. Old and tired. Drawn. Lines scavenging his face, and yet the eyes still luminescent. Shaded now by heavy eyebrows but still quick. Curious. His graying hair puffs out sideways, clown-like if it were not for the majesty of his face.

She sits down next to him on an odd, platter-shaped bench. It seems intended more for lounging than sitting. It requires good posture.

Somehow, she feels more comfortable with this old version of Dickens than she has with all the other iterations. Perhaps she assumes he will be more patient, or it's just the knowledge that he suffered so much. That has always been a part of what's drawn her to him. He's a man who never recovered from losing the woman he loved most in the world, however inappropriate it might have been to fall in love with his wife's younger sister. Mary Hogarth, seventeen years old, who collapsed suddenly after a night with him at the theater. He lost several of his children, both as little ones and as adults. He suffered with physical pain his entire life. Memories of his father's poverty and his mother's betrayal tormented him. Yet he was able to turn all of that into something miraculous. Something that changed the world.

"Merry Christmas," she says.

He nods and turns to her. "Merry Christmas."

She presses her lips tightly closed. She has been overenthusiastic. She sees that now. He is of another time, when things were slower. She must let him take the lead. It's just that there's so little time left. Maybe no more than an hour and then everything will be lost.

He turns away from her and stares instead at a huge lit-up cathedral across from them. It is a gorgeous cathedral and the lighting has turned it gold. She's pretty sure it's Ukrainian, and that it's been a site of protests. In the ordinary course of events, she would adore its sparkle.

"Is that church significant to you?" she asks him. She doesn't think it was there during his time, and he was not a man who went to cathedrals, in any event. He didn't like Buckingham Palace either; he frowned on large institutions. And yet, he seems so intent.

"It doesn't belong there," he says.

"You mean it wasn't there in your time?"

"My time is now," he says. "My time is forever. I will live for as long as time."

Wind has started to gust. She suspects she should feel cold, but she doesn't. Near them a water feature bubbles. It makes a tranquil sound, like the sort of thing you hear at a cemetery. He must not be here to harvest her spirit, she thinks, or he would have done it. He seems more preoccupied with himself than with her. No one ever said the man didn't have an ego. She might have done better with the ghost of Charlotte Brontë.

"Yes, of course. You are eternal."

"I am the Inimitable."

"Yes, I just meant during the time you were actually alive. Before you were a ghost."

"I'm not a ghost."

"You are certainly not an effective one."

He scowls at her.

"Don't get mad," she pleads. "Don't disappear. You are what you are. I don't care. Please, Mr. Dickens, please don't disappear. I can't chase you anymore. I need you, desperately."

Without thinking she goes to put her hand on his arm. He has on a stunning camel color coat, edged in leather, but as she starts to touch him he yanks his arm away, leaving her hand floating in the air. She's not sure what she just felt. Something spongy. Something hot.

"I'm sorry," she says, feeling as though she's exposed something intimate.

He's still there anyway. He hasn't disappeared. He seems to be listening.

"I've lost the magic of Christmas," she says. "I thought when I came here that I would find it again. That being close to the spirit of you, in this beautiful city, at Christmastime, that it would seep back into me. That it would animate me, and my children. Erase the hurts. But instead, I'm further away from it than I've ever been. My family is splintering. I'm falling apart. Literally. No matter what I do, it's wrong."

"Why must you do anything?" He looks quizzical. Bemused. It's an expression she recognizes from one of her favorite portraits of him, created during one of the rare moments of calm in his life.

"Because I'm under a deadline. In every sense of the word. I have just one more day in London and I don't know how many days left in my life." That makes her pause. "Do you know the answer to that?"

He shrugs. "It's not important."

"I beg to differ; it's incredibly important to me."

He shakes his head.

She notices a man looking at her from one bench over. Is that, she wonders, because she's talking to herself, or because she's wearing a hat in the shape of a question mark, or because he recognizes Dickens?

"You are placing importance on the wrong things," Dickens says.

"That's so unfair. I value Christmas more than anything. It's breaking my heart that I can't feel it anymore. That the magic is gone. I can't bear to think of my children living without that magic. That's why I need your help."

He peers at her with those great solemn eyes of his. Those eyes that he believed could mesmerize other people into bending to his will. "Sheila told me that you were quarrelsome."

That is truly the last thing she expected him to say. "Sheila who? Sheila Hobbs?"

Her friend that, last time seen, was sitting on the bronze plaque on Library Way. Who she had lunch with at that horrible diner.

"She's my great-great-great-great-granddaughter."

Sheila was always saying she was related to Dickens, but she said so many things. She said that she'd attended a private school in New Hampshire, that she'd traveled to India, that she'd met the queen. She might have also said she was related to the tsar. The point was that she was a storyteller. That's why Merry enjoyed her so much. But she never thought of her as truthful.

"Is she okay? Is she with you? Has she passed on?

"She's in Virginia. With her brother."

"That's a relief. I assume you mean she's alive in Virginia."

He sighs.

"Okay, okay. But did she ask you to help me?"

"She said you wouldn't listen."

Merry can imagine Sheila saying exactly that. "For a woman living on the street, she has a lot of opinions."

"She told me that you fed her when she was hungry."

"Of course."

For the first time, he smiles at her. His face transforms. She knows he was a man who liked to laugh and party, and so she supposes he must have smiled a lot, and yet in almost all his photographs and paintings he looks languid, delicate, as though looking into another world. She smiles back at him, and she can feel him relaxing alongside her.

"Yes, she is very opinionated." He scoffs. "I refuse to talk to her anymore about *The Old Curiosity Shop*."

Merry nods eagerly. "She and I have had many an argument over that particular book. I love it, just to say. I find the ending perfect, and profoundly moving, and I don't see that you had any other choice."

"And yet I think *David Copperfield* is my best book."

"I know that you felt that way," she says, "but I've always been partial to *Great Expectations*."

He nods in agreement. "Yes, that's a masterpiece."

"Totally."

The bells chime three o'clock. The time when the last of Scrooge's ghosts came to visit him. The time of his great transformation. Daylight is a few hours away. She feels a twist of anxiety that propels her forward.

"Can you help me?" she asks again.

He looks at her strangely. Not with anger. More like confusion. The gold buttons on his coat seem to glare at her, yet he seems calm enough. "But I have helped you," he says.

"How?"

"Do you not see?"

She thinks back over their conversation. No words of advice came from him.

"I apologize, but I just don't see how."

He thinks for a moment, and in that moment, she feels her whole life rush by. She sees her father and hears him reading the book, she sees her mother, she sees Gstaad, she sees Nick, she sees Song Lee arriving, she sees Bessie, she sees Phoebe, she sees all the people that she's loved. She sees Dr. Fiedler. She sees this whole desperate trip and all the things she's tried to do and how she's dragged her children from place to place and underneath it all the nodule. The pulsing, beating pulse of death. And she sees—or rather, she doesn't see—the invisible presence at the end of the line. But what she does not see is Charles Dickens advising her on any plan of action.

"You are impatient," he says. "You are in a rush."

She feels him pulling away. "Who was ever more in a rush than you? You probably died years before you had to because you pushed yourself too hard." He was fifty-eight when he died, not so much older than she is now.

But he's starting to flicker, leaving her, and she knows that once he leaves, she will not see him again. She grabs for his sleeve, but there's nothing there. "No," she says. "You can't go."

He looks startled, as though some larger force is pulling him away from her, stopping him from helping her. He looks as though he's trying to say something.

"Book," she thinks she hears. "Get the book."

And then he's gone.

CHAPTER SIXTY-FOUR

Book? What book?

The only possible book Dickens could be muttering about is *A Christmas Carol*. But she sold it. To the evilest people in the world. Her treasured book is locked up in a safe in a posh house in Mayfair. Or is it locked up? Phoebe had her edition of *War and Peace* out on her bookshelf, and that was worth a hefty amount of money. It would be entirely consistent with what Merry knows of Phoebe that she would want her treasures displayed. She's not one to hide her light under a bushel.

Phoebe's like her mother, come to that. Two people who have to be the center of attention. Who embrace life to the fullest, no matter who is hurt as they rush for what they want. Maybe that's what drew Merry to Phoebe in the first place. And yet, as chronically angry as Merry is at her mother, she doesn't seem as cold-hearted as Phoebe. It occurs to her that there is way more nuance with her mother than she ever realized. That she knows, however mad she gets at her, that if she calls her, her mother will come. Whereas Phoebe is another matter entirely.

Merry is not, in general, a thief. Mr. Hong was always quite rigorous about playing by the rules and she agreed with him. Even paying people fair amounts when they had no idea what their book was worth.

But Dickens said to get the book, she thinks. And that makes sense to her. Truly nothing has gone right for her or her family since she sold the book. Her mind still reverberates with the broken look on Song Lee's face when Bessie spoke those wounding words. *You're lucky we took you in.* As though Song Lee were some form of stray cat. Oh, God. They are the ugliest words she's ever heard. Even worse than *nodule.*

Maybe that antique *Christmas Carol* was some sort of talisman. Maybe when Dickens gave the book to little Nora, he also passed along some of his magic. One thing she knows for sure is that Phoebe will not hand it over. She also knows she doesn't have the money to buy it back, even assuming Phoebe would sell it.

No one would blame her if she stole back her copy of *A Christmas Carol.* Probably.

It's not like she's hurting anyone, and she's not actually afraid of the consequences. At this point, what more can happen? She needs that book. Dickens told her to get the book.

It might even reassure Song Lee to know that her mother is a felon as well. They could be the Outlaw Binghams. And since she would never sell it again, no one would actually know she had it. There are plenty of stolen treasures in safes throughout the world. Even the ethics of the situation don't bother her. The book is hers, in every sense of the word. Except for possession.

She is familiar with the great lengths people have gone to to acquire or reacquire books. They've married unappealing brides or grooms, dug up graves. There was one poignant story in Nicholas Basbane's book about someone who sold off a great collection, then repented and spent the rest of his life trying to buy all the books back. Somehow what she's planning to do doesn't seem so bad if it's part of a great tradition.

Her phone buzzes. Sully. *Where are you? Are you okay?*

She answers, *Yes. Can't talk.* Then she shuts off her phone.

She walks back through Mayfair to the Campion cottage. All the lights are out, except for two reindeer nuzzling each other on the roof. Even Phoebe's reindeer are elegant. They don't go crashing to the ground.

Most of the windows have grilles on them, but there is one near the kitchen that is bare and just about big enough to crawl through.

Merry hesitates. It's so strange for her to be indecisive. Does this mean she's maturing? Getting sensible? Is this the famous sensibility that people have so often pointed out her lack of? She is not a person who hesitates. It's not a word she's ever embraced. She's always felt you should go for what you want. Like her ancestors did.

In fact, she would normally try to channel the Villards at such a moment, but her ancestors don't seem to be responding. She thinks of little Nora, the one she's always liked the best. The little girl who started it all, who was so fearless.

When Merry was little, she liked to imagine herself as Nora. She liked to dress up as her. A collared white shirt that she would squirt with starch. She spent a lot of her childhood damp and smelling of chemicals. She'd mash down her hair so it wouldn't curl. A few times she sprayed starch on her hair until her mother noticed and told her she'd go blind. A black skirt she wore to church. White socks. She desperately wanted to wear a hat, but Nora didn't wear one in the picture, so Merry didn't either. Even as a child, she was a stickler for historical accuracy. She didn't know then how Nora's life turned out. Didn't find out until years later that she died in childbirth. But even without knowing, there was always something about her that portended tragedy. That seemed so romantic to Merry.

Only now does she remember that when she was young and played the part of Tiny Tim, she'd always channeled Nora. Her ancestor was frail. Spindly even, and yet she had such power to her. Merry imagined Tiny Tim being the same way. It took strength to deal with that type of disability. It wasn't pitiful but, rather, powerful. She used to declaim his words as though he had a superpower.

She's been standing outside of the Campion cottage for half an hour.

Merry cannot stay there all night. She knows what she's about to do is a really bad idea. But she's also known, since the moment she thought of it, that she was going to do it. Because she's a Villard. Because she's desperate. Now that she thinks about it, the Villards as a tribe were always more desperate than courageous. Is there a difference?

All she has to do is creep through the window, find the book on the shelf in the living room, take it, and creep back out. Easy peasy.

She walks toward the window. It might well be locked, but it's not. She eases it open, hoists herself up, and climbs in.

CHAPTER SIXTY-FIVE

The police are very kind.

They accept Merry at her word that she did not intend to break into the house, but instead had too much to drink and thought the window was a door.

It helps that the Campions are so, so understanding. They've assembled around her, all six of them, plus the in-law, plus the baby. They stare at her with sad, wilting eyes. They wear matching Christmas pajamas. The fabric is overrun with elves and holly.

"It was just a terrible mistake," Phoebe says to the police. "We had no idea we'd turned the alarm on."

"She's been going through a terrible time," Al Campion stage whispers. "Cancer."

You wouldn't think a man dressed as an elf could be so evil, Merry says—or she would say, if she could speak. If her voice had not disappeared the moment that alarm started.

Of course, they don't want to press charges, they assure the police. Merry's an old friend.

Though Phoebe does just want to dart into the living room for a moment. To "check that everything's okay." She wants to make sure the *Christmas Carol* is still there, Merry knows. Which it is. She never got within an inch of it. No sooner had she squeezed through the window than a siren started blaring and she fell over in shock and wrenched her foot. It hurts like the devil. She wants to cry, but she refuses. Her foot could fall off and she would not give Phoebe the satisfaction of seeing her in tears. She would simply cut her swollen foot off her leg, give it to Phoebe, and say, "Take this. And my heart."

"Is there anyone you'd like to call, ma'am?" the young police officer asks. He doesn't have a line on his face. He has not yet screwed up his life.

"That's all right," Phoebe says. "I've called her husband. He'll be here soon."

"You called Sully!" Merry demands. Now her voice is back.

"You have to have someone take you home, Merry. You can't go home like this."

And proving the argument that it is always possible for things to get worse, Sully shows up at that moment.

"Merry," he croons and wraps his arms around her. For which she is very relieved because he is also blocking her view of the Campions. "Are you all right?"

"Can you get me out of here?" she whispers.

He squeezes her tightly, and then he says to the officer, "Are we all done here?" It is his courtroom voice. The one she's not heard in a while.

The police officer nods. But Phoebe is not done with them yet. She slinks over to Sully. She is the only Campion not wearing elf pajamas. Evidently even Phoebe has her limits. She wears a slippery-looking red negligee that shows off her toned arms and perfect bust. She puts her hand on Merry's arm, though Merry shakes it off. Phoebe's not disconcerted. She proceeds with her agenda.

"I just wanted to say how sorry I am," she says. "You poor thing," she whispers, as she leans forward, intending to kiss Merry on the cheek.

Merry sees that the whole Campion family has lined up behind Phoebe. Even the baby is smacking her lips.

They are going to eat her alive.

"Now," she roars to Sully, and they are gone.

Only in the cab does she notice that Sully is still in his pajamas and socks. The poor man must have been panicked when he got the call from the police. What she has put them all through.

"I'm so sorry," she says. Sully doesn't respond. What can he possibly say? He just pulls her close.

The cab is going surprisingly fast, but then the streets are empty. It's past the time for parties and church. Normal people are asleep now. They stop at a light and Merry, turning, sees a man step from out of a mews. Secret London. Dangerous London. Is it Dickens?

She closes her eyes. She truly does not want to know.

CHAPTER SIXTY-SIX

Thursday

By the time they get back to their bordello Airbnb, Sully is almost sound asleep. His head rests on Merry's shoulder. He's always been a man who needs a lot of sleep. When the kids were little, Merry would sometimes find him leaning against the wall, snoring. Or curled up on the floor, like a cat. Or like her little talking dog, come to that, whom she misses so much.

Merry succeeds in guiding her husband into the elevator, unlocking the apartment door and depositing him into their bed. But there's no way she can go to sleep.

She's shivering with energy. Her ears still ring with the sound of the Campion alarm, or maybe it's a sound coming from within her. Has that roaring gotten worse? She's not sure. She can't find the line between the roaring in her heart and the roaring from outside and the general roar she seems to have become.

There are still two hours to go until dawn breaks. She knows that her last chance for a miracle is gone. She knew that the moment she heard the alarm. But it is not in her nature to give up. If there are two hours to go, she will wait two hours.

The living room is dark and silent. All the lights are off, though the red does sort of seep through the darkness, and there are a number of red lights from various kitchen gadgets, most of which she has not been able to turn on.

Her laminated schedule is on the coffee table and she looks at it as though it were an ancient artifact, though it's less than a week old. But it does represent an ancient time. A time when she sincerely thought she could navigate her family's path through London, that she could solve all their problems, that she could find the meaning of Christmas, that she could persuade them to put on *A Christmas Carol*. It has become a laminated schedule of disappointments and she would rip it up except that it's laminated and won't tear.

She finally takes off her question mark hat. It was possibly not the best idea to try to break into someone's house with such a hat on her head. "Stupid," she mutters, though she doesn't feel angry. She's too empty to feel angry. How perfect the word *drained* is, because that's exactly how she feels. As though everything has seeped out of her.

The feeling is unfamiliar.

This lethargy. Her normal response to any situation is to solve it. Or it least to move. Since she found out about the nodule, she has been in motion, but now there is literally no place to go.

She looks at Facebook, but that's just depressing. Everyone is having a perfect Christmas Eve. No one else seems to be sitting in a room in London while her family smolders around her. And that's leaving aside the virtual boyfriend who may or may not still be in the picture.

She sinks into a soggy chair, which springs into different parts of her back. Ghosts of various young men hover around her, but those ghosts she can push away. Those ghosts are just trying to scare her. They aren't trying to turn her life upside down.

In the quiet, she's much more conscious of the weird sensations in her body, which is probably why she's been running around so much. She's not right. The hammering's louder, the roaring intense, she's got a prickly sensation in her right arm. It's your left arm that means you have a problem, isn't it? This is ridiculous.

It's ridiculous she hasn't called Dr. Fiedler. Ridiculous she's let this go on so long.

She thinks of Mr. Milagro, dying in a bed surrounded by books. How old was he? He could have been sixty or ninety.

One thing she knows is that she cannot sit in this quiet room by herself any longer, terrorized by her own body. The worst that will happen is that he'll say she might have cancer, which is what she thinks anyway. Even Merry doesn't think she's going to die tomorrow. What's most likely is that she will have to have a ton of tests and maybe surgery and things will go up and down for a few years, and then she'll die. It all seems so reasonable when you think of it like that. So distant. *This is what I will do. This is how it will be.*

Though, unfortunately, the moment Dr. Fiedler says the word *cancer* she starts to cry.

He answered on the first ring. She has his private number from his book collecting and although it's late at night, he is up, assembling presents for the grandchildren. She hears Christmas carols in the background. Can almost smell the egg nog.

He is so patient. So understanding. He talks her step by step through what's going on. She's nodding, writing down notes, tears trickling down her face, though everything he's saying feels manageable. Timelines. Plans. She can almost picture laminating the whole thing.

And then he gives her the name of an oncologist and she dissolves. Oncologist. Cancer. Death.

She starts to cry harder. Hot tears that won't stop. She tries to muffle her tears so that her family doesn't hear. She's so afraid.

She has a lot of friends who survived cancer. She knows this can be done, but it just feels so large and dark. Where once her mind glowed with Christmas, now it glooms with cancer. She can see nothing else. The sparkle has gone.

Her hands feel different. Shaky. Old.

She thanks Dr. Fiedler, because she was brought up to always say thank you, even to someone who just told you you probably have cancer. She feels like she's floating through time. She doesn't know what to do, so she decides to call Leroy—the dog. She hasn't spoken to him for a day, at least.

Unfortunately, she does wake up Darcy, but she's good-natured and happy to retrieve her iPad and Leroy. She then plants the one in front of the other and leaves Merry and her dog alone.

"I'm so glad to see you," she says. "I miss you something awful."

He stares back at her, his huge bulbous eyes sinking into her own. Then he begins to scratch his ear.

"Does it hurt? Do you have an infection?"

He slumps to the ground, panting softly. He yawns. She knows the touch of him so well that she can feel him without even holding him. The surprising softness of his golden fur. The way he always smells of her deodorant because he's so often tucked under her arm.

"What have you been up to? How is Sophie the Rottweiler?"

He does not speak, which is really odd. Even if he's still annoyed at her for leaving him with Darcy, she's never before known him to be sullen.

But it goes beyond that, she realizes, as she looks at him more closely. There's something missing in his expression. There's a flatness to him that's never been there before.

She hears Darcy moving around her kitchen, brewing coffee. She's one of those people who drinks coffee constantly though it doesn't affect her sleep or demeanor.

"My friend," Merry says. "Can you not speak to me?"

Has any silence ever been worse than this?

She sees a slight crease of dawn skimming through the window. "I've had such bad news," she whispers to her dog. "I was hoping we could talk together."

But the creature who stares back at her is nothing, more or less, than a dog. He is love, he is gentleness, he is warmth, he is everything to her. But he no longer speaks.

The magic in her life is gone.

CHAPTER SIXTY-SEVEN

So this is what it is to be sensible, Merry thinks.

This is what it's like to grow up.

You don't talk to your dog, or if you do, you talk in an ironic way, because you would not want anyone to think you believe you're actually talking to your dog.

You don't climb onto your roof to put up a reindeer, because you might fall off the roof and hurt yourself and find out you have a nodule.

You don't sell off your most treasured possession, because you're supposed to hoard things that are valuable. It could double or triple in value, or be bought by your worst enemy. You save what you own and do not gamble it.

You do not romanticize your ancestors, who, upon sober reflection, are a bunch of self-destructive maniacs.

You don't seriously plan to have your grown and cantankerous children get along together on vacation. And you do not expect them to dress up in costume.

You do not go chasing the ghost of Charles Dickens around London, and you most certainly do not think that he will offer you a magic solution to your problems.

Because he will not.

He will break your heart.

"You are a betrayer," she whispers to him. She would shout it, but now that she's a sensible person, she knows there's no need to be waking up her children. Better to let them sleep. Maybe they can all sleep right through Christmas, because she doesn't know what else they're going to do. She had anticipated that they would all be joyous and spend Christmas volunteering in a homeless shelter, but that doesn't seem to be in the cards.

There are no presents to unwrap. The trip was the present.

She supposes they could take a walk. Or drink heavily.

That would be sensible.

That is what the world wants of Merry Bingham and that is what she will give it. She will restrain herself. She will accept life for what it is. She will accept that Christmas is something sedate and calm. A reason for overspending on gifts. A retail holiday. A reason to go to the movies. Why is she so caught up in something that everyone seems to have left behind? Why is she expecting something magical and wondrous to happen? It should be clear that she does not live in wondrous times.

She just has to tone it all down. That's what people have been telling her for years. Tone it down. Now even Charles Dickens seems to be suggesting that, a man who was known for his exuberance.

But try as she will to be sensible, she just can't do it.

She's furious. It's all so wrong. So unfair. This is Christmas. Christmas!

She feels like she's going to burst, and suddenly, the room is filled with the sound of something slamming to the ground.

CHAPTER SIXTY-EIGHT

For a moment, Merry thinks that she's gone slamming to the floor. That would be about right.

But no. She's still sitting in the middle of a darkened bordello. Something else must have fallen. She clicks on one of the lamps, which is in the shape of a woman's stockinged leg. A pink glow emanates.

Merry scans the room. All is as it was. The stripper pole in the corner, with a bell on top to ring. The large TV on the wall and the white Formica table that tilts slightly. That's when she notices that Mr. Gaudy's present for her has slipped from the table onto the one patch of hardwood floor that is not covered by white shag rug. *A Christmas Carol.*

Automatically she goes over to retrieve the book. She intends to pick it up and put it back on the Formica table. She has no desire to look at it. Although she would not have said so to Mr. Gaudy, this is not a version she's ever liked. It's so different from the one she grew up with.

That glorious one, covered in soft red cloth, with the title and Dickens's name stamped on the front in gold. The title surrounded by a raised gold holly wreath. How she loved the smooth coldness of that raised gold wreath, the feeling of luxury. The pages edged in gold, so that the whole thing seemed like a treasure box. It was so important to Dickens that this book be beautiful. And then, John Leech's wonderful opening illustration on the frontispiece. *Mr. Fezziwig's Ball.* The old couple dancing in the center, Mr. Fezziwig with his red-and-white striped socks and Mrs. Fezziwig in her yellow dress. The fiddler hovering over them, playing his tune. The old lady in the corner with the children around her and the lone boy to the side. Perhaps Scrooge, looking on.

By contrast, the Arthur Rackham version that Merry holds in her hand was printed some years after Dickens's death. Rackham was a celebrated illustrator, beloved for his ability to capture fantastical creatures, but to Merry, his *Carol* illustrations lack warmth. The book is heavier, bigger, more dour than her own precious version. Dickens's name isn't even on the cover. Just the words "Illustrated by Arthur Rackham." The book is covered with drab violet cloth and there's little gold, only on the elves on the cover that Merry's heard described as playful but really seem satanic. Sharp noses and wicked grins. Most troubling to her is the frontispiece illustration, which, rather than showing a colorful party, shows a frightening depiction of Marley hovering over Scrooge.

She turns to that page now, because although she'd not intended to read the book, it's impossible not to open one when you're holding it in your hands.

She finds herself looking at Rackham's drawing as she never had. The more closely she looks at Scrooge's face, the more surely she sees her own reflected back to her. The irritation in his eyes, the way his slippers press against the floor, the pain in his posture. Never has that drawing resonated quite so perfectly with her. You could make the point that she's become Scrooge.

She can't stop looking at Scrooge's fingers, which clasp the armchair. She remembers how her own hands were just shaking, how she needed to grab on to something to make it stop. There is no sugar coating here. Arguably, no magic. Perhaps Rackham is illustrating the story Dickens intended to tell. After all, he wrote it at a time of disappointment in his life, when his reputation was on the line after the fiasco of *Martin Chuzzlewit*, which sold so poorly that his publisher wanted to deduct money from his monthly stipend, and Dickens's financial troubles were the talk of the literary world. One more failure could have sunk him into oblivion. Dickens was a man who knew bitterness and disappointment.

She turns the page, pulled in in spite of herself. Although the room is dark with only a glowing leg for light, she can still see the words. The first line: *Marley was dead: to begin with.* She smiles, as though meeting old friends, because these words *are* her friends. They've accompanied her throughout her life. She knows each one. She even knows that colon, which always thrilled her.

She knows that the book itself was written in only six weeks, that Dickens was in a mad rush to finish it because he needed money. She's seen the handwritten text at the Morgan Library. Has seen his crabbed fingers stretching across the page. She knows he scratched out word after word, and it feels to her as though each word is carefully chosen. Each word is right.

And so, she keeps turning the pages. How can she stop?

On to dear, gentle, beleaguered Bob Cratchit, who reminds her always of her father. Who could not go down an ice slide, as Cratchit does in the book, but would have loved to. Who loved to wear a top hat, as Cratchit does in the illustration, which brings a healing touch of memory. Of the top hat her father saved for the reading of *A Christmas Carol* and how rosy cheeked he looked when he put it on. How surprisingly silly he always was.

Then on to the arrival of bad old Jacob Marley. Now she has to whisper the words out loud as she reads them, because they are words that must be spoken.

There is more of gravy than of grave about you.

Definitely a part to be played by Al Campion. And Phoebe can be the washer woman at the end, the one who steals the curtains from off the dead man's bed.

But she's getting ahead of herself. Because now it is time for the first of the three spirits to appear. John Leech didn't draw the first ghost. Just a small etching toward the end of that section when Scrooge puts an extinguisher over his head. Rackham hasn't drawn this most invisible ghost either. So perhaps it would be best for Leroy, the invisible boyfriend, to play that part. He who has been so impossible to pin down and know and has disappeared into a bowl of soup.

But even as she thinks of Leroy, she finds herself smelling aromas she hasn't breathed in quite a while. Aromas from the past. Yes, she thinks. The smell of Yankee stadium. Of pretzels and peanuts and gasoline. Of the men who used to chat with her father when he went there. How they'd all laugh. How they didn't seem to see him as someone wounded but as someone who was one of them. A veteran. A fan. And how they fussed over her. How they all seemed to collect cars. Different than book collectors, of course, but the same vibe.

Then on to the Fezziwigs' party, and in Rackham's version the party is muted. More memory than presence. The husband and wife the only ones in the picture, Mr. Fezziwig with a knowing twinkle in his eye. Mrs. Fezziwig is turned away from the artist, but Merry's sure that if she turned around, she'd see her mother's face. Flirtatious Mr. Fezziwig could only be played by Jack Gutiérrez. Has anyone ever loved a party more than the two of them?

Then on to the Ghost of Christmas Present. How quickly the words go by. How completely Merry is drawn into them.

Rackham does not provide an illustration of the second ghost. Perhaps he was not up to the job of drawing someone so cheerful. But Merry remembers Leech's drawings of that ghost quite well. That large, bare-chested figure, swathed in a green fur-lined cloak. How she would love for Nick to play that part. To be that part. To live that part.

And here comes Tiny Tim, riding on his father's shoulders. This Tiny Tim holds his father's strong hand with one of his own, and wraps the other arm around his father's neck. There's fragility about the boy but beauty too. Persistent, wounded, strong, ever-hopeful. It could only be Bessie. In that, her daughter was completely right. She is the perfect person to play Tiny Tim. Not because she is a martyr, but because she breathes hope.

Finally, on to the third ghost. The Ghost of Christmas Yet to Come. The silent one who shows Scrooge his death.

Song Lee and Sully are the only people without roles in this imaginary production of *A Christmas Carol.* It's sort of like playing chess by yourself. Sully's easy, he can be charming cousin Fred, but what about Song Lee? Merry can't imagine her daughter wanting to put a sheet over her head. Plus, it is rather a gloomy role. Though it does point toward transformation. So, it's significant.

Perhaps she could let her play Scrooge, but that doesn't feel like Song Lee. She cannot put on her imaginary play without Song Lee. There's the Cratchit daughter, Martha, who has to work late. Would Song Lee take that as an insult, given the whole work situation? There are the orphans under the robes of the Ghost of Christmas Present. Want and ignorance. That could be insulting too.

But Merry cannot stop turning the pages, because you cannot stop in the middle of *A Christmas Carol.* You have to see Scrooge wake up and see him realize he hasn't missed Christmas. He can buy the prize turkey. He can save the Cratchits. He can turn his life around, he can find his miracle. *And it was always said of him that he knew how to keep Christmas well, if any man alive possessed the knowledge.*

She's read this book a hundred times, and yet she always cries at the end. She always feels something swell inside her. A joy that resides inside her that only Christmas ever seems to bring out. The joy of knowing that you can always start over. That there is always a second chance. That there is so much more buried inside of us than we are ever willing to let out. That the world is a big and miraculous place and we are a part of it.

How does that happen? How is it possible for words, a simple combination of letters, to change your life? She doesn't know, but she's grateful for it.

She smiles at the book and presses it against her heart. Possibly against her nodule.

She will not be sensible. She will not be beaten down. As long as she has this flicker of hope in her heart, she can do anything.

"I will honor Christmas in my heart and try to keep it all the year," she whispers.

Then she goes to the stripper pole, shimmies up, and rings the bell, and keeps ringing it until the doors of the bedrooms open.

CHAPTER SIXTY-NINE

Sully's first out of the room. He flings open the door and says, "Merry, are you all right?"

She's still on the stripper pole, ringing the bell, but she slides down when she sees the look on Sully's face. "I'm fabulous," she says.

Bessie creeps out of her room then. She's a bit like something out of a Stephen King novel. Thinner, whiter, bleaker. And she's not holding her phone, Merry notices. Leroy must have disappeared again.

Then comes Nick, who sleeps with an eye mask and a mouth guard. That's surprising. Is that a millennial thing? He does have on plaid pajamas, which she's pretty sure she gave him years ago. That's touching.

Only Song Lee does not appear.

"Did she come home last night?" Merry asks Nick, faltering for a moment.

"I thought so."

They all turn toward Song Lee's door, which is at the farthest end of the corridor. It's the smallest of the bedrooms, but it has the most windows.

Merry goes to her door and knocks, but there's no answer. What if she's gone? What if she's left the family? What if Bessie's words have pushed her away? She's known lots of families who've been severed like that. Something sharp and cold rushes through her and she pushes open the door so hard that it bangs against the wall, blistering the paint, and there's Song Lee, dressed all in white, with little white booties. Bit of a Miss Havisham vibe but still very elegant. Straight dark hair and heavily made-up eyes.

She's draped across the bed holding a foreign policy magazine. "What?" she says.

"You didn't come out." Merry sits down on the bed. She can't help herself. She grabs Song Lee in an awkward hug. "I was afraid you were gone."

Song Lee pats her back, then pulls away. Somehow, even in this brief period of time, she's managed to make this room her own. Crimson pillows Merry's sure did not start out there. A lavender sachet. A silk blanket. No wonder she had three suitcases. Ten pairs of shoes lined up outside the closet, which means the closet is full.

"Do you think I'm self-destructive?" Song Lee asks.

"I think you drink too much."

She shakes her head. "Not usually. What if I've ruined my life?"

"I suspect you've ruined your career in lobbying, but maybe it's a sign you don't want to be a lobbyist."

"I hated it. I wanted to quit the moment I got there, but I couldn't see how to do it. I beat out thousands of people for that job, and there was nothing else I wanted to do."

Merry understands, sort of, though she thinks a simple resignation letter would have caused a lot less stress.

Song Lee sighs. "To answer the question you're dying to ask, no, I've never plagiarized before."

"I didn't actually think you had," Merry says.

"Though you would have loved me anyway," Song Lee says quietly and when she speaks Merry sees that little girl who tried so hard at swimming. Who always had to be first.

"Always and forever."

"Thanks," she says.

"For what?"

Song Lee looks out the window. What a glorious view she would have, if not for the scaffolding. "You're going to try to get us to put on that play, aren't you?"

Merry smiles. "I do not give up."

Song Lee makes a sound somewhere between a laugh and a snort. "You think a person can be happy working in a shabby bookstore with a bunch of eccentric old people and an abandoned cat?"

"Sounds like the happiest place in the world."

Song Lee smiles now. "Yeah. I think so too." She gets to her feet. Merry always forgets how long and lean Song Lee is. She tucks her hand into Merry's arm. "She's so irritating, isn't she?"

No need to ask to whom she's referring. "Yes. But we love her."

"Yeah. Is there coffee?"

"There could be," Merry says, "if you feel like going to that place on the corner."

Song Lee nods, and Merry feels the shift in her mood. The essential good-natured intimidating person that is Song Lee is back. Then she strides toward the living room, where Bessie is literally cowering in the corner.

"You're an idiot," Song Lee says. "Do you want coffee?"

Bessie erupts with tears. "I don't deserve you," she says.

Song Lee sighs, and then Sully goes over and hugs her. "I'll go with you to get coffee."

But Nick says, "Why don't we just use that coffee maker there?"

"We don't have any coffee," Merry says. "They didn't deliver it."

But he points to a can of coffee right next to the machine.

"That's odd. It wasn't there last night."

She opens up the refrigerator to see if there's milk inside, and they all stop and gape. Merry can't help but think of the shepherds gazing at the manger, though that seems sacrilegious in this context, but it is a thing of wonder because the refrigerator is stocked.

All the food that was supposed to be there when they arrived, but wasn't. Now it is crammed with food. More food than they could ever possibly eat in one day. All the food she remembers ordering and more. Fennel saucisson. Cheese of every color—rich gold and deep orange and swirled white and red. A Stilton with rich blue veins running through it. A charcuterie platter wrapped like a gift. Jars of marmalade and pickled onions. Eggs and pies and milk and bottles of champagne tucked into the bottom. Stacks of biscuits and scones. And grapes. Enough for a vineyard. She's amazed they were able to close the door.

"Bountiful," she whispers. "Bountiful."

Nick grabs a pan and starts to cook, and Sully rolls up his sleeves. Song Lee wraps an apron around her. "Where did that apron come from?" Bessie asks.

Merry, realizing she hasn't showered for two days, darts into the bedroom to take a quick shower, put on fresh clothes, her sparkly diamondish earrings, and her red lipstick. And that crazy hat.

She also tugs out the suitcase that contains all the props. The ledger for Bob Cratchit to write in and the crutch that Tiny Tim needs to walk. The fake eyeball that pops out of Marley's eye. That's not actually in the book, but it seemed a nice touch. The sheet for the Ghost of Christmas Yet to Come and the candle for the first ghost and some fake holly.

When she steps back out into the living room, everyone is holding plates of food. One large stack of pancakes has been set aside for her, filled with raspberries and doused with the best syrup she's ever tasted.

No one mentions the suitcase. But she knows they see it. No one mentions the nodule either, for which she's grateful. She hasn't been thinking about it as much.

"So," she says, smiling. Trying for a look somewhere between desperate and wry. "Would it be possible, do you think, for us to put on this play?"

Clearing of throats.

Sully raises his hand. "I have an idea. What if we draw the roles out of a hat? I'll write up names on index cards and you can pick."

"Can we trade if we don't like our role?" Bessie asks.

"No," they all say.

"And who'll go first?" Song Lee asks, but she's smiling and looking at Bessie, who, mollified, smiles tremulously. Little Nell putting her hand in the basket.

Then Sully starts to make up the cards. He always has index cards with him.

The rest of them go to clear out space for the performance. Bessie and Nick grab either end of the couch. They lift it and immediately one of the legs falls off, which causes Bessie and Nick to lurch off balance, which causes the whole thing to crash to the floor.

"I can fix that," Nick says, but Song Lee goes and gets some cushions and they decide they'll work around the leg and Merry's looking at a mitten that fell out of the couch and that's when someone knocks on the door.

She assumes it's the superintendent, come to ask why they're crashing through the floor.

So she's stunned when she opens the door and sees Mr. Gaudy, in a wheelchair, with Sheila at the helm. Dear Sheila, last seen in a diner in New York City.

"What are you doing here?" Merry cries, though that doesn't come out right. "I'm so glad to see you."

"A little birdy told us you were putting on a play." Sheila winks her eyes outrageously and stage whispers, "Charles Dickens."

"I got that," Merry says. "But how?"

"You mean the ghost of Charles Dickens?" Bessie asks. "Did you find him?"

"Did you lose him?" Sheila asks.

"What? What do you mean?" Bessie looks around wildly, worried that she's the butt of a joke.

"Nick," Mr. Gaudy says, "so good to see you."

"You're looking so much better. How are you feeling?" Merry asks.

He laughs that papery laugh of his. "Amazing the tonic that Milagro money is proving to be." MoMo crawls out from under his arm and scampers over to Song Lee, who whooshes her up and holds her close.

"I think she's going to be very happy with you," Merry says. "Thank you."

"My dear."

Sheila, meanwhile, goes directly to Nick. She's such a flirt. "Now what can I ask you to make me?"

But before Merry can process that development, there's another knock on the door and this time it's her mother and Jack Gutiérrez. Jack's holding the Christmas tree, ornaments and all, from downstairs. "It was just sitting there, doing nothing."

"That elevator felt like a coffin," her mother says.

"Tell me about it," Merry says.

But there's no crushing Lana's essential good nature. Her gold hair is teased up into a rooster coxcomb. She seems to be channeling Johnny Depp. Then her mother laughs. The laugh that is pure joy. A laugh that is almost impossible not to join, though Merry has spent a good portion of her life trying to do just that.

She is starting to think that the only truly joyful person she knows is her mother, who owns up to her mistakes, who loves and loves back, who has never stopped loving her. Who found a way to live her life. Who has the courage to lead her own life.

"Huzzah," Jack says.

"How did you know to come?" Merry asks. "Mother's intuition?"

"No, someone who sounded like a dog called me up and said you were at the end of your rope."

Merry gasps. "Leroy called you?"

"Not the dog. Darcy the dog sitter. That woman must smoke. She sounds like she could bark. Wait, you're not going to tell me you think that dog knows how to use the phone."

"Did someone say Leroy?" Bessie calls.

But just then a bunch of young men, one of them being Vikram from the Apple store, dart through the door. Sully runs over to greet them, then smiles at Merry and shrugs. "Figured as long as we were having a party."

Merry eyes the door, wondering if it's a portal to another world, which, the way this vacation is going, it could well be. Maybe the doorman is actually an angel, instead of an inefficient doorman. Turns out she can ask him because he's just walked into the apartment. Then who's watching the building?

But Merry has no time to think on that because she's distracted by the arrival of Gussie Hong, even more pregnant than she was before, and more fabulous. She wears a sparkly silver dress that Merry envies. She feels a need to amp up her own sparkle, but judging by the way she's smiling, and everyone else is smiling, she thinks a certain amount of sparkle must be emitting from within her.

"Is that Mr. Gaudy?" Gussie says. "I've been hoping to talk to him. You look fabulous, by the way," she says, and shoots off.

"Maybe we should just leave the door open," Sully says and Merry, who is normally a person who likes to man the door, who perhaps is even more controlling than she realized, agrees with him. With the doorman in their apartment, there's not a lot of monitoring going on anyway.

Then a kind-looking young woman wanders in whom Merry honestly doesn't know, but Nick lights up at the sight of her. "Jane," he calls out.

Who is she? Merry wonders. He looks entranced. He looks happy.

Song Lee slinks up. "Doesn't she look like Jane Eyre?"

"No," Merry says. "I can only deal with the ghost of one literary figure at a time. And I definitely can't start introducing fictional ones. The last thing I need is for Bill Sykes to come dashing in."

"Who?"

Everyone is eating. There's prosecco to go around. Laughter and conversation and strategizing.

What Merry hadn't realized until now is that people have brought costumes. Not elaborate costumes, but scarves and hats and aprons and bonnets. It's a bit like a Dickens flash mob. Are they all here to put on the play?

She can't believe it. But she can't think, she can't worry about it, she can't organize it. She doesn't have enough scripts. And then, Leroy the invisible boyfriend walks through the door. He's holding a box of New York taffy. Must have stopped at a duty-free shop. He's skinnier than he looked on the phone, but it was hard to tell because he had on a bicycle helmet most of the time.

Merry expects for Bessie to go leaping into his arms, but she doesn't. She clearly sees him, but she doesn't acknowledge him. Doesn't go to him.

"I'm sorry!" he yells to her, from across the room. "I have commitment issues."

The room silences.

"Then leave me," she says. "Leave me before you destroy me." This is a Bessie Merry has never seen. Part Lady Macbeth, part Juliet. Her posture has changed, her demeanor. She's powerful. Awe inspiring.

"I can't leave you," Leroy says. "I'm obsessed with you."

"You don't deserve me!"

"I *don't* deserve you," Leroy cries back. "But I can spend the rest of my life trying to be worthy."

Bessie absorbs his words. Merry can almost watch them going through her, like when a snake eats a rabbit. They seem to satisfy her because she stretches out her arm to him. He cuts through the crowd, lifts her up, and swirls her around. Everyone applauds. Bessie seems to awake from a trance, surprised to find that there is anyone in the room beyond Leroy. "I didn't know anyone was here."

Song Lee and Nick are laughing so hard they have to leave the room.

Merry follows them, wanting to check the number of scripts she has. Maybe she can find a dusty little shop that's open. There's bound to be a place where you can photocopy pages and buy bananas and souvenirs.

But Nick stops her before she can ask. "Ma, do you think anyone in this crowd *doesn't* know the words to that play?"

"That's a good point."

"Plus, we could always share the scripts," Song Lee says. "That feels Christmassy."

"It does, doesn't it," Merry says, and she heads back into the melee, standing by the door, curious to see who will come next.

Some time goes by with no new arrivals. People mingle and hug Merry and chat. She feels almost like she's drifting.

And then two men walk through the open door.

One is a slight man with big eyes and curly hair. He wears a newsboy cap, brand new jeans that have glitter on them, and a green shirt. He carries a walking stick. Charles Dickens must have gone shopping at T.K. Maxx.

But it's the other man who grabs her attention.

Merry looks at her mother to see if she notices, but she's just smiling at a bartender. Where did a bartender come from? But no one seems to be paying any attention to the man who's walking toward her.

He looks to be in his early thirties. He's a tall man. The word *virile* comes to mind. His outfit is not as colorful as Dickens's, but it's colorful. A vivid blue shirt, surprisingly tight pants. Polished shoes. It's the shoes that truly grab her attention because they are so unfamiliar. Because in all the times she thinks of her father, she thinks of him wearing only socks. He had no use for shoes, and they were impossible to get on him in any case. Cramming a solid unmoving block of foot into a shoe is something she tried to do only a very few times.

But these shoes are sharp. These are shoes made for dancing.

She has a surprising realization that when her mother married Jack Gutiérrez, she was marrying a man like her father.

She feels awkward. She doesn't know this man. He is her father, but he's not. Certainly not the man she grew up knowing. This is who he would have been had things not gone wrong for him. She feels shy. He has occupied such a large part of her mental space for so much of her life; she has come to visualize him as someone shrouded in a dark cloud. But this man in front of her . . . this man is just her father.

He grins then, and that at least is familiar. She'd forgotten how wonderful his smile was. How it was so unfettered. Joyous. Lopsided. Ironic. Red. Loving. Kind.

How had she ever thought this man would not forgive her? It's never been about her father forgiving her. It's been about her forgiving herself.

"Dad," she says, and he folds her into his arms.

The warmth of him, like pancakes.

And she is young again and she is safe and she is loved, but she is also old again and she has a nodule and three children and a husband and she is loved. This is the most magical Christmas she has ever had, and yet she believes—she *knows*—there will be more Christmases to come.

She looks at Dickens, who is eyeing Bessie speculatively.

"No," she says to him, because the last thing Bessie needs is another invisible boyfriend.

He smiles at her, the sort of smile she has never seen from him. Not in his portraits and not during their fraught acquaintance. It's the smile she's always wanted to see. A truly happy smile.

"So," he says. "I understand there is to be a play. I will direct it."

He raises his hands like a conductor, and the play begins.

CHAPTER SEVENTY

The Day After Christmas

They're all sitting in Heathrow Airport, waiting for their various flights. Song Lee to Washington, D.C., to wrap things up before moving to London. Bessie and Leroy to Iceland, to "work things out." They've been bickering like something out of a Tennessee Williams play. Merry can't figure out whether or not that's an improvement in their relationship. Nick back to Oregon to sell his house. To Merry's amazement, he's told her that he's planning to move back to New York.

"That's so lovely," she'd said, "but it's really not necessary."

"No." He'd blushed. "It's not for you. Or it is, of course. But also, I've met this girl."

"Jane?"

"Jane Ayre," he'd said.

"What?"

"Spelled with an A." He'd laughed. "How could you not love a girl with a name like that?"

The waiting room is crowded. Flights have been canceled due to storms in the United States. People are sleeping on the floor, though Merry has managed to snag a cluster of chairs near the little Harrods store. She loves that store. Actually, she prefers this little Heathrow Harrods to the big luxurious one. It's user friendly. She's tempted to go in and buy herself a memento, though she doesn't think she needs one.

She will never need a reminder of this trip.

Her mind swims with memories of the play the day before.

For all the arguing beforehand about who would play which role, it all wound up unfolding organically, each one stepping into the right role at the right time. Almost as though some ghost of a great nineteenth-century genius was masterminding the whole thing.

Bessie played the part of Tiny Tim. She was so perfect, and Leroy was a surprising and yet effective Bob Cratchit. Sully played Scrooge and Nick the first ghost. They were all moved to tears by his evocation of the past. Song Lee actually *wanted* to be the orphans, though it did seem as though she expanded her role; Merry did not recall that many lines about the orphans in the book. Dickens didn't object, but Bessie said if they could all just add lines it would lead to mayhem.

Merry played Mrs. Fezziwig. Turned out that Nick had a yellow shirt she could borrow and Song Lee a yellow scarf. Mr. Gaudy was her spouse. The old man had plenty of energy in him to dance. That was when Dickens scrambled up the stripper pole and turned on the rainbow lights. Who knew? No one seemed to recognize him or her father, for who they were. They were just two more revelers, as far as her guests were concerned. Except for Sheila, of course, who kept making thumbs up signals at Merry whenever she could tear herself away from the bartender.

The high point came when Dickens took out a fiddle. From somewhere. He played exuberantly and at one point her father grabbed her by the hands and they twirled around. Then the music slowed and they rocked quietly together and talked of so many things. Not apologizing. Just sharing. Then dear Sully cut in and they danced even longer.

At one point Merry felt sure she saw a little vampire girl go cartwheeling by.

After a while, everyone got tired and Dickens said there was no need to act out the last part of the play. He would recite it—or no, he said, better that Merry recite it. So he bowed to her and she grabbed up her Rackham edition and read Stave Five. The magic pages of Scrooge's transformation. When they got to the very last paragraph, Merry closed her eyes, the better to live inside those words as she recited them.

He had no further intercourse with Spirits, but lived upon the Total-Abstinence Principle ever afterwards; and it was always said of him that he knew how to keep Christmas well, if any man alive possessed the knowledge. May that be truly said of us, and all of us! And so, as Tiny Tim observed, God bless Us, Every One!

Merry is floating along in a misty froth of memory when she becomes conscious that everyone around her in the airport lounge has gone silent. The space takes on the sullen stillness the sky gets right before a thunderstorm. She half expects to hear a tornado behind her. Everyone looks alarmed. Bessie actually holds her hands over her eyes. Merry turns to see what's coming.

It's Phoebe Campion, dashing toward her, the entire Campion family close behind.

Phoebe looks awful. The kids look awful. Not that awful, but they look wrinkled. They look tousled. In point of fact, they look perfectly normal, but that, in itself, is alarming. The power of the Campions is in their perfection. Without it, they are just any other family.

"Merry," Phoebe gasps. "I'm so glad I caught you. I've felt terrible since the party. You're absolutely right. It was terrible what I did."

She's got a large tote bag roped across her chest, like a seat belt. She's rummaging around in it, which is causing the strap to pull and it looks like she's going to strangle herself. Finally, she finds what she's looking for.

Merry's *Carol*. The family heirloom.

Phoebe's wrapped it up in tissue paper, but part of the maroon cover peeps out.

"I want you to take it back. I can't live with myself."

Merry takes it and holds it for a minute, the touch of it so familiar. So loved. She strokes the raised gold lettering. Breathes in its dusky scent. Pictures herself as a girl, clinging to it.

But it wasn't this book that brought her peace. It was the other, plainer one, that she will always associate with the joy she found on Christmas Day. This one is the past, but the other one is the future.

"I don't need this anymore," she says. "I have something better."

"What is it?" Phoebe's face shifts. She can't hide the greed. She looks like what she will become.

"Something you will never be able to take from me," Merry says.

She hands the book back to Phoebe, who clutches it to her chest. Then Phoebe turns to her children. Merry wonders if her children were upset by Phoebe's actions. If she'd told them that Merry didn't really care about the book. Or that she was just a person who liked to make scenes. Phoebe has the look of someone who's just won an argument.

"Well, if you're sure. As I say, I do feel terrible about taking it from your family."

That's when Nick steps forward and says, "I want the book."

"I didn't offer it to you," Phoebe snarls. Her entire face changes. The genial caring persona has disappeared, replaced by something scrawny. Chicken-like. Ugly.

"It's mine," he says. "It always has been."

He looks so strong standing there. Powerful, even. He looks like he will stand his ground.

"No," Phoebe says, but one of her sons steps forward then and tugs the book out of her hands.

"Take it, sir. With our apologies."

Then the children turn and walk off, leaving Phoebe standing there, bookless.

"Come on, gal," Al Campion says as he tugs on his wife's arm. "Time to go."

The two of them go off, eaten up by the Heathrow crowds.

Meanwhile, Merry stands there, staggered.

"Bravo!" Bessie says, clapping for Nick.

"Indeed," Sully says.

"I took a picture of you, Nick," Song Lee says. "Very ferocious. And I'm going to laminate it."

"You really want the *Carol*?" Merry asks her son, but looking into those dark sincere eyes, she knows the answer.

He nods. "I will treasure it forever."

Then they all squeeze onto three open seats and Merry opens the book to the list of owners. Phoebe has gotten her name on it already, of course, but that's okay. Maybe it will be a reminder of what they almost lost.

Sully takes out a fountain pen. "I knew there was a reason I always carry this around."

Nick takes the pen. He looks at the title page, which is where Dickens's name is written. Then he turns to the front endpaper and they all watch as he inscribes his name on the bottom of the list.

Nora Villard 1867

Nelson Villard 1880

Charles Dickens Villard 1925

Charles Dickens Villard Jr. 1929

Charles Dickens Villard III 1971

Merry Villard 1989

Phoebe Campion 2025

Nicholas Villard Bingham 2025

Merry gazes at all the space there is still under his name. Thinks of all the generations yet to come. Thinks of how she is part of this wonderful, extravagant story, and what a gift this book has been to her.

For just a moment, Merry sees the flash of something green out of the corner of her eye. A twinkling pair of lights, a dancing man. She watches as he twirls on his toes, leg extended. It's so beautiful.

And then he bows to her and spins off, leaving only the slightest trace of something sparkly in his wake.

CHAPTER SEVENTY-ONE

HOME

Merry sits with her nonspeaking dog in her parlor. They're crammed together in her Victorian tub chair. Although Leroy can no longer hold up his end of a conversation, he is still a good listener and Merry has been regaling him with all her adventures. Suffice it to say, he is struck dumb with incredulity.

She's scheduled the first of her doctor's appointments. It sounds disagreeable, but she feels up to the job. She keeps repeating the word *oncologist*. She must get used to it. When you break it down into syllables, the word actually has a nice sort of rhythm to it. "She's there to help me," she says. "I have to embrace her."

Leroy licks his paw.

She loves his paws. They look like long-sleeved gloves; there's something Victorian about them. He is in fact a Victorian sort of dog. In profile she thinks he looks like Prince Albert.

"I'll always love you," she says. "But I do miss hearing you talk."

He looks up at her then. His eyes are fathomless. "Je ne comprends pas," he says.

She starts. "Did you say something?"

"Je suis Le Roi."

"You're talking, but you're talking in French?"

"Oui," he says, cocking his head in a manner she considers very French. It reminds her of a photograph she saw of the great French writer Camus, in a first signed edition she got for one of her clients.

"But I don't speak French."

"Désolé," he says. "Then you will have to learn."

He looks at her severely, and she shrugs. Mais oui. Why not. Why shouldn't she learn French to speak to her French-speaking dog? The world is a miraculous place, full of magic.

She laughs and her dog laughs with her, though not in a guffawing way, because he is French.

"Maybe next Christmas we could take a family trip to Paris," she says.

"Oui, but next time you will take me."

"Absolument!"

The End

DISCUSSION QUESTIONS

1. Merry Bingham decides to sell her treasured edition of *A Christmas Carol* to take her family to London. What do you think of this decision? Would you have made the same choice or a different one?
2. What was your most memorable trip or vacation? Do you find you remember vacations better when things go right or wrong?
3. With which of Merry's three children did you feel most sympathetic? Why?
4. What five words would you use to describe Merry as a character? Have you ever known someone like her?
5. Many of the characters in this novel are dealing with guilt and shame. What are their different coping strategies? Who do you think handles it most effectively?
6. What does the ghost of Charles Dickens add to the novel? What do you think the author's intention was in adding a dash of magic to an otherwise real-world setting? Or is the magic—and Dickens—all in Merry's mind? Have you ever experienced moments of magic in your own life?

7. Building on question number six, do you believe Leroy the dog actually speaks to Merry? Why or why not?
8. Are you an eldest, youngest, middle, or only child? Do you have any personal experience with adoption (international or otherwise)? How has your family structure shaped your life?
9. Merry helps people collect books. Do you collect anything? Why do you think so many people find the idea of collecting so compelling?
10. Merry loves the Christmas holiday season. What is your favorite holiday and why?

ACKNOWLEDGMENTS

This novel got off to a dramatic start. I was lying in a hospital bed, having just barely survived an ordeal, when I got a text from my agent, the fabulous Paula Munier, that said, *I just had a dream that you would write an inspirational book*. Her idea gave me new life. I can honestly say that I would never have written this book without Paula, who then went on to advise/harangue me into writing the best book I could, and then sold it. Thanks also to Gina Panettieri, Amy Collins, and all the other miracle workers at Talcott Notch Literary.

Then along came my editor Jess Verdi, truly the most love-filled person I've ever met, along with being a genius editor. Thank you to all the wonderful people at Alcove Press/Crooked Lane, among them Matt Martz, Rebecca Nelson, Thai Fantauzzi Pérez, Dulce Botello, Mikaela Bender, Stephanie Manova, Megan Matti, Doug White, and Lucy Rose, who designed the cover of my dreams.

Thanks to Keri-Rae Barnum of New Shelves, book marketer extraordinaire. Also, deep gratitude to Debby Gilbert, Darby Gilbert and Lisa Hunter of Outrageous Fortune Technical Services (OFTS), who designed my beautiful new website at www.susanbreenauthor.com

Acknowledgments

I am not a Dickens scholar, but my understanding of Charles Dickens is based on a life-long love. He has been at my side during the worst moments of my life, when I clung to *The Old Curiosity Shop* for dear life, and during the happiest moments, when I laughed along with David Copperfield. *Ain't I volatile.* There are so many wonderful resources for those interested in Dickens, but I especially like Claire Tomalin's biography, Kate Douglas Wiggin's *A Child's Journey with Dickens*, and The Dickensian journals. Special thanks to the people at the Charles Dickens Museum, who have answered my many questions, no matter how foolish, with patience.

One of the turning points in my life came when I was in college at the University of Rochester and happened to wander into an antiquarian book fair. There I found a Heinemann edition of *A Christmas Carol*, illustrated by Arthur Rackham. I bought it for $29.42 and have treasured it ever since. From this experience, I've learned about the sheer physical pleasure of owning a book. I have spoken to many book sellers and book lovers over the course of writing this novel, and read many books on the subject. Favorite resources include Nicholas Basbanes's *A Gentle Madness,* Rebecca Rego Barry's *Rare Books Uncovered*, the addictive Dickens catalogues from Jarndyce Booksellers, any issue of *Fine Books & Collections*, the Morgan Library, and countless seminars at London's Institute of English Studies.

There have been so many people who've helped me on this journey. Thanks to my second family at Gotham Writers: Alex Steele, Dana Miller, Kelly Caldwell, Darren Liang, Stuart Pennebaker, Charlie Shehadi, Emma Stephenson, and Justin Street. Thanks also to the many students who have inspired and taught me. There are too many to mention, but if I were to single out one it would be Jane Carter, a beautiful writer who spent years living in an apartment on Park Avenue by selling off one treasured book a month. Thanks also to Michael Neff and the New York Write to Pitch Conference. Almost every good publishing thing that has happened to me has come out of that.

My church family at Irvington Presbyterian Church has kept me going with their love and prayers. Special shout-out to the IPC daytime book club, which taught me so much about what readers seek: current members being Joyce Chaluisan, Ernestine Glenn, Barbara Hanna, Marge Hone, Kris Liddle, Barbara Mahoney, Fran McLaughlin and Donna Taylor. I also have a medical team family which has kept me going, led by Dr. Abraham Mittelman, Cindy Teeple, and all the wonderful caregivers at White Plains Hospital.

Then there are the friends who have nourished me in every sense of the word: Melinda Feinstein, Robin Freedman, Terry Gillen, Leslie Mack, and Kay O'Keefe. Also my actual family of Breens (Nancy and crew), Brennans, Lujans (Meghan, Chris, Elias, and Robbie), Murcotts, Turchettes, and Zelonys (beloved brother Rob, Beth, and Taylor).

When your mother announces she's writing a book about a family vacation, I can only imagine it instills a sense of horror. But my family has handled it all with grace and love. No surprise there. Special thanks to Tom Breen, Lucy Gellman and little Avi, Kathy and Alex Brennan and little Savannah and Jack, and the London-based wing of the family, Christopher Breen and Camille Petin. Love to my husband, Brad, who has saved my life more times than I can count and who does genuinely love the Heathrow Express. I also have to thank my son Will, who I adopted from Korea. He passed away too young, but his adventurous spirit has fueled me.

Finally, thank you to my parents, Bob and Barbara Zelony, who taught me everything I know about love and faithfulness. As my father loved to say, echoing another long-suffering person, "God bless us, Every One!"